THE
BLUE BEADS

ANCIENT SECRETS BOUND IN GLASS

BY
ELIZA MERRY

This book is dedicated to Harriet, Alastair and Leonora

Apart from the counties of Dorset and Wiltshire, and the cities of Salisbury, London, Durham and Oxford, plus the prehistoric complexes in and around Avebury, and Carnac in France, all active locations in this book are imaginary.

The events in this story are all entirely fictitious.

Likewise all the active characters in this story are creations of the author's imagination

The story is set in the years 1995 -1997

Contents

CONTENTS

CHAPTER ONE

A Necklace

It all started when Cressida found the bead necklace. She was rummaging through the contents of some dilapidated cardboard boxes at the back of one of the second-hand shops on the High Street. An invitation from her best friend Louise to her sixteenth birthday party - which specified fancy dress with a Victorian or Edwardian theme - had sent Cressida on this search of the local charity shops.

It was going to be a very exciting party, because Cressida and her contemporaries at school had just finished taking their GCSE exams. It had been a gruelling few weeks, starting in May and going on intermittently into the first part of June. But now they were over - and Cressida was really looking forward to a few weeks of fun and relaxation.

In her hunt for the right fancy dress she'd started off at home by examining the contents of the old dressing-up box - but she wasn't very optimistic; she remembered most of what was in it. There was a tattered shawl and a pair of buckle shoes, plus a few other limp pieces of cast-off clothing. But the bulk of stuff consisted of costume leftovers from earlier years - animals, superheroes, witches and pirates' outfits - discarded reminders of these all-absorbing fantasy games from a few years back, that she had organised and played with her little brothers.

1

Cressida herself was nearly sixteen. Her brothers, over eight years younger than her, were now much more interested in playing football and making complex Lego constructions than dressing up. Somehow the age-gap between the pair of them and herself seemed to have become much wider than it had been a few years ago. Perhaps it was because she was now finding life a lot more troubling and perplexing than it had been when the three of them romped and rampaged together in the playroom.

She loved her twin brothers. When they were born - tiny and precious - the miracle of IVF producing not one, but two beings out of that final remaining fertilised egg, she had been overcome with excitement and awe. It had been the last chance. Cressida had been acutely aware of the stress her parents were going through as the ongoing cycle of hope and despair took its toll of them, although she hadn't really understood what was going on. She knew it was something to do with them wanting another child. Sometimes she'd tried to plead with them. "Aren't I enough for you?" she had asked once. Her mother had hugged her, crying at the same time, and cuddled her while telling her how precious she was. Cressida never asked that question again.

As she delved into the rumpled contents of the box nearest her, Cressida found her attention wandering so much that she wasn't really making much headway. To draw her mind away from the bitter-sweet memories of the past few years, she turned to the next box, which contained a mixture of clothes and other stuff - fur wraps, trinkets and even a wig or two. She picked up an elaborately coiffured one, the luxuriant powder-white curls piled high and dotted with tiny, different coloured diamante ornaments. Unable to resist trying it on, she tucked her own thick straight dark auburn hair into it and looked into a mirror which was propped up nearby. The girl staring back at her looked like a completely different person - elegant, pale, and beautiful! If only the fancy dress party had specified eighteenth or even seventeenth century costume, it would have been perfect!

There was also quite a lot of discarded jewellery in this box - probably nothing of any worth, but some pretty pieces nonetheless. She found an attractive brooch with an oval turquoise-coloured stone in the middle, surrounded by tiny faux seed pearls set into the gold coloured mount. This could work, she decided, especially since almost immediately afterwards she pulled out a cream blouse with a frilled front. The brooch would look perfect pinned just below the dipped neckline! Now all she needed was a long skirt. A plunge into the depths of a third box, which was full of more expensive looking stuff, yielded a deep blue one in heavy silken fabric, with a ruched hem. This might do, she thought. As she carefully pulled it out she felt something hard and knobbly mixed up with it. Twisted up in the waist fastening was a necklace of blue beads. Cautiously she untangled them and held them up over her two hands.

They were attractive and unusual and would, she felt, complement the blue skirt well. Looking more closely she could see that the beads were slightly uneven in shape, made of some sort of glass, and that most of them had thin streaks of other shades, some darker blue, some yellow, and one or two brown. They were strung on a thin dark thread, and between each bead there was a much smaller flat greyish one which looked as if it was made of clay or stone.

The thread felt very fragile; the beads would probably need re-stringing. She hung them closely around her neck and chest and again regarded herself in the mirror. Yes, they would be perfect – they looked beautiful, and her own deep blue eyes seemed somehow to be enhanced by the blue of the beads. Then something very strange happened. Her fingers started to tingle and her ears began to fill with a muted roaring sound, like water flowing. At the same time her reflected face seemed to be slowly changing. Hastily Cressida undid the necklace and laid it down again. What was going on? Was it some sort of electric shock? Or was she perhaps having an allergic reaction?

That weirdness disappeared as soon as she took the beads off. They were so pretty, so unusual - she *had* to have them! The 'funny turn' must have been a coincidence, she decided, possibly because she had gone out this morning without eating any breakfast. The days always started early at home; even at weekends. Jo-Jo and Mikey were awake by six most mornings, their loud shrill chatter and their exuberant crashing about usually put paid to any chance of a lie-in.

On school days obviously everyone had to get up early; but this was a Saturday. Cressida had planned to have a long luxurious bath and to wash her hair with the apple-scented shampoo which was part of a beauty set she'd won in a raffle at school, before getting the bus into town to search the charity shops. Instead. the twins had erupted into her bedroom early with shouts and laughter, leaping onto her bed and demanding a story.

She'd resisted for a bit, pulling her duvet over her head and keeping her eyes shut, but it was no good, they snuggled up to her and begged her to wake up: "Cressy, lovely Cressy, PLEASE read us a story, you're the best ever story-reader!"

So she'd given in, settling one boy on either side of her and agreeing to read another chapter of the dragon story which she'd started before they went to bed last night.

Cressida sometimes wondered if the boys thought of her as another child or another grown-up. She was of course *growing* up, but she still often felt nearer to childhood than to adulthood. It was difficult at times; she had been involved in helping to look after her little brothers from the start, and she loved their unquestioning affection and trusting dependence. But occasionally she felt quite sad at the role she now seemed to have - big sister, so much older that she was no longer a playmate but more of a carer. It was confusing. There was no way now that she could imagine home life without those dear little boys, but sometimes she couldn't help looking back wistfully to the uncomplicated years of her early childhood.

This morning, to her relief, both her parents had got plans for the day. The boys needed new school shoes, and after that Dad was going to leave Mum in town before taking the twins to the local sports centre for football and swimming. When they'd all gone. Cressida was at last free to have her bath, followed by a long private phone conversation with Louise. After that she too had headed off, to get the mid-morning bus into town.

They lived in Troycombe, a largeish village in mid-Dorset surrounded by picturesque downland countryside. In the summer the village was something of a tourist honeypot, with its attractive terraces of ancient black and white houses, a half-ruined medieval castle on the hill above the village, and a 16th century pub in the central square. There was also a teashop, as well as a Post Office and General Stores, both of which enjoyed a healthy trade even in the autumn and winter seasons.

Her family had moved there a few years after the twins were born, leaving the county town and their cramped Georgian town house for a large but very dilapidated old farmhouse. It had taken several months and a large bank loan to convert it into the comfortable family home it now was.

Cressida thought she was probably the only member of the family to feel an occasional pensive nostalgia for her old home. She missed her attic bedroom and the cosy familiarity of the town house, together with the seemingly uncomplicated lives they all led before the arrival of the twins changed everything. She also missed living in town and being near to the shops, meeting up easily with friends and walking to school. Now she nearly always had to take the bus.

The county town, Chilminster, was half an hour's bus ride away, a journey she made almost every day to and from her secondary school. All the same, today she'd had to admit to herself that it was quite fun to be going in independently on a Saturday, to forage for clothes for Louise's party, then to treat herself to something in a café, and maybe catch up with a friend or two.

Later, thrilled with her success in finding all the fancy-dress stuff and relieved that it hadn't really cost her very much; as planned, Cressida, now very hungry, indulged in a drink and a chocolate brownie. She then wandered round the shops for a bit before getting the bus home. She hadn't seen any friends, but now she didn't mind much, because she wanted to get home and try on what she had bought, before everyone arrived back and family life took over again.

The blouse and skirt fitted quite well. Cressida was tall and slim so she wouldn't have to do much alteration except perhaps a bit of stitching on the two ribbons which were the fastening of the skirt. She swept her hair up into a bun and fixed it on top of her head with hairgrips, fastened the brooch quite low down on the blouse to show a bit of cleavage, then regarded herself in the full length mirror in her parents' bedroom.

Gazing back at her was a solemn, sophisticated looking young woman; recognisably dressed in an outfit which, she thought, looked entirely appropriate for the fashions of the late 19th or early 20th century. She already had a pair of brown leather ankle boots which would do for footwear, and a wide brown belt to buckle around her waist. Now it was time to finish the ensemble with those lovely unusual beads.

She felt slightly anxious. Would that strange sensation come back? The fastening was a bit loose - it was just two interlocking hooks, but to Cressida they looked very fragile. She was actually rather relieved to have an excuse not to put the necklace on again yet, deciding to wait until her mother got home so she could ask her for some advice on securing the hooks.

Without really admitting to herself that she was nervous about the effect it'd had on her in the shop, she also wanted to find out if her mother had any ideas as to where the necklace had come from, how old it was and what the beads were made of. It was possible, she thought, that her skin had reacted sensitively to the touch of the beads; maybe there was some sort of varnish she could put on them to minimise the effect.

"Well - my goodness me - who is this glamorous visitor?"

Her mother had now arrived by bus back from town. She stood at the foot of the stairs smiling as, on hearing the front door opening, Cressida came carefully down, holding the long skirt up so she didn't trip.

"Sweetheart, you look absolutely wonderful!"

It was lovely to have Mum to herself! It was obvious too that Mum was enjoying the opportunity of a one-to-one session with her daughter. They shared a relaxed lunch together - a selection of cheeses, ham, salad vegetables and crisp fresh baguettes, followed by fruit yoghurts.

Over coffee Cressida explained her problem with the necklace.

"Oh my goodness, Cressy, it's beautiful. What attractive and unusual looking beads!" her mother said, as Cressida laid the necklace out on the table. She continued, "They look as if they could be pretty old to me, I've not seen anything quite like this except perhaps in museums. But you're right, they'll definitely need re-stringing. It would be awful if the string broke at the party and they spilled out all over the place."

"Gosh, Mum, do you think they're really old? How old? And what should I do, because if they are very old maybe I need to be a bit careful about re-stringing them myself. And there's something else too, Mummy...."

Hesitantly, Cressida told her mother about the strange sensation she had experienced in the shop when she'd hung the string of beads around her neck.

"I wondered if there was some sort of coating on them - p'raps something psychedelic like drugs or magic mushrooms - or some sort of plant sap which makes you feel weird."

"Well, if they are as old as they seem , who knows what it could be. Have you tried it again? I'll tell you what - why not do so now. I'll stand behind you and hold the fastening together at the back, and if you feel at all funny of course just say so and we'll take them off immediately."

So they did exactly that, but the only thing Cressida could feel was the firm warmth of her mother's hand on the back of the necklace, and her other hand protectively around Cressida's shoulders, reassuring and calming.

"Phew - nothing!" Cressida was very relieved. "Oh thanks, Mummy - that makes me feel an awful lot better! But what do you think I should do now - how can I find out more about them and perhaps get some advice on re-stringing them? The party's next weekend, so I haven't got all that much time."

"Well, I suppose it might be a good idea to take them to the museum in Chilminster. Even if they can't answer all your questions, someone there could perhaps give you some advice as to how you can find out more. You could pop in after school on Monday. I must say, I'm really intrigued, I'd love to be able to come too!"

"Why don't you, Mummy? Leave work early maybe." Her mother was employed part-time in the archive department of the County Council.

"If only! I have to get back in time to pick the boys up from school, then get them home and give them their tea! But maybe we can make a plan once you've found out a bit more. Who knows what you might discover? And now I think I can hear them all arriving back! Hello darlings! Did you have a lovely time swimming?"

The tranquil mood of the day was suddenly transformed as the two little boys erupted into the house and, flinging their coats and outdoor shoes off, rushed excitedly up to their mother and big sister to tell them about everything they'd been doing. Following them was their father, a football under one arm and a bag of wet swimming things and damp towels in his other hand.

"They should be exhausted, they literally haven't stopped!" he said with a smile, putting the football into the small cupboard by the front door where boots, shoes and other outdoor kit were kept, then pushing the contents of the bag of swimming stuff into the washing machine.

He continued, "Boys, could you hang your coats up and put your shoes away, then perhaps go and play in the garden or in the playroom. I need a cup of coffee and I also want to hear all about what Mummy and Cressy have been getting up to."

CHAPTER TWO

In the Museum

On Monday morning before school, Cressida gently folded the necklace into a few layers of bubble-wrap, then put it carefully into the small pocket on the front of her school rucksack. She'd decided not to mention it to any of her friends; they would certainly want to see it. Too risky, she thought, imagining the string breaking and the beads scattering all over the floor, rolling into inaccessible corners of the classroom.

It was difficult to concentrate in class, and in a way lessons seemed rather pointless now the exams were over. Her mind kept going back to the discovery of the necklace, the strange effect it'd had on her, and her mother's reaction when she showed it to her. The school day seemed to drag on interminably. Luckily few of the staff seemed to have noticed her abstractedness, although she was pulled up sharply in Science when she knocked a test-tube full of liquid onto the lab floor, not breaking it, but spilling its contents.

"Wake up, Cressida," was the exasperated comment from Miss Sellars, but as Cressida was normally quiet and competent she got away lightly, clearing up the mess then getting through the rest of the session without further mishap.

At last the bell signalling the end of the school day rang out. Instead of leaving as usual with Louise, who lived on the outskirts of town, Cressida grabbed her bag and hastened away down the hill towards the city centre.

"Sorry Lou," she said as she left, "Something I've got to do - I'll have to get a later bus. See you tomorrow."

Chilminster was an attractive old city, with a picturesque centre featuring some fine stone buildings, a market place, an impressive Norman cathedral with added side chapels, a medieval cloister and a row of almshouses nearby. The Chilminster County Museum, a red-brick Victorian building dating from the 1880's, wasn't all that far from the cathedral - along a cobbled lane and past a row of small shops. Further on was the High Street, where Cressida had been two days earlier, searching for second-hand clothes.

The museum was open until 6pm, and, it being a weekday afternoon, was not very busy, so there would be plenty of time to find out what, if anything, she could discover about the necklace. Feeling slightly nervous she went in and walked over to the reception desk, her heart beating a little faster than usual. Suppose they laughed at her for bringing the beads in, and told her it was a worthless modern necklace, or a piece of synthetic costume jewellery.

"Hello. How can I help you?" The man behind the desk seemed friendly and quite approachable, so she laid the bubble-wrap package carefully in front of him and explained what was there.

"My name's Cressida Curtis, and this is a bead necklace that I bought at a second-hand shop. My mother said she thought the beads were quite old, so I wondered if anyone here would be able to tell me a bit more about them."

"Let's have a look."

He unwrapped the package to reveal the necklace, and was immediately intrigued. His eyes widened and he let out a gasp of surprise.

"Well, my goodness me, yes, your mother was right. They are indeed old - very old. They look to me like a set of Ancient

Faience beads, possibly of Egyptian or Greek origin. Let me call my colleague Penelope Emerson, she's the Keeper of Historic Decorative Artefacts and Jewellery - she can probably give us a bit more information. I'm Matthew Harding, by the way, and my speciality is the Middle Ages, so I could also do with learning something from Penny's ideas and expertise!"

Leaving an attendant in charge of the entrance desk, with care he picked up the package and took Cressida through into a small book-lined room. It was a relief to be taken seriously, but slightly intimidating to be dealt with by two experts. By now she was feeling a mixture of excitement and apprehension; excitement about the possible rarity and antiquity of the beads, coupled with apprehension lest she was going to be told that they were much too rare and precious for her to keep.

What she learned when the colleague arrived was both unexpected and astonishing. Miss Emerson confirmed that they were indeed faience beads. Antique Faience, she explained, had been invented by the ancient Egyptians - who discovered that they could grind quartz or sand crystals and mix them with various other ores to make a powder. They then added water to the mixture which turned it into a sort of clay - which could be shaped into beads, ornaments, little sculptures and so on.

Once all those different hand-made artifacts had set hard, they would have been buffed up and polished to give them a shiny surface. Could it have been some sort of substance to do with the polishing that had given her the strange feeling in the shop on Saturday, Cressida wondered again.

There wasn't really time to think about that now, because as Miss Emerson continued, what she was saying was so interesting and extraordinary that Cressida was entranced. To imagine that all this had happened hundreds - maybe thousands of years ago - was quite overwhelming! That her beautiful bead necklace had been created so long ago and had survived to be found by her in a cardboard box full of discarded clothes and other stuff - it seemed improbable and incredible - indeed, almost miraculous!

"I think," continued Miss Emerson, holding up the string of beads in her right hand, and gently cradling the rest of it in her left one, "that this particular necklace could be Greek. You see, Cressida, by the early Bronze Age the Mycenaean Greeks had learnt the technique of creating faience from the Egyptians - and to me this looks like Greek work."

Cressida had learnt a bit about the ancient world in history lessons at school. They had done the Greeks and the Romans in Year Eight. But the starting point for those lessons had been much later than the Greek Bronze Age, she remembered. They had learnt about the first Olympic Games, the rise of Athens, wars with Sparta and the Persians, and something about the great philosophers, before going on to Rome. She wasn't even sure when the Greek Bronze Age had been - but it seemed to have been much earlier than the British Bronze Age.

"We're probably talking late Bronze Age as a roughly possible time for your beads - during the thirteenth century BC - that is, the twelve hundreds BC," Miss Emerson went on, realising that Cressida was out of her depth with regard to dates. "This was also around the time that the Trojan War is supposed to have happened - though we should bear in mind that it's a story largely made up of legend, fantasy and folk tradition, passed down through the ages by storytellers before being written down in about the eighth or seventh century BC. Not really verifiable history, although fascinating."

Unbelievable! Cressida was astounded to hear that her necklace could have been made so long ago. Who had worn it, she wondered, mentally creating a shadowy visualisation of a nymph-like girl from the distant otherworld of the far past.

Miss Emerson continued: "What we do know is that the Mycenaean Greeks were an early Greek civilisation, they spoke an archaic form of Greek and were a pretty sophisticated lot, skilled in arts and crafts, constructors of cities and palaces, and experts in ship building and warfare. To the later Greeks of the classical period they seemed like a race of legendary heroes - perhaps almost like half-gods themselves. As I say, it's possible that this lovely set of beads dates from as long ago as the thirteenth century BC; between twelve-eighty and twelve-twenty or so. Certainly similar beads were found on the Uluburan shipwreck."

Both Cressida and Mr Harding were fascinated at this glimpse into the mists of ancient history.

"The Uluburan shipwreck - what was that?" he asked.

Miss Emerson explained that it was a wrecked late Bronze Age ship that had recently been discovered accidentally by a young diver, who found it on the sea floor off the coast of Turkey. It was full of high status goods, including decorated weaponry, glass ingots, ivory, jewellery, gold, tin, storage jars, bronze figurines, and lots and lots of Ancient Faience beads!

"On the ship were some high-ranking Mycenaean passengers, and there were also Mycenaean goods such as the typical Mycenaean double axes which we see depicted on the pottery of the period. Of course we can't be sure, but it is entirely possible, Cressida, that your beads might have been part of that cargo."

Cressida could have stayed for hours asking questions about the previously quite unknown but tantalisingly intriguing ancient historic world Miss Emerson was showing her. But time flew, and glancing at her watch, all too soon she saw that it was after five o'clock and she had a bus to catch. At this point too she remembered that she had intended to ask for advice on re-stringing the beads. Hesitantly she began to explain.

To her surprise Miss Emerson was able to be more than helpful! She said she would love to have a bit more time to examine the necklace, and suggested that Cressida leave it with her for a few days. Also, as a jewellery specialist, she had a large selection of strings and yarn and was sure she could find something entirely appropriate for re-stringing the beads.

"It won't be Bronze Age," she said, "but it will look very like the one they're on now - and there will be no danger of it breaking, I'll also fix the fastening at the back."

Cressida didn't dare mention what she was also privately thinking - of the 'funny turn' which had happened when she first tried the necklace on. Would Miss Emerson have a similar experience, she wondered. Surely she wouldn't be able to resist trying the necklace on once she'd fixed it.

Arranging to return to the museum in three days' time she thanked both Mr Harding and Miss Emerson for all their help and kindness, grabbed her school bag and rushed off to the bus stop to get home.

Sitting in the bus, her head was in a ferment of excitement and curiosity. It felt as if a mysterious door had been opened and given her a glimpse into an exotic past she hadn't even known existed. Without doubt she knew now that she had to find out more - not just about the mysterious Mycenaean Greeks, but also about the Trojan War. History had always been her favourite subject at school, and all this hitherto unknown information had really fired up her imagination.

The turmoil of home life engulfed her as soon as she arrived back - her little brothers clamouring for her attention and her mother needing help with their baths and bed-time. Cressida managed to feed her new-found fascination with the world of ancient Greece by reading bedtime stories to the boys from an illustrated book of Greek Myths which she'd enjoyed when she was younger. They loved the tales, and because of what she now knew, those old stories took on a new significance which made reading them aloud more of a pleasure.

Then, at last, once the twins had settled down, she was able to tell her parents about her experience at the museum and the unforeseen revelations of the afternoon. They were as intrigued as she was. What she didn't mention again was the strangeness of the feeling she'd had when first trying on the necklace. She had almost convinced herself that it was just one of those weird fleeting sensations which sometimes happened.

CHAPTER THREE

The Party

Cressida collected her necklace from the museum after school on Thursday. Miss Emerson had done a wonderful job! Not only had she re-strung the beads and repaired the clasp, but she had also given them a meticulous and careful clean and polish. She assured Cressida that she had used a very mild liquid soap and warm water, just to lift off the accumulated dust and dirt of thousands of years. The necklace looked absolutely beautiful - glowing and iridescent as it lay spread out in front of Cressida. The little clay spacers between the beads had been left alone - they were much too fragile for such treatment.

"Oh wow, it looks totally amazing! Thank you so - *so* much!"

"It was a pleasure," Miss Emerson replied, smiling at Cressida's awed delight. "It's been a real privilege to work on something so ancient and so beautiful. Now, off you go and enjoy your party this weekend - but do treat the beads with care! They are very special and very unusual - and I think you'll be surprised when you put the necklace on at how it makes you feel."

On the way home Cressida pondered over this last remark. Had there been a hint there that Miss Emerson too had experienced some strange effect coming from the necklace? Or was it merely a kindly comment about how stylish and elegant Cressida would feel with the beads around her neck?

By Saturday morning she had almost forgotten about the odd sensations from the necklace. She was feeling excited about the party and confident about her carefully chosen outfit - it was both flattering and in keeping with the theme of the event. Louise had asked her to come early so they could get changed together.

There would also be boys there. Lou had two older brothers, Duncan and Charlie. Cressida knew them both well, in fact Charlie had been just one year above her and Louise in primary school, and when she lived in town the three of them had often played together. The other brother, Duncan, was a few years older, now completing his last year at school. Perhaps, she thought, with a slight thrill of anticipation, some of his friends might be at the party. She had not yet had a boyfriend, although every now and then she had seen a boy she fancied, and of course she had also fantasised about some of the gorgeous young men she'd seen on television or in films. Might she now meet someone who could bring to reality her secret romantic dreams?

She and Louise were students at the Chilminster Girls' High School, which was the sister school to the Boys' High School in the city. Both schools got together for events like plays, concerts and school trips; and the sixth forms were largely amalgamated, sharing lessons on both school sites.

Having two little brothers of her own had given Cressida a few insights into the world of boys - but of course the twins with their superhero games and garden kickabouts were miles away from the handsome, kind, funny and clever male inhabitants of her secret imaginings. She had often envied Louise's familiarity and easy-going camaraderie with her brothers' friends.

So it was with a pleasurable flutter of anticipation that she arrived at Lou's house early on Saturday afternoon, and was immediately caught up in the atmosphere of excitement. Louise was celebrating her sixteenth birthday; this seemed like a huge milestone to both of them - very near to being properly grown up.

The house was colourfully decorated with posters and flowers, with glittering paper chains and decorations strung up across the hall and around the large front room. Already, music was playing and the room had been cleared of furniture to make room for dancing. On the wall at the back was a collage of photographs and pictures, depicting Louise from babyhood to the present day.

It was headed 'LOUISE ANNA JACOBS BORN 20TH JUNE 1979' in arresting colour calligraphy, and below, inside a painted circle of flowers, was a photograph of Lou's mother in hospital, cradling the tiny newborn Louise. Cressida was fascinated as she looked round the photographic panorama of her friend's life so far - developing from a little blue-eyed baby proudly held in the arms of Duncan - himself then just four years old - to a fair haired laughing toddler, a skinny seven-year-old and so on all the way to the pretty blonde teenager she was now.

"Welcome, Cressy darling!" Louise's mother appeared in the doorway while Cressida was looking at the photos. "Lovely to see you! Wasn't she a dear little thing?"

"Hello Mrs Jacobs - yes, really sweet!" Cressida replied with a smile. She was fond of all Lou's family but particularly of her kind easy-going mother, who had been both practical and sympathetic a few years ago when Cressida had unexpectedly started her period for the first time while staying with them. She had felt utterly mortified and horribly embarrassed, but Mrs Jacobs' help, discretion, empathy and kindness was something she would always remember.

The Jacobs's were a tolerant, relaxed family, seemingly free from the anxieties and stresses which often troubled Cressida. She loved visiting them and sometimes secretly wished that her own more highly-strung mother could be a bit more laid-back. She couldn't imagine Mum and Dad being anything like as lenient as Lou's when the time came for her own sixteenth birthday, only a couple of months away. Lou's parents, once they'd organised everything, were tactfully retreating for the duration of the party to the attic - which had some time ago been converted into an en-suite guest room.

The family had prepared and laid out a tempting-looking buffet supper in the dining room at the back of the house, with a large barrel of non-alcoholic fruit punch for refreshments. The problem of alcohol was dealt with simply - a few bottles of champagne were waiting in the fridge to be opened and dispensed by Duncan and Charlie when the cake was cut and everyone sang 'Happy Birthday.'

Lou's parents had also established a few rules and regulations, and would be on hand in case of any sort of emergency, but they didn't anticipate trouble. Nineteen year old Duncan was tasked with supervising things and generally keeping an eye on the proceedings.

Louise, slightly embarrassed by her mother's effusive comment about the picture display, was anxious to get changed and to have some private time with Cressida.

'Come on Cressy, let's go upstairs and get dressed up. Can't wait to show you what I'm wearing, and to see yours. Oh, thanks so much!" Cressida had handed over her present - a carefully chosen pair of earrings for Lou's recently pierced ears, a CD, and a glossy magazine.

Looking back on the events of the party afterwards, Cressida realised that the time upstairs, with giggles and whispered confidences to one another as they dressed up, and with all the anticipation of the excitements still to come, had been very much the most carefree part of the afternoon. Lou admired the unusual necklace, and was intrigued by Cressida's account of how she'd discovered it in the charity shop, then had later visited the museum to find out about its extreme antiquity. What Cressida didn't mention was the strange effect it'd had on her, even though she'd again felt a slight fuzzy sensation just now when she put it on. But she had no idea yet of the strangely challenging, and ultimately life-changing experience which lay ahead of her.

When the two of them emerged just over half an hour later, Duncan and Charlie, waiting at the foot of the stairs, broke into spontaneous applause at their transformation into a pair of elegant young ladies. The boys' efforts had been much more cursory; each one in reasonably smart clothes and both sporting top hats which they swept off in exaggerated admiration as the girls came downstairs.

Soon the other guests started to arrive, including friends from school as well as some of Louise's many relations - she had a large extended family and several teenage cousins. As Cressida had hoped and feared simultaneously, there were boys there too, schoolmates of Charlie and Duncan plus a few others who were unknown to her. She felt shy and awkward to start with, but soon relaxed as she chatted with Mandy and Clare from school. The three of them congratulated one another on their costumes - Mandy in a stately outfit enhanced with a very grand purple feather boa and Clare in a long summer dress and a pretty hat decorated with artificial flowers.

"Don't we all look glam?" Clare said, as Duncan came round with a tray of punch and some cheese straws. "Love your necklace, Cressy."

"Well, Mandy's feathers are pretty amazing too, and what a brilliant hat, Clare. Did you make the flowers yourself?"

At first everyone stuck together with those who he or she already knew. But soon, thanks to the friendly relaxed sociability of Duncan,

Charlie and Louise - none of whom were in the least bit shy - the ice was broken and the room filled with eager chatter. Charlie had spent the morning creating a musical playlist which had been running softly in the background - now, with the volume turned up, people started to dance.

"Come on Cressy, let's bop!" he said, grabbing Cressida's hands and whirling her into the centre of the room. It was fun dancing with Charlie. whose cheerful exuberance was irresistibly infectious! In fact, the whole party was turning out to be delightful. Cressida felt her awkwardness disappearing as she spun around with Charlie then was claimed by a succession of other partners, known and unknown, until breathlessness made her flop onto one of the chairs around the edge of the room.

She sat there panting and laughing, watching the stamping and twirling dancers slow down as the music moved to a more leisurely tempo. And as the party careered on in full swing Cressida felt a growing sense of contentment and enjoyment; she needn't have been so nervous after all! Everybody was really friendly and the atmosphere was effervescent and exhilarating!

As the afternoon progressed, Charlie and Louise began to encourage people to move into the next room for the buffet, where an attractive array of food awaited them. The French windows at the end of the room were open, fairy lights had been strung between trees, and an assortment of garden furniture was set out. The afternoon was lengthening towards evening, but it was a warm early summer day, so most people were taking their plates outside.

"Hey Cressy, come along and meet my mate Tolly!" Duncan greeted her as she was stepping out into the garden, intending to join a group of girls she'd been talking to earlier.

Beside Duncan was a tall boy, unknown to Cressida. He looked very much the part, in a long black jacket over a grey waistcoat, narrow dark trousers and under the waistcoat a white shirt with an elegant maroon knotted cravat. Emboldened by the way things had gone so far, she smiled at them both, for the moment not feeling too ill at ease. After all, Duncan was an old friend.

"Hi Duncan. Hi Tolly."

"Tolly's one of my friends from orchestra," Duncan explained.

Cressida had forgotten about Duncan's music - he was a talented cellist and played in the Chilminster Youth Orchestra. She turned to Tolly; "Would I have seen you then, at CYO concerts? What d'you play?"

"Well, I play the clarinet, but I'm no longer in the CYO because I'm at University now. I'm in the woodwind section of my college orchestra."

Cressida realised with a sudden spurt of recognition that Tolly was as nervous as she was. His voice was deep and pleasant, but despite his elegant appearance, the way he was fiddling with his watch and his slightly diffident expression showed her someone who was a bit ill at ease. In a way this was heartening; she wasn't alone in being shy.

Duncan, having done the introductions, now left them to it. He'd noticed Tolly's glances over at Cressida while she'd been dancing, he knew both of them well and he rather fancied himself as a matchmaker. Part of his responsibility in ensuring that everything ran smoothly was to introduce people to one another, after all. This was a pairing he thought could work very happily.

The next few moments were awkward for Cressida and Tolly. They both started to talk at once, stopped, laughed nervously, and tried again.

"I noticed you when you were dancing, and wanted to meet you. From what Duncan told me you sounded amusing and interesting, so I asked him to introduce me, I hope you don't mind!" Tolly said. Cressida was flattered. This could be exciting!

"Of course not. Any friend of Duncan's is sure to be a nice person!" she replied, quite surprised at how self-possessed she sounded. "Shall we get some food and go out and sit down over there."

"Yes, let's - and I must also get rid of some of these layers of clothing - they're far too warm for a summer afternoon!"

They carried their plates to the bench she had indicated and she held his while he hung his jacket and waistcoat over the back, and loosened his cravat. "That's better", he said, smiling at her.

As they began to eat she couldn't help covertly glancing at him from time to time. He really was very good-looking, with dark curly hair and brown eyes, a straight nose and a friendly smile. Soon they were chatting quite easily. Cressida began to feel a sort of happy effervescence rising inside her as they ate, talked and laughed. They were starting to feel much more at ease with one another, relaxing while sharing anecdotes and comparing what music, books and films each of them liked. It seemed that they had a lot in common.

"Tolly - that's an unusual name, " Cressida said, "Is it short for anything - or is it perhaps a nickname?"

He gave a slightly rueful grin.

"Well, it's a bit embarrassing really. It's the shortening of a family name. I come from a long line of medics. My grandfather was quite a distinguished surgeon, Sir Bartholomew Henderson; in fact he'd been named after Barts Hospital in London - St Bartholomew's. The name was carried on into the next generation - my granddad insisted that it should be handed down the family. So my father is also

Bartholomew, and he's a doctor too; he's always called Bart. And I, for my sins, am Bartholomew as well. But when I was little I couldn't say it, so I called myself Tolly - and it stuck. I'd rather stay as Tolly than be Bartholomew, especially since I'm certainly not planning to become a doctor! Nor am I planning to saddle any son I might have one day with such a cumbersome name!"

Cressida laughed. "Well, I think it's rather a sweet story. I like nicknames. I've got two little brothers whose names are Michael and Joseph, but they've always been Mikey and Jo-Jo!"

It was all going so well, but the conversation was soon to take an unfortunate turn. Still on the subject of names, Tolly said, "Anyway, yours at least is much more normal than mine. Though I suppose Chrissie could be short for Christine, Christabel or indeed Christina?"

Cressida shook her head. "None of those. I'm not Chrissie, I'm Cressy, short for Cressida."

"Cressida! Wow, that's uncommon! A lovely name - but thanks to Chaucer and Shakespeare not one that many people would choose! I wonder what made your parents opt for it?"

Cressida was baffled. She had always loved her unusual first name and its meaning - Gold. She knew it had Greek origins, and because of her new-found interest in Greek history she had lately felt even prouder to have such a name.

"But what d'you mean? What's it got to do with Shakespeare and Chaucer?"

Her class had studied Macbeth and most recently, Romeo and Juliet, in English lessons at school, but Chaucer was little more than a name, although she vaguely remembered learning a bit about the Canterbury Tales in her first year at secondary school.

Tolly, who was at university reading History and English Literature, tried to explain.

"She was a Trojan girl at the time of the Trojan War. Chaucer called her 'False Criseyde' - because she had a lover, Troilus, but she ditched him and went off with a Greek warrior called Diomedes. Chaucer's 'Troilus and Criseyde' is all in Middle English so a very challenging read - but really great stuff. After that, Shakespeare is a piece of cake!"

Cressida began to feel an odd mixture of dread and excitement. Suddenly, to be hearing about a long-ago tragic story of love and betrayal from the time of the Trojan War - a subject which had preoccupied her ever since that first visit to the museum - was more than a bit disturbing.

Here she was, a modern Cressida, sitting with those ancient Greek beads now buzzing ominously round her neck. Extraordinary too, that Tolly should have referred to the Trojan War. She felt somehow that what he had said might indicate something fearful lying ahead of her.

Part of her wanted to leave it all behind, to go back and simply enjoy the party and gossip with her friends. But she was also finding Tolly very attractive and desperately wanted to stay talking to him and get to know him better. And the fact that he had some knowledge about that ancient story - myth, legend or fantasy though it might have been - seemed somehow to link him into her own preoccupations. Could they perhaps try to solve the enigma of the beads together?

"At my school we did 'Troilus and Cressida' for A Level," he was saying. "Shakespeare isn't quite so hard on Cressida but it's still a story of betrayal. It's pretty brutal - all the bloody events of the Trojan War plus the swopping of girls from Troy to the Greeks and vice versa - poor Cressida didn't really have any choice in the matter. Anyway, actually I don't think it's a true story, and apparently there's no mention of it in Homer. Our teacher said it probably originated in the Middle Ages."

He glanced over at her. Her expression had changed. She seemed to be terrified, her eyes wide open and staring blankly, as if she was experiencing some appalling inner vision. Suddenly she got up.

"I'm sorry, Tolly, I don't feel well. I need to go. So sorry..."

While she was saying this, she was again experiencing that strange buzzing sensation from the necklace, but now it was much stronger, and she was also feeling a sort of rushing in her ears and a tingling in her fingers.

Her ears then became full of shouting and the clashes of weaponry, and there seemed to be shadowy figures of warriors materialising in front of her. They encircled a youth and a girl who were facing one another with hands clasped together - but two soldiers were pulling them apart and the girl was then dragged away by another warrior. It was a frightening and distressing scene.

Suddenly she knew she had to escape. She gathered up her long skirt, jumped up and fled down the garden.

CHAPTER FOUR

'What's in a Name?'

Tolly was totally taken aback. What on earth was going on? She'd seemed absolutely fine until they started talking about her name - what was all that about? He wondered whether he should go after her; it was both worrying and inexplicable that she should suddenly have become so agitated. Was she ill? Had it perhaps been his fault - by telling her about the Cressida of the old stories, and how she betrayed her lover? He realised all too late that this might have been rather a tactless response to her after she'd told him her name.

And despite the fact that they had been getting on so well, and that they were undoubtedly attracted to each other, of course they really hardly knew one another. He didn't want to make things worse by unwittingly blundering in on what might be some sort of private distress. He decided the best thing to do was to find Duncan or, better still, Louise, and explain what had happened, and perhaps see what he could do to help.

Meanwhile Cressida reached the bottom of the garden and made her way through the trees at the end, searching for an old wooden gate which she knew led into an adjoining field. It was heavy and decrepit but in the end she managed to push it open, then nearly fell into the tangle of overgrown vegetation on the other side. Her heart was thumping and her breath coming out in great gasping sobs as she collapsed onto the ground.

What was happening to her? Why had she suddenly become so agitated and frightened? Fumbling at the back of her neck she managed to unfasten the necklace and remove it. The buzzing and shouting, the noises and visions of a long-ago conflict all faded away and she was in control of herself again, but still very anxious and very scared.

The worst thing was what Tolly must have thought. They had been having such a happy time together, getting to know one another and sharing impressions and experiences. Now he would think she was just a silly temperamental adolescent. He was nearly grown-up - eighteen or nineteen at least. No way was he going to be interested in a hysterical teenager still at school. And all because of her name.

As she began to calm down she started again to ponder over that name, and what it signified. Her parents had obviously had no idea that the name they had chosen for her had meant anything more than its 'gold' origin. She remembered her mother telling her when she was very little that the Greek word for gold was Chrusos or Chrysos, which was the source of her name, and that she was their own golden treasure.

She looked down at the string of beads lying on her lap, beautiful and mysterious. What was the secret that they held? What ancient sorcery had been stirred into life when she found them in that second-hand shop? Had they been waiting for her, waiting for a modern-day Cressida to reawaken the unfinished business of that long-ago betrayal?

But Tolly had said it probably wasn't a true story anyway. He seemed to imply that it dated from Chaucer's time or thereabouts. She recalled her conversation with Miss Emerson at the museum, about the Mycenaean Greeks in the twelve-hundreds BC, and the suggestion that the necklace could have come from as long ago as that. Miss Emerson had also mentioned the story of the Trojan War, but had added too that it was probably a mixture of legend, fantasy and folklore.

So what was it that had activated the hallucinations which seemed to emanate from deep inside the bead necklace? And was her own imagination also playing bizarre tricks on her, creating illusions stimulated by the effect of the beads?

She needed to talk to someone who might understand, and would listen to her description of those disturbing experiences without judgement. Into her mind again came Miss Emerson. She was the only other person who understood the historical significance of the beads, and who might be able to shed a bit of light on their disturbing effect. There had also been the very slightest hint of some mystery, when Cressida had collected the necklace from her, and she had then said that Cressida might be surprised at how it might make her feel.

Calmer now, Cressida stood up. When she got home she would get in touch with Miss Emerson again and tell her what she had experienced. Meanwhile she needed to get back to the party. With any luck she would be able to apologise to Tolly and get things back on track. She didn't put the necklace on again but dropped it carefully into her little make-up bag which hung over her shoulder. If anyone asked, she would pretend that the fastening had become loose.

"Hiya Cressy, oh great - you're OK!" Louise greeted her when she came back through the garden and into the house again. "Are you all right? We were getting worried about you - Tolly said you suddenly felt ill and then you rushed off. Is everything alright?"

"Yes, sorry, I felt sick and weird for a bit. But I'm fine now. Poor Tolly - he must have thought I'd gone crazy. Where is he, I need to explain."

She tried to keep her voice matter-of-fact and casual, neither wanting Lou to make too much fuss of her nor to let on how very much she cared about putting things right with Tolly. She repeated, "Where is he? I must go and apologise."

"Oh, he went home," Louise replied. "He said he had to go. Shame really, I thought you and he were getting on so well together!"

Cressida was devastated. She had obviously offended him by her behaviour and he didn't want anything to do with her any more. Trying not to let her acute disappointment show on her face she shrugged her shoulders. "Oh - what a pity. He was really nice. Anyway, how's the party going? Have I missed much? "

"No - you made it back just right! It's cake and champers time!"

Louise, sensing how upset her friend was, linked arms with Cressida and drew her further into the dining room, where Duncan and Charlie were handing out glasses of champagne. Then, keeping Cressida with her, Louise moved forward to the middle of the room where a large square cake lay on a silver tray. It was beautifully iced and decorated with flowers and fruit made of sugar candy, with LOUISE piped across the middle, and a large number '16' displayed below. Positioned around the cake were sixteen candles, ready to be lit.

As the candles flickered and they all sang 'Happy Birthday', Louise cut the cake. Cressida, watching, now abandoned herself to a sort of recklessness. Tolly was gone and she might never see him again - but the cake was delicious, Lou her very best ever friend - and the fizzy champagne tasted wonderful! She pushed away her sadness and worries for the time being and decided to drown her sorrows.

It was a decidedly unsteady Cressida who was collected by her father later that evening when the party drew to a close. She had downed several glasses of champagne and for the first time in her life was drunk. Her mood had swung from wild effervescence down to a sort of maudlin misery. She hardly remembered Dad escorting her to the car, she crashed into bed when they got home, and woke up the next day feeling awful.

Luckily Dad had been understanding and kind. "It's not a cordial, darling, although it tastes like one!" he'd said as he drove home. "But it's happened to all of us one time or another - a 'rite of passage' - part of growing up!" He promised to minimise things when talking to her mother, who was likely to be much more disapproving.

In fact, when Cressida rang Lou later that morning with thanks and apologies, it turned out that she wasn't alone - several others had also drunk rather too much champagne. On the whole though, the party had been a huge success, no real damage had been done apart from a couple of broken glasses and some spilt food. Cressida nursed her hangover and her sadness, but began to feel slightly better as the day went on.

Resolutely trying to put Tolly out of her mind, she remembered her plan to talk to Miss Emerson, which might offer a way forward. It could also be a way of injecting some productive positivity into the whole time spent with Tolly, because if he hadn't talked about Troilus and Cressida she would still be even more in the dark than she was already.

CHAPTER FIVE

Nepenthe

"**H**ello. My name is Cressida Curtis and I wondered if I could make an appointment to see Miss Emerson sometime."

Mustering up her courage, Cressida was ringing the museum. It was Monday afternoon, two days after the party. At school that day she'd had to put up with a fair bit of teasing from her friends.

"So what happened, Cressy? Did he try and kiss you?" " Why did you run away? Wasn't he as nice as you thought he was?" "Come on, Cressy, tell us! What was it all about?" " You certainly made a good job of drowning your sorrows anyway!"

"It wasn't like that," she responded repeatedly and sadly. "He was really nice. It was me that ruined it. I got scared and rushed off."

Even to herself this sounded like a weak excuse, but she couldn't face trying to explain what seemed to be the absolutely unexplainable reality of what had happened to her. She clung to the hope that Miss Emerson would get her message and ring her back. This didn't happen for several days, during which time she tried to conceal her anxiety but was all the time battling with an ongoing feeling of dreary depression. She had packed the beads away in bubble-wrap again, the enchantment she had felt when she received them back from Miss Emerson now replaced by a sort of nervous fear.

She found herself getting increasingly irritable with her little brothers, and really annoyed by her mother's repeated enquiries as to her mood and behaviour. She couldn't possibly explain the sad ache in her heart and her thoughts of Tolly.

"Whatever's got into you, Cressy? You've been sulking for days now. If that's the effect going to a rather special party has had on you, you'd have been better off staying at home. What on earth has happened to put you in such a bad mood?"

Even her father, usually fairly equable, was getting fed up with her moodiness. His attempts at remonstrance were equally fruitless. She responded angrily, "Oh, please, please - why can't you both just leave me alone? There's no point in telling you anything, you wouldn't understand! I need to be on my own. I'm going upstairs and I don't want the twins following me."

She knew that this was typical temperamental teenage behaviour and that it wasn't fair to take it out on her parents or her little brothers, but she couldn't help it. At least when she was alone in her bedroom she didn't have to explain herself to anyone. Day after day as soon she got home from school she rushed upstairs and put her headphones on, listening obsessively to music on her Walkman to blank out her troubles.

It was a week after the party when her mother came upstairs to find her.

"Phone call for you. Penelope Emerson from the museum," she said briefly.

Mrs Curtis was now thoroughly fed-up. She was increasingly irritated by Cressida's ongoing sullen moroseness, but at the same time she felt a natural frustrated concern. Her daughter's evident and unexplained misery was hanging like a black cloud over the whole household.

On hearing about the phone call, Cressida gave a huge sigh of relief. At last!

"Thanks Mummy, thanks so much!" With these words, the first civil ones she had uttered for days, Cressida jumped up and rushed downstairs to the telephone.

"Hello - is that Miss Emerson? Oh thanks awfully for ringing back."

"Hello Cressida. Yes, this is Penny Emerson. How did the party go, and how can I help you?"

"Well, it's a bit complicated, but I wondered if I could come and see you soon. It's about the necklace."

She had her fingers crossed that Miss Emerson wouldn't fob her off.

"Of course. My apologies for not responding sooner, I've been away at a Fine Art Symposium. What about tomorrow? I'll be in the museum all day. Say about 2 o'clock – would that suit you?"

"Yes, yes - that would be fine! Thank you so much again." What a relief!

And with that, Cressida felt some of the burden of stress and sadness which had been hanging over her for the last week lifting slightly. There was still her misery over Tolly, but that had become a sort of dull regret, completely different from the terror and panic which had overcome her at the party and which had haunted her ever since.

She found her mother and gave her a hug. "Sorry I've been so horrid. There's something I need to sort out, but I think it might be OK soon."

"Alright lovey. If you think the lady from the museum can help, that's fine."

Mrs Curtis privately felt rather hurt that her daughter hadn't felt able to confide in her, but was relieved that there seemed to be a solution. The obvious reason for it all might well be some sort of boyfriend trouble, or a falling out with one of her friends, but how the museum came into it all she had no idea.

It was with a beating heart and a sense of mingled hope and dread that Cressida arrived at the museum the following afternoon. Miss Emerson was waiting for her in the little back office where they'd had their first meeting. That had been less than a couple of weeks ago, but it seemed like a lifetime to Cressida, who had gone through such a roller-coaster of emotion in the meantime.

"Hello Cressida, nice to see you again. Would you like a coffee or a cup of tea while we chat? There's a staff canteen here."

"Oh yes please, thank you. Tea would be lovely. It's really kind of you to let me come and talk to you."

"It's a pleasure," said Miss Emerson with a smile. "I've been longing to hear about how you got on with wearing that beautiful necklace at your friend's party. I'll just order our drinks and then you can tell me about it. Did you have a good time?"

"Well, yes, sort of - the party was lovely - and lots of my friends said the beads were beautiful - but they made me feel very strange. That's why I wanted to come and see you."

Miss Emerson's expression changed slightly, and she nodded her head slowly.

"I wondered if that was the trouble. Tell me about it."

So Cressida launched into a full account of everything which had happened, starting with the beginning of it all, when she had felt peculiar and seen her face changing while trying on the necklace in the second-hand shop. She then went on to describe the final catastrophic and fearful episode which had overcome her as she and Tolly were sitting together In Louise's garden. As she recounted these experiences, she couldn't stop herself becoming emotional, almost tearful, as she remembered how terrifying that last episode in particular had been.

"Am I going crazy?" she blurted out, now feeling tears spilling out of her eyes and rubbing them furiously.

"No, Cressida, you're absolutely not going crazy. Here, take a tissue and have a drink of tea. I completely understand both how alarming it must have felt, and how unexpected and incomprehensible it must have seemed. And the reason I understand is because it happened to me too."

Cressida gasped, staring at her - wide eyed and open mouthed.

"What? REALLY? ... When ...what... how did it happen?"

" It was after you left the beads with me to re-string and clean. I did feel a bit light-headed when I was working on them, but I just thought I must be overtired and perhaps coming down with a touch of cold or flu. However, of course I couldn't resist trying them on when I'd finished cleaning them and had put them back together again. They looked so beautiful, laid out in front of me! I was absolutely thrilled at how gorgeously luminous and bright they'd become after a bit of gentle TLC. So, as I say, I put the necklace on, and it all looked marvellous! But that woozy buzzing feeling came back, and then I started to feel very odd - I was hearing strange noises and thinking I saw shadowy moving people behind me in the mirror. I took the necklace off, and everything stopped and went back to normal. But it had given me a terrible shock!"

This was an amazing revelation! A feeling of release had begun to spread slowly over Cressida as she listened to Miss Emerson's account. She wasn't going mad! It wasn't all in her head! There had to be some external reason for all this strangeness.

"What is it, then, do you think? When I told Tolly, the boy I was with, that my name was Cressida, he started talking about Troilus and Cressida and the Trojan War, and how Cressida betrayed her lover. I couldn't help wondering if somehow I was being punished for what she did, because I'm Cressida too. I know it sounds silly – but... "

Miss Emerson was comfortingly reassuring. She smiled at Cressida.

"No, I don't think it sounds silly at all. But having a lovely Greek name doesn't make you responsible for whatever did or didn't happen all those hundreds of years ago. And anyway, the story of Troilus and Cressida is a medieval fiction - there's no trace of it in Homer. Actually I too have a Greek name - Penelope - but that doesn't mean I have to wait ten years for my wandering husband to come back from the Trojan War, and resist the advances of a whole crowd of suitors while waiting! Especially since I'm not even married!"

Cressida couldn't help laughing at this. She had read the tale of the return of Odysseus from the Trojan War quite recently; it was retold in the stories of Greek mythology which she'd been reading to her little brothers.

Her obsession with Greek literature had really taken hold; she was now also reading translations of The Iliad and The Odyssey. The Odyssey was more approachable and indeed very exciting, but realising that the Iliad was more relevant to her current concerns, she was determined to get to grips with it too.

All this kind reassurance came as a tremendous relief. It felt as if a great weight had been lifted from her mind, but there were still baffling unanswered questions. She tried to approach it more rationally, saying,

"I still don't get why it happened. I remember wondering after the first time I tried the necklace on, when I was in the shop, if the beads might have a coating of some drug - p'raps like magic mushrooms or some sort of juice from a plant, or something like LSD. D'you think that's possible?"

"Well, yes, it could be," Miss Emerson replied. "But could such a substance have kept its potency for so many hundreds of years? And I'm pretty certain that glazed faience beads aren't at all porous. In any case, of course, after I'd cleaned them, surely that would have got rid of any residue. However, there is undoubtedly some sort of psychedelic effect which we've both experienced. And the ancient world was no stranger to the use of mind-altering drugs. Have you heard of Nepenthe?"

Unsurprisingly, Cressida hadn't. What Miss Emerson now described was another fascinating revelation into that long-ago ancient Greek world.

Nepenthe, she told Cressida, had been a plant-based cordial used by the ancients as a cure for grief and suffering. It was thought to induce forgetfulness and thus to get rid of pain or sadness. There were references to it in the works of Homer, for instance in the Odyssey, when the Trojan prince Paris gave it to Helen after abducting her from her home and husband in Greece, in order to make her forget all about her old life.

"It isn't clear today," Miss Emerson continued, "which plant was the origin of that ancient drug, but later herbalists thought it could have been opium. Opium comes from poppies, and was believed to cause forgetfulness. Nowadays there is still a family of plants called Nepenthes, but I don't think they have any psychedelic qualities."

Cressida had been brought up by parents who had a zero-tolerance attitude to the very idea of mind-altering drugs. She had never been tempted to try them, but until now she'd had no idea how ancient the use of drugs was.

Miss Emerson went on talking.

"There are other candidates," she explained. "For instance, LSD is supposed to have been developed from ergot, which is a fungal disease of wheats and grasses; and of course marijuana or cannabis also comes from plants. The archaic drug Nepenthe could have originated from any of these, or from some as yet unknown other plants which have psychedelic properties. But what seems clear is that both you and I, Cressida, seem unwittingly to have been exposed to the traces of some ancient hallucinogen."

"Oh my goodness," said Cressida, simultaneously fascinated and alarmed. It was all really interesting, but also quite worrying.

"Do you think I'd better not wear the necklace again," she went on, "even though I love it so much and also, weirdly, sometimes when I've worn it, it hasn't had any effect at all. But it frightened me so much ..."

"That might be a wise decision," Miss Emerson agreed, "at least until we find out conclusively what it is that has been causing these effects. But don't worry, Cressida, we will get to the bottom of this sooner or later."

On the bus going home Cressida's head was once again spinning, alight with today's revelations. She decided not to share the substance of what she had learned with her parents; she could imagine them becoming horrified and angry, perhaps even vetoing any further investigations into the provenance of the necklace and its hidden powers.

It was not until nearly a week later, when she was playing in the garden with her little brothers, that she suddenly she realised how the hallucinogen might possibly have remained in the necklace.

CHAPTER SIX

Mud Pies

Over the next few days Cressida tried to make amends for her week of sulks and bad temper by being helpful at home and making an effort with the little boys. She certainly felt far less upset and scared about the necklace after that chat with Miss Emerson, but there was still plenty to worry about. She wasn't sleeping at all well. In the dark hours of the night all her troubles crowded in - and most prominent among these was the loss of Tolly.

She tossed and turned, obsessively re-living the friendly rapport they seemed to have had, before she'd destroyed it with her hysterical outburst. Tears trickled down her face as she struggled to come to terms with bleak reality. He was by far the nicest boy she'd ever met, and the first boy she'd felt like this about. She was nearly sixteen, so one day perhaps there might be others. But the tears kept on welling out. She didn't want anyone else. She only wanted Tolly, and he was gone. As she agonised over everything, she toyed with the idea of asking Louise to find out from Duncan how she might get in touch with Tolly to apologise, but in the end she was too nervous to do so. He would probably say he didn't want to have anything more to do with her, and that would do away with the tiny shred of hope she was still clinging to.

Meanwhile life went on; school, homework, helping with the boys, doing her household chores and so on and so on. It was a dreary routine, there was nothing at all to look forward to, as her ongoing depression and misery continued to dominate her emotions.

Her mother, while relieved that Cressida was now behaving more normally, was nonetheless very much aware that all was not well with her daughter. Until now the relationship between them had been on the whole a peaceful and happy one. Cressida had always shared her worries, confided in her mother and appreciated her advice and support. But now, it seemed that she was turning away. It had to happen one day, Mrs Curtis told herself with a sigh, aware that her adolescent daughter was changing. Really, she thought, they had all been lucky that Cressida had reached her mid-teens so far without much drama.

In the end it was the little boys who managed at least partly to break the deadlock. Mikey and Jo-Jo adored their kind big sister and couldn't understand why she always seemed to be so unhappy now. They sometimes heard her crying in her bedroom, and that made them also feel sad and somehow unsafe. They decided to do something to try and cheer her up, so one day after school they spent an hour in the playroom creating a big picture for her.

Working together carefully, they made a large white sheet of paper by sticking four blank A4 pages together. Then they drew a border of animals and leaves and flowers. Starting at the top, each of them filled in that decorative border using thick coloured markers, working in opposite directions and meeting again at the bottom, Jo-Jo on one side, Mikey on the other. The twins were used to doing things together and liked to share everything.

In the middle they drew and coloured a giant picture of their sister and themselves, she had a huge smile on her face and held a hand of each of them, one on either side. Underneath they wrote, in large capital letters in alternated colours: 'Don't be sad we love you

Cressy', and put lots of kisses underneath. They took turns with all this too, each doing one letter, then the other doing the next one in a different colour, and so on till the message was complete.

When it was finished they felt very proud of themselves. They rushed excitedly to the kitchen where their mother was making their tea.

"Look Mummy, come and look what we've made for Cressy to help her feel better."

She followed them back to the playroom.

"Oh darlings, it's beautiful! What a lot of hard work you've done. I think she'll love it. Shall we call her downstairs to see it?"

But the twins had their own plan. Cressida was upstairs in her bedroom, still depressed, half-heartedly listening to music and apathetically looking through the list of post GCSE reading recommendations her school had provided .

Their mother helped them roll the picture up carefully, then the two of them crept upstairs as quietly as they could and pushed it under the gap at the bottom of Cressida's door.

"Surprise, Cressy!" they called in unison, then scuttled away again giggling with excitement, to wait on the landing while she opened the surprise.

Cressida heard the shuffling and whispering outside her bedroom door. Those annoying little boys again - why couldn't they leave her alone? She jumped up, meaning to fling open the door and tell them to go away, when she saw the flattened roll of paper sticking out below. Picking it up, she unrolled it and was overcome with emotion, simultaneously touched and amazed. Her eyes filled with tears as she beheld the colourful creation the twins had so lovingly made for her.

Then they burst in, exultant. Why was she crying? It was meant to cheer her up. They hesitated, suddenly unsure. But Cressida rushed over to them, laughing and crying at the same time. "They're tears of joy! I love it! Thank you, thank you so much, you darling clever boys!" she said as she hugged them both.

And for the time being, it really did feel as if the world had become a happier place. Her little brothers, with their unconditional love for her, and the painstaking and affectionate picture they had created, had achieved something truly heartwarming.

"You are both sweethearts," she said. "You've made me feel much, much better. And at the weekend I'll take you to the park on Saturday after swimming, and we'll also do something nice together on Sunday, I promise." She hugged them again and they all went down to tea, Cressida for the time being feeling almost like her old self again.

She kept her promise and pushed them tirelessly on the swings at the park on Saturday afternoon, chased them up and down the climbing frame, had a kickabout with them in the empty tennis court, and ended an energetic afternoon with a wildflower hunt in the field by the playground. Despite feeling exhausted as they trailed back home, all that outdoor activity had delivered Its own tonic. Although nothing had really changed fundamentally, Cressida felt more in control of her emotions and less fragile, and at last, thanks to the fresh air, had a much better night's sleep.

During the night it poured with rain. Cressida had planned to create a sort of treasure trail in the garden for her little brothers, but everything was so wet and soggy that this wasn't going to work. Instead, as by the next morning the sky was clearing, she came up with another idea.

"Let's go outside and dig up some clay from the mud pile and play that we're Stone Age people. We'll make plates and cups and other things, and while they're drying we'll make a bonfire. Then we'll roast marshmallows and pretend we're having a sort of Stone Age feast."

She knew this would involve them all getting very messy, but the little boys had always loved the games she invented for them. They were delighted and excited, and rushed off to find their wellies. Then she kitted them out with the waterproof overalls they used for painting.

"We can pretend they're robes made of animal fur," she said.

Luckily, the boys were still young enough to believe in the power of fantasy, and before long they were chattering happily about mammoths and cave bears, while digging away at the mud with their small seaside spades until they had quite a large amount. Cressida also provided them with old picnic knives, skewers and a bowl of water for smoothing out and decorating their creations. Lopsided clay animals began to take shape, and were laid out on the stone paving to dry, as the sun rose in the sky and the garden too dried out.

Cressida herself, seeing that the boys were much more interested in creating models than crockery, made a few flat plates and some little bowls. It was at this point that she started to ponder the porous qualities of clay. As the clay dried out and became hard, it shrank slightly. The boys' bulkier models took longer to harden, but her plates dried out quite quickly. She noticed how they stayed absorbent, even when dry, if they came into contact again with any spilt water.

Suddenly she remembered the greyish clay spacers between the beads in her faience necklace. Suppose the ancient craftsmen, once they had fashioned those little clay beads and laid them out to dry in the hot Mediterranean sun, had then soaked them again in a solution of something like Nepenthe before letting them dry out again. The clay would then be impregnated with the liquid with its hallucinogenic qualities. Could this be the clue to the strange secret of the necklace?

CHAPTER SEVEN

Ideas and Questions

For the time being, Cressida was unable further to explore this idea - the Stone Age marshmallow feast by the bonfire had to be organised. It was a full-time job! She and the boys collected dry wood from the garden shed, then, with her brothers eagerly helping, she supervised the creation of the bonfire on the paved part of the garden. Their anxious mother, watching nervously by the back door, had to be reassured that the twins wouldn't be allowed too close to the flames.

Cressida assured Mum that she would be punctilious and careful, and would keep a strict eye on the bonfire. First she drew a large chalk ring around it on the paving, and said this was a magic circle. Then, after lighting the fire she told the boys that they had to stay on the circle and mustn't move any nearer to the flames. She gave them each a long skewer and a bag of marshmallows and oversaw the roasting. To ensure no-one got a burnt mouth she temporarily removed the sweetmeats when done, to cool them down before being eaten. The twins, sticky and happy, loved it all!

One more idea crossed her mind as she busied herself doing all this. She knew that clay and earthenware had to be fired before it was fit for use. Would the firing have made a difference to whatever substance might have been impregnated into the ancient clay spacers? Just to test the firing qualities of her bonfire she popped a couple of her dried clay plates right down into the heart of the flames. She planned to check on them tomorrow morning before school.

The little boys didn't want their clay animals to go into the fire because they'd decided to paint them when completely dried out. Kind Cressida said she'd help them with that one day after school next week. At present, as she supervised the fire, she continued to think about those ancient clay spacer beads. There was still so much she didn't know, but this afternoon with the boys and the bonfire, while at times rather stressful and demanding, had undoubtedly provided her with plenty of ideas and a lot of food for thought.

"You've given them such a happy afternoon, lovey, well done," her mother said as they all went inside again, leaving the charred remains of the bonfire smouldering in the garden. There was another brief shower forecast later, which would probably get rid of any remaining cinders, but Cressida was hoping it would hold off for a few more hours at least, so her little clay plates could have enough time to be fired in the heat of the embers.

The boys, grubby but contented, went to watch television before tea, and Cressida escaped upstairs to her bedroom after what had turned out to be quite a tiring and laborious but oddly enjoyable day. It felt good to have wiped out the gloomy malaise of the last ten days or so and to be on normal terms with her parents again. The activities with her little brothers over the weekend had also partly allayed her private troubles as well as giving her a possible clue about her mysterious necklace.

Early next morning before breakfast she went into the garden to retrieve her bits of fired clay. The remains of the bonfire, now a gritty pile of black charcoal, were damp after the brief night-time shower, and she had to scrape away at the dead ashes with a hand rake before discovering any traces of her little clay dishes. To her surprise the embers below were still dry, glowing and warm, despite the night's rain.

When she found the clay plates, the results were disappointing. They had been broken by the heat of the fire and were now in pieces. However, they did feel different when she picked them up; the fire had changed the clay so it felt more like stone or brick. Also, it definitely felt that the shards had become much less brittle. She rinsed them under the outside tap then wrapped them in her handkerchief.

As she did this another idea came into her head. What if clay retained some of its porous qualities *after* firing? If it did, the ancient hallucinogen could have been absorbed later, after the little spacer beads had been fired. By that process they would of course have become much more robust. Maybe she should tell Miss Emerson about this little experiment, she thought.

Her initial disappointment on finding the broken clay shards faded away as Cressida now realised that they might provide a lead to solving the enigma of the necklace. She stood dreamily by the dead bonfire, imagining those ancient craftsmen fashioning the tiny round clay spacer beads, pushing a fine point into the middle of each while they were still soft, then once they were dry laying them down carefully on some sort of stone or slate tray into an oven or kiln for firing.

She had no idea what materials would have been used to make such trays, or what an ancient firing kiln was like, but her imagination was conjuring up an extraordinarily vivid image. There was so much she needed to find out. Did the Mycenaean Greeks have kilns for firing pottery? How did they mass-produce the myriad spacer beads needed for jewellery? What tools did they use?

How extraordinary, how very extraordinary, that she, thousands of years later, should be considering these things and visualising that long-ago world. It seemed incredible that she should have become somehow linked to that ancient time through her possession of the faience necklace. How many necks had it encircled in its long existence, and how many of the wearers had been drawn into inexplicable visions manifested by its secret powers?

Everyday life suddenly pushed itself urgently into Cressida's reverie. Inside the house the usual Monday morning rush and bustle was in full swing. The little boys were finishing their breakfast while their mother dashed about retrieving shoes and school bags.

Today their father was dropping them at school on his way to work, as their mother had to go off in the opposite direction for an early meeting, but where was Cressida?

"Cressida! CRESSIDA! You'll miss the bus if you don't come in for breakfast now! It's well after eight o'clock and everyone's ready to leave. I need to lock up the house."

"Sorry Mum, coming." Cressida shoved the little package of broken clay pieces into her pocket and rushed inside. Grabbing a piece of toast and gulping down a mouthful of tea she hauled her school bag over her shoulder and dashed to the bus stop.

She had been so absorbed by her ideas about the ancient clay beads that it was hard to concentrate on the everyday demands and routines of school. On the whole she enjoyed school and was a hardworking, diligent and able scholar, and now that the exams were over, lessons had become much more relaxed. She also had a nice group of friends, of whom the most important was Louise. In many ways they were very different; Lou was confident, outgoing and bold, Cressida quieter, shyer and much more reserved. They'd been friends for years and despite the differences in their characters - or perhaps because of them - they were devoted to one another.

Cressida half-wanted to confide in Louise about all the peculiar things which had been happening to her lately, but couldn't bring herself to do so. It was all so incomprehensible, so inexplicable and so strange; the last thing she wanted was for Lou to think she had gone a bit crazy. At the moment her only reliable ally and confidante seemed to be Miss Emerson from the museum. However, she did feel she could trust Lou enough to bring up the subject of Tolly. Later, after school dinner, trying to sound calm and casual, she mentioned him as if in passing, as she and Lou made for the garden at the back of the school where they tended to hang out together in their breaks between classes. Louise was not taken in for one moment.

"Come on Cressy, don't act like you couldn't care less either way. I can tell that you fancied him. And I think he really liked you too. Whatever happened at the party to make it all go wrong?"

Cressida sighed, then said, "Alright, I'll tell you. But you'll think it's pretty weird. Out of the blue I suddenly started to feel very shaky and scared - I don't know how to explain it .... but I sort of had to run away. I had this awful feeling of danger. And before you ask, no, I hadn't taken drugs or anything."

This was, she knew, not strictly true. But she hadn't known then about the hidden psychedelic qualities of the necklace. It was hard to explain things to Lou without giving away the frankly unbelievable reality of the hallucination caused by the beads.

"OK, OK, I do believe you." But Louise was both baffled and concerned. What could have suddenly occurred to create such an extreme reaction?

Cressida went on,

"You're right, of course I fancied him - and I really liked him too. We were getting on so well, he was sweet and kind and interesting and funny - but basically I blew it. I'm not surprised that he went off so early, I expect he never wants to see me again."

Her emotions were again getting the better of her. Her voice faltered as she felt tears coming. Lou immediately hugged her.

"Don't cry Cressy, I'm sure he fancied you too and I'm also sure things will work out. Tell you what - I'll do a bit of very casual probing through Duncan if you like. And actually, thinking about it, I'm pretty sure Tolly always intended to leave early. He had to get back to University the next day, and I know that it's a long journey away - Durham - right up in the north somewhere. I think Duncan said something about Tolly needing to get back there for first year exam results."

Louise's sympathy and robust common sense did act as a bit of a tonic. Cressida calmed down and they carried on chatting.

"Thanks, Lou. It's really helped, talking to you; sorry I'm being such a drip. But please don't give away too much to Duncan - I'd hate for Tolly to think I'm chasing him. Anyway maybe you could be right - it might just be that he had to leave early. I'll try and make myself be a bit more positive and optimistic about it all. Oh - there's the bell!"

Together the pair of them turned and headed back into school and the afternoon's classes. Lessons were much less pressurised now GCSE's were over, but still quite challenging for both these girls and those of their contemporaries who were also staying on to start A level courses next term.

CHAPTER EIGHT

A Secret Plan

Cressida decided to pop into the museum again after school to see if Miss Emerson was available. After that emotional session with Louise at lunchtime it helped to have something else to think about, something which continued to be baffling, fascinating and intriguing. She was eager to share her ideas about the porous qualities of the clay spacer beads. The more she thought about it, the more plausible this theory seemed.

She felt a bit diffident as she arrived once more in the foyer of the museum. Would they think she was wasting Miss Emerson's time with these frequent visits? Mr Harding was again at the front desk.

"I'm really sorry to keep bothering you, but I wondered if Miss Emerson was available."

"You're Cressida, the girl with the necklace, aren't you? That has proved to be a really fascinating find! She's very excited about it! She's probably upstairs in her office - I'll phone through and see if she can spare you a few minutes."

Miss Emerson was indeed in her office and busy, cataloguing a collection of miniature late 18th century silhouette portraits which had been left to the museum. To Cressida's relief, she didn't mind being interrupted.

"She says that's fine," said Mr Harding, "just go down the passage that way, then left up the stairs, straight along the corridor at the top, and her office is the second door on the right. Sorry I can't take you up there myself but at the moment there's no-one to take over the desk."

Mis Emerson was waiting for her. "Hello again, Cressida. How are things going?"

Cressida plunged straight in.

"Fine, I think, thank you. I just wanted to tell you about an idea I had about the beads, and the effect they had on me - and on you too."

"That's intriguing. Have a seat and tell me what you've discovered."

"Well, it was at the weekend. I'd been organising games for my little brothers in the garden, but because it had rained in the night, we were reduced to making mud pies the next day, once the rain had stopped, and pretending we were in the Stone Age." Miss Emerson smiled at this. "Sounds fun! I bet they loved it!" she said.

"Well, yes they did, they made lots of clay animals. And of course I noticed that even when clay has dried out, it still absorbs water. I remembered the little clay spacer beads between the main ones of the necklace, and I wondered if it was in *them* that the hallucinogen liquid had been absorbed."

"Goodness me, that's a really interesting and clever suggestion, well done! I hadn't thought of that, but you could easily be right."

"But that isn't all," Cressida continued, "I realised that the little spacers would have been very fragile when they were first made - they would've just crumbled away - so they'd have to be fired before they could be used. Well, we'd built a bonfire to roast marshmallows, so I put a couple of the clay dishes that I'd made right down into the middle of the fire, to see if the heat might toughen them up. When I got them out this morning they had broken, but the whole texture had changed. Look!"

From her pocket she pulled out her carefully wrapped shards of pottery.

Miss Emerson picked them up and felt them, turning them over in her hands. "Yes," she said, " I see what you mean. They feel much stronger and harder than they would have done when they were first made. The fact that they broke doesn't really matter - even in a proper kiln sometimes pottery breaks - it's caused by air bubbles inside the clay."

Cressida went on, "Then I thought, that if the pottery stayed porous even after it was fired, that would be a much better way of applying whatever the druggy liquid was, by soaking the hardened spacers in it. They would absorb it without destroying the strength of the fired clay. But I don't know if fired clay stays porous."

"Oh yes indeed it does, after the first firing. The way it becomes watertight is by being put through a second firing at a much higher heat. My goodness, Cressida, you clever girl! it looks as if you might have come up with a possible solution to our mystery."

Cressida felt herself blushing at these words of praise. To be congratulated by a real scholar - someone who, as a member of the museum staff, was in charge of a whole department - felt quite overwhelming! She didn't know how to respond but mumbled a few hesitant words of gratitude,

"Oh thank you - it was just luck really. I've been thinking about it all so much. I'm really glad you think it's possible."

"Not just luck, Cressida, but a rational and intelligent assessment. Very well done indeed."

Miss Emerson's praise was sincere. She was truly appreciative of the logical process through which Cressida had reached her conclusions. She smiled and added, "I think we have a future researcher on our hands. I'm really impressed!" Sparing Cressida's blushes she continued,

"Now we need to decide what to do next. I suppose it might be possible to get a scientific examination of the necklace to try and identify what the substance is. But it's so ancient, and also quite fragile – so I'm not sure. What do you think?"

Cressida was flattered at being consulted like a colleague. She responded as thoughtfully as she could,

"I don't really like the idea of it going to some unknown lab where it might get lost or damaged. What about if we remove a few of the spacers and send those for analysis. Actually p'raps it would be better if you took them off, as you've already done some work on the necklace. I don't want to send the whole of it away."

Miss Emerson nodded. "That sounds like a good plan. Would you like to bring it over after school one day? Tomorrow or Wednesday would be best as I'm away on Thursday, and Fridays are always busy. I'll also trawl through my academic colleagues and contacts and see what any of them can come up with. Meanwhile, thank you, Cressida, for involving me in such a fascinating area of interest."

They agreed that Cressida would come back the next day with the necklace, and would take it home again with her after Miss Emerson had carefully removed some spacers.

On the bus home Cressida's mood was buoyant and triumphant, her lovesick misery temporarily eclipsed by a feeling of elation. How exciting to be involved in a real research project!

There was a bit of explaining to do at home when she arrived back later than usual, but her mother couldn't really disapprove of all these visits to the museum. She would have been much more concerned had she been able to read her daughter's mind and find out what Cressida was planning next.

After a hurried cup of tea Cressida rushed upstairs, ostensibly to do some of the post GCSE reading recommended by her school, but really to scrutinise the necklace again. She tied a handkerchief around her face before laying it out carefully on her bed, then examined it meticulously, bead by bead, being careful not to get too close to it in case the hallucinogen began to affect her. She now noticed that some of the spacer beads were chipped or broken - could this be why sometimes wearing the necklace had no hallucinatory effect? Unless enough of them were actually touching the wearer, perhaps nothing would happen.

She also found herself wondering if the particular manifestations of strange things caused by the drug-soaked spacers had been in any way affected by what was going on in her mind at the time. When she'd put the necklace on for the very first time, at the charity shop, she'd been looking at herself in the mirror and her face had seemed to be changing. But the entire purpose of her search then had been to alter her appearance and re-invent herself as a Victorian or Edwardian lady, in keeping with the theme of Louise's party. Had her own intentions affected the subject of the vision she saw appearing?

Then she began to consider, in a much more calm and detached way than previously, that terrifying illusion which had upset her so catastrophically as she sat with Tolly in Louise's garden. She had heard the sounds of fighting, the clash of weaponry and the cries of warriors. She recalled how she and Tolly had been talking about Troilus and Cressida and the Trojan War. Again, had her own imagination influenced the content of what she saw? Had her mind created that distressing scene of the girl being wrenched away from the young man, after hearing what Tolly had been saying about Troilus and Cressida?

There was only one way to find out, she realised, which was to subject herself again to the powers of the necklace. She would need to wait until she was alone in the house - she couldn't risk her parents knowing what was going on. More seriously, she'd have to make sure her little brothers were out of the house too. There mustn't be any possibility of them interrupting what could be a hazardous and upsetting experience, or, worse still, getting hold of the beads themselves. With regard to herself, nothing, she felt, could be more shocking than what she'd already undergone, and she was now beginning to feel better informed and more mindful of the strange qualities of the ancient necklace.

This time, she would focus very carefully on thinking up a scenario of images or activities with which she could occupy her mind, so she could judge how much effect it had on whatever she might see or feel. Should she concentrate on the ancient past, the time in which the necklace had been created?

Her growing fascination with the Mycenaean period, and her ongoing explorations into ancient history and translations of the Homeric epics, had given her a wider understanding of what had obviously been a brutal, vicious era. She'd been particularly shocked when Tolly talked about the trafficking of girls between the Greeks and the Trojans. Poor Cressida - the original Cressida - 'False Criseyde' - didn't really have a choice, he had said.

Since then she had read many other legendary accounts about the abduction of women and girls in the ancient Greek stories: the rape of Europa by Zeus the king of the Gods, the capture of Persephone by Hades the king of the underworld - and also the kidnapping of Helen by the Trojan prince Paris, which had been the trigger for the Trojan War. As well as these there were numerous other tales of nymphs and maidens, pursued, captured and raped by Gods, heroes and warriors. Again she envisaged the girl in the horrifying hallucination she'd had while sitting with Tolly at Lou's party, realising now that what she'd seen was another abduction. No, thought Cressida, she would form her fantasies around a much less violent scenario.

Racking her brains for examples of gentler subjects to focus on, she remembered an enclosed garden, with overhanging trees, a waterfall, and lots of flowering shrubs. Not long ago with her family she had visited that garden. It was in the grounds of a nearby stately home; a seventeenth century mansion which had been the family seat of an aristocratic family, but was now run by the National Trust.

The garden was a charming place, with espaliered fruit trees and rambling roses climbing up grey walls, pathways laid out between beds of colourful flowers and shrubs, and a decorative splashing water feature in the middle. Apple and pear trees laden with young fruit, gooseberry and raspberry bushes and a small kitchen garden lay at one end, and at the opposite end there was a little lawn and a seating area.

Cressida had brought her camera with her on that trip, and had taken several photographs. These pictures, and the memory of that lovely garden, she decided, would be her inner vision. Meanwhile she would wait for an appropriate and safe time, when once again she would subject herself to the mysterious alchemy of the beads.

Downstairs, she could hear that her father had arrived home, while in the background the clash of kitchenware and crockery meant that supper was being prepared. The boys, whose shrill chatter was punctuating the other sounds, were on their way to bed and would be demanding bedtime stories from her as usual. Reluctantly, she abandoned her plans and went down to make herself useful. If she played her cards right Dad might give her a hand with the maths puzzles they were doing at school - intended to be a bit of fun now that they were free of GCSE pressures. So far she'd hardly done any of them and wasn't finding them fun at all.

CHAPTER NINE

The Experiment

It was over a week before Cressida was able to complete her daring experiment. The necklace, minus a few of its spacer beads (which had been carefully removed, as planned, by Miss Emerson) lay ready on the desk/dressing table in her bedroom. It was Saturday morning, and she was alone in the house.

Her father had taken the twins to the fun-fair and circus. This particular event took place in parkland on the other side of Chilminster in the early summer and remained there for a few days. To add to the delights awaiting the boys, in a nearby field there was an exhibition of steamrollers, tractors and other vintage farm machinery which Dad promised they would visit after the circus. The little boys had been in a state of almost uncontrollable excitement for several days now; all in all, it promised to be an unforgettable experience for them both!

Their mother was away for the night, visiting an elderly great-aunt in the Midlands. She'd suggested that Cressida accompany the others to the circus, or maybe arrange to spend the day with one of her friends, rather than stay by herself at home. Cressida, however, opted to stay where she was. She had other plans, secret plans.

She had assured her parents that she would be fine at home alone. Her explanation was that she wanted to listen to music, watch daytime television, try out some cooking experiments and generally relax with no distractions and no real homework. She also felt she deserved some time off. The current school year had been academically demanding in all subjects, and normally when she was at home she was helping with chores or looking after the twins.

As soon as everyone had gone Cressida set out to test the strange magic of the beads. Before putting them on she laid out the photographs she had taken of that exquisite garden she had recently visited. She scrutinised each picture intently, trying to imprint its content on her visual memory, creating an internal panorama of the plethora of rich colour, foliage and fruitfulness depicted in the photographs.

Next, her heart beating slightly faster than usual, she gently picked up the necklace and fastened it around her neck. She waited, looking at her reflected image in the mirror. Nothing happened. Had the removal of a few of those little spacers destroyed the weird powers of the beads?

Then, almost imperceptibly at first, the mysterious buzzing sensation she remembered from her previous experiences started to develop – first very faintly, then louder and louder until her ears were full of it and her hands were tingling. She stared at her pale reflected face, and at the floral panorama behind her.

At first, she didn't realise that what she was seeing there was an illusion - for one mad moment she had thought it was a surprise display of real flowers in her bedroom! Then realisation kicked in. It was working!

The developing vision of an enchanted garden, more beautiful than anything she had seen in real life, expanded and gradually filled the mirror in front of her. Each flower and leaf seemed to be edged with a rim of gold. She could see rainbows in the water fountains and hear birdsong as the buzzing faded away. Then, entranced, she found herself walking slowly down a grassy pathway towards a seated figure at the end. Who was it? It looked like Tolly. Why was he there? She was transfixed, awe-struck and full of longing as she gradually moved towards him.

But before she reached him the panorama began to fade and the colours to dim; gradually she realised where she was - standing in front of the mirror in her bedroom at home.

Cressida then began to try and pull herself back together. She sat on her bed, her head spinning with wonder at the extraordinary and enthralling revelation which the beads had delivered to her. She unclasped the necklace and started to reflect on what had just happened. It was several minutes before she felt anything like her normal self again.

That, she realised, was the power of mind-altering drugs. They gave you glimpses of paradise - but could also lead you into scenes of horror and violence. They preyed on your subconscious and could inspire you to untold heights of ecstasy and creativity, but could also draw you into depths of despair and degradation. What had just happened to her was something she would never forget, but she wasn't going to seek it again.

Slowly she stood up and enfolded the beads again in the bubble-wrap pouch where she had been keeping them. It felt almost as if she had become a different person, that she had been taken on a strange journey, and that she wasn't quite the same girl she had been earlier.

Still reeling slightly from the effect of the drug, and feeling lightheaded and fragile, she decided to go downstairs and make some coffee. It was going to be a challenge to apply herself to the everyday tasks which she had planned to do, but they must be done.

Cressida therefore took herself in hand. She made herself a large cup of milky coffee and cut herself a hefty chunk of fruit cake. When she had finished that she felt physically much less shaky. The next thing was to have a soothing bath with plenty of scented bath lotion, then to go for a short walk before tidying her room and preparing the supper for later.

Next week she would get in touch with Miss Emerson again, who might by then have received news about the spacers. But now, as far as Cressida was concerned, any more revelations or discoveries about the origin of the drug were not important. She knew now from her own experiences that it was a very powerful and potentially dangerous hallucinogen.

When her father and the boys got back late that afternoon she had done some reading, tidied her bedroom and prepared a welcoming early evening meal for them all. Jo-Jo and Mikey were almost incoherent with happiness as they jointly told her about their exciting time at the circus, describing the brilliance of the acrobats, the antics of the clowns, and the cleverness of the dancing horses!

Then, at the fair, they'd both had goes on the helter-skelter and the dodgems, been up on the big wheel, and each won a prize from the tombola. Lastly - and perhaps most excitingly of all - they'd both had rides on an enormous tractor and a steam roller.

"And we've got two goldfishes. Daddy won them on the coconut-shy!"

Dad grinned ruefully at this, "I didn't expect to win anything, but once I'd got one goldfish, I had to keep on trying over and over again till I got another. They now have one each, haven't you, boys!! And the coconut-shy manager has done rather well financially after all my efforts!"

Gradually the normality and routine of everyday life was returning, replacing the bewitching imagery of the phantom world which Cressida had visited that morning. For the time being she was completely contented with this peaceful state of affairs. The twins' exciting day had tired them out, and after they had been tucked up in bed Cressida was able to enjoy a rare relaxing evening with her father.

It wasn't often that the two of them spent time alone together, but in general they had a very easy, companionable relationship. After the otherworldly events of the morning it was lovely to chat to Dad and to hear his account of the high and low points of his day with the twins.

"On the whole they enjoyed everything, but they had their moments," he said, "They were both actually pretty scared on the big wheel, and I was terrified that they'd try to climb out before it had stopped. Mikey had an accident when queuing for the loo; luckily I had spare pants and shorts at the ready - thanks to instructions from Mum! Jo-Jo dropped his ice-cream, then as soon as I'd bought him another, he almost immediately dropped that one too! They were both alarmed by all the wasps whizzing around everywhere but luckily no-one was stung.

"And there was huge anxiety when I tried and tried and *tried* to knock down another coconut for the second goldfish. If I hadn't succeeded in the end, I think I would have had to give the first one back - you know how vital it is to them to be equal in every way!"

He refilled his glass of wine and smiled at Cressida. "It's really nice to be home, darling; to relax and have some rational conversation with my lovely daughter! How has your day been? Not too boring, I hope!"

CHAPTER TEN

Resolutions and Solutions

When a few days later Cressida told her mother that she'd yet again be late home after another visit to the museum, Mrs Curtis couldn't help wondering what was going on. Up till now she had accepted her daughter's excuses for those frequent late arrivals home from school, but now she had begun to think that maybe there were things she didn't know about.

Could Cressida be involved with something she knew her parents would disapprove of - perhaps meeting a boy in secret - and be using the museum contact as an excuse, she wondered? She hesitated to make any accusations, but was becoming increasingly concerned about the secretive manner Cressida seemed to have acquired lately. No longer did her daughter confide in her as she had done previously, up until only a few weeks ago. Although Mrs Curtis recognised that Cressida wasn't obliged to tell her everything, the fear was that she might have become mixed up in something illegal or dangerous, or perhaps more likely, got involved with a boy who she knew her parents would disapprove of.

She discussed it with her husband, who was on the whole fairly reassuring. He acknowledged that Cressida's moods had become more volatile lately, but he was sure this was all part of the emotional turmoil of adolescence. She was still helping with the twins, doing her post GCSE reading and generally behaving normally on the whole. The last thing they should do, he said, was make any sort of unfounded accusations. He had an idea, which might provide proof of what Cressida was up to.

"I'll tell you what we can do. Why don't we suggest asking this Miss Emerson over for a drink, or dinner one day? After Cressy came home after that initial meeting, when she first took the necklace in, she was full of excitement and curiosity about what she'd learned. And since then, she's been reading up about ancient Greece and even working her way through bits of Homer in translation. Hardly the actions of someone who's up to no good! It could be that we owe Miss Emerson thanks for inspiring our girl with this new and obviously enthralling interest. And remember, at that age, one does go rather over the top about stuff - it's either all or nothing!"

These were wise words, and his anxious wife at once began to feel calmer.

"You're right love, I'm probably over-reacting as usual," she said. "It's an excellent idea to invite Miss Emerson over. We'll suggest it to Cressy when she gets back later on."

Cressida, meanwhile, had again taken the necklace to school with her, safe in its bubble-wrap pouch. Sitting at her desk trying to concentrate on the current lesson, she had to keep stopping herself from speculating about what might happen later. Miss Emerson would have heard back from the lab where she had sent the spacers, which had probably now also been returned to her, ready to be replaced in the necklace when Cressida brought it back.

Exciting, and at the same time worrying for Cressida, was going to be the result of the scientific examination of that group of little grey clay spacer beads. It seemed ages since Miss Emerson had carefully removed them from the necklace and sent them off for analysis. What would the scientists have discovered? Would they have been able to identify that mysterious hallucinatory drug?

A nudge from Louise bought her back to the decidedly un-hallucinatory reality of her geography lesson. Their teacher, Mr Beresford, had devised some quick-fire question and answer quizzes to keep the class busy.

"Cressida Curtis - wake up! This is the third time I've asked you," he was saying. "What's got into you today? Are you away with the fairies! Name five commodities which are regularly imported to Great Britain from the Far East."

" Er - Tea, coffee, clothing .....(Louise's whisper gave her two more answers) .... "minerals and chemicals."

"At last. Thank you, Cressida. Keep your mind on the subject, please, No more day-dreaming."

"Yes sir, sorry sir." she responded humbly.

As Mr Beresford moved on to someone else, Cressida mouthed her thanks to Lou. She managed to keep herself focused for the rest of the school day, but had to dissuade her friend from accompanying her to the museum. She would have loved to be able to tell Lou about the whole mysterious business, but until a clear resolution was reached she didn't feel she could. There was no better or more loyal friend than Lou, but she was also very gregarious and sociable. It might be hard for her to keep this secret, Cressida thought. In fact, she was wrong in this; later she was to learn that Louise was eminently able to keep important confidences to herself.

"I've got this meeting with the museum lady again, Lou. Once the whole thing is sorted out I'll tell you everything, I promise. Sorry - I wish I could, but I can't yet."

Louise couldn't imagine what it was all about, although she had some vague idea that it might somehow be connected to the strange episode which had upset Cressy during the birthday party. Sometimes, when someone had a secret they didn't want to talk about, it turned out that they were pregnant, or had a terminal illness, or their parents were divorcing. None of these seemed likely as regarded Cressy.

Visits to an academic at the museum obviously couldn't indicate any sort of pregnancy scare! In any case Lou knew that Cressy had never yet had a boyfriend, and the interlude with Tolly had been too fleeting to be significant. Then, as far as Louise knew, Cressy's health was good, and as for a possible parental divorce, you only had to look at Mr and Mrs Curtis to see that they were devoted to one another.

Nevertheless, Louise was worried. Could Cressy have some sort of invisible mental illness? Again, that wouldn't really fit with visits to the museum. It must be something she'd discovered - perhaps something in the distant past which had turned out not to be true, or some historical anomaly which didn't make sense and needed an academic to sort it out. That might possibly be nearer the truth, but it was such a vague idea that Louise couldn't take it any further. Nobly, she resolved not to pester her friend, but to wait until Cressy was ready to share her secret.

Cressida arrived at the museum, which was now so familiar to her that she knew quite a few of the staff and was on friendly terms with them. As she entered the building she saw a poster on the wall by the entrance desk. It was headed **"Volunteers Wanted"**. While she was waiting for Miss Emerson she started to read it.

"University of Wessex Archaeological Excavation to take place at Troycombe Castle between 24th ***July and 18***th ***August 1995."*** was the sub-heading. Cressida was intrigued. Troycombe Castle was the semi-ruined medieval castle on the hill above her village.

"Hello Cressida. Thinking of doing some digging?"

She turned round. Miss Emerson was standing just behind her.

"Oh, not really - but it does look interesting. Troycombe Castle's very near to where I live."

Miss Emerson opened the door to the little back room, now also very familiar to Cressida, saying meanwhile,

"Well, do have a think about it. If you're interested, have a word with Matthew Harding. He's going to be in charge of the whole thing - and of course he'll also be on the hunt for medieval stuff. Cup of tea?"

"Oh yes please. And here's the necklace - I hope you can get the spacers back on OK."

When she had ordered tea and biscuits Miss Emerson took the necklace and laid it out carefully on the table. She then unwrapped a small package and spread it out. The small group of spacer beads lay inside. Next she took a surgical mask from her pocket and put it over her nose and mouth. Cressida stared, astonished.

"Don't worry - it's to stop me getting woozy from the drug, I've got one here for you too if you want it."

"Should I?" Cressida felt a bit self-conscious. She hadn't expected this.

"It might be a good idea. After all, both you and I know what effects this ancient drug can have."

While she was talking, Miss Emerson was delicately unpicking the fastening on the necklace and, with a pair of fine tweezers, unknotting the string and very gently lifting the faience beads off so the spacers could be returned to their places. Cressida, as advised, also put on a mask, watched, and waited.

While Miss Emerson was concentrating on this meticulous restoration work, Cressida decided that she would tell her about that final secret experiment she had initiated on the day she was at home alone. Meanwhile she gazed in fascination at Miss Emerson's skill and care as she returned the necklace to its original form.

"There! All done!" Miss Emerson breathed a sigh of relief and rewrapped the necklace. "Now we can take off these masks and enjoy our tea!"

"So was the drug definitely in the spacers?" Cressida said. "What did the lab discover?"

"It was indeed. They identified a very strong hallucinogen, still potent despite the extreme antiquity of the necklace. They were able to identify opium as part of the content, but there were other elements too. These they couldn't recognise, but they have taken scrapings so they can continue their investigations."

"Oh, my goodness!" Cressida was simultaneously excited and alarmed. She then began to tell Miss Emerson about the private experiment she had conducted at the weekend, in order to find out if the visions produced by the drug were influenced by the thoughts of the wearer.

Describing how she'd put the necklace on, feeling the strange buzzing at first, then gradually being drawn into the illusion of the enchanting paradise garden, she said,

"It was all so gorgeous and so magical, but when it faded away I felt strange and shaky. And then I realised how dangerous it could be. This time I'd deliberately focused my mind on something beautiful, because previously, interpretations of what I was thinking about had been pretty frightening. But those other times had only lasted a few seconds, as I was so alarmed that I took the necklace off as fast as I could; actually the second one was so terrifying that I had a real panic attack. On that last time, though, the garden that appeared was so wonderful and inviting that I stayed there for several minutes.

"When I came out of it I not only felt weird, but I actually got quite scared, thinking I might become a drug addict if I went on trying it out. So I decided I would never do it again."

She felt herself becoming emotional as she spoke, and took a mouthful of tea to calm herself down.

Miss Emerson was, as ever, understanding and kind.

"You're absolutely right, Cressida, like all such drugs it has the potential to lead to degradation, addiction and misery. That's why we need to decide on a way forward. One solution could be the removal of all the spacer beads. and replacing them with modern copies. That would make it safe, but it would of course mean the partial destruction of this extraordinary and unique piece of ancient art. What do you think? After all, it belongs to you."

Once again Miss Emerson was treating her as a colleague, an equal, not an emotional teenager. This time Cressida was clear with her response.

"I've been thinking about that. I'd like to give it to the museum and for it to be kept on view in a strong glass display case, in one of the galleries here which has stuff from Greece and Rome. I do love it, but now it has frightened me too, and I think the place for it is somewhere where it can be seen but not touched."

"Bravo, Cressida! That's a perfect solution! And a very generous decision on your part. I'll talk to my colleagues and see what they think. It may be, of course, that it's considered to be too unique and precious to stay in a provincial museum like this one. I'm sure the British Museum would absolutely love to have it - but we'll do our very best to keep it here! For the time being, if you agree, I'll lock it up safely in a drawer in my office."

"Yes that's fine - I don't want to take it home again. I had a bit of a scare a few days ago thinking what might happen if my little brothers found it and started playing around with it. I'll be sad in a way to part with it, but I know it's the right decision. And if it stays here I'll be able to see it whenever I like."

CHAPTER ELEVEN

A Dinner Party

"What do you want to invite her over for?" Cressida asked sullenly.

Her parents had suggested, as they'd previously agreed, that since Miss Emerson had been so helpful to their daughter in researching data about archaic Greek history and the faience necklace, they would like to invite her to come for a drink or a meal.

"We've heard so much about her, darling, we'd like to thank her for all the help she's given you. Why don't you like the idea?"

Her father had made the proposal but it was echoed by her mother, also very much in favour.

The plan did not please their daughter at all. Without really knowing why she found it so irritating, she felt distinctly unenthusiastic. Somehow she didn't want Mum and Dad to become part of the different space she entered when she visited the museum. It was something she had discovered completely independently, and Miss Emerson's help, sympathy and knowledge had made Cressida feel that she had been admitted into a new grown-up world of wisdom and learning which was both enlightening and exciting.

She imagined her parents making polite conversation over glasses of wine or sherry, while she herself once again became the ungainly adolescent, the awkward teenager, no longer the young historian whose research had aroused the admiration of a real academic. It could be really embarrassing! And worse still, there were those rumbustious little boys, who'd no doubt be wanting her to play with them, demandingly curious about visitors to the house, and loudly insisting on stories before bedtime.

It was also a fearful possibility that Miss Emerson might inadvertently give away something about the necklace itself, letting out its strange secret and thus incurring horror and anger from her parents. If they found out anything about what she and Miss Emerson had been dealing with, would they ban her from ever visiting the museum again?

Cressida's more rational self took over at this stage. Miss Emerson was wise and self-controlled, and very unlikely to make any indiscreet utterances. But it still felt embarrassing to visualise her as a guest at their house.

Although unable to suppress her negative feelings, Cressida nonetheless begrudgingly agreed to deliver a note of invitation to Miss Emerson at the museum after school the next day. She had to admit, it was a kind and friendly message. Her parents had given Miss Emerson a choice of dates, asked her whether she would prefer drinks or dinner, and also said that if she had a partner or friend she would like to bring, he or she would be most welcome too. Their home phone number was at the bottom of the note.

It did fleetingly cross Cressida's mind, as she got onto the school bus that day, that she could get rid of the invitation then tell her parents that Miss Emerson couldn't come on any of the suggested dates. But that idea was a step too far for the generally law-abiding Cressida, she knew she would feel guilty and awful if she did this. So after school she went to the museum and self-consciously handed the note over to Miss Emerson, feeling both uncomfortable and apologetic. Miss Emerson, however, was delighted.

"What a lovely idea! How very kind of your parents - of course I'd be thrilled to come, and so I think would Matthew. I'll give them a call later."

Cressida had half-hoped that the invitation would be declined; that Miss Emerson would say she was too busy, or going to be away, or some other excuse. The fact that she actually wanted to come, and to bring Mr Harding as well, made Cressida feel that maybe it didn't seem such a bad idea after all. However, she did hesitantly mention her worries over the necklace and her fear of her parents' reaction if they knew what had been going on.

"Don't worry Cressida, we'll just stick to history and chat." was Miss Emerson's easy-going response.

Relieved, Cressida headed for the bus stop. In the end, she thought, the dinner party might actually turn out to be quite enjoyable!

Saturday evening a week ahead was decided on, coinciding with the beginning of the school summer holidays. The prospect of several weeks of freedom, with no holiday homework now the exams were over, had made a huge difference to Cressida's state of mind. When the day came she cheerfully threw herself into helping her father tidy up the house then took her brothers to the park while their mother prepared the evening meal.

Jo-Jo and Mikey were fascinated by the prospect of visitors coming to dinner, and begged and begged to be allowed to stay up.

"No chance, chaps," their father said, "It'll be much too late, and anyway you'd find it pretty boring. But I expect there'll be some ice-cream and meringues and other treats left so you'll be able to have a bit of a feast tomorrow."

What should she wear, was Cressida's next worry. Miss Emerson and Mr Harding had only ever seen her in her school uniform. Miss

Emerson's work clothes tended to be either a trouser suit and shirt, or a blouse and skirt - very sober, very professional. Would she dress up a bit more for a dinner party? She probably would, Cressida thought to herself. These considerations might seem trivial, but they were anxiously occupying Cressida's mind. She must try to look her best too.

She decided on a patterned Indian cotton summer dress, a gift from her mother's sister who had brought it back from Delhi, and her Roman style summer sandals. Regretfully she thought briefly of the Greek necklace which would have complemented this outfit perfectly - but instead she did have a pretty gold chain which would have to do. She added a bit of makeup and some earrings, which made her feel both more attractive and more sophisticated.

By seven o'clock everything was ready. It was a warm sunny evening, so the plan was to start off with drinks in the garden. Cressida was reading bed-time stories to the little boys when she heard the doorbell ring, and the clamour of voices as the visitors arrived.

"Welcome," she heard her father say as he opened the front door. "Do come in. I'm Graham Curtis and this is my wife Helen. Lovely to meet you both, we've heard such a lot about you from Cressida."

From her position upstairs in the boys' bedroom Cressida then heard Miss Emerson and Mr Harding responding with their own first names.

Briefly she wondered whether she should go on calling them Mr and Miss, or whether she should address them as Penny and Matthew. This was one of the perplexing aspects of being a teenager. When were you grown-up enough to be on first-name terms with adults much older than yourself?

"Why've you stopped reading, Cressy? Go on - tell us what happened next?" Mikey demanded severely.

"Sorry - where was I?"

She was still reading to them from the book of Greek myths, and had reached the Gorgons. The twins were fascinated by those three witches who had snakes for hair, as indeed they had been by all the stories of other monsters. Cressida held the picture up so they could see the fearful trio. Neither boy was at all scared by them, or by any of the fantastical creatures they'd encountered in the pages of the book. The more grotesque, the more exciting, as far as they were concerned!

She'd been hoping that tiredness would overtake them quickly so she could go and join the others downstairs, but it was well over twenty minutes before she could shut the book. Her mother then arrived, to draw the curtains and tuck both boys up.

Cressida, rather nervously, went down the stairs and out into the garden where her father and the two visitors were comfortably chatting, There was a bottle of wine, a jug of fruit juice and a dish of canapés on the table in front of them.

"Here she is!"

"Hello!" she said, shyly. She could feel herself blushing, as Mr Harding stood up and pulled out a chair for her.

It was all a bit nerve-racking, but she received a friendly smile from Miss Emerson (should she now call her Penny?) That was soon sorted out.

"Let's dispense with the Mr and Miss, shall we, Cressida," she said. "Call us Penny and Matthew - that makes things much easier, doesn't it?"

"Oh, yes, thank you so much - I'll try to remember." It was typical of kind Miss Emerson, thought Cressida, to make her feel like an equal, not just a mere teenager.

When she looked back on the dinner party after it was over, she recognised that all her misgivings had been unnecessary. It had been fun! It was lovely to sit outside in the evening sunshine enjoying delicious food and being included in the conversation. Miss Emerson - or rather Penny - had been very complimentary about the reading and research Cressida was doing about Mycenaean Greece, and also about the fact that she'd been studying the Iliad and the Odyssey.

"She's even got her little brothers hooked on it all, haven't you, Cressy?" commented her father, with a smile at his daughter. "They are obsessed now with giants and Gorgons, monsters and Furies!"

"Have you thought about getting involved with the Wessex University dig that's taking place this summer?" Matthew Harding asked Cressida. "It'll be very near here, based around the castle, and I think you'd find it really interesting. There is some evidence, I believe, of Mycenaean trading with western Britain in the period you've been reading about."

Penny Emerson nodded.

"Yes, there's certainly a theory that the ancient Wessex culture was influenced by Mycenaean ideas, but the jury's still out really on that one. However, Ancient Faience beads have been found on early Wessex sites, so who knows! But you might really enjoy it, Cressida - digs are very exciting! It's an amazing feeling when you unearth something from hundreds of years ago! The site's very rich one, all around the castle - obviously there will be medieval stuff as well, and later deposits too."

It sounded fascinating! And the dates, between July 24th and August 18th would fit in well, as they weren't having a family holiday this summer. Maybe Louise might like to get involved too! Cressida began to feel both intrigued and excited.

"But I don't know anything about what you do on digs, for instance what equipment I would need, and so on. Also, would it matter that I've never done it before?" she asked.

"Not in the least. You'll learn on the job," Matthew explained. "Most volunteers are new to it. I'll be running it - I'm an archaeologist myself, and as you know, my period is the Middle Ages. So I and a couple of colleagues will be keeping an eye on all the volunteers, showing them how to excavate artefacts without damaging them, and how to clean and store them safely. The only equipment you'll need to bring is a mason's pointing trowel - the ones with a triangular blade that builders use. Oh, and make sure your anti-tetanus vaccine is up to date. So, d'you think you'd like to do it?"

He turned to her parents, saying: "She'd be in safe hands, I can assure you, and as you live so nearby she wouldn't have to camp as most of the volunteers do, but could come home every evening."

Graham and Helen Curtis, both feeling rather as if they were being swept along in an unforeseen tide, exchanged glances. How could they refuse? It seemed like a blameless and interesting way for their daughter to spend a few weeks. The little boys would be at Summer Holiday Club some of the time anyway. It was far better for Cressida to be productively occupied than wandering round the shops in town, drifting purposelessly around the house, glued to her Walkman, or watching too much television.

Also, as they had all spent ten days in the Netherlands at Easter for the wedding of Cressida's uncle to a Dutch girl, there were no plans for a family summer holiday. This dig could be just the thing to give their daughter an interesting and enriching experience - and it was more or less on her own doorstep.

"Oh, please, Mum and Dad - I'd really, really love to do it, " Cressida begged, clasping her hands together. "And I'd still be home to help with the twins first thing in the morning and in the evenings too."

"Sounds fine - and fun as well!" said her father. "What d'you think, Helen?"

Mum, always more cautious and anxious than Dad, hesitated briefly, but bearing in mind the fact that Matthew would be there overseeing it all, she agreed.

"Yes, I think it's a wonderful idea. It could be an amazing experience for you, Cressy. Of course you can."

For Cressida the rest of the evening passed in a sort of dream. What an exciting prospect! And how wonderful to have the chance of digging up precious relics from the past, meeting lots of other volunteers, and perhaps making new friends. Might someone new come into her life who could be as attractive and unforgettable as Tolly? Better still, she fantasised, if Duncan and Louise got involved with the dig after their holiday, maybe Tolly too might be there.

When Penny and Matthew had gone she drifted off to bed in a trance of anticipation. What discoveries and experiences could be lying ahead?

CHAPTER TWELVE

The Dig

O ver the next week, whenever she could, Cressida climbed up the steep hill towards the half-ruined castle, to watch the groundworks taking place in preparation for the dig. If he had time, Dad sometimes came with her, bringing his binoculars; he seemed to be almost as interested in it all as she was. Large trenches were being marked out in a wide square grid pattern on the flat part round the castle, which would be the focus of the first stage of the excavation. On the far side of the hill was a long gentle slope leading down to the river valley below, and was much less steep than the approach from the village.

Around the castle, tarpaulin shelters and a marquee were going up. Here, finds would be catalogued and stored, and the marquee could provide shelter if it rained. It would also be used for meal times and coffee breaks if necessary, as well as being the venue for regular lectures from the archaeologists, focusing on particularly interesting finds and the wider history of the area.

A water supply was established from the section of the castle which wasn't ruined, enabling temporary outside toilets to be installed for the use of the work-force. That part of the castle had been inhabited until the late eighteenth century, and, over two hundred years ago, an early water-pumping system had been set up from the river in the valley, with wooden pipes and steam pumps. Obviously this was now no longer functional, but water engineers had been brought in to instigate a modern pumping system linked to the mains water supply in the valley.

Those volunteers who intended to camp would be based on the level area down the slope, near the valley, Another toilet block was being set up there, with running water from the mains supply. Cressida found it all irresistibly fascinating, watching these preparations and observing the gradual transformation of the entire hillside into a working archaeological site.

She'd asked Louise to volunteer with her once the dig got going, but to her disappointment, the entire Jacobs family was going to be away on holiday for most of the period. Lou hoped to join in with it in the final week, when she was back, and she said Charlie and Duncan might also get involved.

That would be fun, Cressida thought. By then perhaps she herself would be quite experienced and might have some interesting finds to show them! It might all be a bit nerve-racking at first, as the other volunteers would be strangers to her, and most of them were likely to be older than her, but Matthew had been reassuring.

"Digs are really friendly places, you'll soon get to know people," he'd told her. "There's nothing like working together on a project like this to make new friends."

Unfortunately, a last minute crisis at home meant that Cressida wasn't able, to her great disappointment, to start on the first day of the dig as planned. It was Monday morning. Her father had gone to work, and both the twins were unwell. Her mother had an important meeting in the archive office, so instead of heading off up the hill with her carefully packed rucksack containing sandwiches, water bottle, newly bought trowel, and binoculars borrowed from her father, poor Cressida was stuck at home looking after her ailing brothers.

She tried not to take out her disappointment on the rather pathetic little boys, who had both been sick and were feeling extremely sorry for themselves. Whenever they were ill, they seemed to regress back into babyhood. They moaned and complained, wanted constant attention including lots of cuddles, and cried whenever she left the room. By the afternoon, to her relief, they had dropped off to sleep. Cressida, feeling extremely martyred, then gave way to tears herself. It was to a very woebegone daughter that her mother returned later.

"I'm really sorry, lovey, but thank you so much for looking after them. Are they feeling any better?"

'What about me?' Cressida wanted to shout, but of course she didn't.

"They're both asleep. I'm going for a walk," she responded shortly.

She needed to go up to the dig and explain to Matthew why she hadn't shown up. Would he be annoyed by her unreliability so early on in the proceedings? Would she be barred from taking part after all? Cressida could hardly bear to think about such a possible disaster.

Of course she wasn't barred! Matthew, who she found writing up field-notes in the marquee, was kind and understanding. She hadn't missed much, he said, and went on,

"Now, first I'll give you the briefing that I gave the others this morning, and then we'll go over to the trenches where everyone is working, and I'll show you what to do when you come back tomorrow. Don't worry, Cressida - of course you had to stay and look after your little brothers."

Cressida started in the dig the next day. Arriving at the site early she found Matthew and a few others already at work. Talking to Matthew was a middle-aged man she didn't know. Unsure what to do next, she hesitated.

"Ah, here she is," Matthew said with a smile of welcome. He turned to his companion. "This is the girl I was telling you about - Cressida Curtis. Cressida, this is Dr John Hanbury from the British Museum. He's here for the day to have a look round the site. I've been telling him about your Greek necklace."

"Good morning Cressida. Dr Harding's been talking to me about your extraordinary find. I would very much like to see it sometime."

This was all a bit overwhelming. Dr Hanbury must be a pretty high-powered archaeologist if he came from the British Museum. How was she to respond?

"Oh - yes, it's at our local museum in Chilminster now. It isn't on display yet ... She looked over at Matthew, who continued, to her relief,

"My colleague, Dr Penelope Emerson, is Keeper of Historic Decorative Artefacts and Jewellery at our museum; she and I will be curating the display we're planning to create, to showcase the necklace. I think the best thing would be for you to contact her there. But meanwhile, I'll give you a guided tour round our site here, once I've taken Cressida to where she'll be working today. Come along, Cressida."

Dr Harding; Dr Emerson! It hadn't crossed Cressida's mind that these two would have academic titles. All that time she had been addressing Penny as Miss Emerson - how humiliating this mistake now seemed!

"Oh Matthew - I'm so sorry. I didn't realise you and Penny were both Doctors. All the time when I've been calling her Miss Emerson - I feel awful about it," she blurted out as they set off towards the dig trenches.

"It couldn't matter less, Cressida, truly! They are just our academic qualifications - how on earth were you to know! Don't give it another thought. Anyway, you now know us as Matthew and Penny, which is much friendlier!"

"Oh thank you so much. And could you give my apologies to Penny too. She's been so kind to me and I would hate her to think I had been rude."

"She won't have minded at all, I assure you, Penny is the least pompous person I know. But I'll mention it when I tell her about John Hanbury's request to see your necklace. Much more important for us all is to insist on the necklace staying here in Dorset. I know John will be keen for it to go to the BM - the British Museum. So I think that Penny, you and I have to put our heads together to create a stunning display about Mycenaean Greece, with the necklace at the centre of it. We can also include some of the theories about Mycenaean connections with ancient Wessex, information on faience beads, and some ideas about the Trojan War."

"That sounds amazing! I would absolutely love to help it happen. And I suppose it's possible that some more relevant stuff might be found through work on this dig!"

"Yes indeed. So let's get you digging. This is the trench which I thought would be a good place for you to start." He indicated a deepish trench where three others were already working.

"Hello all. Here's Cressida come to join you. Any finds so far today?"

Cressida stepped down into the trench where two other girls, Lucy and Suzanne, and a boy, David, were working. They were all a bit older than her, but as Matthew had promised earlier, they were very friendly. As they scraped away gently at the impacted earth in the trench, the three of them told her about what they had already discovered.

"It's post-medieval period stuff mainly here," said Lucy, "In fact, yesterday we found some broken decorative pottery which Dr Harding - Matthew - said was quite late, probably 17th century. As we're so near the castle there's quite a lot of stuff from that time."

"Yes," added David, "We were quite excited about it - that's what I love about this work - it feels like finding buried treasure!"

"Well, I suppose in a way, that's what it is," Cressida said, "I mean, getting glimpses of the past - but also seeing and finding things which might once have been people's treasured possessions."

She was thinking of her ancient necklace; but really it would be almost as magical, and a lot safer, if they were to find anything here of value or interest. Suzanne was the first to unearth what might be a significant item that morning.

"Look!" she said. There was a gleam of something where she had been scraping. Very carefully, using her fingers, she shifted the earth aside to reveal a gold earring.

They all gazed at it in silence. How amazing was that! Suzanne wrapped it in a tissue and took it over to the tarpaulin shelter where finds were being meticulously cleaned, analysed, classified and stored. Meanwhile the others, fired up by this discovery, returned to their work. Would the second earring turn up, Cressida wondered. Thinking of how often she lost one earring, and visualising the contents of her little jewel box at home, which contained several lone remaining ones, she was doubtful. But it didn't matter - she was beginning to realise that the earth around here must be full of these lost relics.

Because the castle had been partly inhabited up till the late eighteenth century, that earring had probably belonged to one of the ladies who had lived there. Like the pottery which had been dug up yesterday, after comparison with similar jewellery, it seemed that Suzanne's find was also from the seventeenth century.

The next find was very different. It was a fork, but nothing like the ones they were all accustomed to in their home cutlery drawers. At first David had thought it was some sort of weapon, as he started to uncover something thin and silvery. Then Cressida, next to him, noticed two spikes emerging from the soil. As he pulled it out they all saw that it was a two-pronged fork.

Again, they were enthralled! To think that this had been used by the long gone inhabitants of the castle centuries ago, perhaps while eating an al-fresco meal! When it was examined by the experts the four of them learnt that forks hadn't really been common in England until the early seventeenth century, and even then use of them was limited to the wealthy. It wasn't till several decades later that forks began to have more prongs – or 'tines', as they were called. The one they had just found was obviously a luxury item, they saw that its silver handle was decoratively embossed and the two tines were elegant and tapering.

When her first working day at the dig was over, Cressida headed off home feeling tired but very elated. It had been a wonderful day! She had made new friends, helped to unearth fascinating relics, and had entered a world of discovery like nothing she had ever experienced before.

Over the next few days she became more familiar with excavation techniques and began to appreciate the spectrum of historical periods covered by the dig. The trenches nearest to the castle yielded the most recent finds; further down the hill medieval and even earlier stuff was being unearthed, including some broken Roman potsherds. Cressida explored the whole site, discovering an overgrown walled area outside the castle which had perhaps once been a kitchen garden, and from there she could enter the part of the castle which had remained inhabited.

One morning during the coffee break she walked through the castle entrance and down a long corridor, reaching a sizeable and once elegant drawing room. She went in. Its large windows were still intact, and as she knelt on a window seat to look out, she heard a voice behind her.

"Hello Cressida!" She whirled round. Standing before her was Tolly.

CHAPTER THIRTEEN

Explanations and Hopes

For a few seconds, they stood staring at one another. Cressida felt a blush rising in her cheeks and her heart thumping in her chest. Tolly moved towards her, his hands held out.

"There you are!" he said, "I've been looking for you all over the place. How are you doing?"

Cressida, who had firmly pushed her sadness about Tolly and their brief and ill-fated previous encounter into a deep recess of her mind, felt all those emotions and memories rushing back. She tried to get a grip on herself.

"Oh, fine really. I'm loving working on the dig. Are you volunteering here too?"

There were so many questions she wanted to ask, so much explaining she needed to do, but at the moment her mind was in chaos. Tolly, much more self-possessed, nodded.

"Yes, a notice went round at university for volunteers to join this dig. As I don't live all that far away, know the area well, and took Archaeology as a first year subsid. subject, I thought it would be fun to get involved. I'm camping down in the valley."

"I can't believe you're here!" Cressida said, managing to regain a bit of composure. "I'm really sorry, you took me completely by surprise! But also I feel so ashamed of myself for running out on you that day. Will you let me explain?"

"Yes of course - I thought you must have had some sort of panic attack or maybe were suddenly taken ill …. Shall we sit down?"

So they sat on the window seat, where Cressida told Tolly all about the necklace - how she had found it, the disturbing effect it'd sometimes had when she put it on, and the revelation of its hallucinogenic qualities.

"I was so scared, I thought I must be going mad," she finished.

Tolly was simultaneously fascinated and appalled.

"Oh my goodness," he said, "it must have been awfully frightening! Poor you, and there I was blundering on about Shakespeare and Chaucer and 'False Criseyde', and showing off talking about Middle English. How tactless can one get! When you rushed off I just thought that as well as feeling ill you were also upset by what I'd been saying about your name. I felt dreadful about it."

Cressida shook her head.

"I only thought about that afterwards; at the time I was hallucinating and terrified, and didn't know what to do. And also, as I say, I felt awfully ashamed of myself. In the end, a week or so later I went back with the necklace to the museum, and talked again to this really lovely lady there, Penny Emerson , who's in charge of ancient art and jewellery. She'd already been very interested when I took it in the first time, to show it to her and to find out more. She'd said then that it was really old, dating from the twelve hundreds BC! Can you believe that! And she was so kind, she'd already changed the string for a stronger one and polished the beads up for me, so I could wear it safely at Louise's party - but neither of us knew then about the drug which had been impregnated into the little clay beads between the coloured faience ones.

"Anyway when I went back there again after my traumatic experience at the party, she told me that the same thing had happened to her when she tried it on, after she'd repaired the old string. It was *such* a relief to realise I wasn't going crazy after all and it was something to do with the necklace!"

"Oh go on, go on - this is all so extraordinary and amazing!"

So Cressida brought him up to date, leaving out the private experiment she'd engaged on at home to test the mysterious power of the drug-infused necklace, and ending with her decision to donate the necklace to the museum where it could be displayed safely.

He turned to her and took her hand, as if he was about to say something, but at that moment the door burst open and two girls and a boy rushed in. Tolly and Cressida stood up hastily.

"Tolly, where on earth have you been all this time. Coffee's been over for ages and we need you back at the dig. We've found loads of pieces of what look like Roman pottery."

"Sorry - just catching up with an old friend. Cressida - these are Mike, Linda and Serena. Yes, I'm coming - see you later, Cressida."

Cressida's friendly "Hello" to the newcomers made no impression at all, as Tolly was almost dragged away by the two girls.

"Who's she?" Cressida heard one of the girls asking, and then the voices faded into laughter as they disappeared.

Cressida too went back to work. Her mind was in turmoil after that completely unexpected meeting with Tolly. Had he really been looking for her? It was a huge relief to have been able to give him a full account of the episode at Lou's party, but she'd been so determined to clarify the reason for her behaviour that she hadn't really given him a chance to tell her anything about himself or what he'd been doing.

What had he been going to say when his three friends rushed in? Had he just taken her hand in a friendly gesture of comfort, or did it mean more? He had, after all, referred to her as an old friend. But then, the way Linda and Serena had almost captured him, was that an indication of either of them having some sort of romantic connection with him? They had certainly seemed to be rather proprietorial as they hurried him away.

Her experiences of the last few weeks had toughened her up a bit. She resolved not to repine over the uncertainty of her position with Tolly. In a way it was enough to know that she had cleared up any misunderstanding over her behaviour at the party. It was also a great comfort to know that he was here, working at the dig as she was, so she would definitely be seeing more of him. More than that at present, Cressida wasn't going to allow herself to consider.

She returned to her trench full of apologies. By now she'd been moved to an area further from the castle, together with her three new friends from the old trench. To Matthew Harding's delight, as the days went on, bits and pieces from the Middle Ages were beginning to turn up here.

Even more excitingly, there seemed to be some sort of a wall appearing as they all scraped away at the side of the trench. Over the next few days they revealed the remains of a grey brickwork structure.

"It looks as if it could be the ruins of some building," David said. "Maybe a house, or could it possibly be a farm building?"

"A bit too close to the castle for a farm, I should say," put in Lucy.

"What about some sort of boundary wall, like the one round the kitchen garden next to the castle," suggested Suzanne.

"The brickwork is different, though," Cressida said. "Oh - I wonder if it could be the remains of a church or chapel. Shall we get Matthew to come and have a look?"

They all agreed that this was a good idea.

"You're his mate, Cressida, why don't you see if you can hunt him down?" David said.

Cressida was always happy to take a walk round the site. She continued to find the whole complex of trenches, the covered work areas and ever-increasing collection of finds endlessly fascinating. She loved exploring different parts of the dig - and also now, there was the added excitement from time to time of meeting up with Tolly.

They had now become good friends, and whenever they met they had plenty to chat about, wandering around the site together in comfortable companionship, exchanging impressions and ideas. Both of them were fascinated by the variety and diversity of the stuff being excavated.

She was determined to keep a grip on her emotions, but couldn't help hoping for some sort of relationship with him. They might just end up as friends, she told herself firmly. That would be better than nothing, and at least their meeting in the castle a few days earlier had banished any remaining misunderstanding between them.

Cressida arrived at the improvised museum space which had now been created under one of the tarpaulins, where she found Matthew. He confirmed her suggestion that their wall was part of a chapel.

"There are now bits of it coming up all around that area," he said. "We'll be doing a full geophysical survey of the site, but it's already clear that there was a chapel built here, probably in the 13th or 14th century. If we find anything organic in or around the chapel, we can get some radiocarbon dating which will give us a more accurate estimate. But well done, all four of you, Once I've finished what I'm doing here I'll be over for a good look at it, probably early this afternoon."

Cressida was elated! She had been right! They had found the remains of a medieval chapel! Feeling buoyant as she made her way back, she noticed that people were now getting sandwiches out and stopping for lunch. So after she'd got back to the others and told them Matthew would be over later to have a look at what they had discovered so far, she grabbed her rucksack, deciding to do a bit more exploring on her own, and maybe find a new place to eat her sandwiches.

To start with she searched out the other places where parts of the ruined chapel had appeared. She wasn't specifically looking for Tolly, she told herself, but it would have been fun if she came across him again and could show him what they had unearthed.

A little later, while still not really admitting to herself that she'd hoped he might show up again during this particular ramble, she looked down at the camp site near the valley below. She had long been intrigued by the tented community there, where several of the volunteers were staying, so she decided to go down the slope to get a closer look.

When she got there it all looked such fun and so welcoming that she felt slightly wistful that she wasn't part of it. She was accustomed to returning home at the end of each day, and resuming her normal life with Mum and Dad and the twins. The little boys were always delighted to see her again, clamouring as usual for games and stories, and her parents very much enjoyed hearing her news about the events and discoveries going on at the dig. But each morning she awoke with a fresh feeling of joy and anticipation about her daily escape to the excavations..

Now, as Cressida wandered round the camp site, she couldn't help wishing that she too could be part of that free and easy outdoor world, relaxing with fellow volunteers in the evening and sleeping under the stars. It felt that, despite really enjoying her work on the dig, she was missing out on a whole world of fun and conviviality down here.

"Hi Cressida!" There were Lucy and Suzanne, sitting outside their tent eating sandwiches.

"Come and join us," Suzanne said. "Why didn't you tell us you were coming here - we could have all gone down together."

"Oh, sorry - I was just wandering about and it looked so nice down here that I thought I'd check it out. Are you both camping, then?"

"Yes, and Dave's tent is just over there." said Lucy. "We've got a cosy little community here - it's so nice! Often we have campfires, drink beer and cook sausages on the fire. A couple of the boys play the guitar, so we sometimes sing and dance as well. Why don't you come and stay for a night or two - we could probably make room for you in our tent."

"That's really kind of you - I'd absolutely love to. I wonder if my parents would let me - I live very nearby in the village, you see."

"Oh do ask them," Lucy said. "It's very friendly and completely safe here, and it's a bit of a shame that you're missing out on all the fun we've been having."

As she ate her sandwiches and chatted to the girls, Cressida, who'd previously been entirely satisfied and happy about all aspects of her experience so far on the dig, was now feeling envious. It would be wonderful to be part of all the freedom and sociability the campers were enjoying! But she doubted if her parents would let her join in. As far as she could gather, nearly all the campers were older than her, and most of them were sharing tents with friends.

Somewhere, as a member of this camping community, was Tolly. Was he sharing with anyone? How much of the cheerful conviviality of those evenings in the open air was he enjoying? Her imagination conjured him up, a bottle of beer in one hand, and his arm around the shoulders of an unknown girl - perhaps one of those two who had erupted suddenly into their companionable and fascinating tête-à-tête over a week ago.

"I *will* ask my parents," she said. "Maybe I can get my Dad to come down here at the weekend, so he can see how nice and friendly it is - and that there isn't anything for them to worry about. Or perhaps I could ask Mum if I can invite you both over one evening so she can meet you first. I would really love to stay here for a few days!"

They left it like that. As they all made their way up the hill again for the afternoon's work, Cressida almost wished she'd never gone down to the camp. So far, she had been contented and indeed excited by everything, but now that she'd had a glimpse of the cheerful community enjoying life in the camp site, she yearned to be part of it.

CHAPTER FOURTEEN

The Castle

"Cressida, Cressida - wait!"

It was Saturday evening, and Cressida was just about to walk down the steep slope away from the dig on her way home. She turned round, her heart jumping as she beheld Tolly running towards her.

"Caught you again at last!" he said. "What an elusive person you are – nearly every time I get a glimpse of you, I seem to lose you again as you disappear off into the ether. Where are you going now?"

Cressida was thrilled to see him! He had been looking for her! What did this mean? Was it just about their occasional companionable rambles around the dig site? She tried to sound calm and casual. "I'm going home. No more digging till Monday."

"Let me walk back with you. I've been hoping we might be able to spend some time together this weekend. And I've got something to show you."

That was intriguing. He wanted to spend time with her! She tried to contain the leap of hope his words had instigated.

"Oh - what is it? Have you discovered something?"

"Look!" Tolly held out his hand. In it, half-wrapped in a handkerchief and still partly covered with earth, were a few faience beads. "They turned up in one of the trenches," he said, adding, "Don't worry, I haven't stolen them, I'll return them on Monday. But I wanted you to see them first."

"Oh goodness, Tolly, wow - what a find! How on earth did they get there I wonder. Nothing that early has been found anywhere here yet..."

"Hang on, Cressida. There's a story behind them. Do you have to be back at a particular time or can you come with me to the village pub and I'll tell you all about it?"

"I'd love to! And I can phone home from the pub and tell my parents I'll be back a bit later than usual. They'll be fine about me going there, as long as I don't drink anything alcoholic. I'm still underage, you see. They'll go bonkers if they think I've been illicitly boozing."

"Oh, of course - I suppose you must be about the same age as Louise?"

"A bit younger - I'm very nearly sixteen."

"OK, - well I'm nineteen - so *am* allowed to drink, but it doesn't matter at all - we'll both have a soft drink. I must say, you seem a very sensible and mature nearly sixteen-year-old!"

Cressida remembered getting drunk at Louise's party. 'Not always,' she thought to herself as she shrugged her shoulders with a smile. Had Duncan told Tolly about that, she wondered.

"Come on then, give me your bag and let's go." He slung her rucksack over his shoulder, grabbed her hand and they ran down the hill together.

Was it just that he had found some beads, or did all this mean more? With her hand in his firm grasp as they ran, again she felt the happy effervescence she had last experienced when they'd met at Louise's party, before everything changed so disastrously.

They reached the bottom of the hill and paused to get their breath back. Tolly didn't release her hand. "Hey Cressida," he said, "I'm so glad I've found you again."

"Me too," she responded, smiling shyly and still feeling a bit breathless. They then proceeded together into the village.

The pub, 'The Troycombe Arms', was in the central square just off the village High Street. While Tolly was getting their drinks, Cressida went to the telephone to ring home, then returned to her seat and sat staring out of the window but not really seeing anything, trying to pull herself together after the extraordinary events of the last few minutes.

"Here we go." Tolly was back with two glasses of sparkling elderflower and a packet of crisps. "First things first," he said, "Here's to friendship!"

He took a swig of his drink as did Cressida, clinking their glasses together.

"Now, " he went on, "I can't wait to tell you about these beads!"

They were not, he explained, proof of rumoured ancient links between prehistoric Wessex and Mycenaean Greece. He'd found them with a cache of other bits of more recent jewellery in one of the trenches nearest the castle.

"I've been doing quite a bit of ferreting around since you told me about your necklace. It seems that these beads were part of the jewellery collection of one of the ladies of the castle in the eighteenth century. Have you ever wondered why your village is called Troycombe, after the castle?"

"I have thought about it, yes, but I thought it was just a coincidence. There's a place not all that far away called Troytown, and that name was associated with a nearby ancient turf maze - apparently there's a Welsh word - 'droia' or something like that I think , which means 'turning round and round'. Also, an ancient Mediterranean wine jar with a maze pattern on it was excavated around there. However, there doesn't seem to be any sort of maze connection here. But all this investigating is why I love history and archaeology so much - exploring the past is endlessly exciting!"

"Oh yes - I absolutely agree - and I've found out quite a bit about the Troy connection in this village. In a way it was all because of you really - I'd felt such an affinity with you when we met, and was sad and worried after you dashed off. When I got back to Durham I moped about thinking of you, and looking up your village and its history and surroundings as a way of keeping a sort of link with you."

"Oh Tolly - I was doing the same - thinking about you but also feeling so cross with myself and so guilty about everything. I thought you must think I was a hysterical idiot!"

Tolly smiled slightly and shook his head, continuing,

"Actually it was Duncan - well, really Louise - who made me feel a bit better. She'd told Duncan about a conversation you'd had with her and how upset you were about it all. Thank goodness for that - I felt it gave me hope! So I must confess now that it was really when I heard you'd be joining this dig, that I decided to volunteer too. I've been on digs before, and, like you, I'm pretty addicted to exploring the past - so even if things didn't work out with you, I knew it would be an interesting experience. But you weren't at the initial briefing, when Matthew filled us volunteers in about everything. I was really disappointed - I'd hoped I might see you there. Matthew had said you probably would be."

"I was really disappointed too - my little brothers were ill and I had to stay at home and look after them that day."

So he had been attracted to her from the start! Wonderful and amazing! She told herself that she mustn't get carried away, it was very early days. Trying to keep her voice calm and casual, she smiled, saying,

"Gosh, Tolly, how extraordinary, that things have actually turned out to be OK between the two of us after all! What luck - I'm so glad!" She paused briefly, then went on, "But anyway, go on, go on please - tell me about the Troy connection you discovered."

"OK. Well, you know about the Grand Tour - the trip that rich young men used to do as a sort of 'coming of age' tradition, from the end of the seventeenth century till about the mid-nineteenth?"

Cressida nodded, and Tolly continued,

"The heir to the castle at the time was a chap called Sir Anthony Marlington. Until the early seventeen hundreds it was called Marlington Castle after that noble family, they'd lived there since they were given the castle by Henry the Eighth after the Dissolution as a reward for their loyalty. Actually you probably know all this already."

"Yes, I knew about the Marlington family and the change of name, but not why it was changed," Cressida said.

"Well, on his Grand Tour travels in the early eighteenth century Sir Anthony became fascinated by historical accounts of the Trojan War. He visited lots of different parts of Greece and Turkey in the hope of finding the site of ancient Troy. At the time no-one knew exactly where it had been, though there were lots of theories. In fact it wasn't till the nineteenth century that the actual location was discovered, long after his death. It's such an exciting story, the search for Troy! Like Sir Anthony, I've become pretty obsessed with it and I've been reading all I can to find out more about it."

"I knew nothing about that period of ancient history, till I found the necklace, so when Penny Emerson told me about the Greek Bronze Age, the Mycenaeans and the Trojan War I was absolutely gripped. Since then I've been reading translations of the Iliad and the Odyssey as well as stuff by other ancient historians. But I still don't know anything about the more modern searches to find Troy." Cressida admitted.

"Well, unlike Sir Anthony, all my knowledge came from reading, and I had the advantage over him of up-to-date conclusive data. Even though he spent ages exploring the area, he never found Troy. But what he did an awful lot of anyway, was collecting stuff which he thought might be connected to the Trojan story.

"He visited lots of places, buying antiquities which might be relevant; he had no compunction about accumulating artifacts - sculptures, jewellery - presumably including your necklace - plus pots and vases and all sorts of things, which he shipped back to England. Then when he inherited the castle he filled several of the rooms with Troy-themed stuff, he commissioned murals depicting some of the key events of the Trojan War, he even paid a wood-carver a huge sum of money to recreate a massive wooden Trojan Horse to be placed in the grounds of the castle. And surprise, surprise - he renamed Marlington Castle to Troycombe Castle - after the real Troy!"

"Oh, gosh! I wonder what happened to that horse! No sign of it now!"

"Who knows? But I understand there's a nineteenth century painting in the City Art Gallery in Chilminster, of Troycombe Castle with Sir Anthony's Trojan Horse standing right in front of it. I thought we might go and see it together tomorrow, if you have time. I believe the gallery's open on Sundays during the summer holiday period."

"Brilliant! I'd love to do that. And we could maybe pop in to the museum as well - I'd like to introduce you to Penny Emerson so you can show her your little cache of beads. She's often there on Sundays."

Tolly smiled at her, saying, "That would be great. Anyway, back to Sir Anthony - once he'd renamed the castle he also renamed your village, which was then part of the castle estate. It used to be called Towcombe or something like that I believe."

"Yes, Torcombe - it's in the Domesday book. I've always just thought it had morphed into Troycombe over the centuries."

They grinned over the table at one another, then carried on chatting, united in their shared fascination about the events of the past, and simultaneously each finding the other increasingly interesting and attractive. Tolly was on the point of saying something more, when there was a sudden interruption.

"This has been a very long half hour, Cressida."

Her father had come into the pub and was standing in front of them, his arms folded and a rather stern expression on his face.

"Oh Dad, sorry - we got a bit carried away, talking about history. This is Tolly - he's also on the dig. He dug up some faience beads like the ones in my necklace."

Mr Curtis's face relaxed and he looked over at Tolly. "Hello Tolly. So you too are a history enthusiast! That's nice for Cressida. But I trust in your enthusiasm you haven't been plying my daughter with alcoholic drinks."

"Of course not, Dad," "We were drinking elderflower," Cressida and Tolly spoke simultaneously.

Tolly stood up, polite and self-possessed. "I'd better be getting back," he said, then turned to Cressida. "I'll get to the Art Gallery by about ten in the morning, if you're able to make it. 'Bye, Cressida, 'Bye Mr Curtis - very nice to meet you."

"Bye Tolly, thanks for the drink," Cressida said, feeling rather cast down at the abrupt curtailment of their comfortable tête-à-tête.

However, Tolly had been composed and civil, surely there was nothing for her father to disapprove of there. She linked her arm into Dad's, and as they walked back home she gave him an account of some of the events of the day, including the ongoing excavation of the chapel walls and Tolly's revelations about the castle and the Trojan War.

CHAPTER FIFTEEN

The Picture Gallery

Tolly, making his way back along the street towards Castle Hill to return to his tent, turned round to watch Cressida and her father heading for home. They looked a contented and animated pair as she, her arm through his, chatted to him enthusiastically, his head bent towards hers as he listened. Tolly couldn't help feeling rather bleak and lonely - even a little envious - as he watched them. The dig site would be almost empty; most of the volunteers would have gone home as there was no work on Sundays. His own home was a bit too far away to go back to for just one night. In any case his father would probably still be working - he often did extra-long shifts at the hospital on weekends.

Life had changed a lot for Tolly in the last few years. When he was twelve his mother, who had been unwell for some time, had been diagnosed with advanced breast cancer and, after three years of intensive chemo- and radiotherapy, as well as a double mastectomy, had died just after his fifteenth birthday. His father's way of coping with this terrible tragedy was to immerse himself in work. Tolly had done the same - dealing with his grief and loneliness by obsessively burying himself in his studies. He achieved very high grades in all his subjects.

This had resulted in unconditional offers from both Oxford and Cambridge, but he had opted to go as far away as he could from where all the suffering had taken place. He'd accepted a place to read Joint Honours in English Literature and History at Durham University.

Tolly had fallen in love with Durham. He was enchanted by its massive, majestic Romanesque cathedral and its magnificent Castle - which was also University College and had now become his second home. Just as evocative and romantic to him were the three ancient bridges over the beautiful river Wear, the long history of the city, and the spectacular scenery round about; all these had partly helped to heal his lonely soul.

But his real salvation, he recognised, had largely come from the care and kindness of the Jacobs family. He and Duncan had become friends when they were thirteen, having both just been accepted into the Chilminster Youth Orchestra. Tolly grew very fond of all the family and was always welcome in their home. His mother was undergoing treatment at the time, and although there was still hope, he remembered the feeling of permanent underlying anxiety which lay inside him like a hidden sore. Duncan, Charlie and Louise became almost like the siblings he'd never had, and Mr and Mrs Jacobs like a kind and caring uncle and aunt.

After the tragedy of his mother's death, when he had finished his GCSEs he'd then been sent away to boarding school. His father had tried to make a new beginning for them both, by selling up and moving to Salisbury, where he became a senior consultant at one of the hospitals. It was near enough for Tolly to keep in touch with the Jacobs family, but not near enough to visit them regularly as he had been able to do previously. Sadly, neither his nor his father's grief was diminished by the change of scene, although they had moved there because it was where Tolly's mother was buried. Salisbury had been her home city.

Now, thanks to Duncan, Cressida had come in to his life. He had noticed her immediately at Louise's party. He'd thought her very pretty, and had tried to make eye contact with her, sensing something more, some sort of special quality about her that made him want to get to know her. When they were introduced to one another soon afterwards he felt there had been an instant rapport between them; he was now remembering the carefree conversation they had been enjoying before everything went so disastrously wrong.

She was only sixteen - well, not quite sixteen, he kept reminding himself. He felt hopeful and elated at finding her again, and imagined putting his arms around her, stroking her hair and kissing her. But, he told himself, he must be patient. In any case, she was far too young for anything really serious. It wouldn't be fair on either of them to precipitate any sort of more intense relationship too soon. It was miracle enough that they had, after all, found one another again, and that it seemed that they really might be kindred spirits, with shared opinions, interests and values.

Her parents, he sensed, were understandably protective of her, and there was no way he wanted to threaten that. A loving friendship had to be enough for the time being. If their relationship did stand the test of time, Tolly hardly dared think of what might transpire. But at the moment he felt an awakening love and longing which was adding hope to his saddened soul and rekindling some of his natural optimism. That was a gift in itself.

As he mused over these things he remembered suddenly that Duncan and his family would now be back home from their summer holiday. Quite soon it would be the final week of the dig, and Duncan had said he might come and take part for the last few days. 'He can share my tent,' thought Tolly. Why should he not ring Duncan now and see if they could meet up, or - better still - maybe he himself could go over to their house. Kind Mrs Jacobs - Stella, as he knew her - had said he was welcome at any time, and could stay whenever he needed to.

With renewed optimism, Tolly therefore headed for the phone box. If he was able to go to the Jacobs's, he might get Duncan to tell to him a bit more about Cressida, what she'd been like as a little girl, how long had they known her, what did she enjoy doing.... There was so much he wanted to find out!

Meanwhile at her home Cressida's parents were discussing their daughter's new friend.

"He seems a nice young chap, very well-mannered and personable," Graham Curtis told his wife, while Cressida was upstairs reading a late story to the sleepy twins.

"Maybe, but from what you say he's obviously quite a few years older than her. She's a bit young to be getting involved with a boy."

"She's very nearly sixteen, love - at her age it's absolutely to be expected. I wouldn't mind betting that you weren't oblivious to the opposite sex yourself when you were that age."

"Well, yes - it's true - I did have a bit of a crush on the music master at school, and I also fancied one of the greengrocers in the market! But it was really just fantasy stuff - I didn't actually go out with anyone till I was well over sixteen."

"That was then, this is now - times have changed. And it seems to me that Tolly is a well-educated, pleasant young man spending his university vacation working on an archaeological dig and having conversations with our daughter about ancient history. They want to meet up tomorrow to visit the City Hall Art Gallery. We can't really object to any of that!"

"No - of course you're right. Anyway I think she's finished reading so she'll be on her way down soon. We'd better stop talking about her."

"Yes, we must. The twins seem very tired, so I'll just pop up quickly and tuck them in and kiss them goodnight, while you catch up with her. Don't worry, she's a sensible girl."

He went up, Cressida came down and the evening progressed as normal.

Cressida chatted happily to her mother about how she and her co-diggers had come across the medieval wall which had turned out to be part of a chapel - and how she and Tolly were planning to meet in Chilminster tomorrow to visit the City Art Gallery.

The next morning she awoke full of excitement as she contemplated the day ahead. She tried very hard to keep her feelings in check, and to stay temperate and calm, as the family sat down together over breakfast, although she didn't feel like eating much. She then made herself spend a bit of time playing football in the garden with her little brothers, before leaving to catch the bus into Chilminster.

She was free! The day was hers and Tolly's, lying ahead of them like a shining gift - a magical multicoloured rainbow of anticipation. Arriving in Chilminster a bit early, she popped briefly into the museum, which was just opening for the day. There she left a note for Penny saying she and her friend Tolly would call in later, with more news about faience beads. Then, her heart beating a little faster, she headed for the gallery.

"Here she is!"

There stood both Duncan and Tolly waiting by the entrance. Fond though she was of Duncan, Cressida was slightly disappointed to see him there. He gave her a brotherly hug while Tolly stood by, smiling at her.

"Tolly came over to ours last night, pining for you, Cressy, so I thought I'd come in with him to say hello. The gallery doesn't open till 10.30, so why don't we all go for a coffee, then I'll leave you two to yourselves," said Duncan with a grin. "I've got to go and pick up some music anyway, lots of practice to do."

He had left school and had been offered an undergraduate place at the Royal College of Music in London.

"Good idea, let's do that," Tolly agreed, again smiling at Cressida and now taking her hand as they crossed the road to the coffee shop on the other side.

Over coffee Duncan made them laugh with his account of his family holiday, which had been a mixture of fun and disaster. Their hire car had broken down in a remote village, where they were stranded in the heat for several hours waiting for a replacement. The gîte they had booked had a very eccentric power system which failed on several occasions. But the weather had been wonderful, the countryside beautiful, and the food and drink delicious. He had also engaged in a mini-flirtation with a pretty French girl. "Great for my French," he said, obviously in no way repining for her now he was home.

When he had gone Tolly and Cressida exchanged glances of relief. Much as they both loved Duncan, it was good to be alone together again.

"Typical Duncan!" Cressida said, "I think he feels a bit proprietorial about us because he originally got us together".

" Yes I know - but I wasn't going to stop him coming. You see, I do owe him and his family an awful lot, much more than just introducing me to you. Later on I'll tell you about it and how kind they've all been to me. But now - let's go and find the Wooden Horse."

With these words, Tolly had given Cressida a glimpse into something unknown, serious and possibly sad. She felt a frisson of concern as she looked over at him, but he was smiling again as they left the café to go back to the art gallery. It had only just opened, so with very few other people around they could take their time. Together they wandered around, looking at and exchanging reactions to several of the pictures, quietly enjoying one another's company, but also both keeping an eye out for the painting of the Trojan Horse.

Suddenly, there it was, in an alcove all on its own, right in front of them! Cressida and Tolly stood side by side gazing at the huge canvas; the dark walls and turrets of the castle almost dwarfed by the monstrous wooden horse which stood in front of it. The creature was gigantic and menacing, its fiery eyes blazing and its mouth open in a snarl, revealing two rows of threatening yellow teeth. The angle was slightly oblique, so viewers could see the huge door on the side of the horse. This was of course the door though which, according to Homer, the perfidious Greeks had emerged from hiding in the horse's belly, to sack Troy, slay its warriors, and lay waste the city.

"Oh, goodness me! Quite terrifying!" Cressida said as she gazed at the scene. "I don't know much about art but it does conjure up incredibly vividly the mentions of it in the Odyssey."

"There's also a longer description of it in Virgil's Aeneid - Book Two, I seem to remember. It was one of my set books for A Level Latin."

Cressida, who had only just finished her GCSE's, began to feel a bit in awe of the young man by her side. Latin wasn't even on the curriculum at her school.

"Gosh, Tolly," she said, "I didn't think Latin was taught in secondary schools any more. Did Duncan do it too?"

"No, Duncan and I weren't at the same school - we met when we joined the Youth Orchestra together at the age of thirteen, and became mates from then on. But not long after my mother's death, when I'd passed my GCSE's I was sent to a private boarding school to do my A Levels. That was where I learnt Latin. I did A Levels in Latin, History and English. Actually I also studied Greek, but didn't take it as an A level subject. By then my father and I had moved to Salisbury, where we still live."

All at once Tolly seemed to Cressida to have become very grown-up.

"Oh goodness, you're way ahead of me! I thought I was becoming a bit of a swotty geek, but you're in a different league."

"Well, no, not really - just a few years older than you. I reckon all that research and reading you've been doing lately definitely qualifies you conclusively for membership into the school of swotty geekdom!"

They both laughed at this, then wandered separately round to look at more paintings. There were plenty of portraits of past local dignitaries as well as a long panel with a vertical sequence of some picturesque views of the town, its cathedral and the meadow behind it.

Cressida then stood in front of a late eighteenth century painting of Troycombe Castle. It was beautiful - depicting the castle against a pastoral background of hills and sky, and in the foreground a parterre with symmetrical patterns containing flowers, and bounded by box hedges. In its sweet romanticism it was a complete contrast to the raw brutality of the Wooden Horse painting of that same building.

"Come and have a look at this, Cressida."

Tolly, a few yards away, was indicating a portrait. It was of a man and a woman. The man wore a straw coloured satin waistcoat and knee breeches under a long black cutaway coat, with a frothy neckcloth at his throat, and the woman was in a heavy lilac silk gown, tight around the waist and with a low-cut neckline trimmed with a lace fichu. A powdered wig completed his ensemble, and her hair, also powdered, was swept up high above her head and decorated with pink and lilac coloured ornaments.

"Sir Anthony and Lady Marlington," said Tolly.

Together they stared at the painting. Then Cressida noticed something.

"Look Tolly, look at her necklace."

Lady Marlington was wearing the faience bead necklace! There it lay, on her chest, above the lace trimming of her gown.

"Oh my God!" They stared at one another, she clasping both hands together and he with one hand to his mouth at the shock of discovery.

"Is it really the actual one?" Tolly asked, slightly breathlessly.

Cressida had spent so much time looking at the necklace since she had found it, that she knew the exact layout of the beads, and how, while the blue colour was predominant, there were streaks of other colours on most of them. She recognised the order in which they were strung, and how colours on a particular bead were followed by ones with a streak of a different colour. In her mind's eye she compared the necklace in the painting with the real one - which she had last seen laid out on the table at the museum, when Penny was completing the re-setting of the spacers.

"I know it off by heart," she said, "It's definitely the same necklace. I wish we could take a photo of it - but anyway we're going to see Penny this afternoon and she can go and see for herself. If only we could find out a bit more about what happened to it, what happened to Lady Marlington. Could it have had that same effect on her .....? Oh Tolly, there's so much we need to find out."

Tolly had an idea. "There's a little shop here, I think. Maybe they've got some info, and possibly a booklet about the art collection, let's go and check it out."

"Brilliant! And also, Tolly, they might be selling postcards of some of the pictures. I wouldn't mind getting some copies of the Wooden Horse one for my twin brothers. They'd be thrilled!"

They were in luck. There was indeed a booklet for sale about the art displayed in the gallery, and Cressida was also able to buy two postcards of the Wooden Horse painting - one for each of her little brothers.

After all that excitement they decided to stop for an early lunch. There were things Tolly needed to tell her about, sad things, he said.

CHAPTER SIXTEEN

Some Sad Stories

Cressida felt rather apprehensive as she and Tolly arrived at the little café near the museum to have some lunch. What were the sad things he wanted to tell her about, and how did they somehow relate to Duncan and the Jacobs family? Tolly had already mentioned his mother's death; was he going to tell her more about that?

When they'd ordered their food he began to explain.

"Don't look so worried, Cressida - it's just some stuff about my life which I think you ought to know, if we're going to continue together. One of the things I like so much about you, but can't help feeling a bit envious of, is your happy family life. You seem to have a great relationship with your parents and obviously adore your little brothers."

"Well, yes, on the whole you're right, but they do all drive me round the bend at times. Sometimes I really resent the amount of childcare I'm expected to provide. Of course I love the twins, but they can be incredibly demanding and annoying!"

"I'm sure. But let me give you a bit of an insight into my family - if it can be called a family. There are only two of us in it - me and my father. And I hardly ever get to spend much time with my father, because he's a workaholic. He's a brilliant surgeon, no doubt about it, but since my mother died he doesn't seem to have much interest in anything other than his work."

Tolly paused - trying to explain without being disloyal. He went on,

"Don't get me wrong - he doesn't treat me badly or anything like that, he provides for me, he paid my school fees and now pays my University ones, and gives me a generous allowance as well. But when I saw you walking home so companionably with your father yesterday I couldn't help feeling a bit wistful. Sorry..."

His voice cracked a little as he said this. Cressida was horrified. Her own gripes about her family seemed petty and self-indulgent as she listened to what Tolly was saying. A rush of sympathy brought tears to her eyes as impulsively she stretched her hands over the table to grasp his.

"Oh Tolly, I'm so sorry, I had no idea. When, and how did your mother die? How utterly dreadful for you - can you bear to tell me about it?"

"It was breast cancer. I was about your age when she died, but she'd been ill for years before that, She was a lovely kind mother, but, I realise now, never very strong. I think she'd had a pretty awful time giving birth to me, and had been advised not to have any more children. But my father adored her - so did I. And she was only forty. So after that, in a way I had to grow up very quickly. Like my father, I immersed myself in work - studying, in my case. School work was a lifeline really."

"And there was me teasing you about being a geek. Oh Tolly, Tolly, you poor thing. I'm amazed that you manage to be so cheerful and sane – some people would go under...."

"Well," he continued, "It was really Duncan and his family who got me through. Cressida, I can't tell you how good to me they were - and still are. His mother - Stella she's called - listened to me, encouraged me to rage and cry and rant, she hugged me and comforted me as if I were her own child. She told me that while she could never replace my mother, she would always be there for me - and she is. Duncan, Charlie and Louise were wonderful as well, they said I was to consider myself an extra brother in every way. And their father Marcus was also amazingly gentle and understanding, he made me promise that if ever I felt that I couldn't cope, I was to get in touch immediately. They still look out for me. I truly believe that they saved my sanity."

"They really are a lovely family," Cressida said, remembering how kind and understanding Stella Jacobs had been, when her first period started while staying with them. "And they've been loyal too," she went on, "Lou's my closest friend, but she never told me anything of all this."

"They were protecting me, you see, helping me to rebuild myself, while still respecting my right to privacy. So they didn't talk to others about it. And actually, on the whole I think they did a pretty good job! "

Tolly smiled as he said this, lightening the mood now that he had shared his sad story. It was as if his natural self - optimistic, positive, creative and enthusiastic - had reinstated itself.

"Of course they did. It's amazing, not just how good they were to you, but how brave and determined you've been. I'm really impressed, Tolly."

"Thanks Cressida, that's very kind of you. I'm so glad I've told you, and I do feel much better now I've spoken to you about it."

It was an emotional conversation, leaving both of them close to tears at times. Then they relaxed, each in a different way feeling a sense of relief. As they finished their lunch Tolly told Cressida more about his childhood, focusing on happier times before his mother became ill. He showed her the photograph which he kept in his wallet. A dark haired, brown eyed, gently smiling face looked out at her.

"She's beautiful," Cressida said, "And she looks lovely and kind too. Actually you're very like her - the same dark eyes and thick curly hair. No wonder you and your father adored her. Thank you so much for telling me all this, and for showing me your mother."

She was very much aware that her own family situation had been in contrast, enviably tranquil. Nevertheless she recalled to Tolly the stressful time when her parents were going through IVF and their emotional roller-coaster of hope and anguish, which she, as a little girl, had found so intensely worrying, mystifying and upsetting. It wasn't in any way comparable to what he'd been through, but it had left a shadow.

They then both reflected on the baffling, disturbing, helpless and sometimes frightening aspects of their childhoods, when things had happened which they couldn't understand and had no power over.

Soul-searching done, the two of them paid for their food and went off to the museum for their meeting with Penny Emerson.

She was waiting for them in her office, and greeted them kindly.

"So this is your young man, Cressida! Hello Tolly, lovely to meet you. Do sit down, both of you. I'm really intrigued to hear about what you've unearthed or discovered! "

Cressida felt a combination of embarrassment and pride to hear Tolly described as her young man. "Show her, Tolly!" she said, hoping she hadn't started to blush too obviously.

Tolly put his hand in his pocket and withdrew the little heap of beads, still wrapped in his handkerchief.

"We found a cache of jewellery in one of the trenches nearest the castle," he said, "There were necklaces, brooches, hair ornaments

– and these ..." – he unfolded the handkerchief and revealed the handful of faience beads. Looking slightly shamefaced he added, "As I knew you and Cressida had done so much research on the necklace, I - well - sort of borrowed them - to show her and you. I will of course return them tomorrow."

"Don't worry, you needn't do that. I can hand them over to Matthew later. I'm delighted to see them!"

Penny picked up the beads one by one and scrutinised them through a small magnifying glass, while Tolly and Cressida waited.

"Yes, they are contemporary with your necklace, Cressida, and they almost certainly came from that same necklace. While I was repairing it I wondered if the cord had been cut. I expect the wearer wanted it slightly shorter."

"And we've identified the wearer!" Cressida burst out, unable to contain herself any longer. "We've just come from the City Art Gallery. There's a big portrait there of Sir Anthony and Lady Marlington - and she's wearing the necklace!!"

Penny was as surprised as they had hoped!

"REALLY! I haven't visited the gallery recently - not for at least a year or more - but I do remember that portrait. I suppose at the time I just wasn't looking closely enough, also I hadn't then become quite so obsessed with Ancient Faience beads as I am now! How absolutely fascinating! I must go back there and take a closer look! What a find - and just on our doorstep, as it were."

She paused, then continued, "Sir Anthony was a great collector of Objets d'Art and brought piles of archaic treasures back from Greece, Italy and Turkey; that's how they would have got here."

Tolly nodded, "Yes, I've done quite a lot of research about Sir Anthony and his Grand Tour. He was fanatical about locating the site of ancient Troy - but of course he never did. But as you say, he brought masses of stuff back, renamed the castle after Troy, and filled the rooms with Mediterranean and Aegean artefacts."

"Absolutely, Tolly. And I think also that the pair of you may have unwittingly stumbled on what might be a clue to Lady Marlington's descent into madness."

Tolly and Cressida turned to one another, then back to Penny, simultaneously aghast and intrigued.

"What d'you mean? What happened?"

Cressida had a sudden inkling of the direction in which this was going.

"It was the necklace, wasn't it? The hallucinogen in the necklace."

"Yes, Cressida, it must have been the necklace. Poor Lady Marlington - it's a very tragic story I'm afraid."

Tolly and Cressida exchanged glances. Another sad story - it felt as if something silent and sombre had slipped into the room.

"Can you tell us about it," Tolly asked, glancing slightly anxiously at Cressida, who knew better than anyone what the necklace could do.

"I don't know all the details, but apparently Lady Marlington began to have episodes of delusion and insanity. She had recently given birth to a baby which sadly hadn't survived for more than a few weeks, and that was considered to be the cause of her intermittent dementia. In those days, ideas about the causes and treatment of mental disorders were very different from what they are today. Insanity was considered dangerous, and it was thought that sufferers should be isolated. Hence the incarceration of them in insane asylums."

"What happened to her?" Tolly's voice sounded anxious.

"Sir Anthony had her committed to an asylum for the insane, and never saw her again. He paid for her but never visited her. He then had a succession of mistresses who bore him a few illegitimate children, but there was no legal heir. That was the end of the Marlington dynasty."

"But that's absolutely awful!" was Tolly's appalled reaction, "What a horrible, cruel thing to do, to discard his wife when she was ill and to commit her to a life of solitude and misery, while he cavorted with other women. Utterly selfish, disgusting behaviour. Makes me feel sick."

Even though she hadn't known him for long, Cressida felt it was unlike Tolly to react so vehemently. She was sure he was thinking again of his own mother, and of the emotions raised while they'd been having lunch together. She linked her hand into his.

"We need to find out more, Tolly." she said, "We need to see what we can discover about mental health treatment at that time. Perhaps we can bring her story to life a bit - put the record straight."

There was a brief silence, then Penny said,

"Quite right, Cressida. Another bit of research for the pair of you. I'm sure there are records in the town archives, all sorts of data you could explore. I know that the building which used to be the local asylum here still exists. It's gone through several incarnations since then - workhouse, remand prison, children's home, hospital, and now I believe it's a care home. And Tolly, I completely understand your anger. It was an appalling thing to do. We can't change the past, but we can study it and learn from it, as you two are already doing so diligently. Thank you both so much for coming - and as I say, don't worry about getting the beads back to the dig."

They said their goodbyes, Tolly apologising for his outburst, then left the museum. Outside, he was silent, still distressed by what they had heard. Gently Cressida patted his arm, saying,

"Tolly, Tolly, don't be sad. I know it's a really upsetting story, and after telling me about your mother it must have been extra awful for you to hear all that about poor Lady Marlington, Let's go and find somewhere where we can sit quietly, and calm down and pull ourselves together."

For a moment he turned away and covered his face with his hands. Then he looked up and suddenly took her hand and kissed it.

"Yes, let's do that. Why don't we go to the Minster Gardens near the Cathedral?"

"Great idea, they're always lovely but especially so at this time of year."

The gardens were blooming in the full fruitfulness of high summer. Flowering trees, blossom-filled bushes and colourful flowerbeds between meticulously manicured lawns were spread out in front of them. At one end was a playground, the shrieks of the children there floating over to Tolly and Cressida through the clear summer air. Further round they could see the towering mass of the Norman cathedral. As they sat, they heard the solemn, sonorous sound of the bell tolling the quarter.

For some time they sat silently, each holding the another's hand, not saying anything, just content to be together. Then Tolly spoke.

"I wonder how many other poor souls have been victims to the effects of that necklace? Thank goodness you decided to give it to the museum. And thank goodness we're living now and not two hundred years ago. That could have been you, put into the asylum."

Cressida decided at this point that she needed to tell Tolly about the secret experiment she had conducted, which had resulted in her handing the necklace over to the museum. Sitting in the pretty Minster Gardens, she recollected for him that phantom garden she had summoned up when she wore the beads for the final time.

"You were there, Tolly, sitting on a seat at the end of the garden waiting for me," she said.

Tolly had never taken drugs. There were plenty of them around at university, and several of his fellow students regularly smoked weed. But as the son and grandson of doctors he had long been aware of the capabilities and dangers of drugs even for medical use, and had been repeatedly warned about the disastrous consequences of addiction. In any case, in reality, the psychological toll of enduring his mother's decline and death had made the idea of any sort of recreational indulgence - such as experimenting with drugs or alcohol - irrelevant and unacceptable to him.

He therefore felt shocked and anxious, remembering Cressida's terrified flight at Louise's party that evening in June, as he listened to her account of her secret test of the hallucinogen.

Now she was describing for him the vision of a paradise garden and the mystical beauty which the necklace had conjured up from her imagination, and the inclusion of himself in the illusion. He looked intently at the girl he was falling in love with, listened to her vivid and articulate account of the whole experience, and in conclusion heard her eloquent explanation of how she now understood the treacherous quality of the seductive beauty she had encountered.

"So I decided I would never, ever do it again, nor would I unwittingly enable anyone else to do so. It was too dangerous, and it made me feel too weird. That's why I've given the necklace to the museum. Apart from Penny, you're the only person I've told. I hope you aren't too shocked, Tolly, does it make you feel differently about me?"

Without speaking Tolly picked up her hand and kissed it again. He felt extremely emotional. The effect of the day's events had been overwhelming and distressing, but also simultaneously auspicious and promising. Their relationship seemed suddenly to have become much more profound and meaningful after those revelations. Words failed him, but he put his arm around her and kissed her cheek. They sat again in silence, close and peaceful.

The sound of the cathedral clock striking the hour interrupted their reverie.

"Four o'clock, time to go home" said Cressida.

CHAPTER SEVENTEEN

Last Week of the Dig

Things were beginning to wind down at the dig site. Some of the trenches, those which had yielded few or no finds, were already being filled up again and re-covered with the thick patches of soil-backed grass which had been cut away to create them. Others, mainly those around the castle, stayed open and were still producing a range of finds dating mainly from the seventeenth and eighteenth centuries, but some from earlier periods. It had been very exciting when a few religious relics appeared around the remains of the medieval chapel which Cressida and her friends had found.

An improvised field museum was now well established in the marquee, and Matthew and his colleagues had been giving daily talks about the most important finds. Most of the volunteers, including Cressida and Tolly, attended these talks; it was fascinating to learn about the function, antiquity and in some cases, rarity of what had been dug up. For Cressida and Tolly, it was particularly interesting, because of their own explorations into the history of the castle and its inhabitants.

The camping community in the valley had shrunk as some of the inhabitants had already left, but to Cressida's delight, Duncan and Louise came over to join the camp for the final week. There was room for Duncan in Tolly's tent, and, if her parents agreed, Cressida was hoping to go in with Louise. Charlie also planned to pop over for a day - he was involved in a cricket tournament but hoped to visit the camp if he could. It all depended on how long his team managed to stay at the crease.

Cressida's parents did, to her great joy, consent to her camping down in the valley with Louise. With Lucy, Dave and Suzanne also staying on till the end, plus several others who she was now getting to know, Cressida anticipated a happy, convivial wind-up to what was turning out to be in so many ways an unforgettable experience. Most important, and most exciting in all this, was of course her developing relationship with Tolly.

The penultimate day of the dig also promised to be a momentous one because it was the seventeenth of August, her sixteenth birthday. Word soon spread, thanks to Lou and Duncan, both of whom were so outgoing and friendly that they quickly seemed to have got to know most of the other campers.

She soon found out that there were plans afoot for an al-fresco party on the evening of her birthday, with a bonfire, music, singing and dancing, and plenty of party food and drink. It would be a celebration mainly for her birthday, but also a general festivity to end the dig. Cressida, while touched by all the effort being made, was also feeling a bit nervous. Naturally rather shy, she wasn't used to being the centre of attention. But the presence of Lou, Duncan and possibly Charlie, as well as now having Tolly by her side, would make all the difference.

Under the watchful tutelage of Duncan, Cressida and Louise pitched Lou's tent and sorted their stuff out. They then escaped for a long walk together. There was lots to catch up on, and now that Cressida knew what an important part Louise's family had played in helping Tolly cope with the tragedy of his mother's decline and death, she felt doubly fond of them all.

"He said you've all been amazing to him, and that it's because of your family that he's basically OK," she told Louise, after filling her in on the increasingly serious relationship which was developing between herself and Tolly.

"We always knew that you two would hit it off," Lou admitted. "I suppose Duncan did sort of choreograph getting you together, but I'm so glad it's worked out. He's a lovely guy, Cressy, also a really brave and good person."

"I know, he truly is. But can I live up to it all? At the moment we're pretty besotted with each other, but I worry about the almost four-year age gap between us. There's also the fact that he's so clever and handsome, and that he knows so much more about stuff than I do, and of course that he'll soon be going back to Durham. I imagine him leading a grown-up studenty life with lots of girls around, all much nearer his own age, while I'm still at home with Mum and Dad and the twins, going to school and studying for my A levels."

"Don't worry, Cressy - he isn't that sort of person. He's really keen on you too - anyone can see that. And just because he's good-looking doesn't mean he's a womaniser! I've known him for ages - he's almost like an extra brother - and I can tell you that he is - well - quite humble really - he certainly doesn't run around after girls, thinking he's God's gift! He's actually rather quiet and serious, quite geeky in fact, but also generous and funny and lovely. A bit like you in a way."

"Thanks Lou - oh, it's really kind of you to say that! Goodness me, it's so nice to talk to you about it all! But haven't *you* actually ever fancied him? Being such a close friend of your family, Duncan's best mate etcetera, etcetera?"

Louise laughed, "No way! I love him dearly but he's far too intense and swotty for me! And as I say - he's like an extra brother -

so certainly not romance material! Anyway I'm not on the look-out at the moment - I still just want to have fun."

Cressida laughed too, "He and I both agreed that we were fully paid-up members of the school of swotty geekdom!"

"There you go! One more thing, though, Cressy. He's coped amazingly with the awful things that have happened, he's kind and gentle - sad but not bitter. In many ways he's one of the most competent and caring people I know. But he's also quite vulnerable. He doesn't seem to be able to confide in his father, and although we all cherish him in our family, I think he's actually pretty lonely a lot of the time. So maybe bear that in mind. I'm not saying you're likely to do so, but for instance if you two-timed him or wanted out of the relationship ....."

Before she could finish Cressida broke in, "I never will, Lou, I'm in as deep as he is. And I do know about his vulnerability."

She was remembering how upset he had become that day they'd spent together in Chilminster, and how protective and compassionate she had felt as she tried to comfort him.

"OK Cressy, you know yourself best, I just thought I'd better mention it."

"Of course - yes, sorry - and thanks too, Lou, I didn't mean to sound snappy - you truly are the very, very best of friends. But oh my God, who would have thought it? Before your party I didn't even know he existed - and now look where we are! We both know we have to go slowly and carefully and not rush things at all, but already he's changed my life."

She paused, then went on, realising that her concerns had dominated the conversation. "Anyway, enough of me, How was France? Duncan told us about the disasters, but said it had been really fun as well. Any holiday romances for you, or even flirty flings like the one he had?"

When the girls got back from their walk they found Tolly and Duncan, both stripped to the waist and hard at work filling in trenches which were no longer needed.

"Skivers!" Duncan shouted jokingly as they walked past. "We've already filled two trenches while you've been gossiping."

"I'm just showing Lou round the site!" Cressida said, delighted to see them both, and secretly thrilled by the sight of Tolly's rippling muscles as he wielded his spade.

"Keep at it, boys," Louise added, "Keep up the hard graft! We're off to the marquee; Cressy wants to show me some of the stuff they've dug up, as well as bits of the chapel she and her mates found."

"Meet for lunch maybe?" Tolly suggested, sticking his spade into the ground and wiping a grimy hand over his forehead.

"Of course," from Cressida. "Maybe, maybe not," was Louise's more teasing response; "Come on, Cressy, let's leave these sons of the soil to their toil."

Meanwhile, at Cressida's home in the village her little brothers were making plans for her birthday. They had each created a birthday card for her, Mikey's depicting the Greeks coming out of the Wooden Horse, and Jo-Jo's showing a very bloodthirsty battle going on between a pair of ferocious fighting men with shields and swords.

They'd been thrilled with the postcards of the Wooden Horse painting that Cressida had brought back for them, and since then had spent quite a lot of time in the garden inventing games about those warriors hiding inside the horse, and their battles with their Trojan opponents.

Suddenly Mikey had an idea. "Why don't we go up the hill on Cressy's birthday to see the castle, and pretend that the horse is still there. And after that we'll go and give Cressy our cards for a Happy Birthday surprise."

"Yesss! But will Mummy and Daddy let us?" said Jo-Jo.

Mikey thought for a moment. He knew that they probably wouldn't.

"I know! Let's do it secretly," he suggested. "We'll make ourselves wake up very early on her birthday morning when they're still in bed, and creep out through the kitchen door. Then we'll climb up the hill and go to the castle and play a game about the Wooden Horse."

"Yes, then we can go down the other side and find Cressy in her tent!"

They went very willingly to bed a few days later, on the evening before the birthday, hardly able to contain their excitement about their secret plan. The next morning they were awake well before 6am, got dressed as quietly as they could, and crept downstairs. As usual the kitchen door was locked, but as usual too, the key was still in the lock on the inside. Breathless with anticipation, Jo-Jo turned it, opened the door and they stepped out into the grey dawn air of the back garden, shutting the door quietly behind them.

A track outside the garden gate led past the side of the house towards the street. The sun wasn't quite up yet, so it was only just getting light. There was very little traffic, and no people about, but the twins knew their way, and trotted along the pavement, hand in hand, towards the hill and the castle. This was the biggest adventure they had ever had!

With a mixture of excitement and nervousness they hurried towards the track up to Castle Hill as fast as they could, hoping that none of those driving the few cars and delivery vehicles along the main road would recognise them. They had their story ready if anyone did stop: they were going up to the castle to meet their big sister who was camping there.

"It's not really a lie," Mikey said, "We *are* going to see her today aren't we, just later than now."

Both felt relieved, though, when the road veered off to the left and they arrived at the beginning of the track leading up to the castle. Excitedly they set off to climb up the steep hill.

On the other side of the hill where the camp was, the volunteers who hadn't yet left the dig were still asleep, all except one. Tolly had awoken early. Sometimes when this happened he managed to get back to sleep, but today, perhaps because it was Cressida's birthday, he couldn't settle. He decided to get dressed and go for a walk, something he often did when he couldn't sleep. Moving quietly so as not to disturb Duncan, he pulled on his jeans and jumper, laced up his boots, and left the tent.

Outside, the dawn chorus was getting under way as the sun began to make its daily journey across the sky. Tolly always enjoyed the ethereal, almost magical atmosphere of these early morning walks. White wraiths of mist drifted around the camp site and hung over the river, but as he climbed up towards the castle he came out through the mist and saw it rising out of the haze like a mirage, or an enchanted vision from a fairytale. He decided to walk all the way round the dig site, still empty of people in the early morning light, then to go around the outside of the castle before heading back down to the camp. By then, he thought, the others might be waking up and he would be able to get some tea or coffee on the go.

CHAPTER EIGHTEEN

Little Boys Lost – and Found

Mikey and Jo-Jo had reached the castle. They were both breathless and, though neither would admit it, quite scared. All of a sudden it felt rather frightening up there - bleak and empty. They tried to pretend that the big Wooden Horse was still standing, as it was on their postcards, but somehow the fantasy didn't work. Mikey thought of his warm bed and his Mummy and Daddy, and felt as if he might cry.

Jo-Jo, trying to be brave, said, "We *are* still hero-warriors, but it's a bit cold and horrid isn't it? I wonder if we can get inside. Come on Mikey, let's explore round a bit."

They started to walk round the semi-ruined building, soon coming across the overgrown kitchen garden which their sister had discovered a few weeks earlier, and from there they reached the open passageway leading into the castle.

"Let's go inside," suggested Jo-Jo, "It won't be so cold, and we can play a game there!"

Mikey, beginning to feel more cheerful, agreed. In they went, soon arriving at the half open door leading into that large empty chamber where, unknown to them, some weeks back, Cressida had first met up again with Tolly. It seemed much safer there, so they went in, then leant against the huge heavy door till it closed behind them, and started to explore the room.

As Tolly came to the end of his early walk and his circumnavigation of the castle, he felt much invigorated and was also by now very hungry. He decided to head back downhill to the camp and make a fry-up on the camping stove he and Duncan had been using. A bacon sandwich and some hot coffee was just what he needed, and by then Duncan and the girls would probably be awake for a convivial breakfast in the open air.

He turned to go down the hill, but was arrested by a noise which sounded like a child crying. Was it a bird, or an animal - a fox perhaps? The screeching call of a fox often sounded hauntingly like a human being crying for help.

Tolly paused, looking around him. Nothing. Then, out of the side of his eye he glimpsed some movement near one of the castle windows in that big empty room where he had found Cressida a few weeks ago. At the same time he heard the wailing noise again. Turning round to look fully at the window, to his astonishment he saw two little faces. There were children in there, sobbing and banging on the window panes.

Horrified, Tolly rushed back to the castle and made his way inside through the passage near the old kitchen garden.

At home in Troycombe village Graham and Helen Curtis were waking up. It was just before seven o'clock. Every morning, before Cressida and the twins awoke, they liked to enjoy a private cup of tea in bed, with a bit of one-to-one time chatting about this and that before the demands of the day took over. They took it in turns to go down and make the tea. This morning it was Helen's turn. She went down and put the kettle on.

Meanwhile Tolly, now inside the castle, had reached the door of the large chamber where he had seen the children. He opened it and went in, arriving into what was obviously a very sorry state of affairs. Two small boys were sitting on the window seat, crying their eyes out. One was holding his ankle and was clearly in pain. The other was sitting beside him with an arm round him.

"Hello! What's happened? What's going on here?" asked Tolly, moving quickly towards them. He had a brief flash of déja-vu, remembering that memorable meeting with Cressida, and almost simultaneously realising that both little boys had a look of her.

"Are you Mikey and Jo-Jo?" he asked, coming up to them. They gulped and sniffled. "Y-y- yes," they said together. Then one of them added, trying to control his sobs,

"We came in to play and to pretend about the Wooden Horse, but we shut the door behind us and then we couldn't get up to the handle to go out again."

He sniffed again, rubbing his eyes, then went on,

"Jo-Jo tried to climb on my back to reach it, but he fell off and hurt his foot." They were both patently very distressed and frightened.

"We want our Mummy," they wailed.

Tolly sat down beside them. "My name's Tolly and I'll look after you. Let me have a look at your foot, Jo-Jo. And don't worry, I'll take you down the hill and back home to your Mummy and Daddy. Try to be brave boys and don't cry, everything's going to be alright."

Jo-Jo's ankle was swollen, he had obviously twisted it when he fell. "But it hurts," he moaned, as Tolly held it and gently felt it to check if anything was broken. "I can't walk on it, it's too sore."

"It'll be a lot better in a day or two," Tolly assured him. "And you won't have to walk on it, I can carry you on my shoulders. You can pretend I'm your horse - but not the Wooden Horse! Are you OK to walk if I hold your hand, Mikey?"

Both little boys were beginning to feel much better. The kind and calm presence of Tolly was immensely reassuring, and had the effect of turning their escapade from a catastrophe into an adventure again.

"You're a very nice man," said Mikey happily. Tolly felt himself blushing slightly, as he hoisted Jo-Jo onto his shoulders, took Mikey's hand and set off out of the castle to walk downhill to the village.

Jo-Jo, thrilled to be up so high, soon forgot his sore foot and shrieked with excitement. Remembering a song he used to sing at nursery he chanted "Horsey, horsey, don't you stop – just make your hooves ago clippetty clop..." and twisted his hands into Tolly's thick dark curly hair as he bounced up and down.

"Hey - steady on, that's my hair you're grabbing!" protested Tolly. Mikey, virtuously walking by Tolly's side, started to sing a different song that they'd learnt at school. Jo-Jo joined in, and Tolly, remembering it from his own childhood, added his deep bass voice to the chorus. Thus they proceeded down into the village and towards the twins' home.

Meanwhile Helen Curtis, completely unaware of all this drama, had taken the tea tray upstairs, and she and Graham were in bed enjoying their morning tea and chat together.

"The twins must have been really tired," she said to her husband, "I haven't heard a peep from them."

"Probably because Cressy's up at the camp, so no noises of birthday excitement. I'll go and look in on them in a few minutes," Graham said, lying back against his pillows.

"Thanks, darling."

They finished their tea then got dressed before checking on the twins.

That relaxed and peaceful state of affairs came to an abrupt and traumatic end when Graham, popping into the twins' bedroom, saw the two empty beds. Both parents rushed downstairs to see if the boys had got up and gone into the playroom. It was empty. They each began to feel a horrendous panic rising and their hearts jumping, as a host of disaster scenarios suddenly rushed through their heads.

"They may have just woken early and gone outside to play," Graham said hopefully, looking out through the kitchen window. But there was no sign of the boys. They realised, however, as they reached the kitchen door to go into the garden, that it was unlocked.

"Where have they gone - has someone taken them?" cried Helen, panic-stricken with fear and dread.

"They must have got out of their own accord," Graham said, "that door has been unlocked from the inside. No-one except either of the two of them could have opened it. But where they've gone I have no idea. I think we need to call the police."

At that moment the front door bell rang. Helen rushed to open the door. There stood Tolly, Jo-Jo on his shoulders, Mikey holding his hand.

"Good morning Mrs Curtis. I'm Tolly Henderson, and here are your twins."

Helen, white faced and trembling, felt tears of relief spilling down her cheeks.

"But what - but where - where have they been?" she asked shakily.

Graham, close behind her, was equally agitated.

"Come in boys, come in all of you. What's been happening?" he said.

All was confusion for a few moments as Tolly lifted Jo-Jo down, and the two little boys rushed into the arms of their distraught parents.

Then Helen, regaining a bit of composure, turned again to Tolly.

"Yes, *please* come in, and tell us where they've been, and how you found them."

Graham realised at this point that he had seen Tolly before. This was the young man Cressida had been with in the pub some weeks previously. Letting go of Mikey, he held his hand out to Tolly.

"Hello again Tolly," he said, "Thank you, thank you, thank you!" He grasped Tolly's hand and holding it in both of his, he continued "Yes indeed, come on in. How can we possibly express our gratitude and relief? Will you come through and join us for breakfast and tell us where and how you found them."

Tolly was discomfited. He was also extremely hungry and was feeling tired and light-headed after his long walk and his rescue of the boys, with his back and shoulders aching from the transportation of sturdy little Jo-Jo down the steep slope. After the turbulent outpouring of emotion in the last few moments the thought of breakfast was very appealing, but he felt slightly awkward about it - after all, even though they were Cressida's parents he hardly knew them. He didn't want them to think he was accepting hospitality in order to gain their approval of his friendship with their daughter.

It was the little boys, who had recovered their equilibrium much more rapidly than anyone else, who clinched things. They each grabbed one of his hands and Mikey said,

"Yes, Tolly, please, please, *please* come to breakfast with us," while Jo-Jo, letting go of Tolly's hand, put both arms round him and added,

"We love you Tolly, you're our best friend now!"

How could Tolly resist such artless affection? He couldn't!

Remembering Jo-Jo's foot, he told the parents about that slightly sprained ankle and reassured them that it wasn't serious - in fact Jo-Jo seemed already to have almost forgotten about it. Within a few moments Tolly found himself sitting in an armchair with a mug of hot coffee in his hand and the irresistible aroma of frying bacon assailing his nostrils. The hero-worshipping twins leant against him, one on either side of the chair.

Over breakfast he described how, unable to sleep, he had gone out for an early morning walk, and how he had then heard the boys crying and found them inside the castle. They hadn't been in any danger, he assured their parents, but they'd been very frightened and upset, because the huge room they had wandered into had a large heavy door which they had pushed closed behind them, and the handle was set too high for them to reach to get out again.

"How very, very lucky for them - and for us - that you woke up so early and went for a walk. They could have been stuck there for hours," said Helen, who was still feeling shaken up by the whole episode.

"I suppose someone would have found them eventually, once the day's work on the dig got going," Graham added, "but by then we would have contacted the police - the whole episode would have blown up massively and we'd have been living through a nightmare scenario until they were found. As well, it would all have been much more traumatic for them - and absolutely ruined Cressida's birthday!"

As the talk continued the twins began to get impatient. They had finished their breakfast and wanted to show Tolly the playroom and their den in the garden, imploring him to come and play with them. But Tolly stood up. It was time to go. He addressed the two of them,

"I really must be off, I'm afraid, chaps. They'll be wondering where I am, back at the dig. Also. as it's your big sister's birthday today I want to say hello and Happy Birthday to her before we all go back to work doing the big clear-up at the dig."

He was longing to see Cressida again, and was hoping that they might get some time alone together before the planned party celebrations got under way.

Suddenly a wail rose up from the twins.

"Our cards! We made cards for Cressy and we brought them with us to go and surprise her." "We left them in the castle. We forgot to take them with us."

"I'll tell you what, boys," said Tolly, "When I get back I'll go and pick them up from the castle, and be your postman to deliver them to Cressida. Would that be OK? I promise she'll have them just as soon as I see her, once I'm back at the dig. And thank you all so much for that delicious breakfast!"

"That would be fine, wouldn't it, twins? How very kind of you, Tolly," Helen said firmly. She was feeling much more like her normal self. "And, boys, you'll be able to see Cressy later anyway because we're all going to come and visit the camp this afternoon."

Graham, suddenly looking rather stern, added,

"Now, say goodbye to Tolly and let's all get on with the day. Before anything else, Mummy and I would like to know whatever made the pair of you embark on such a thoughtless and reckless escapade."

Tolly left them to it, thankful to get away from the domestic day of reckoning which looked likely to follow.

CHAPTER NINETEEN

The Birthday

Cressida awoke in a mood of mingled excitement and nervousness. She was sixteen! Somehow this felt like a real milestone, a much more mature age than fifteen. She sat up, leaning over to see what sort of a day it was. The sun shone down from a cloudless sky, with no vestige left of that early morning mist that Tolly, unbeknown to her, had experienced over two hours earlier.

When would she see him? Lou was still asleep, but she could hear some movement from the adjacent tent where the boys slept, and wondered whether she might pop her head through the opening and say hello. She was forestalled by Duncan, who appeared suddenly with a cup of tea in each hand.

"Rise and shine girls - and Happy Birthday Cressy! Hope you slept OK. It's a lovely day - Tolly's obviously making the most of it - he seems to have gone off for one of his early morning walks."

Quelling her slight disappointment, Cressida got dressed, came out and thanked Duncan. She drank her tea and chatted cheerfully to him and to Louise, who emerged a few moments later, ready for breakfast.

As the morning wore on and there was still no sign of Tolly, Cressida began to feel a mixture of apprehension and dread. Had something happened to him? Or had he perhaps been called home by his father - was there some crisis there? Or, most worrying, maybe he'd decided that he didn't want to be with her after all?

"Cheer up Cressy, he'll be back. He's probably scouring the village for flowers and other birthday stuff for the party," Louise said confidently, patting Cressida on the back. After a pause she continued,

"Anyway, I suppose we'd better all go off now to see what needs to be done in the big clear up. Let's get over to the marquee and see what Matthew wants us to do."

Cressida's mini-panic was very soon over, because there in the marquee was Tolly, in conversation with Matthew. He seemed to be explaining something. Matthew was nodding and smiling, as he clapped Tolly on the shoulder. Tolly then turned towards the way out, his face lighting up as he beheld Cressida, Louise and Duncan coming in.

"Hello all," he greeted them cheerfully, "And Happy Birthday Cressida! Actually Matthew's just agreed to the two of us having a bit of time off, so we'll see you all later. Will you come with me, Cressida, I've got some things to show you." Cressida's anxiety was instantly replaced with excitement and delight!

Taking her hand, Tolly headed out of the marquee, leaving Louise and Duncan slightly surprised, but relieved for Cressida's sake that no disaster had occurred. Indeed, quite the opposite, it seemed, judging by Tolly's upbeat manner.

"I hope you don't mind me dragging you off, but I've got so much to tell you. Let's go down to the bit of woodland behind the camp site," Tolly said. When they reached the camp he asked her to wait for a moment while he collected his rucksack. Then they continued into the wood.

Relieved and happy, she would have gone anywhere with him! It was enough to be back together again, with the prospect of a birthday celebration to come later, and Tolly by her side. It was all very exciting and very mysterious! They didn't say much, but from time to time they exchanged smiles.

"Here we are," he said, leading the way to a little patch of grass surrounded by a copse of trees. There was a fallen tree in the middle, where they sat down. She turned to him expectantly. What did he want to tell her about?

"First, I need to give you these." He felt in his pocket and handed over the two birthday cards so painstakingly created by the twins, which he had retrieved from the room in the castle where they had left them.

"Oh goodness, from the twins, bless them!" she exclaimed, smiling at their gory depictions of warriors and the Wooden Horse. She continued,

"But how come you've got them? What's been going on?"

So Tolly related, to a spellbound Cressida, the saga of his early morning activities, starting with the walk he took when he couldn't sleep, the crying he had heard, leading to his discovery of the trapped twins, then his rescue of them and the trek down into the village with Mikey by his side and Jo-Jo on his shoulders, and their arrival at her family home.

"Your mother opened the door - she was in a real state, poor woman. They'd discovered that the twins weren't in their beds, and they'd been frantically searching for them. In fact your father was just about to call the police when I turned up."

Cressida was astounded. He had rescued the twins! He had been to her home! He had met both her parents! And all this time she had been fast asleep and completely unaware of the drama going on.

She begged him to fill in every smallest detail of what had taken place. Everything was interesting, from his finding the trapped boys crying in the castle, to the three of them singing nursery songs together as he brought them down the hill, and how the twins had claimed him as their best friend and hugged him and persuaded him to stay for breakfast.

"Those bad little boys!" she exclaimed, but couldn't help laughing too. "I suppose in a way it's partly my fault, for getting them so fired up about Greek mythology and giving them those pictures of the Wooden Horse. I bet once you'd gone they got a very stern telling off. But also, I can't help feeling that in the long run your meeting my parents like that must have shown them what a kind, capable and good person you are, which can only make things easier for you and me."

"Thanks Cressida, oh thanks so much," he said, touched by this, putting an arm around her. "Actually I was worried that they might think I was staying for breakfast only in order to get on the right side of them. I would have left, but it was the twins who made me stay. In fact Jo-Jo put his arms round my waist and wouldn't let me go!"

"Mum and Dad wouldn't think that. They would have been so utterly, utterly relieved - and all they would have wanted to do was to show their gratitude with a bit of hospitality. I hope it was a good, tasty breakfast, you must have been starving!"

"It was a superb breakfast! And they were both really welcoming to me; they seem like great parents. Anyway, they're coming over to the camp with the twins later, presumably with birthday stuff for you, so you'll hear their side of the story then, I'm sure. But now, Cressida my darling, I have some things for you."

He had not called her 'darling' before. Cressida felt excited and happy!

Tolly rummaged in his rucksack, which was lying by his feet, and brought out a small parcel and an envelope. "Could you open this first?" he said, handing the package over to her.

He watched nervously as she unwrapped it, to reveal a jewellery case containing a gold bracelet inlaid with opals of iridescent milky bluish white, streaked with faint shades of pink and green, and a pair of matching opal earrings.

Cressida was overcome. Tears of joy filled her eyes and she looked at Tolly, her voice full of emotion.

"Oh, Tolly, Tolly - They're beautiful! They're so beautiful - and the pale stones with those faint colours remind me a bit of our faience beads."

Tolly nodded. "Yes, that's why I thought you'd like them, and it would make up in a way for you giving up the necklace. And no danger of hallucinogens here!"

Cressida slipped the bracelet over her wrist and turned it this way and that, watching the opals gleaming with their pale colours in the dappled sunlight.

She then put the earrings on and smiled at him. "How do they all look?"

"Gorgeous, just gorgeous," Tolly said. "I found them in an antique shop in Salisbury. I remembered my mother wearing an opal necklace which she loved, so I thought how much I'd like to give you some opals too."

"They're wonderful!, I absolutely adore them, dear Tolly - thank you so, so much!"

Her eyes were shining as she turned to him. Then he took her in his arms and kissed her, a long, deep, loving kiss. Cressida had never been kissed like that before. She felt a little breathless, and was conscious of her heart thumping as they clung together. It was all very new, very wonderful, and very overwhelming.

Then, gently, Tolly loosened his arms and smiled at her, before picking up the envelope and handing it to her. "Don't forget this, my love. Another little surprise."

Inside was a card with a caricature of Cressida on the front, sitting at a desk scribbling away, with piles of books around her, her hair chaotically secured with a clip but with tendrils hanging down on either side, and a headline above, reading "Swotty Geeks' Academy". Then, when she opened the card out she saw an equally disordered scene inside, depicting Tolly, his hands sticking up through his hair, his shoulders hunched over an enormous volume, and again stacks of books all around him. The message read thus:

'From one Swotty Geek to another keeping up the good work! Happy Birthday to my beloved fellow geek with all my love - Tolly xxxxx.'

Cressida burst out laughing. "Brilliant, Tolly - you are clever! You've managed to get a bit of a likeness of us both, even in caricatures. I didn't know you could draw."

"Well, it's not exactly fine art but I do quite like doing cartoons. Anyway, there's also something in the envelope. I'll tell you my idea once you've opened it."

There was a leaflet inside, with the heading 'National Shakespeare Theatre 1995 Autumn Programme'. Cressida looked down the list of performances, between September 1st and the end of November.

Tolly began to explain.

"The NST is based in Farleighurst, not far from Oxford, as you probably know. One of my mother's cousins lives nearby, and I've often been to the theatre there - it's quite an easy trip from

Salisbury. They're a really good company, and I'd so much like to take you to a performance. When I saw that they were doing both Troilus and Cressida *and* Romeo and Juliet on subsequent nights in early September and again in late October I thought how wonderful it would be if we could go together. We could stay with cousin Charlotte, in separate bedrooms of course! What d'you think?"

"Oh gosh, Tolly, I would absolutely love it! But would my parents allow it - I don't know. Also, school starts again on September 11th, so it would have to be before that, or more likely during half-term - which *is* actually in late October. When do you have to be back in Durham?"

"Well," said Tolly, "Michaelmas term starts in early October, but it's quite easy to get an exeat in termtime, especially for Shakespeare, so that wouldn't be a problem for me. I just thought it seemed so right for us - first Troilus and Cressida - after our bitter-sweet early meeting at Lou's party - and your faience beads, and our shared explorations into the Trojan War. And then Romeo and Juliet - well, they were teenagers like us, weren't they? I know I'm a bit of a romantic - and there's no way we're going to end up as they did, thank goodness, but it is the most poignant and haunting love story isn't it?"

Cressida nodded. "Yes - and actually it's nearly always on the GCSE syllabus. It was, this year, so I know it pretty well off by heart. It seems to be the play of choice for adolescents! And of course I'm just as much of a romantic as you are. Oh, it would be SO brilliant! I must admit I'm dreading the end of the summer, me back to school and you going back to Durham, I shall miss you so much, Tolly! If we went in October it would be something to look forward to. I'll certainly sound out my parents; perhaps if they could talk to your mother's cousin on the phone ... that might help."

"I'll miss you just as much, Cressida. It's been an idyllic time for us, hasn't it? Of course we'll write, and talk on the phone a lot, but things are going to be very different for us both. Let's keep hoping, and see what your parents think. Anyway, we do still have over three weeks left before you go back to school, so for the time being at least, we can carry on spending as much time together as possible. And we also have that further research to do - checking out about poor Lady Marlington. I'll need to go back again to Salisbury quite soon to see my father, but maybe you might be able to come with me and meet him. Who knows, he might lighten up a bit when he sees how lovely you are!"

Cressida blushed slightly. From what Tolly had told her about his life, she was nervous about meeting his father, but at the same time she couldn't really believe that any relative of Tolly's could be all that formidable. She thought too that Dr Henderson being a consultant surgeon must mean that he was also a humane and caring person, despite, as she now knew, still overwhelmed with sadness about his dead wife.

They carried on chatting, sitting close to one another. Tolly had one arm around her and his other hand was clasped in with both of hers. It was a tender, affectionate and peaceful interlude, with time seeming to stand still for them both. But inevitably reality took over, and at last Tolly said,

"I suppose we'd better both go back again now and do our bit on the dig. I wish we could stay here all day, just the two of us alone together."

Cressida agreed, adding,

"We always have so much to talk about, don't we? Oh well, I'd better put this lovely jewellery away and get back to work. It was really kind of Matthew to give us some free time. See you later, and thanks again so much for my wonderful presents, dear Tolly."

They kissed again, then parted to climb back up to the dig and resume their jobs - Tolly to continue filling in trenches and Cressida to help with wrapping the finds which had already been washed, examined and classified, ready to be transported to the museum. Two of her co-workers, Dave and Suzanne, were also there. The third of them, Lucy, had left that morning as she had unexpectedly been called home.

Also there, to Cressida's surprise, was Serena, one of the girls who'd burst in on hers and Tolly's first tête-à-tête when they'd met up again in the castle.

Cressida was wary of her. She remembered how Serena and her friends had hustled Tolly away that morning a few weeks ago, and how very unfriendly they had all seemed. But, now secure in her happiness, she smiled at Serena and said "Hello, I'm Cressida."

"I know exactly who you are." Serena responded. "You're the girl who's after Tolly."

Cressida looked at her in surprise, but decided not to engage in further conversation. Instead she turned to Suzanne and Dave who were busy sorting finds.

"Hi you two. Shall I make a start on this lot here?"

They toiled away companionably and after a while even Serena became more friendly.

An unexpected visitor arrived early that afternoon as they continued their work in the marquee. Penny Emerson, accompanied by Matthew, came in to say hello. Cressida was thrilled to see her again, and eager to tell her how much she was enjoying the dig.

"I've just popped over to see how it's all going," Penny said, "and to wish you a happy birthday, Cressida. Have you found anything interesting?"

"Oh yes, it's all been absolutely brilliant - *so* exciting and fun! We've found lots of stuff! These are my friends - Dave, Suzanne -

and Serena. Dave and Suzanne and another girl, Lucy - who's sadly had to leave - were all with me when we discovered the first bit of the wall of the chapel. "

"And what about that nice young man of yours, Tolly? Have you made any more progress on your joint researches?"

"We were talking about it earlier today. When the dig's over we'll get back into all that, while we still have time. Oh - and Matthew - it was really kind of you to let us both off for a bit this morning - thank you so much."

Soon after this Penny and Matthew departed, Cressida having said she would visit the museum again once she and Tolly had resumed their unfinished investigations around the fate of poor Lady Marlington.

When they were out of earshot Serena turned to Cressida.

"Could we have a bit of a chat outside?" she asked.

"Of course." She followed Serena out, wondering what this was about.

Serena, looking slightly embarrassed, then began to speak.

"Thank you very much for introducing me as a friend. I want to apologise for being so hostile to you, and for what I said earlier. To be honest, I did fancy Tolly. Lots of us do, but he isn't interested in any of us. He's always nice and friendly, but we've all realised it's no-go with him. He doesn't play the field at all. At first we thought it was probably because he had a girlfriend at home, but now I completely accept what I must admit at first I didn't want to believe - that it's definitely you. I feel awful now about being so unfriendly. I'm really sorry, I would like us to be friends."

This was a generous and courageous confession, Cressida thought. She responded with equal generosity.

"Thank you for saying all this, it was a kind and brave thing to do and I really appreciate it. And I hope you and your friends will come to my birthday party this evening, down at the camp. I think it's going to be great fun!"

"That would be lovely, thank you."

They ended the conversation with a spontaneous mutual hug and went back to work - the invisible cloud of awkwardness between them gone as if it had never been.

The next visit, during the afternoon, was to be the expected arrival at the camp of Cressida's family. By this time all the finds had been wrapped and labelled and the marquee was being emptied, ready for dismantling the next day.

When Cressida had left the marquee to return to the camp she couldn't help feeling slightly wistful now it was all nearly over. It had been an unforgettable experience - the excitement of search and discovery, the purposeful atmosphere of working together to find out more about the past - as well as learning different techniques, making new friends, and sharing in the general ambience of camaraderie and fun.

For her personally, the time had also been illuminated into something truly magical, as her relationship with Tolly had developed and deepened. She thought she would never, ever forget the enchantment of these few weeks. But it wasn't all over yet, she told herself, as she arrived back at the camp.

"Hi Cressy! Happy Birthday!" came greetings from various of the other campers, some of whom were busy beginning to build a large bonfire on a flattish grassy area halfway down the slope which led down to the camp site and the river and woods beyond.

"Cressy, Cressy!" came a familiar shriek. The twins were rushing along up from the river valley towards the camp, their parents following more slowly. Dad must have brought them all in the car, she thought; he'd have driven it out of the village and parked it somewhere further down on the winding road, part of which ran along close to the river.

"Hello lovely boys," Cressida held out her arms and hugged her little brothers as they ran into them.

"Did you get our cards?" "Is Tolly here?," they burst out simultaneously.

"He's working, but I'm sure he'll be along soon. And yes, he gave me your cards! Thank you so much - they're wonderful - I'm absolutely thrilled with them! What clever boys you are to have made them!"

By this time her parents had arrived, Mum carrying a large cake tin and Dad bearing a bag full of what Cressida assumed were birthday presents.

"Happy Birthday, Cressy darling!"

Hugs and kisses followed, while the little boys bounced around excitedly. Their energy had clearly in no way been diminished by their early morning adventure!

"Where's your tent? Can we go in your tent!?" was their first request.

Both twins were intrigued by the cosy space where she and Louise had been sleeping, and would have liked to have been allowed to wriggle down inside the two sleeping bags and pretend they were caterpillars. This, however, was firmly vetoed by their sister. Instead, she suggested they help collect sticks for the bonfire.

"Remember our Stone-Age bonfire at home? Well, now that you're both so good at making bonfires you can help with this one - it's going to be much, much bigger than our garden one. Why not see how many sticks you can find."

The arrival of Tolly on the scene shortly afterwards turned this task from rather a boring chore into one that they were suddenly thrilled to take part in. Thoughtfully, Tolly ensured that Cressida and her parents could have some time on their own together by helping the twins search for firewood, encouraging them to make neat heaps of it ready for use, and tactfully discouraging them from too much interference in the building of the bonfire as the edifice grew.

Meanwhile Cressida provided her parents with a pair of camping chairs borrowed from Duncan and Louise, and was herself sitting on a camp stool chatting to them and opening her presents - a pleasant selection including some books and CD's, a new pair of slippers, a pendant inlaid with a green tourmaline gemstone, some bath foam and other toiletries, and a box of expensive looking soap.

The cake, made by her mother, was a delectable looking confection decorated with an artistic depiction of a flowering tree. Piped icing letters spelling 'Happy Birthday Cressida' circled the tree, and a border of sugar flower petals were set all the way around the edge of the cake.

"It's lovely, Mum. I didn't know you were so good at cake decoration."

"Well," Helen admitted, "I did get a bit of help from my friend Lisa who's much more skilled than me, she gave me the sugar petals and created the tree. But obviously I baked the cake, iced it and did the writing."

Duncan and Louise then came over with cups of tea and biscuits for everyone. At this point Tolly joined them, followed by his two small devoted acolytes, who positioned themselves one on either side of him and partook of orange squash and chocolate biscuits.

"What about the cake? Mikey asked, "When can we have some cake?"

"We'll definitely keep you some, for when I come home. We can have another little party then," Cressida said, hoping this wouldn't cause an outburst. After all, the cake was really intended for the campsite birthday party later.

"Will Tolly come too? Will you come to our house again then, Tolly? Please, please, PLEASE, " the twins begged him.

"I will, if that's OK," was Tolly's kind reply, glancing over at Cressida with a smile. If agreeing to attend a repeat tea party in a couple of days' time meant he could forestall a noisy protest from the twins, it was worth it. And, most importantly, it would make things easier for Cressida.

Graham Curtis obviously agreed.

"Thanks Tolly. You're certainly doing your bit for this family these days, isn't he, Cressy? But now I think it's time we left you to your celebrations, and took these two lads home."

"Wow Tolly - what a hero," teased Duncan as Cressida's family departed. Tolly had told him about the early morning adventure while they were working together that afternoon. Now, the four of them sat on the grass in the late afternoon sun, chatting about the dig, planning for the party to come, and musing together on what lay further ahead.

Duncan was both excited and nervous about going to music college; a completely new chapter would shortly be opening in his life.

"I'll have to polish up my piano playing," he said, "Cello's OK. That's what I got in on, but I'm doing piano as a second study. Lots of practice every day for me till I go to London. Do you still play, Tolly?"

"Not as much as I should," Tolly confessed, "I'm in the college orchestra, but I don't practice enough. At the moment I've got other

stuff on my mind - including quite a lot of reading and researching."
He smiled again at Cressida as he said this.

"And meanwhile we two girls will be back at the boring old grind before either of you," Louise said. "It must be lovely to have the short terms and long holidays that you get, Tolly! Can't wait to get my GCSE results and into the Sixth Form where we can at least choose what we want to study. I hope we've done OK."

"You'll be fine, Lou," said Cressida, " I hope I will too, although the maths papers were a bit of a trial - and results are due quite soon! Help! I must admit I won't be sorry to be leaving maths behind - if I've got through. Otherwise it would be a re-take - can't bear to think of that!"

She looked briefly over at Tolly with a slight smile, and then went on,

"One thing I really wish, is that we could do Latin at our school - I would love to be able to read Virgil in the original. Ideally, Homer too - but no chance of that. OK, OK - I know that all sounds pretty geeky. But you get it, don't you, Tolly?"

Duncan stood up, saying "Enough, enough, enough of geekdom, exams, Latin lessons, music practice and research," he said, "It's still summer, we're all still on holiday, and it's Cressy's birthday. Let's toast her and one another and drink to the future for us all. Wait here, all of you."

He went over to his tent and fetched a bottle and four glasses. "Left over from Lou's party," he explained. "It's been in the fridge at home and in the coolbox since we got here, so it should still be nicely chilled."

"To Cressida, and to the future for all of us," he said as he popped the cork and poured the champagne. Then they all clinked glasses and echoed his words.

Cressida remembered with a flicker of secret embarrassment the first and only time she had drunk champagne before. Now she took her glass calmly, with a feeling of gratitude and contentment. As she sat with these three good friends, one of whom had brought so much wonder and joy into her life that she felt she had almost become a different person, she moved closer to Tolly and slipped her hand under his. He linked his fingers through hers as she raised her glass in a private tribute to him.

"Thanks Tolly," she said softly, "Thanks for everything."

As the afternoon dwindled into evening, preparations for the party accelerated. All those who had camp stools and chairs brought them out. Others provided groundsheets and spread them on the grass. Some of the boys had been up to where the tarpaulins were, and had begged the loan of a couple of trestle tables, now empty of excavated relics. The dig was effectively over; only the final clear-up remained, to be completed tomorrow. But that was all in the future - tonight was party time!

Cressida and Louise spent quite a long time getting ready, helping one another with costumes, hair and make-up. Choice was obviously limited, but Cressida had brought the pretty Indian patterned dress she'd worn for the dinner party with Matthew and Penny. She completed the ensemble with her Roman-style sandals, the pendant her parents had given her, and Tolly's opal earrings and bracelet - much admired by Louise.

Lou herself looked arresting and glamorous in black harem pants, a glittery top and an embroidered red Chinese jacket. When they emerged everything was ready - and the party began.

A sumptuous and diverse array of food, with plenty of both alcoholic and non-alcoholic drink, variously contributed by everyone in the camp, had been laid out on the tables. There was a heap of disposable plates, a pile of paper napkins, packets of plastic cutlery and two long cardboard tubes containing plastic beakers.

Cressida's birthday cake lay in pride of place at the centre of one of the tables. Drinks were poured, the fire was lit, everyone gathered around it and Duncan, never happier than when making music and overseeing a party, brought out his guitar and started to play.

One or two other guitar players joined in, harmonising with him. Then to everyone's surprise, Tolly, who'd disappeared sometime earlier saying he needed to fetch something, returned with his clarinet, which he'd been keeping at the Jacobs's house. He added new sounds, improvising and jamming along with the other musicians. The clarinet, capable of producing the most haunting and complex classical melodies, now sounded more like a saxophone as Tolly churned out a dazzling succession of jazz riffs.

While the dancing and singing was at its height Cressida, dancing with Duncan, found herself grabbed away from him in a sudden embrace. In front of her was the cheerful face and wide grin of Charlie!

"Hey Charlie - oh; brilliant! You made it - I'm so glad!" she said, "What happened at the cricket. Did you score?"

"Less said about it the better - we were flattened!"

But he didn't seem too downcast; like his siblings Charlie loved parties and was soon absorbed into the very heart of it all. He had brought a sleeping bag and hoped to be able to squeeze into someone's tent later.

Once people started eating and drinking, things quietened down a bit. The birthday cake was cut, shared out and enjoyed, Cressida carefully cutting and wrapping up part of it for the twins. Everyone then sang Happy Birthday, and the celebrations continued, albeit in a slightly more muted form.

To her surprise, Cressida received quite a few more presents - small gifts from the new friends she'd made, as well as a lot of birthday cards. It was very exciting and very delightful!

Much, much later on into the night, Cressida herself slipped away alone down the lower slope to look back at the joyful spectacle.

'All this for my birthday' she thought. 'I'll always remember this amazing, magical time.'

She could see the moon rising in its last quarter phase, the sky so clear that she could make out the craters and crags on the unshadowed part of its surface. She stood for some time gazing at it, transfixed by its otherworldly silvery mystery and its pale cold light.

Turning to walk slowly back she noticed that a few others were venturing further out, often in couples, perhaps pairing up to enjoy a bit of night-time romance. She thought she recognised Serena going off hand-in-hand with Duncan. That was a surprise! But after Serena's honest and open-hearted apology to her earlier in the day, Cressida was glad to see her happy. She'd be fine with Duncan.

As she paused, she saw Tolly coming towards her to join her again. 'Here he is, my own true love,' she said to herself. Never before had she felt so uplifted, yet so peaceful, so calm, so happy.

CHAPTER TWENTY

Aftermath

Next morning the area around the campsite looked messy and chaotic. Waking early, Duncan ventured out, and found himself facing a very dismal scene. There were discarded plates, plastic beakers rolling about on and around the tables, bottles - some empty, some still partly full - half-eaten food, cigarette ends, food and sweet wrappings, plus more general mess and rubbish left over from last night's celebrations.

As well as all this, there were some even more unwelcome leavings. More than one person had been sick, and it looked as if a fox or two had come out of the woods and been feasting on leftovers during the night, spreading much of the unfinished food far and wide. The animals had also left their own unwelcome offerings ready for unwitting people to step on.

Duncan, despite having partied into the small hours and enjoyed a lighthearted tryst with Serena, was feeling reasonably normal. He'd done a lot of dancing, played a lot of music and eaten a lot of food but, prudently, had limited his alcohol consumption. He had also, thinking ahead, yesterday asked Tolly to buy a roll of plastic sacks when he went back to Chilminster to collect his clarinet. While Tolly was still asleep Duncan managed to extract the roll from his rucksack without waking him.

Trying to keep as quiet as he could, Duncan first collected all the used plates, cups, paper napkins and cutlery, and bagged them up ready for disposal. The more noisy clearance of bottles could wait till more of the campers surfaced. Little by little, some of them did - Louise was the next to arrive, rubbing her eyes and blinking in the early morning sunshine. Although definitely feeling not quite her usual cheerful self, nevertheless she too began to gather up rubbish and fill up more plastic sacks. Gradually others turned up, and slowly the area began look more normal, apart from the burnt patch where the bonfire had been.

When Cressida appeared she seemed to be the most energetic and lively of them all. She had enjoyed the singing and dancing last night but had neither eaten nor drunk very much. It had been a wonderfully romantic night; she and Tolly had both been so enamoured of one another that they had lost their appetites for anything except the food of love.

So they had talked and talked, kissed and kissed again, sung songs to one another, quoted poetry, wandered in the darkness with their arms around each other, and laughed and cried about the times they'd had together and the separation soon to come. It was another of those transformative times, they agreed, when their "star-crossed" love affair seemed to have become even more meaningful.

Tolly himself was the last of all to emerge. The previous day had been a very long one for him, starting before dawn with his early walk and his discovery and rescue of the twins, and ending in the small hours when he and Cressida parted at last, to go and get some sleep. He was very apologetic when he finally appeared, seeing that most of the clearing was done.

"So sorry everyone - can I do penance by making tea, coffee and breakfast for us all?"

"I'll help," Cressida offered, happy to be together with him again.

So the two of them served up hot tea and coffee, boiled eggs and bacon sandwiches for the flagging workers. Everyone was aware that the next task was the final dismantling of the dig. There was a slightly melancholy 'fin-de-siècle' feeling in the camp.

A few people were already looking forward to getting home, picking up the threads of real life and sleeping in a proper bed again. Others felt sad at the ending of what for many had been a fascinating and enriching experience. Not only had they made new friends and learnt new skills, but they had also unearthed fascinating glimpses into the past - insights into the lives and concerns of people long dead.

Louise and Cressida went for another of their private walks before heading back to the dig site to help with the final clear-up. Both agreed that the party had been a great success, and each eagerly begged the other for an account of her experiences. Lou was first.

"I had a brilliant time," she said. "Lots of dancing, lots of singing, lots of chat, lots of flirting and quite a few kisses! Lovely food and plenty to drink - though on the whole I wasn't too heavy on the booze. On the minus side, also a fair bit of looking after people who'd overdone it booze-wise! For instance, Duncan had to help me to evict a couple who'd settled down in yours and my tent for a good old smooch! We managed to decant them onto a groundsheet in the end; luckily they were too pissed to resist and equally luckily they weren't pissed enough to throw up on our beds! But what about you, Cressy? You seemed to have gone AWOL most of the time."

"Well, yes, I suppose we did, really. But not all the time - I was there for the music and dancing. Weren't Duncan and Tolly fantastic with their playing! I know Duncan's really good - he seems to be able to play so many instruments and in so many styles - but Tolly! I had no idea he could do jazz clarinet!"

"Yes they were both brilliant - but come on Cressy, don't hedge! What did you and Tolly get up to?"

"Well, not what you might be thinking," Cressida said. "Yes, we did go off together, but we really just found a quiet place to be alone, and yes, of course we did kiss and cuddle, but we also looked at the moon and stars, walked together in the silvery light, we sang songs to each other, talked about poetry and history and our families and friends - really just enjoying the romance of the night and being on our own together. We need to make the most of the time left to us before we have to go off in our different directions."

As she finished talking Cressida felt her voice breaking up a bit. Facing the future was going to be a trial in many ways. It would also be a challenging test of their relationship. Both she and Tolly felt they had established a bond which could be a binding and long-term one, time would tell if this really was so. The thought of being without him was something she could hardly bear to contemplate, but confront it they must - and that long parting was only a few weeks away.

It was a paradoxical situation. If she had never met Tolly she would still just be thinking about going back to school, still secretly and innocently dreaming about meeting a nice boy, and carrying on as she had always done. She didn't want to return to that stage of life, but until now, she hadn't realised that emotional turmoil and anxiety was as much a part of falling in love as the joy and elation she'd been experiencing. The old, naïve Cressida was gone forever, she was moving into a more intense, complex, wonderful yet challenging phase of existence. She listened to what Lou was saying.

"I suppose if a relationship can't survive the separation of the two partners it isn't one worth having. But I'm sure that won't be the case with you and Tolly, it seems obvious to me that you were made for one another. I can see your family phone bill rocketing up and the postman weighed down with long screeds of fervent correspondence between the two of you! And just think how marvellous it'll be when you do get together again in University and school holidays!

"Also, time passes quite quickly, Cressy. This time next year we'll both be over seventeen, working on our A levels, and thinking of the future - University or College or whatever. And Tolly will be nearly twenty-one and starting his final year at Uni - that's something to think about! Real, true adulthood! Only just around the corner for him, and not all that far off for all of us, Freedom, independence, and adventure! And as far as you're concerned, Cressy, yes, separation will be challenging, but what you won't have to worry about is Tolly falling for someone else. Like his poor dad, he's a one-woman-man – and you're that woman!"

Cressida was cheered by this vigorous and sensible rejoinder. Of course Lou was right. If she and Tolly remained true to one another, kept in touch and carried on working towards their ideals, one day they would be free to face the future together. She gave her friend a grateful hug.

"Oh, thanks so much Lou, no-one could have a better or a wiser friend than you. I'll try to be as wise and useful to you if you need it, once you fall in love!" As they walked back, Louise couldn't help feeling amazed at the transformation of her hitherto quiet and retiring friend. Until a couple of months ago, as Lou knew, Cressy had never had a boyfriend and had certainly never been kissed by a boy, other than friendly platonic greetings from Duncan and Charlie.

Now, however, Cressida was deep into a romantic partnership, sincere and wholehearted, loving and being loved, sharing intimate confidences and contact with someone she had only known for a few weeks, but managing it with an assurance and poise which seemed to have become a natural part of her. Louise was impressed and happy for her much-loved friend.

The two of them returned to the camp, where tents were being taken down as people packed up, ready to return to their normal lives. Most of the boys had gone uphill to help with dismantling the marquee and tarpaulin shelters, as well as finishing filling up the remaining trenches. The castle, scene of so many emotional encounters, both in the past and in the present, was locked up again and the water supply disconnected. Engineers were due to arrive later to dismantle the two toilet blocks.

Cressida was not alone in feeling a general nostalgic melancholy as all this activity was completed. For her, the castle on its hill above the village would now always hold a special sort of magic. It was where, over the ages, much suffering and injustice had taken place, but it had been, for her, the setting for the awakening of the miraculous love affair which had changed her life.

It felt strange and sad later to be going down the hill for the last time. Louise, Duncan, Charlie, Tolly and Cressida, together with several others who weren't being picked up by car, all trudged down the steep hill into Troycombe village. Most of them were laden with heavy backpacks crammed full of stuff; also with boots, rolled up tents and other gear suspended from the backs of their rucksacks.

They all paused at the bus stop. Everyone but Cressida was getting the bus to Chilminster, where most of them would head for the station to get trains home. The others - Duncan, Charlie, Louise and Tolly - would walk together back to the Jacobs's house on the edge of town.

Cressida had the least baggage, having spent most of the dig commuting from home, but she did have a sizeable haul of birthday presents and cards, plus the tin containing the rest of her birthday cake. She would have given anything to be going back with her friends, but she knew how eagerly her little brothers were anticipating her arrival, and how pleased her parents would be to see her and to hear all about everything. And Tolly would be coming for tea and cake tomorrow as he'd promised.

Trying to stay cheerful, she hugged them all, then reached up, stroking Tolly's hair as they kissed. Then without a backward glance she picked up her stuff again and headed down the street towards her own home.

And it was a delighted and welcoming family which was awaiting her there! The twins, collaborating again in artistic creativity, had made a big banner to go over the front door - with 'WELCOME HOME CRESSY' on it, and a lopsided but recognisable painting of the castle below. Tolly was gone, but there was plenty of love here. She felt like a returning hero!

For Tolly, being able to go back with Duncan, Charlie and Louise - in effect to his second home - offered him a sort of lifeline. He knew that in a couple of days' time, after the tea party with Cressida and the twins, he would be returning to his own real home in Salisbury. He'd rung his father earlier saying he would be back by Sunday, and had been relieved to hear that Pa was not working that day. Perhaps, Tolly thought, they might be able to spend some father/son time together, when he would be able to tell his father not only all about the dig, but, more importantly, about Cressida.

One of the things he was hoping to do before going back to Salisbury was to have a private talk with Mrs Jacobs - Stella. She had been a kind confidante since before his mother's death, and her wise counsel even now often helped him when facing difficulties. He would welcome her views on his relationship with Cressida, and any suggestions she might have about how to face the future. He knew she would be frank, and that perhaps her advice mightn't be what he wanted to hear, but he felt he really needed some wise guidance.

The next morning, having as usual awoken early, he got dressed and went quietly downstairs to make a cup of tea, when he noticed that Stella was out in the garden. Seizing his chance, he abandoned the idea of tea and went outside to join her.

" 'Morning Tolly - isn't it a lovely one - I often feel that the early morning is the best of the day!"

"Yes I agree - I quite often go for walks about this time. And actually, Stella, if you've got time I wondered if we could have a bit of a chat - just a few things I need to get my head round. Would that be OK?"

"Of course, Tolly. Let's have a wander around the field at the bottom of the garden and you can tell me what's on your mind."

So the two of them headed down the garden to the rickety old gate which led into the field beyond - that same field to where, unknown to them both, several weeks ago Cressida had fled in terror.

"It's about Cressida," he said, and told Stella how sincerely and overwhelmingly he and she had fallen in love. As soon as he met her, at Louise's birthday party, he said, he had known that she was the girl for him. The amazing and miraculous thing was that she felt the same about him.

But how on earth were they going to be able to manage, given their very different stages of life, the hundreds of miles which would shortly be between them, and, most seriously, her youth? Was it fair to expect her to wait for him for several years, until they were both old enough to make their own life choices? Should a sixteen year old girl be asked to commit to such a serious relationship? Tolly could feel himself becoming emotional as he said all this and his voice ground to a halt.

Stella tried to comment as reasonably and honestly as she could.

"Yes, Tolly - of course you're right to be concerned. As you say, Cressida is only just sixteen, and although it's now legal at that age, I think that it's really far too young for any sort of meaningful intimate physical relationship. And as I'm sure you're aware, the last thing you both need is worries about contraception and pregnancy."

Tolly nodded, "Oh, I know, I know, Stella - and we haven't - we won't.."

"That's good, because you should try and hold yourselves to that for the time being, however hard it is. However, on the plus side, I do think that both you and Cressida, in your different situations, are in many ways mature beyond your years. I know, of course, you poor boy, all about how you had to grow up quickly, as it were,"

She paused for a moment, putting an arm round him as she recollected that awful time, and the intense misery and distress Tolly had suffered, then went on,

"But Cressida, in a very different way, has also had to take on responsibilities at an early age. She's been involved in helping to care for and look after her little brothers since she was eight years old. No criticism of her parents implied, but for years she has played a very active role in those boys' nurture and upbringing."

"She does adore the twins, she wouldn't want to be without them."

"Of course she does, Tolly, because she's a good, kind, loving and conscientious person, and obviously the twins have brought great joy to the whole family. But I remember her as a very anxious little girl when her parents were going through IVF, she didn't really understand what was going on but she was aware of some sort of emotional roller-coaster happening. No child can cope rationally with his or her parents crying intermittently and repeatedly about strange and perplexing things. Understandably, little Cressida might have wondered whether it was some inadequacy or flaw in herself, although again I would completely absolve Graham and Helen from knowingly making her think that was the case. They were always caring and kind."

"She did tell me a bit about all that after I'd told her about Mum. We both agreed about how as a kid there's so much about adult behaviour and the things they say and do, which is incomprehensible and often pretty frightening."

"Quite so, Tolly. You've obviously both already had quite a few serious and important discussions together, and this, I think, augurs well for your future. The next few years will be a challenge for you both, but for anything that's really important, it's absolutely worth having to cope with such challenges. Just reflect on the positive side! You and this kind, clever and charming girl have fallen in love. Both of you have had to deal with adversity, but haven't been embittered or corrupted by your different experiences. In fact, I think we all learn much more from getting through the hard times than the easy ones. There is, of course, the possibility that the relationship might dwindle away, but somehow I doubt this. It seems to me that you may well have each found your soulmate, and with luck, in a few years' time you'll be able to live your lives together."

Tolly was immensely invigorated and heartened by this discussion.

"Thanks, thanks so much, Stella, you've been really helpful, and so kind. I feel miles better about it all!" He gave her a hug.

"Good. Keep at it, Tolly, don't lose hope, and the very, very best of luck to the pair of you! And now let's go and have some breakfast! I don't know about you, but I'm dying for a cup of tea!"

CHAPTER TWENTY-ONE

Intermezzo

By the time Tolly arrived at Cressida's house later they were each feeling calmer and more philosophical about what lay ahead. The conversations with Louise and Stella had proved helpful and had given both Cressida and Tolly a bit of a positive internal 'road map' to manage their love affair.

The tea party with the twins took place in the Curtis family garden. The cake was much enjoyed by the little boys, and before his departure that evening Tolly delighted them both with some football coaching. By the end of the session they'd mastered various techniques including the 'nutmeg', which made them immensely proud of themselves!

The other, very important thing that happened on that short visit, was that Tolly, extremely politely, had asked Graham and Helen Curtis if they would allow Cressida to come and stay with him and his father at their home in Salisbury for a few days. He explained that his father had lived alone since the death of his wife, and was a busy surgical consultant, but he was taking some time off while Tolly came home. It would be wonderful, Tolly said, if he and his father could show Cressida around Salisbury together. She would be well looked after, and Tolly would see her back onto the train to Chilminster when the visit was over.

They both avoided looking at one another but Cressida had her fingers crossed as Tolly was making this request. Her parents, exchanging glances, agreed to consider it. They couldn't really think of any reason to refuse, but felt they needed to talk it over first.

Cressida walked to the bus stop with Tolly when it was time for him to go. It wasn't a final farewell, they agreed. They were very much hoping she'd be able to come to Salisbury to meet his father, then not long after that Tolly would be in Chilminster again, when they would have some more time together before Cressida went back to school. That five day period in early September was when they were planning to continue with their research into the sad fate of Lady Marlington and the enigma of the bead necklace. Their hope was that they would manage to connect up the missing links in this historical mystery.

"Bye, darling Tolly," Cressida said as they exchanged a final embrace and last kisses before going their separate ways. "Goodbye, my love, see you - hopefully - very soon," replied Tolly, boarding the bus.

Then Cressida went home, fervently hoping that her parents would agree to the Salisbury visit. To her joy and excitement, they did! It was a very happy and excited Cressida who got onto the Salisbury train at Chilminster Station one morning about a week later.

Tolly had been quite anxious about his reunion with his father - and telling him about Cressida - but Dr Henderson had been understanding and kind. Remembering every day the joyful early years of his own courtship with, and marriage to Tolly's mother, he could only hope for his son's sake that the girl Tolly had met would be the right one for him. Tolly had never brought a girlfriend home before. It might, thought his father, possibly be the beginning of a more naturally carefree attitude of mind for his serious, studious son.

"Cressida, Cressida!"

Tolly came running up to her as she emerged onto the forecourt of Salisbury station. She was whirled into an excited embrace, then he grabbed her suitcase with one of his hands. and her hand with the other.

"Come on, come on - oh, it's so exciting that you're here. Thank goodness your parents were OK about it!" he said, his face all smiles.

It was a surprise for Cressida when Tolly led her to a dark blue car sitting in the station carpark. He opened the boot and put her suitcase inside.

"Oh, goodness, Tolly, do you have a car? I didn't even know you could drive."

"Well, I passed my driving test a year ago, but this car is my father's. He lets me use it when he doesn't need it, and he's promised me a car of my own for my twentieth birthday at the end of October. So after that I'll be able to drive up to Durham with all my stuff rather than taking the train. And while you're here, I can borrow Pa's car and take you to visit lots of interesting places around. What do you think of that! "

"That's brilliant! How exciting! I never imagined being taken sightseeing by car!"

Cressida was privately a little daunted by this revelation. She had been so used to walking everywhere with Tolly, or going on the bus with him; it had never crossed her mind that he might have taken his driving test. It made him seem much more grown-up. Also, his mention of his oncoming twentieth birthday was somehow slightly unnerving.

He glanced over at her as they got into the car, sensing an element of unease.

"Don't worry, I know what I'm doing! Later on we'll go for a walk round the town together, there's so much I want to show you. But now I need to get you home - my Pa is looking forward to meeting you."

"And is it OK with him - I mean, when you told me about him being wrapped up in his work and also still feeling really sad – won't he find me a bit of an encumbrance?"

Tolly, who had been about to start the car, stopped and turned to her.

"Oh Cressida, of course he won't. He's not an ogre - he's just still quite a lonely and unhappy man. But please don't be afraid of him; he's been sweet to me this last few days, and as I say, he's very much looking forward to getting to know you. He's so glad for me that I've found someone special at last."

Cressida found herself in tears, suddenly ashamed of her misgivings.

"I'm sorry, I'm so sorry, Tolly" she sobbed. "Of course I didn't mean to imply anything like that. I don't want to hurt your feelings, or to upset you - forgive me Tolly... " and she tried to pull herself together, scrubbing at her eyes with a handkerchief and trying to dash the tears away.

"Darling Cressida - please, please don't cry. I'm sorry too - I put it badly, my father's a good man and is really, really glad that I've met a girl who I care about enough to bring her home with me."

Tolly too was getting emotional now. They turned to one another in the cramped space of the car, and held each other as best they could. Cressida was the first to pull herself together.

"I can't wait to meet him, Tolly, honestly and truly. Anyone related to you has to be a good and kind person. I suppose I was suddenly overwhelmed by everything - the car, a new place - and feeling a bit shy too, about meeting your dad for the first time and hoping I make a good impression. Sorry again for being such a drip."

"Thank you. I'm also sorry - I didn't put it well. Let's go."

Tolly's home was a Victorian terraced house within walking distance of the town centre and the Cathedral Close, As Tolly carefully parked the car, the front door opened and a tall, grey-haired man emerged, coming towards them with a warm smile and his hands held out.

"So this is Cressida! Welcome to Salisbury, dear. I'm Bart Henderson and I'm delighted to see you."

Tolly, retrieving Cressida's suitcase from the boot of the car, felt a lift of the heart as she went straight up to his father and put her hands in his.

"It's lovely to meet you too, Dr Henderson, and thank you so much for having me to stay."

Following them in, Tolly heaved a sigh of relief. It was going to be alright!

In fact, it turned out to be more than alright. The three of them sat round the kitchen table with coffee and biscuits, and Cressida was soon chatting away with ease. Tolly's father was interested in everything she had to say, asking her about her family, how she and his son had met, what subjects she liked best at school, and how had she enjoyed the dig.

She told him about some of the more exciting finds they had dug up. including the seventeenth century fork, Tolly's cache of jewellery, and of course the remains of the medieval chapel they had uncovered.

"Truly, Dr Henderson, it's like finding buried treasure. I love how, by finding things and learning about them - how ancient they are, what they were used for - and so on - well, it somehow brings the lives of those people in past ages vividly to life, doesn't it, Tolly,"

Tolly nodded, saying, "Cressida's as keen on history as I am, Pa. We've both got hooked on researching aspects of the past experiences of some of the people we've been finding out about - most particularly the inhabitants of Troycombe Castle during the eighteenth century. But Cressida's also drawn me into another of her areas of interest - going back over three millennia, to the Greek Bronze Age."

"Oh, yes, Dr Henderson - Tolly and I have got involved with the local museum in Chilminster and are hoping to collaborate on a display there about stuff from that period." Cressida then enlarged on their plans.

"It all sounds fascinating! I'd love to hear how you get on; what you're both trying to achieve seems pretty impressive. Oh, and by the way, Cressida, 'Doctor Henderson' is a bit of a mouthful isn't it - do you think you could call me Bart?"

Cressida felt the same slightly confused gratitude she had experienced when Penny and Matthew urged her to use their first names. She also remembered the mortification she had felt when she realised they both had academic titles.

" Oh, oh - thank you - yes, yes, I will. Actually someone once told me that high-up doctors like consultants should be called Mr, not Doctor, so I expect I was getting it wrong anyway. Bart will be much easier!"

When she and Tolly left to visit the cathedral and the city centre, Bart returned to his paperwork, writing patient assessments and checking case histories, but also thinking about the girl Tolly had brought home. It seemed to be a very harmonious partnership, and Cressida a charming, interesting and attractive girl, but anything might happen, going forward. Tolly had been through enough suffering in his life so far; his father hoped fervently that as time passed this wouldn't all end for him with a broken heart.

Tolly and Cressida walked towards the city centre. "Your dad is lovely," Cressida said, feeling rather ashamed of her anxious tears earlier.

"Yes, he was on good form. I'm so glad you both got on well, you were great with him, I think he really likes you. And he also seemed to be interested in our research plans, didn't he? I should make sure I talk to him more about the things we find out about. I must confess I hadn't realised that he would be as interested as he seemed to be."

"Well, I really like him too, and there was no need for me to get so worked up earlier." She paused for a few seconds, then continued, "And where are we going now, Tolly? The sign says 'City Centre' over there."

"Yes, but first I'm taking you on a little detour. I hope you don't mind."

"Not at all, I never mind little detours with you by my side, Tolly."

He kissed her for that, happy that the shadow of their earlier emotional exchange had gone away. They came to a track leading away from the pavement they had been walking along.

"We just go down here for a bit," Tolly said, leading the way down the narrow gravelled path. At the end was a small, ancient church, with a grassy lawn in front, at either end of which stood a grey wooden bench.

"Here we are." Tolly took her round the back of the church, to the graveyard. He went on, "I hope you don't mind me bringing you here, Cressida. You see, it's where my mother is buried."

Cressida had wondered, when she saw the church at the end of the path, whether this would be so. She realised that this was a significant pilgrimage for Tolly, and sharing it with her was important. She took his hand and went with him to the grave. The headstone read:

Eleanor Madeleine Henderson, née Parry 1951-1991
Beloved wife of Bartholomew Henderson
and loving mother of Tolly
Warm summer sun shine kindly here
Warm southern wind blow softly here
Green sod above lie light, lie light
Good night, dear heart, good night, good night

"Oh Tolly, it's heartbreaking," Cressida said softly, her voice full of pity. "So heartbreaking, but so beautiful. Where did the poem come from?"

"Well, actually I found it," Tolly said. "I'd seen it in a Mark Twain novel that I'd read a year or two earlier - I was keen on his stuff when I was about twelve or thirteen. That short poem was in the introduction - his little son had died as a baby. After Mum died I remembered it - and my Pa and I both agreed that it was both gentle and loving - like Mum."

At this point Tolly broke down. Cressida put her arms around him and waited silently until he raised his head again. " Sorry - sorry . Every time I come here it overcomes me. But somehow I have to keep on coming, so does Pa. And then we usually sit quietly and talk and think about her."

Cressida said gently, "You can do that. I don't want to intrude - would you like me to go back and sit on one of the benches at the front so you can have some private time, just you and your Mum?"

"No, no, Cressida, don't go, stay with me. I wish, oh I wish so much, that you could have known her. She would have loved you, I'm sure. And she would have been so glad to know how happy you've made me."

"Perhaps she does. As Shakespeare says, "There are more things in heaven and earth...than are dreamed of in your philosophy"..

"Who knows? But thanks, Cressida, I'm so glad I brought you here. Let's just hang on for a little longer while I sort out my emotions - then we'll go back to the original plan and head for the city centre and the cathedral."

So, after sitting peacefully for a while, the two of them moved on, stopping for a sandwich and a drink before reaching the cathedral. After that emotive visit to Tolly's mother's grave, Cressida was particularly touched by the bronze Walking Madonna statue on the lawn in front of the cathedral. It was a modern sculpture, by Elisabeth Frink, poignant in its austere solitude, and for some reason it brought tears to her eyes.

Next they entered the cathedral itself, where they spent a long time looking round. Tolly, used to the massive magnificence of Durham Cathedral, nevertheless admitted that he now found Salisbury just as impressive. He gave Cressida a guided tour, first telling her about the spire - the tallest in England - and pointed out how it was slightly leaning, due to having been built on marshland.

"It's not quite as skew-whiff as the Leaning Tower of Pisa," he said with a grin, "but it's still pretty amazing, isn't it?" - and then he explained how it had been reinforced by columns to stabilise it and prevent any further tilting.

Next they climbed up the stone staircase to the base of the tower. There Cressida was fascinated by the inner view far below, down into the long nave of the cathedral, then equally entranced as she looked out over the wide panorama of the surrounding Wiltshire countryside.

Back down in the nave, Tolly next took her to the Chapter House so she could see the cathedral's copy of Magna Carta, one of only a few originals. This was a great wonder to Cressida, who was amazed that something so fragile could still be complete and legible after hundreds of years.

"I know my Greek beads are much, much older," she said, "But they are of hard faience - presumably this is just parchment? "

"Yes, vellum parchment - calfskin I think," Tolly confirmed, and he tried to translate some of the Latin script, but the text was so close and the lettering so archaic he had to give up.

The last thing he showed her was the cathedral's extraordinary clock. What looked like a tangle of ironwork was, Tolly explained, was actually one of the oldest medieval working clocks in the world.

"I'm really glad you've found everything so fascinating, Cressida," he said as at last they emerged into the sunshine again. He continued,

"When we moved to Salisbury after Mum's death, one of the things which helped me cope was exploring the history of everything here. Mum had in been born and brought up here, she went to the famous girls' school in the city, and when she knew she was dying, she said she wanted to be buried in Salisbury. Pa and I moved back here quite soon afterwards, to be near her."

Cressida knew that this hadn't been a happy move for Tolly, and she felt that being sent away to boarding school for his A levels must also have been very emotionally harrowing. She could hardly bear to imagine him, aged only about sixteen, lonely and miserable. Now that she had met his father, and found him so kind and welcoming despite the tragedy of the last few years, she felt sad and sorry for them both.

There would perhaps come a time when she might be able to understand why Dr Henderson had sent his son away, but she wasn't going to ask. She'd had an inkling earlier of delicate ground regarding Tolly and his father, and didn't want to put her foot in it again. One day, one day, she told herself, it might all become clear.

She linked arms with Tolly as the two of them then wandered around the beautiful Cathedral Close, looking at the elegant Georgian houses there. Tolly pointed one of them out to her.

"Not long before I was born, and a bit longer before you were, the Prime Minister was a bloke called Edward Heath. When he retired he moved into this house, where he still lives. I remember what both Mum and Pa liked about him wasn't his politics - which they didn't agree with - but the fact that he was very musical. He has a huge concert grand piano there, and is very involved with music. Rather illogically, I always feel that someone who loves music must be basically an OK person."

Everything was fascinating and enlightening, but Cressida was by now beginning to feel rather footsore, and they were both in need of food. They'd left Tolly's home just before midday, it was now nearly six o'clock and they realised suddenly that they were both very hungry. Tolly rang his father from a phone box to tell him they were on the way home, and came back looking pleased.

"Pa's going to take us out to dinner tonight. There's a nice restaurant not far away, and he's booked a table for seven-thirty. That'll give us time to unwind a bit and get changed. Is that OK with you?"

" How lovely - that's so kind of your father! You're both making such an effort for me - what an exciting time I'm having! Thanks again, Tolly!"

CHAPTER TWENTY-TWO

Prehistory

C ressida awoke the next morning wondering where she was. She had slept so deeply that it took a few seconds to re-orientate herself. She lay in an unfamiliar but comfortable bed, in a simply furnished room with large sash windows. Of course - she was in Salisbury, in the spare bedroom at the Hendersons' house.

She sat up, happily remembering yesterday evening. Dr Henderson (Bart) had taken herself and Tolly to an Italian restaurant, where they had all enjoyed prawn and mushroom risotto, salad and a bottle of red wine, followed by delicious Italian ice cream. It had been a carefree and relaxed couple of hours. So far, she thought, everything was going well.

But she still felt a bit shy, and was slightly self-conscious about going to the bathroom in nothing but her thin nightie. She slipped a cardigan on and crept out. Both men were up, she could hear them talking downstairs. Then, not long after she'd returned to her room and got back into bed, she heard the clink of crockery and a knock on the door as Tolly arrived. He had a tray of tea and was smiling.

"Good morning my love, I've bought you some tea. How did you sleep?"

"Like a log, thanks, Tolly - I didn't realise how tired I was, and it's such a comfy bed. I feel a bit lazy lying here when you're already up and dressed - but what a treat to have morning tea brought up to me."

"What a treat to have you here! When I woke up this morning, just for a second I didn't know why I felt so happy. Then I remembered! Anyway, there's no hurry - enjoy your tea, and just come down when you're ready."

When he had gone Cressida propped up her pillows and looked around the room as she sipped her tea. She'd been so tired last night that she hadn't really noticed much about her surroundings. Now, she could see that there was a bookcase full of books, some pictures hanging on the wall, and through the windows a view of a slightly overgrown garden.

Suddenly she wanted to be up and about. She only had today and tomorrow here - she had to make the most of it! Finishing her tea she grabbed a towel, had a quick shower, got dressed and ran downstairs.

Bart was alone in the kitchen.

"'Morning, Cressida my dear, I hope you slept well. Tolly's just gone out to pick up the paper, so he's delegated me to get you your breakfast. Would you like more tea, or coffee; muesli, toast or a full English - eggs and bacon ? The choice is yours!"

"Oh, thank you so much. I slept wonderfully! And coffee and toast would be great. After that delicious supper last night I don't think I could manage a full English!"

When Tolly returned he found Cressida and his father chatting companionably around the kitchen table. It did indeed seem that any secret concerns he'd had about Cressida and Pa were unfounded.

"Ah, here he is! More coffee for you, Tolly? Cressida's just been telling me about her interest in the archaeology of prehistoric Wessex. I think we should take her to Avebury, don't you? It's somewhere I've often thought of visiting but somehow never got round to it."

Tolly had envisaged himself and Cressida spending a romantic day alone together, visiting a country mansion like Wilton or Bowood House, wandering hand in hand around the gardens, from time to time sharing kisses, and enjoying the magnificence of the estate. He hadn't imagined his father coming too, but suddenly he felt rather ashamed of himself. The plan seemed rather a self-indulgent one.

It was wonderful that Pa wanted to be with them both, rather than staying at home on his own. It was also right; Pa was making such an effort to be hospitable and welcoming - of course he should be included in whatever plans they made. The very fact that his father actually wanted to be part of these plans might be the first step to a happier state of mind, Tolly realised. After all, for himself, meeting and falling in love with Cressida, and everything that had happened since, had led him into a much more hopeful and optimistic emotional landscape.

All these thoughts rushed through Tolly's mind in a torrent of revelation. He kissed Cressida on the cheek, put an arm round his father and said,

"Great idea, Pa. Let's do that. Have you ever been there, Cressida?"

"No, Tolly, never. Of course I've been to Stonehenge - but there are so many places further north which I would love to explore. Avebury, Silbury Hill, the West Kennet Long Barrow - oh, the whole area is steeped in prehistory! I'm thrilled just to think of them all!"

That was the day planned. Cressida and Tolly put together a substantial picnic lunch while Bart examined the route. It turned out to be quite straightforward - about three-quarters of an hour's drive almost due north from Salisbury, and all the places Cressida had mentioned were in the same area. She was very excited about it all; from childhood she had been fascinated by these remnants of the long distant past, and had read all she could about the standing stones, henges and chamber tombs left by the prehistoric inhabitants of the region.

Tolly, who had so far focused his studies on the more recent past - from the medieval period onward - now also found himself infected by Cressida's enthusiasm. He had already been fired up by her explorations into very ancient history due to her discovery of the faience necklace. This even more ancient world was pretty well on his own doorstep. How come he'd never considered it before?

The drive to Avebury through Salisbury Plain was both picturesque and interesting, roughly following the course of the nearby river Avon and passing through several pretty Wiltshire villages. Cressida was thrilled anew each time she noticed a prehistoric burial mound en route.

Avebury was a revelation! It was an enormous stone circle, so huge that it enclosed two smaller circles as well as the major part of the village which had developed there in the Middle Ages. The massive sarsen stones were spectacular - towering far above Tolly and his father, who were both over six feet tall. Some were missing or had been broken, but the effect was still magnificent. As they all wandered round the site it was intriguing to find stones from the two inner circles popping up in people's gardens. There were, they learnt, one or two houses which had actually been built around individual stones - enormous ancient relics of a long gone era - now standing, immovable, in someone's parlour. When Cressida had visited Stonehenge with her family a few years ago, they hadn't been allowed to get anywhere near the stones; here at Avebury they were free to roam wherever they liked all over the monument. They all three dispersed to explore in different directions.

Like many of the other stone circles and henges in the British Isles and further afield, it seemed that there had been some sort of religious significance about the whole area. As with Stonehenge, the Avebury complex could have been associated with the themes of fertility, death and rebirth, the rising of the sun and the phases of the moon, the turning of the seasons and the significance of midwinter and midsummer.

Cressida remembered her imaginative musings over the powers hidden in those grey spacer beads from her faience necklace. She couldn't help wondering if this ancient community, some millennia earlier than the Greeks of the Mycenaean late Bronze Age, had also found some secret wisdom from plants; perhaps how to create mind-altering drugs. What sort of ancient mysteries lay behind their rituals?

She was so wrapped up in the atmosphere of the place and her own thoughts that at first she didn't notice Tolly looking upwards, equally absorbed, just a few paces away from her. She went over to him and took his hand.

"Isn't it extraordinary, Tolly. I've never been anywhere quite like it. What did they do here – what does it all mean?"

His hand tightened round hers as he looked down at her.

"I was thinking of the significance of the sun and moon, and how terrifying an eclipse must have been. Oh, Cressida, it's so mysterious, so strange - so 'other'. And, thousands of years on - think of it - we are both Wessex born - we could be their descendants, generations upon generations later."

They stood in silence together for a moment, considering this possibility. Then reality took over again, so off they went to find Bart, who'd said he would be waiting for them in the museum.

Somehow, that museum felt almost familiar, due to the displays of finds there - many of which reminded them of things that had been unearthed in their own dig at Troycombe. There were also lots of animal bones, as well as flints and antlers, which had been used as tools. And in one showcase, forlorn in its stark simplicity, they saw the complete skeleton of a small child, thousands of years old.

"Hello, you two!" Bart appeared from the other gallery. "What a fascinating place," he went on, "Thanks so much, Cressida, for suggesting we come here. To think I've lived in this part of the country for years and never got round to visiting! Now, how about some lunch?"

After their picnic they headed back to the car for the short drive to the other sites, and parked near Silbury Hill. There it was, a perfect conical mound with a flat top, rising up in the downland countryside. Cressida said that it was the oldest man-made prehistoric mound in Europe, but no-one knew what its purpose had been. It wasn't a natural hill or a burial mound, she explained, it was a structure completed by human labour over a period of several hundred years, starting in the third millennium BC. She told them about the legend of the mythical King Sil, who was believed to have been buried there on his fabled golden horse. But, she added, when soundings were taken of the hill, and probes made into its interior, nothing had been revealed except the complex Neolithic building techniques.

Cressida found she was much enjoying the role of guide and mentor! It was wonderful to be visiting these ancient places from an era which had fascinated her since childhood, and to be able to share the experience with these two appreciative followers was a joy. She was equally knowledgeable about the nearby West Kennet Long Barrow. Even the first sight of it was astonishing - a long, long raised mound stretching away across the landscape.

There were avenues, she said, leading from Avebury to significant sites in the surrounding areas - one of which came up to where they were all standing now. Chamber tombs like West Kennet were obviously of huge importance - dating from the fourth millennium BC – again much more ancient than many of the chamber tombs of the ancient Greeks! Like the Greek tombs, these were family mausoleums and would have been used to house generations of deceased clan members. The bodies of people of all ages, from infancy to old age, would have been interred there.

Tolly knew about Cressida's interest in ancient history, and was much impressed by her knowledge of the prehistory of the area. He was eager to know more.

"Shall we - can we go in?" he asked, thankful that he had his small torch with him. It lived in his pocket, to be always readily available for his early morning walks.

"Yes, let's. I think the first part of it is accessible. Shall I go first, then Bart, and you last, Tolly, so you can illuminate the passage for us all."

Bart also had a pocket torch, but he wasn't all that keen on going in. He handed it over to Cressida.

"I'm not sure my back is up to all that bending," he said, laughing slightly. "But off you go, you youngsters. Leave anything you like behind with me - tell me what you find - and don't get lost!"

So in they went. To their surprise, after stooping to get through the entrance, the interior was a wide, high passage, so even tall Tolly could stand upright comfortably. The massive stones - sarsens, like those silently standing in the Avebury circles - made up the walls of the passage and were bridged overhead with equally massive stones piled on one another to make a corbelled roof. On either side were chambers which would have housed the interred remains of family members of the ancient clan. Modern visitors to the barrow had sometimes left offerings of their own - including shells, unusually shaped stones, and even sprigs of rosemary.

Cressida turned to Tolly, her eyes gleaming in the light from his torch.

"There's rosemary, that's for remembrance," she quoted, continuing, "remembering all those people, so long ago - those different families -parents, children, babies - who lived their lives and are buried here. And now, how weird is this, Tolly - you and me in a prehistoric burial chamber, surrounded by the ancient dead!"

"So weird, but somehow not scary at all. I suppose most of the bones and stuff have been removed from this part, but I wonder if the more inaccessible end is housing more of the sleeping remains of the dead. I suppose too that there must have been grave goods in the chambers. How fascinating it all is - and how brilliant of you to have thought of coming here!"

They emerged, blinking, into the afternoon sun, feeling both moved and inspired by the experience. Waiting for them outside was Bart, who had walked all the way round the perimeter of the Long Barrow while they were inside. Then, once he heard that the ceiling was high enough for visitors to stand upright, he too disappeared into it. Cressida and Tolly sat down together on the grass, peacefully sharing impressions and enjoying the view.

They'd been lucky to have the place to themselves. Just as Bart came out again a large group of sightseers appeared, led by a guide.

"Looks like a coach party," Bart said. "Lucky for us that we didn't arrive at the same time. Shall we go?"

It had been a wonderful day.

CHAPTER TWENTY-THREE

The End of the Idyll

Two days later Cressida was on the train back to Chilminster. She and Tolly had arrived at the station early, so they could eke out the last half hour or so of her visit by having a coffee together at Salisbury Station.

It was going to be an emotional farewell. Although they knew that Tolly would be back in Dorset in a few days, they both also knew that their time together was nearly over.

The last day in Salisbury had been a pleasant one. Tolly had taken Cressida to Stourhead. It felt strange to be wandering round the planned perfection of the house and garden, enjoying its Palladian beauty, after the ancient mysteries of yesterday's experiences. This time they'd been alone together; Bart couldn't come with them as he was at a medical conference in town that day. Somehow his absence made them both feel a bit sad. He had been a delightful companion - cheerful and kind - treating Cressida not only as a welcome guest but also as someone rather special.

That evening Tolly and Cressida decided they would take charge of supper. They'd got back from Stourhead too late to make anything complicated, so Tolly suggested takeaway curry or pizza might fit the bill, but Cressida really wanted to make a bit more of an effort as a 'thank you' to Bart for his hospitality. They compromised; Tolly would pay for the takeaway as well as making a lavish fruit salad for pudding, and Cressida meanwhile set about creating a selection of little home-made canapés as starters. Tolly then went out to order the curry, and also to buy some beer and wine. He left his father and Cressida in the sitting room chatting companionably together.

It was an attractive room, with paintings on the walls, lots of books, a desk by the window, and a baby-grand piano. There were also several framed photographs on display. Cressida had immediately noticed the original of the photo Tolly kept in his wallet, the picture of his mother.

It was, however, another photograph which caught her attention, showing a solemn little boy with big brown eyes and a head of dark curls sitting on his mother's lap. His mother was smiling, her arms protectively around her small son. It was a beautiful portrait, and for some reason brought tears to Cressida's eyes.

"That's a lovely picture," she said to Bart, then, because she didn't want him to think she was trespassing uninvitedly on sensitive ground, she added, "Tolly's told me such a lot about his mother, and he took me to see her grave the other day. I found it - well - heartbreaking, but also beautiful."

"She was a beautiful person," Bart replied. Cressida didn't know whether it would be too upsetting for him if she said much more, but she couldn't help asking how old Tolly had been in the photograph.

"He was three. It was such a happy time for us. Of course we thought he was perfection in every way – we absolutely doted on him! And he was the most charming little boy, very sweet natured - and also very bright. We were so proud of him! Those years after his birth and before poor Ellie became ill were the happiest I've ever experienced."

Cressida responded gently, choosing her words carefully,

"I'm sure Tolly feels the same, he's often talked to me about his mother and how much he adored her. But he's still that same person - sweet natured, clever, charming and kind. I hope it's some comfort to you to see so much of her in him. Some people who'd been through as much tragedy as that might have completely gone off the rails. It seems to me that both you and he have managed somehow to deal with it without that happening. Sorry - I hope I'm not speaking out of turn. Really I just wanted to say how much I respect you both for coping with it all."

"Thank you for that, my dear. You seem to have quite a gift of empathy for someone so young; no wonder you mean so much to Tolly. I wasn't much older than he is when I first I met Ellie, so I understand how he feels. But I'm afraid in my case you are being much too kind. I became reclusive, obsessional and angry. I realise now that I was on the verge of a mental breakdown, and I made decisions which I now regret - sending Tolly to boarding school was one of them. I thought it would be better for him to be away from such an unhappy home, with a grieving father who couldn't cope. I was wrong, And I can never forgive myself for that."

Inside herself, Cressida was sure that Bart was right to have realised that this decision had been a mistake. But at the same time she could see why he'd thought then that he was doing the best thing for his son. She was beginning to feel slightly out of her depth as she continued to converse with this kind, complex man who she had come to like and respect, but who she had only known for a couple of days.

Because he was her beloved Tolly's father, she felt it was vital to find a way of expressing herself in a way that was both honest and sensitive. She listened intently as he went on talking about that unhappy time and how he felt his relationship with his son had been affected. It seemed to be important to him to say all these things - perhaps it was best for her to keep quiet for the time being and just carry on listening.

When he stopped and, with a slight smile, apologised for saying so much, she tried to come to some sort of ameliorative conclusion.

"I suppose," she began, "I suppose that what everyone has to come to terms with, in life, is that we can't change the past. So all we can do is try to get things right in the present and for the future. I've seen, while I've been here, what a relaxed and congenial relationship you and Tolly now have. And oh, goodness me, I think it's sometimes impossible at the time to get things completely right! I've often done and said stupid things which still embarrass or upset me when I look back on them, and which I totally regret. Well, I can't undo or unsay them, but I can make sure I don't make the same mistake again. That might sound a bit of a trivial example, but...."

"What kind of a trivial example? What have you two been nattering about?" Tolly was back. He had ordered the curry and it would be delivered when it was ready. He'd also bought beer and a bottle of nicely chilled Chablis.

The mood lightened as Cressida got up to fetch the tray of canapés she'd made earlier, while Tolly went in search of glasses. The remainder of the evening passed in cheerful accord as they ate, drank and chatted, ending up with some live music, with Bart on the piano and Tolly on the clarinet.

Cressida found herself wishing she hadn't stopped having piano lessons after Grade Five. Maybe, she thought, starting them up again might help with the challenging prospect of life without Tolly, when he was back in Durham. Music might offer another, subliminal way to link with him.

As she and Tolly left for the station the next day she felt quite sad to be saying goodbye to Bart, who had been so kind and hospitable. After yesterday's conversation she felt especially fond of him, and she hugged him as she would her own father. That reclusive, depressed, fanatical workaholic of her imagination had disappeared into thin air.

While she was on the train Cressida found herself revisiting her conversation with Bart, with some doubts creeping in. Had she overstepped the mark? What was she thinking of, at the age of sixteen, to be giving advice to a man who must be at least three times her age, and who she hardly knew? And how trite, in retrospect, her example about her own mistakes seemed. Thank goodness Tolly had come in when he did, and stopped her floundering around further.

She'd mentioned the gist of that conversation while having coffee with Tolly before getting the train. He had been reassuring, saying his father wouldn't have minded anything she said, and he would have probably been touched by her attempts to be helpful.

"He thinks you're great, he really likes you and thinks I'm lucky to have you. Which I am!"

Cressida had to accept that. She knew too, that she was lucky to have been welcomed with such warmth and love by both father and son. Hers and Tolly's all too brief tête-à-tête at the station ended with hugs and kisses and tears, then Cressida took her suitcase from him, boarded the train and waved to him, blowing more kisses as the train began to move and his figure on the platform receded, then disappeared.

It was a wonderful surprise, therefore, after all that soul-searching and intensity, to see the familiar figure of her own dear father waiting at the barrier for her, when the train arrived at Chilminster.

"Hi Dad, oh, how kind of you to come and meet me," she said joyfully as his welcoming arms went round her. She'd been prepared to get the bus.

"Of course I was going to collect you, darling. You look wonderful! We've enjoyed your phone calls, but it's lovely to have you back!"

And, despite the sadness of leaving Tolly, Cressida realised that it felt good to be home! She had a rapturous welcome from the twins, and a quieter but equally heartfelt one from her mother.

"We've all missed you, Cressy. The house isn't the same without you. But it sounds as if you've had a marvellous time."

After the entirely masculine company of the last few days, it was lovely to sit drinking tea with Mum and talking to her about all sorts of things, just as they had often done previously. To Helen it felt a bit as if that familiar, younger Cressida was back - albeit probably temporarily - but for the moment ready to share confidences again.

She knew that things had changed for her daughter, and that the relationship with Tolly would probably continue to intensify as time went on. However, both she and Graham liked and respected Tolly, and had realised that his love and care for their daughter was sincere and serious. They had discussed it together repeatedly while Cressida was away, and had concluded that there wasn't much to worry about at the moment.

After all, the reality was that Cressida belonged here at home with her family, and would do so for at least the next two years. Time would tell whether anything would eventually result from the Tolly situation; meanwhile they'd decided that he should be a welcome visitor in their home. It was providential, they agreed, that their daughter's first romantic relationship was with such a decent, personable and well-mannered young man.

So it was a happy and united family that came together over supper that evening - earlier than usual, so the twins could be included.

CHAPTER TWENTY-FOUR

Preparing for their Quest

Cressida had just received her GCSE results. She'd collected them from school that morning, meeting up with Louise and her other friends, all at first huddling together in a sort of collective semi-hysterical nervous fear. Then as the envelopes were distributed and opened, most of them reacted with relief. Hugs and shrieks followed, also a few tears. Both Lou and Cressida had done well, Lou had straight A's, and Cressida also had a string of A's, plus, to her astonishment, A-stars for English, History and French, but a B for maths.

"I didn't even expect a B so that's actually a relief!" she said. They were all effervescent with joy, parading through the High Street with linked arms, singing and giggling. They then went to a coffee bar for drinks and cakes, chat and laughter before gradually dispersing to go and celebrate with their families.

When Cressida got home everyone was waiting to hear her news. As soon as her mother saw her she realised all was well, giving Cressida a massive hug when she heard the glad tidings. The twins, catching the mood of excitement, pranced around gleefully, especially when they heard their mother saying that they would have a proper celebration tomorrow, Saturday, as today Dad was working late and wouldn't be back till after the twins' bed time.

"But do ring him, Cressy, and leave a message, he'll be so proud of you!"

Cressida was just about to do so when the phone rang, Her mother answered it, fully expecting it to be her husband - but it wasn't.

"Tolly on the phone for you, Cressy."

Helen was getting used to Tolly's deep voice on the other end of the line. He and Cressida had talked on the telephone almost every day since she'd been home after the end of the dig, apart from the three days of her Salisbury visit. Tolly had been working on a long essay as part of his history course, while his father was back at work at the hospital. When the essay was done, Tolly was hoping to come back to Chilminster for the last few days with Cressida before her return to school, to complete their planned shared project researching the fate of Lady Marlington.

"I've got my results, Tolly - all A's and A stars except a B for maths!" squealed Cressida in excitement.

Tolly was thrilled for her!

"Oh, fantastic! Well done - well done, you clever girl! What brilliant news! I'm *really* excited for you! Can't wait to see you and give you a big hug! And, with that in mind, I've got what I hope is more good news. I've nearly finished my assignment, and should be able to come back to Dorset on the fourth of September, just after the weekend, and for a few days after that. I'm dying to see you again!"

While at home Tolly had taken over some of the household chores like food shopping and cooking, so when Bart was also at home the two of them had more free time to spend together. Since Cressida's visit their relationship had become easier and much more companionable. Tolly had realised that reaching out to his father was helping both of them to deal with the sadness of the past and face the future with more optimism. Some evenings they would go to the cinema or to a concert together, or just to the pub for a companionable drink. Bart was also planning a short break in France as a surprise for Tolly. He would miss his son very much when Tolly returned to Durham next month.

Cressida and Tolly had been punctilious about taking turns to ring one another, so each household's phone bill would not be unfairly burdened, but when a call went on for more than forty-five minutes Cressida's parents tended to get a bit edgy. Surely, they thought, the pair must have exhausted all possible topics for conversation by now!

It seemed not; daily letters had also been flying to and fro between Salisbury and Troycombe. Tolly's were all carefully locked away by Cressida after she had read them. Sometimes they contained inserts, like press cuttings about things she and he were interested in, as well as photographs, sketches and love poems; hers to him might also include pieces of poetry and sprigs of lavender and rosemary, symbolising romance and remembrance.

Still on the phone, after the excitement of those GCSE results, they continued talking, blithely oblivious of the fact that Cressida's father was trying the phone repeatedly to find out how his daughter had done in her exams.

"Oh Tolly, that's brilliant! I'm dying to see you too - although it's not been long since I came back from Salisbury it's seemed ages! But thank goodness for the phone and the post! It's so much better than nothing, and I suppose it's also getting us into practice for when you go back to Durham."

"Absolutely, we've proved we can do it! Anyway, as I say, I'll be back on the fourth, all being well with the Jacobs's, so shall we meet in Chilminster?"

"Yes, yes of course - I'll be at the station waiting for you, Tolly. Let me know which train you'll be on." And at last the phone was free!

Everything seemed to be going according to plan, so it was horribly disappointing when Tolly phoned again the next morning with some depressing news.

"I don't know what to do, Cressida, because I can't stay with the Jacobs's in Chilminster after all. They're all going to be in London, helping Duncan sort out his lodgings before the RCM term starts. They'll be away for several days, they're also planning to go to some of the Proms, and to the theatre as well. And honestly, I can't begrudge them that - they absolutely deserve a bit of a break. Maybe I could camp somewhere...."

"Oh no, Tolly, I can't bear to think of you camping all alone - anyway the nearest camp site is right away over the north side of Chilminster so it would be a huge trek in and out of town each day. No, Tolly, you must stay here, with us. I'll talk to my parents and ring you back. We've got a little spare bedroom at the top of the house, with its own bathroom and loo, so it should be OK. Fingers crossed, I'll be back in touch very soon; don't despair. Leave it to me, I'm sure I can sort it out."

Cressida found her mother in the garden. It was Saturday, so Mum wasn't at work. Dad had taken the twins swimming, and afterwards they were all three going on to take part in a children's nature trail, making it an ideal time for Cressida to have a one-to-one chat with her mother.

"I'm just going to make some coffee, Mummy, would you like a cup? I'll bring it out, it's such a nice day. And I think there are still some of those little shortbreads left that I made the other day. I want to talk to you about a few things."

Helen was weeding the vegetable patch, but was quite happy to leave it for the time being to have a chat with her daughter. When Cressida called her 'Mummy' not 'Mum' she usually wanted help with something! It was obviously going to be about Tolly's latest phone call; however, Helen was happy that Cressida was again prepared to confide in her. Also, after those impressive exam results she felt relieved as well as proud of her daughter, so was quite willing to help with whatever Cressida wanted.

"Of course, Cressy, that would be lovely. I'll just go and wash my hands."

As they sat in the sun together Cressida started by telling her mother more about the research that she and Tolly had undertaken. She described how they had found the painting of Sir Anthony and Lady Marlington in the City Art Gallery, and how she had noticed that in the portrait Lady Marlington was wearing the faience bead necklace. Cressida was certain it was the same one, she said; she was so familiar with the necklace.

She went on, next describing their visit to the museum to talk to Penny Emerson about this discovery. This, she said, had led to Penny's mention of the death of the Marlington baby, and the subsequent mental illness which had resulted in Lady Marlington being sent by her husband as an inmate into the Chilminster Asylum for the Insane. What Cressida didn't mention was the hallucinogen in the spacers; that, she knew, had for the time being to be kept as a secret between herself, Tolly and Penny. She didn't want any awkward questions about drugs and 'tripping' to be gleaned from her reporting. She did, however, reveal how very upset Tolly had become after hearing about Lady Marlington's incarceration in the asylum. Cressida then explained that before they'd arrived at the museum that day he'd been telling her about the tragic early death from breast cancer of his own much loved mother a few years ago when he was only fifteen.

"Just about a year younger than I am now, Mummy - I can't begin to imagine how awful it must have been. Even thinking of it makes me feel really sad for him and his father - and oh, Mummy, what would I do if it happened to you?"

The thought was unbearable to them both, they suddenly hugged one another in a simultaneous emotional impulse. Then Cressida continued,

"Anyway, Tolly and I have decided that we need to find out what sort of a life poor Lady Marlington would have had in the Chilminster Asylum, and what happened to the necklace. If she took it with her, why wasn't it found after she died? We know she'd had it shortened, because on the dig Tolly found some of the beads from it, discarded in a cache of jewellery near the castle. Also, Penny said that when she was working on it she'd thought perhaps it had originally been longer.

"And, Mummy, this is where you come in, as you work in the Council archive department - because we think that maybe we can get some of the information we need by going through the City archives. Also, if we have time, we want to visit the site of the old asylum. Penny said it's on the outskirts of town, and it's now a care home. Is there any way you can help us with some of these things?"

Helen was much intrigued by all this, as well as being impressed by the serious and sincere motivation of both young people. She was touched by their concern for the fate of a long dead woman.

"Goodness, Cressy, what a very interesting but tragic story. Poor Tolly, no wonder he was so upset; I can see that thinking about the fate of that poor woman would bring back the all too recent and heartbreaking death of his own mother. Of course I'll do all I can to help you both. I'm at work on Monday, so I'll try and make time to trawl through the historical archives and see if I can find some relevant papers. There will almost certainly also be stuff about the old asylum. Have either of you any idea as to dates when all this took place?"

"Well, no exact dates, but Sir Anthony brought the necklace back in the early eighteenth century, I think. Tolly will be more accurate on that, as he's done a lot of research about Sir Anthony's Grand Tour; how he brought the necklace, together with lots of other treasures, back from Greece and Turkey. The portrait must have been done soon afterwards, when Sir Anthony was home again and had succeeded to the castle, presumably when they got married."

"Well, when Tolly's back in Chilminster I suggest you both come to County Hall and meet me at the archive department. Tuesday morning would be best, as I'll have sorted out relevant data by then. I can show you what there is, and you may both want to look through other stuff too – registers of births, marriages and deaths, for instance."

"Brilliant, Mummy - thanks so much! Oh yes, and there's one other thing. Poor Tolly can't stay with Lou's family in Chilminster this time as he usually does, because they're all going to be in London. Would it be possible for him to stay with us - in the little spare room in the attic? The only alternative would be camping, but the dig campsite has all been dismantled and the nearest proper campsite is miles away. He wouldn't be any trouble, I promise, and it would only be for a few days - Monday to Friday next week. So I'd still have plenty of time the following weekend to get sorted out for school."

Cressida felt a little nervous as she made this request. She was sure that Tolly would be a considerate and polite guest, but she knew how protective and principled her parents were. Would they think it was inappropriate to have her boyfriend staying in their home? As well, perhaps they would think it was too near the beginning of term .....

"After all you've been telling me about your investigations, and of course remembering how wonderful he was when he rescued the twins, I don't think I could possibly say no!" Helen said with a smile. "I think we can trust you both enough not to spend too much time hugging and kissing, especially when the twins are around. In fact, Tolly might end up wishing he was staying somewhere else, because the twins have such a crush on him they probably won't give him a moment's peace. So the answer is yes, Tolly can stay, so long as Dad agrees - and I'm sure he will; on the whole he tends to be much more easy-going than me!"

"Thanks, oh thanks, Mummy! And I promise we'll be on our best behaviour. Actually the main thing we do is hold hands, and I expect most of the time the twins'll each grab one of Tolly's hands and I won't get a look-in! Oh goodness, Mummy, you've been really helpful and so kind, thank you so, so much!"

Cressida gave her mother a hug then picked up the coffee tray and rushed into the house to phone Tolly with the good news.

"My mother was brilliant! I told her all about our plans, she was really interested in what we're doing - and she's fine about you staying, Tolly! As I said earlier, at the top of our house there's an attic bedroom with its own bathroom and loo, so you'll be able to escape up there whenever you want to be on your own. And you might need to sometimes, because, I warn you, you will be lionized by the twins - they're both mad about you!!! Well, I suppose including me that makes three of us!!!"

Tolly was overcome with gratitude; he sounded very relieved as he replied,

"Oh, thank goodness - That's absolutely wonderful! And as long as I'm back with you I can cope with anything - including the twins - anyway they're charming boys really! Thank you so much for fixing it, and give my thanks to your parents for letting me come. So, see you on Monday - I can't wait!"

CHAPTER TWENTY-FIVE

Planning

C ressida was at the station by mid-morning on Monday, in good time to meet Tolly. They had agreed that after he'd arrived they would go straight to the museum and update Penny on their plans, so it was frustrating when his train was delayed. In the interim Cressida rushed back to the museum to postpone their visit till later, and was back at the station to find Tolly patiently waiting for her, his rucksack at his feet.

"So sorry Tolly, I just had to dash to the museum to change our appointment - have you been waiting long?"

"Only a few minutes, all worth it to see you running up to me!" he said, as they hugged one another. It was wonderful to be together again.

He hoisted his heavy rucksack onto his back and they walked down into town, having decided to start with a coffee and a catch-up now that their appointment with Penny was delayed. She'd been very accommodating and had said that actually an afternoon meeting suited her better.

"Even though we've talked so much on the phone, to have you here again, in the flesh, real and lovely as ever, makes me utterly joyful!" Cressida said as they made their way along the street.

He bent down to give her a quick kiss for that, then they linked arms and headed to the café. For the moment, each of them felt full of perfect happiness. Facing one another across the coffee table suddenly reminded Tolly of their first real tête-à-tête in the pub at Troycombe.

"What a lot has happened since then", he said. "It was such early days for us - but I think we both somehow knew, even then, that we were meant for each other, didn't we?"

"Yes, I remember thinking as I walked back with Dad that I was at the start of something magical which could change my life. And it has!"

"Mine too, for then, for now, and hopefully for the future too."

Tolly paused, holding both her hands firmly in his across the table and smiling at her. Then their coffee arrived and practicality took over as they turned their attention to plans for the next few days.

Cressida updated him in with the gist of her conversation with her mother a few days ago.

"Idiot that I am, I'm so used to Mum going to work that I'd half-forgotten what she actually does. In fact she works at County Hall in the archive department! Just what we need! When I remembered that, I realised how much help she might be able to give us. She was really interested in our plans, by the way. Of course I didn't mention the hallucinogen because that would have freaked her out - but I told her all about the necklace and Lady Marlington, your research on Sir Anthony, and our discovery of that painting in the Art Gallery."

She paused to gulp down some coffee, then continued,

" Anyway, she's going to look out any relevant archive material in the historic records, and she also suggested we check out info on Births, Marriages and Deaths during the eighteenth century, as well as any data we can find about the Chilminster Asylum. I was thinking too that there might be some newspaper or broadsheet archives; also maybe census stuff. Did they have newspapers and censuses in the eighteenth century? In any case, as you see, we have plenty to get our teeth into!"

Tolly nodded, "You're telling me!" he said. "Let's hope between us that we can get hold of enough data to produce - well - a reasonably coherent narrative of how things happened. But, oh, Cressida, it's actually really exciting isn't it! You and I, working together to investigate, as far as we know, unanswered questions - and then to produce a completely new report about a series of events which no-one has yet explored!"

"SO exciting! I can't wait to get started! We must make notes about everything, rather like the field notes they produced on the dig. In fact, maybe we should both make a list now of everything we need to find out, as a sort of starting point. Perhaps we can run it past Penny this afternoon. Then tomorrow we can come back into town and spend the whole day researching. By then Mum should have sorted out some data for us. And later on in the week we can check out the asylum - the Minster Care Home. as it's now called. It's a bit of a way out of town, but there's probably a bus we can get; after all, the residents must sometimes have family and friends to visit."

They still had about an hour before they were due at the museum. Tolly ordered some sandwiches and a slice of cake for each of them, while Cressida popped across the road to the stationer's to buy a pad of paper, then they both set to work on their lists of tasks. By the time they left, they had pooled both lists into a comprehensive amalgamation, which they photocopied at the shop across the street.

"We'll give a copy to Penny too," Cressida said, "she might have some more ideas. She's very wise, Penny is, so she might be able to give us some advice on asking the right questions, and tell us who would be useful people to contact."

When they reached the museum they were pleasantly surprised to see Matthew. He was designing notices about the next exhibition he would be curating, focused on the findings from the Troycombe dig.

"It won't be officially open for quite a time, but do come and have a quick look round and see what we've done so far," he said.

They followed him into the Victorian Hall where exhibitions took place. It was intriguing to see much of what had been dug up now piled in shallow boxes on long tables, in preparation for display. There were also diagrams of models yet to be created - of the castle, the ruined chapel, the eighteenth century drainage system and other constructions, as well as plans for posters and information sheets.

"I'll ensure you both get an invitation to the opening ceremony, probably sometime in the spring," Matthew promised, as they left to go upstairs to Penny's office. School and University might mean neither could make the official opening, however they thanked him and promised to come anyway, when it was open to the public.

Up in her office Penny was waiting for them. At first, Tolly felt slightly awkward, remembering his angry outburst when they were last there, but Penny was, as usual, her hospitable and kindly welcoming self.

"Hello both - lovely to see you again. Tell me how you've been getting on with your researches. And how were your exam results, Cressida?"

Blushing slightly, but also feeling proud, Cressida told her, and received the appropriate congratulations. "Though I'm not surprised," Penny added, "I was sure you would do fine!"

The two of them then explained what they were proposing to do, giving Penny a copy of the list of tasks they had set themselves.

She added one or two suggestions but was clearly impressed by their planning so far.

She continued, "It would be really useful if each of you could write a paper about your investigations and findings. As you know, we're planning to mount an exhibition about the necklace, its antiquity and context, and the extraordinary, much more recent history, involving the Marlington connection and related aspects. Now, I know you are both busy, Tolly, you with your degree course and Cressida, now with A levels ahead. But we don't anticipate this exhibition to be ready at the earliest until the end of next year - December 1996, probably more likely to be later, sometime in mid-1997 - so there's plenty of time for you to produce your papers. And of course you'll both be important guests at the opening! What do you think?"

Tolly and Cressida exchanged delighted glances. This was absolutely in keeping with their plans and ambitions. They spoke simultaneously "Oh yes - that would be brilliant!" from Cressida, and "We'd love it! Of course we will - how exciting!" from Tolly.

Discussion followed about what they would cover, and also how to deal with the discovery of the hallucinogen without causing alarm. Before they left, Penny said she had something else to tell them regarding the hallucinogen. She was now able to give them the latest conclusions from the scientific examination of the drug in the little grey spacer beads.

"They've identified traces of something which is certainly related to features of some plants today, but the exact plant seems no longer to exist. So far, certainly in Greece and surrounding countries, they've found no trace of it. It's possible that it was used so much that it became extinct, or that it mutated or hybridised with other different but similar organisms. But botanists are always on the look-out for previously unknown plants, so it may well yet turn up in some remote corner of the world."

After all this, and a pleasant chat with Penny and Matthew over a cup of tea downstairs, the pair decided that it was time to go home. They would return tomorrow to carry on with their investigations, starting with a visit to County Hall and the archive department. Meanwhile, there was plenty to think about.

Together they made their way to the bus stop, pausing at a florist's shop for Tolly to buy an elegant bouquet of pretty flowers for Cressida's mother. He was feeling a bit nervous about the prospect of staying with Cressida's family; much as he liked them all he didn't really know them very well, and he was also secretly wondering how much time he would have to spend playing with the twins.

However, he told himself, it was extremely kind of the family to have offered to host him for a few days, and, weary of the weight of his heavy rucksack on his back and shoulders, he was looking forward to shedding it and unpacking his stuff.

CHAPTER TWENTY-SIX

Further Investigations

Tolly was rather taken with his little attic bedroom at the Curtis's house. It reminded him slightly of his study bedroom at Durham Castle. That room too was situated high up, and he remembered how excited he'd felt to be housed somewhere so ancient. Later, standing down by the river, he'd also been enchanted by the famous view of the 11th century castle and the Romanesque cathedral.

Now, here in Troycombe, he could look out through a little dormer window over green Dorset hills towards another castle - Troycombe Castle - the one he had got to know so well over the last few weeks. This coincidental symmetry pleased Tolly and made him feel quite at home.

He pointed it out to Cressida who had come up the attic stairs with towels and some necessary toiletries for the tiny bathroom. She'd assured her mother that she would prepare the room for Tolly and was now providing the finishing touches.

"Oh yes, it's a lovely view isn't it! And of course that castle's a really special place for you and me! Anyway, let me know if there's anything else you need. I must go down now and help Mum with the twins' tea, and our supper. See you downstairs when you're ready, Tolly! Oh, goodness - I can't believe how amazing it is to have you here!"

When Tolly came down, the flowers and a box of chocolates in one hand and a bottle of wine in the other as presents for the household, he realised fairly quickly that the domestic atmosphere here was very different from his quiet home life. Any hope he'd had of sitting down with Cressida and her mother later to talk about archives was probably way off the mark.

The twins, who were in the kitchen having their tea, greeted him with shrieks of joy and would have leapt up forthwith had they not been reprimanded by their big sister. The sight of Cressida, stern and firm and in strict control, threatening them with early bed and no time with Tolly unless they stayed put at the table and finished their meal, showed him an authoritative and assured young woman very different from the relaxed, joyous girl he now knew so well! Trying to keep a straight face he urged the little boys to do as they were told and promised to play with them once they had finished eating.

Cressida then suggested he go into the sitting room where there was a cupboard full of toys and games. If he was prepared to play with the twins there when they'd finished their tea, she could help her mother with supper. Soon afterwards it would be the boys' bed time - earlier than usual because they were going back to school tomorrow; the primary school term started nearly a week before hers.

A little apprehensive about what was in store for him, Tolly acquiesced and busied himself sorting out a selection of possible entertainments. He settled on an animal jigsaw, Dinosaur Snap, and one of his old favourites, Cluedo.

He was surprised to find, once he and the twins had got stuck in to doing the jigsaw, that he was really rather enjoying it! He'd suddenly been transported back to half-forgotten happy memories of game playing when he was their age. When Cressida arrived sometime later, to usher the boys up to bed, she was charmed to see her beloved sitting on the floor with her brothers, solemnly discussing what was fiercer, a Tyrannosaurus or a Pliosaur.

"Bath time now, boys, so say night-night to Tolly and thank him for playing with you."

To their delight, Tolly lifted each twin high in the air, holding first Jo-Jo, then Mikey right up above his head and 'flying' them around the room before giving both of them a hug and promising to play with them again after school tomorrow.

Cressida was now temporally off duty, as supper was in the oven and her mother was managing the boys' bed time routine. She and Tolly were alone, free to relax together on the sitting room sofa.

"You were wonderful with the twins, Tolly, you're so kind," Cressida said, looking at him lovingly.

"Well, nothing like as impressive as you, darling. I'm full of admiration at how firmly and competently you managed them at tea time!"

"Don't forget, Tolly, I've had years of practice. I was changing their nappies when I was eight, and have been entertaining them, telling them stories, and helping to look after them more or less ever since!"

It was all very different from what he'd been used to, but he thought her family life was probably a more normal one than his had been. Despite at first having been rather overwhelmed by such an atmosphere of busy domesticity, he now found himself beginning to enjoy it - while at the same time recognising that he was probably in for a few days of demanding hero-worship from the twins. But he also realised that he now felt rather fond of them, remembering how frightened they'd been when he found them trapped in the castle - and of course he couldn't help being both touched and flattered by their ongoing devotion!

Cressida's parents he knew less well, and he'd at first been slightly wary of them. He remembered Graham arriving suddenly at the pub, when he and Cressida were deep in conversation and were just beginning to realise that something wonderful and special was developing between them. Thank goodness that neither he nor she had even considered drinking anything alcoholic - if it had been otherwise, would he have been forbidden from seeing her again, destroying their love-affair before it had even really started?

Then there was Helen, Cressida's mother, so different from the gentle, ghostly memory of his own beloved mother, but someone who, he felt, was probably equally kind and caring. He had a picture in his mind of how she had looked when he first met her; her face agonised and fearful, her cheeks strewn with tears, as she opened the door to him on that memorable morning when he'd brought the lost twins back home.

Her welcome to him today, when he and Cressida had arrived home, had been warm and kindly. So far, thought Tolly, everything was going well. He suppressed a small pang of anxiety about his father, alone in Salisbury, and planned to phone him later. Meanwhile, here he was, in the Curtis family home, together with the girl he loved, invited into the very heart of her family. He settled himself more snugly into the sofa, moving closer to Cressida. Just now, at this moment, he felt entirely contented, with no sense of the lurking intermittent loneliness which he had kept hidden inside himself for so long.

The family was shortly to whirr into action again, when a few minutes later the two of them heard the click of the front door unlocking as Cressida's father arrived back home from work. Hastily disentangling themselves from one another they leapt up, shook and replaced the cushions, and went into the hall to greet him, Tolly hovering a little uncertainly behind Cressida.

"Hi Dad," she said, "You remember Tolly, don't you? Here he is. Oh, and Mum's upstairs with the twins - and I'd better just go and see to the supper in the oven."

Left to themselves, Graham took his coat off and shook Tolly's hand.

"Welcome, Tolly - I'm glad to say this household is in better shape than it was on your first visit to us! I still have a vivid memory of your arrival on the doorstep with our naughty twins!"

"Oh, yes - well, it was just lucky that I happened to be where I was when they got shut in. Anyway, since then they and I have become firm friends! I've just finished playing Dinosaur Snap with them! And I wouldn't be at all surprised if I get co-opted into the odd bedtime story!"

"Nor would I! However, I think you've done your bit for today. How about a drink before supper?"

When Helen came down all was order and tranquillity. Cressida, Tolly and Graham were in the sitting room with drinks and a tray of olives and nuts between them. In the dining room the table was laid and supper was keeping hot in the oven.

"What a peaceful picture," Helen said, with a smile and a kiss for her husband. "The twins have settled beautifully. If this is the effect you have on them, Tolly, you'll have to come and stay more often!"

That night Tolly slept well and awoke later than usual. When he got out of bed to go to the bathroom he could hear the noise and bustle of a busy family getting ready for the day ahead. He identified the shrill chatter of the twins as they were being hurried into their school clothes by their mother. He could also hear the deep voice of Graham and the softer one of Cressida downstairs as they sorted out breakfast, interspersed with instructions called down from Helen to them about school bags, shoes, pencils, exercise books and other such necessities.

Much as he would have liked to go down and offer to help, he realised that his presence would probably be an added complication at such a busy time, so he stayed put, lying in bed. Would that be considered lazy? All being well, he thought, there might be ways in which he could make himself useful to this hardworking household over the next few days.

Family life was hectic but strangely appealing, made all the more so for him by the presence of Cressida. She was a remarkable person, he realised anew, not just as his own beloved soulmate, but also as a kind, competent and obviously indispensable member of her loving family.

As if on cue there was a tap on the door and Cressida arrived with a mug of tea for him.

"My turn to bring you morning tea!" she said, putting the mug on his bedside table, and continuing,

"How did you sleep? Were you warm enough? I hope we didn't disturb you with the morning rush?"

"Not at all, actually I rather enjoyed hearing you all. What a nice family you are! It's all new to me - and much, much more appealing than the morning rush I used to endure at boarding school with queues for the bathroom, cold showers, and all the other dismal trappings of institutional life."

Cressida sat on the bed, slightly saddened by this unexpected glimpse into Tolly's past.

"Oh, Tolly, how horrid it all sounds. But it's over, thank goodness, and we love having you to stay here, darling Tolly."

Impulsively she leaned over and squeezed one of his hands, then stood up again, saying before she left,

"I just need to finish doing the twins' packed lunches, but then I'm free, so shall we have breakfast together in about half an hour? And then we can plan our day."

"Of course, and thanks."

She dashed away again and Tolly was left to drink his tea, to shower, to shave and to get dressed, feeling a pleasurable anticipation about the day ahead.

They were back in Chilminster by ten o'clock, and headed straight for County Hall, where Helen was awaiting them in the archive office. She had a sheaf of papers for them.

"!'ve been through the records and photocopied everything that might be relevant. No census details I'm afraid - the first national census wasn't until the beginning of the nineteenth century. But I've found some interesting information in one or two of the broadsheets and newspapers of the time - there's a fascinating article in the Wessex Courant dating from 1750."

"Oh wow! Thanks Mum!" "Great! Lots to get on with!" Cressida and Tolly responded simultaneously.

"Well, good luck to both of you. By the way, you'd be better off going to the cathedral for data about Births, Marriages and Deaths - Church records have been kept since the sixteenth century, but civil registers didn't get going till the eighteen thirties."

"What about the asylum?" Tolly asked. He had a particular interest in this, feeling a tender concern about the fate of Lady Marlington.

"Again, before the nineteenth century there was no national system for the treatment of the insane. The most destitute of them - 'pauper lunatics', as they were called - might end up as outcasts and vagrants, and were sometimes imprisoned or put in the workhouse. It's a painful fact that the mentally sick were considered dangerous, and it was thought that they should be kept away from normal society - basically isolated, in effect."

There was a short pause after this, as the two of them took in the bleak reality of what she was saying. They exchanged brief anxious glances, then turned back to listen to what else she had to tell them. She continued,

"For a person of status, like Lady Marlington, things would have been marginally better. Her husband would have financed her care, but incarceration in the Chilminster Asylum - or 'madhouse' - as it was known - came under the jurisdiction of the local JP - Justice of the Peace, rather than any national authority. Sometimes these were good people, but not always. I'm afraid that the treatment and conditions were often cruel and inhumane, with inmates sometimes put in chains or straitjackets, underfed and often beaten."

Helen paused again, glancing at the two young people standing facing her. They were holding hands and looking very solemn.

"It's a sorry chapter in our history - one of many, I'm afraid. You'll have to visit the Minster Care Home just outside town to find out more. Things are, of course, very different there now, but when you see it you get a ghostly inkling of its past because of the tiny barred windows. I know they've turned one of the outhouses there into a small museum about the history of the place."

Cressida was the first to speak,

"Mum, thanks so much for all this. We knew the asylum stuff would be harrowing, but we both feel it's important to find out all we can, don't we, Tolly?"

"Yes, absolutely," he said. "With any luck we'll be able to fill in a few gaps at the very least - and thank you very much indeed for all the data."

Helen, facing them both, stood up and briefly put a hand on each of their shoulders.

"Good luck, children, don't let it all make you too sad! Here are all the documents!"

She gave them the sheaf of photocopied papers and they left the office.

"Whew!" exclaimed Cressida, "Strong stuff! Are you OK, Tolly?"

"Yes, love, but thanks for asking, Your mother was great, wasn't she? We've certainly got plenty to go on, so shall we go and find somewhere to sit and work out how we're going to proceed - in what order we should tackle things?"

"Yes, and we've got our lists from yesterday to help. Let's find a bench so we can work out our next step."

After that they headed for the cathedral. They'd decided to leave the Care Home till tomorrow, but planned to phone there to make an appointment to visit. Later, when they got back home, they would scrutinise in detail the documents Helen had printed out for them, and make notes about any relevant information, but now, they agreed, they needed to see what they could find out from the cathedral.

After the unhappy glimpse they'd been given of past life in an asylum for the insane, things felt much more comforting and peaceful when they reached the Cathedral Green. Here stood this immense ancient building, calm and serene; assured and steadfast in its hundreds of years of ministry to the people of the city. Neither Tolly nor Cressida was particularly religious, but they both felt a sense of optimism and hope as they entered Chilminster Cathedral.

Inside, the building was almost empty of people, apart from an unseen musician high up in the organ loft practising Bach preludes, and a couple of women at the front of the nave where there was an information desk. Smiling, they both greeted Tolly and Cressida and welcomed them to the cathedral.

Were they visitors to the area, one woman enquired. The other asked if they'd like to buy a copy of the guide book, with details of the history of the cathedral as well as information about the stained glass, chapels, monuments and other notable aspects of the building.

"I think we would, wouldn't we, Cressida," said Tolly, thinking that there might be information there about a plaque, or even a small side chapel dedicated to the Marlington family.

"Oh yes, definitely," Cressida agreed, then added, "I live in Troycombe, not far away, and Tolly here comes from Salisbury, so we know the area well, and we're doing some research about the Marlington family of Troycombe. We wondered if there was a register of births, marriages and deaths for the eighteenth century that we could have a look at."

"That all sounds interesting," said the second woman, "The historic Register is kept in the Chapter House, which is locked at the moment. But we are expecting the verger a bit later so maybe he'll be able to help you. Meanwhile, why not take a look round the cathedral. You'll find much of interest here, both historical and spiritual!"

Tolly paid for the guide book, saying,

"Thank you, we'll do that. What a splendid building it is! And what wonderful stained glass! It's fascinating to compare it to Salisbury, where I live - but this cathedral is even more ancient, I think. And the organ sounds absolutely magnificent."

"Yes, we're very proud of our organ," the first woman said. "It's eighteenth century, made by a German craftsman and installed here a hundred and fifty years ago."

Cressida and Tolly sat down on one of the old oak pews in the nave and opened the booklet. Tolly, more familiar with church practice due to his knowledge of Salisbury Cathedral, as well as those daily chapel services at boarding school, was genuinely captivated by the peaceful beauty of the place. The rich sonorities and rippling cadences coming from the organ added to his feeling of uplift.

To Cressida, scrolling through the guide book, the cathedral seemed to be a great historical repository of past lives as much as a living place of worship. She stood up and began to walk round, first looking into side chapels, then casting her eyes upward to the medieval stained glass windows and the magnificent fan-vaulted roof.

Flags and pennants commemorating past and recent conflicts hung from the ceiling above the side aisles, and on the walls were memorial plaques. On either side of the nave were stone monuments - statues of long-ago knights and citizens lying on their tombs. One was particularly touching; a knight with his lady alongside him, serene in their timeless dignity, with their adjacent hands clasped together and small reliefs of three infants above.

As she stood looking at this, a warm and living hand enfolded hers as Tolly came to join her. She looked up at him, smiling.

"Isn't it amazing! I've only been here for concerts and carol services and never really looked around properly before."

"Yes, it's really stunning! No sign of Sir Anthony, though, so far. Shall we go and check the other side?"

In the end they did find what they were seeking - a memorial relief in one of the side chapels. The inscription read: *'Here lyeth the remains of Sir Anthony Marlington of Troycombe, Baronet of the Realm. He departed this mortal life the sixteenth of June, 1763, aged fifty nine years'.*

It was decorated with carved scrolls and curlicues, and the Marlington armorial bearings were displayed over the top of the monument.

"Not a mention of his poor wife," Tolly said. "Why am I not surprised?"

"I know, it's as if she never existed. But she did, and we are going to make sure she's not forgotten," Cressida said robustly. "It's probably unlikely, but she might even have outlived him. With any luck we'll be able to find out tomorrow when we go to the Care Home."

"You could be right; anyway well done for staying optimistic! I have to confess I'm not looking forward to the Care Home," Tolly admitted. He paused, then brightened up again, saying,

"Oh, look, I think that's the verger now, up at the front desk - maybe we can get a look at the Register of Births, Marriages and Deaths. Could she at least be listed there, I wonder?"

The verger was prepared to let them see the historic Register, under his supervision. He let them into the Chapter House and put on a pair of white cotton gloves. Fascinated, they waited while he lifted the huge volume from its wooden case and carefully opened it, searching for the page which would have registered the deaths in 1763. They found Sir Anthony quite easily, in the middle of a spidery black-inked list, but without a death date for her they couldn't check on his wife.

However, Tolly then remembered the poor little baby who had died in infancy, so he asked the verger if they could look at the births. Judging that Sir Anthony might have been in his mid-twenties to early thirties when he married, Tolly requested that they might be able to scrutinise the birth entries from 1729 till 1739. The obliging man agreed, but added that after this he really had to get on with his work getting the chancel ready for choir practice then Evensong later that afternoon.

In the end they had to give up. There didn't seem to be anything relevant, though there was a smudged patch around some very faded entries in early 1735. Among them was a baby '*E..... S....a*' who had been born to '*A...... a.d S....a Ma.lin....*'

"It *could* be Anthony and Sara Marlington," Tolly said hopefully. But the verger thought it unlikely.

They thanked him for his time and trouble and each put a donation into the offertory box. They then left the cathedral. Both were now hungry and thirsty so they decided to take a lunch break, and to have a quick look through the stuff that Cressida's mother had given them from the Archive Department. They also planned to ring the Care Home to make an appointment to visit the next day. Sitting on a bench on the Cathedral Green and eating the sandwiches Cressida had prepared earlier made for a peaceful interlude in the early autumn sunshine.

"It's a lovely cathedral, isn't it," Cressida said, "And they were all so friendly and helpful. And we are making some progress, Tolly."

"Yes, we really are, it's all so interesting, and such fun to be doing it together. Actually, I wouldn't mind going back there for Evensong this afternoon, I'd love to hear the choir and that gorgeous organ again."

CHAPTER TWENTY-SEVEN

The Care Home

The following day both Cressida and Tolly embarked on the next stage of their quest feeling rather less enthusiastic than they had done until now. Neither of them was really looking forward to what might be quite a distressing experience, as they contemplated the hours ahead. They were also both aware that already they were nearly half-way through the precious few days of Tolly's visit. This time next week, Cressida thought to herself, she would be back at school and Tolly would be gone.

Both were rather silent as they took the bus into Chilminster again, this time staying on all the way to the bus station, where they could pick up another bus to take them to the Minster Care Home.

"You OK, Tolly?" Cressida asked as they took their seats.

"As OK as you are, I think," he responded, with a slight smile, then squeezed her hand, saying, "We've got to do it, but we'll feel better when we have, and it mightn't be as depressing as we're expecting. And afterwards, let's go and reward ourselves with ice creams and relaxation in the Minster Gardens near the cathedral."

"Great idea, Tolly! It's always nice to have a little treat to look forward to! And I know that there's delicious Italian ice cream on sale nearby."

The setting of the Care Home was, after all, not too grim. There was a wide grassy lawn in the front where several elderly people were sitting out in the sun; some on benches and chairs and some in wheelchairs. They noticed those small barred windows that Cressida's mother had mentioned, but the building looked well kept, with fresh white walls and even some window boxes. Tolly and Cressida came round to the main entrance and walked in though a wide doorway into a reception area.

"Hello, how can I help you?"

A youngish, very pretty woman in a blue dress gave them a smile of welcome as they came up to the reception desk. An oblong badge was pinned to her dress headed "Reception', and below that was her name: 'Priya Chowdhury'.

"Oh, yes, thank you. We rang yesterday," said Cressida. Despite her misgivings, she was beginning to feel more encouraged as she looked round. There were pictures on the walls and vases of cut flowers set on tables and pedestals. The general impression was one of welcome and kindness. She went on,

"I'm Cressida Curtis and this is Tolly Henderson. We're doing some research into the history of what things were like here during the eighteenth century." Cressida paused, glancing at Tolly, who continued,

"We understand you have a small museum about the place's past, which we would love to visit, and we also wondered if there was someone here who could tell us a bit more about history and background."

"Yes indeed," said Priya, smiling again. "We're expecting you. We're going to be introducing you to Professor Jonathan Sheldon, who's one of our residents. He's a retired college lecturer and since he moved in here two years ago he's been working on a book about this building, its different functions over the years, and some of the people who were here during the three hundred years or so since it was built. Do take a seat while I call someone to take you to Jonathan. Can I order you a cup of tea or coffee while you're waiting?"

Tolly and Cressida exchanged a quick glance. They'd had coffee just before getting the bus. They both spoke at once,

"Thank you so much, but we've just had one." "It's very kind of you, we had some before we got the bus so we're fine, thanks."

While Priya was on the house-phone the two of them looked at one another and grinned. Quite suddenly, their forebodings had diminished, due to Priya's friendly welcome.

When a young man in a blue shirt arrived and came towards them they stood up. This was obviously the person who was going to take them to Professor Sheldon. He also wore a badge, Cressida noticed, which was headed "Care Worker," with his name below: 'Jake Binstead'.

"Hello, I'm Jake," he said with a smile.

"Hi Jake. We're Tolly and Cressida".

They all shook hands, then Jake led them out of the reception area, through a door, along a passage, though another door and into a spacious carpeted room with book-lined walls, a large television, several armchairs, and a cabinet covered with a selection of magazines and newspapers. There was a table and chairs at one end and a big picture window overlooking a pretty garden at the other.

Awaiting them was a very elderly man, sitting in a wheelchair with a rug tucked over his knees. Fixed to the wheelchair on one side was a small foldable table with a pile of handwritten papers lying on it; and on the other was a cup-holder attached to the arm of the chair.

The man held out his hand in greeting.

"Welcome! I'm Jonathan. I understand you want some help in finding out about the history of this place."

"That's right."

Between them Cressida and Tolly told Professor Sheldon about their research into Sir Anthony Marlington, his obsession with the Trojan War and his search for relevant artefacts during his Grand Tour. They concluded with a description of the tragic outcome of his wife's mental illness after the death of their baby.

"He sent her here when she became sick," Tolly explained. "We don't know how long she was here, or when she arrived, whether she died here, and if she outlived or predeceased him."

"We think it was sometime in the mid-1730's that she got here. We were shocked that he never wanted to see her again, and we wondered what sort of a life she would have had after being incarcerated," Cressida added.

Professor Sheldon was old and disabled, but there was nothing at all wrong with his brain. He was delighted that these two young people had come here in search of historical information. Since he had become so physically incapacitated that he could no longer live independently, he'd moved in here. He had then made it his mission to find out all he could about the history of the building which was now his home, hoping that he would live long enough to see his work published.

"Do sit down, both of you, and I'll tell you all I can."

They thanked him, pulled up a couple of chairs, and sat down. They'd agreed that they would each take notes and then pool them afterwards, deleting any duplicate data.

The professor began with a more detailed account of the information Cressida's mother had given them the previous day. He launched into a vivid and harrowing description of the miserable existence led by most 'lunatics' as they were called at the time.

Country asylums like this place, he told them, would probably have been marginally less hellish than those in cities. He referred to the infamous Bedlam in London, where inmates were often kept in chains, beaten and subjected to all sorts of painful, humiliating and abusive treatments, often as punishments, but sometimes categorised as cures. They were also frequently the objects of assault, derision and violence by crowds of voyeuristic spectators from the outside world, who paid to come and gawp at the 'lunatics'. As an unwanted extra, he added, these visits would also expose those inside to disease and infection. The death rate in such places was high.

That at least was lower in the countryside, as was the practice of admitting paying visitors to view inmates as a sort of hideous sideshow of human misery. However it wasn't until the next century that attitudes to mental health care began to become more humane. Acts of Parliament, medical advances and individual philanthropists were all heralds of change and reform.

Cressida and Tolly were simultaneously fascinated and horrified by what they were hearing. They both felt a sense of relief when the professor moved on to talk briefly about some of the improvements which began to take place during the nineteenth century. He then focused on the sort of experience a 'wealthy lunatic' like Lady Marlington might have had at the Chilminster Asylum. Tolly and Cressida leaned forward, pens in hand. This was at the heart of what they needed to know.

The professor explained that there had been a separate wing of the building where those people who could afford to pay, or were being paid for, had been housed. It was more comfortably furnished, sleeping accommodation for inmates was not as crowded, and the care was intended to be kinder and less punitive. These more privileged inmates also had access to a walled garden at the back of the building. Family visitors were permitted, but the professor confirmed that although Lady Marlington was funded by her husband, she was never visited by him. This was upsetting but not unexpected. Tolly, while still feeling indignant on her behalf, kept his emotions to himself this time.

Professor Sheldon couldn't provide much more specific data on Lady Marlington, but it was clear that, as a rule, life for wealthier inhabitants was rather more tolerable. Nevertheless they would sometimes have been subject to such inhumane practices as restraint in irons or straitjackets, if they seemed to be behaving irrationally or violently. As Tolly and Cressida both knew that it was almost certainly the necklace which had been the cause of poor Lady Marlington's supposed insanity, they hoped that she had been able to avoid such punishments.

That was more or less the sum of what Professor Sheldon was able to tell them, although, sensing how much he was enjoying talking to them, Tolly and Cressida, exchanging glances, tacitly agreed to stay a bit longer. In the end, looking at his watch, Tolly stood up, followed by Cressida.

"Thank you so much, sir, it's been so interesting and really helpful listening to you, hasn't it, Cressida? But we really must go now; we want to visit the Care Home Museum before we leave."

They both shook hands with the old man before departing to make their way back along the passages to Reception. Priya was still behind the desk. They thanked her again for facilitating the meeting and asked her where the little museum was.

"You will have made Professor Sheldon very happy with your visit," she said, "I am so glad he was able to help you. And the museum is at the back of the building, where the old walled garden used to be. You just need to go out again and walk round the side till you see it. I hope you also find it interesting."

"The old walled garden," Cressida repeated, as they walked round outside as instructed. "That was the part where posher inmates could spend time, wasn't it? Oh, Tolly, it's all proving to be really interesting, isn't it - and, despite the grim history, not all that depressing at all, because everyone here is being so nice and helpful."

"Yes, and what a sweet man the professor was. I do hope he manages to finish his book. This must be the place, don't you think?"

They had arrived at a large shed with a corrugated iron roof and an open door. Above the doorway it read "Minster Care Home Museum". Stepping inside, they found themselves in a long narrow room with glass display cases on the wall on either side, and several long glass-covered tables placed end to end down the middle. Sitting at a desk just inside by the door was an elderly woman.

She smiled at them, and said, "Good morning - or should I say afternoon, I see it's past midday. Welcome to our museum."

"Oh, thank you," said Cressida, "We've been talking to Professor Sheldon this morning, and are now hoping to find out more about what life in this place was like during the eighteenth century."

"Is there an entrance fee?" asked Tolly, putting his hand in his pocket.

"No, dear, no entrance fee, but when you've looked around, any donation would be very welcome. I'm Mary Gardiner, one of the residents here - we run a rota system between us to curate the museum. Now, take your time, have a good look round, and if you want any more information, please don't hesitate to ask. I'll do my best to explain anything you need to know. Oh, and the toilets are at the other end of the room."

Tolly and Cressida then split to each side of the museum. The wall displays had some interesting pictures, including, Cressida soon noticed, a portrait of Lady Marlington alone. In style it was reminiscent of the joint portrait they'd seen in the City Art Gallery. In it Lady Marlington was again wearing the faience bead necklace.

"Look, Tolly!" He came over immediately. "Oh, my goodness!" he said, then turned to Mary.

"This picture - it's similar to one half of a portrait we saw in the gallery in town. We know Lady Marlington was an inmate here in the eighteenth century - can you tell us anything more?"

"That portrait came with her when she was sent here. There are also a few of her things on the middle table, and a bit of information on display in the wall cabinet over there, but I'm afraid most of her possessions disappeared; it was thought that one or more of the maids stole the more valuable stuff. We do have some photocopied leaflets somewhere, which I think should give a bit more information. I'll see if I can find one for you."

While she was doing this Tolly turned to Cressida, saying quietly,

"Quite significant, I think, that she took the solo portrait with her when she came here; presumably Sir Anthony had no interest in keeping it."

As Mary rummaged through the drawers of her desk, they paused briefly. Were they getting somewhere at last? They each crossed fingers before proceeding to the cabinet she had indicated. The first thing they noticed was a framed paper entitled "Wessex Courant", and dated April 18th 1765.

"Didn't your mother mention a page from the Wessex Courant?" Tolly asked Cressida, thinking of the sheaf of papers they'd been given the previous day.

"Yes she did - I suppose it must have been the local newspaper at the time. But I'm pretty sure the one she had was for an earlier date. We haven't yet finished looking through all the stuff she gave us, have we?"

While she was talking Tolly was scrutinising the paper in front of them. The print was tiny and close-packed into three columns, but it was easy enough to read the headlines above those closely written columns. They were entitled "Death of a Lady" with the brief sub-heading below: "Sophia Elizabeth, Lady Marlington: 1714 - 1765."

He turned to Cressida, his voice a bit unsteady.

"It's her, Cressida, it's Lady Marlington. Oh, if only we had a magnifying glass, I can't really read much of the script, can you?"

"No, but look, I can tell you something, Tolly, She outlived Sir Anthony. He died in 1763 - remember the memorial plaque in the cathedral?"

At the same moment Mary called out from the desk.

"I've now found some copies of the old leaflet - there's more about Lady Marlington in it."

By now both Cressida and Tolly were feeling a combination of excitement and trepidation. Nervously Tolly took the leaflet from Mary and together they pored over it,

It quoted largely from that unreadable article in the Wessex Courant. Lady Marlington, born Sophia Elizabeth Granger in 1714, had died of typhus fever at the Chilminster Asylum on March 15th, 1765. She had left no issue; her only child, a girl, had been born and had died in April 1735. Shortly after the baby's death Lady Marlington had been committed to the asylum.

"Typhus," said Tolly, "I think it comes from infected fleas or lice. I suppose in an institution like an asylum it would spread very quickly, and I would imagine that hygiene standards wouldn't have been great even in the posher part where she was kept. Poor woman. Poor, poor woman."

Cressida was continuing to read further down the leaflet.

"Lots of the inmates got it, Tolly - it says here that typhus epidemics were common at the time and that it was very infectious. At least she outlived him - that'll probably be the reason why she's not on the memorial."

Once they had absorbed all this they moved on to look around at the central tables, which had glass covers fitted over them to protect the contents. These tables were spread with some of the possessions and relics of inhabitants of the place over the years. There was a rather touching display of Victorian toys and tattered picture books from when it was a Children's Home.

Spread out on another table were a few examples of clothing, dating from the time when it was a Workhouse. There were drab coarse cloth trousers and jackets for men and boys, flannel petticoats and shawls for women, and shapeless grey dresses and pinafores for girls.

Of most interest to Tolly and Cressida, however, was the table displaying stuff from when it was an Insane Asylum in the eighteenth century. As well as the utilitarian crockery and cutlery provided by the management for the inmates, there were broken but obviously treasured reminders of life before incarceration: cups decorated with flowers and birds, handmade wooden platters and boxes, dog-eared chapbooks and pictures - all poignant and pathetic relics of lives long gone. More grimly, there was a straitjacket and some punishment chains on display. They also noticed a few written fragments - mainly notes about inmates or lists of tasks.

To their surprise and delight, they found part of a page which could have come from a letter or a report, mentioning Lady Marlington. It was a tantalising fragment, reading, "*...Lady Sophia continues kindly and gentle with the most deranged souls and is able* *to calm....*". Tolly copied it and folded the copy into his wallet. They were both touched by this testimony, which seemed to give a tiny glimpse of the sort of person she had been, even while confined in the asylum.

There was nothing of monetary value left there, which made both Cressida and Tolly wonder whether thefts of inmates' more precious possessions were commonplace. Was that, they wondered, the fate of Lady Marlington's ancient faience bead necklace - and perhaps many more of her treasures? Who had stolen them, and had the thief then become another victim of the drugged beads?

Both were now beginning to feel hungry, a bit spaced out and in need of some downtime. Tolly had one more question before they left.

"What happened to the inmates' clothing and other possessions after they had died," he asked Mary, thinking about the blue skirt Cressida had worn at Louise's party, and the necklace which had been tangled into the waist fastening.

"It was dependent on condition," Mary replied. "Most of the garments were too shabby and old to be kept, they would either have been burnt or cut up to use as floor cloths. Higher quality stuff would be collected and washed and eventually sent to other institutions. Also, it's inevitable, I'm afraid, that various members of the asylum staff would have purloined some - in fact it's likely that most of the better pieces of clothing as well as jewellery and other possessions of any value were almost certainly stolen."

After a brief pause, she then added, "I understand too, that during the eighteenth century a lot of second-hand dealing went on, stalls selling clothing to the poor were very much part of merchandising at the time. So some items would have probably been handed over to stallholders and resold. Really, I suppose in a way it's still happening today, isn't it? Here, for example, if a resident leaves or, sadly, passes away - his or her clothes (unless the family wants to keep them) mainly end up in local second-hand and charity shops if they're in reasonable condition."

Cressida and Tolly each put a contribution into the donation tin, thanked Mary for all her help and kindness, and set off, slightly wearily, to the bus stop to return to Chilminster.

CHAPTER TWENTY-EIGHT

An Interlude

There was no-one else waiting in the bus shelter when they got there, and the next bus wasn't due for several minutes. Thankfully they sat down on the plain wooden bench and turned to one another.

"Fascinating, but sad, so sad, wasn't it, Tolly," Cressida said. He nodded, still feeling shocked as he thought about the ordeals and tribulations suffered by these long gone people.

" 'Man's inhumanity to Man'," he said soberly. "And it's still happening, Cressida - cruelty to children, abusive relationships, war and torture. What a flawed lot we are."

"Some of those past abuses must have been - and perhaps still are - due as much to ignorance as to cruelty, but - yes, you're right - one despairs sometimes for the future of humanity. But, oh Tolly, we mustn't give up! We can't change the world, but we can just try as best as we can to get things right in our own way, to be kind, truthful and compassionate. And in a way that's what we're doing together - trying to solve a mystery and find the truth behind historic abuses and misdeeds."

"Of course, my love. Come here." He put his arms around her and they hugged one another while pledging themselves to continue striving in their search for truth and justice.

That embrace proved soothing and gentle, making them both feel better. Returning to practicality Cressida said,

"Silly me, I meant to make us some sandwiches again but didn't get round to it. But we need lunch, and what about those ice creams you mentioned this morning? I suggest we get off the bus near the cathedral and give ourselves a break - lunch at the nice little Greek bistro on the Cathedral Green, then ices in the Minster Gardens - a bit of leisure time. After all, we still have the whole of tomorrow left."

"Excellent idea, I love the Minster Gardens. And yes, I agree - we do need a bit of downtime. It's all been pretty intense, hasn't it? Having said that, first, if it's OK with you, I'd like to quickly go back into the cathedral again. I don't know if you noticed, but that leaflet Mary Gardiner showed us quoted the Wessex Courant, and gave Lady Marlington's full name - she was born Sophia Elizabeth Granger. Look."

Tolly pulled his copy of the leaflet out of his pocket, and pointed out the relevant passage. Cressida glanced at the paragraph he was indicating.

"It also mentions that poor little baby," she added, then suddenly she realised what he meant.

"Oh, Tolly - yes - I see what you're thinking of - the smudged entry in the historic Register of Births, Marriages and Deaths - we saw a name that could have been Sophia, not Sara, as we thought."

"Yes, and it was in 1735, I'm sure. Perhaps we could pop in again and show them this, and if the verger is around maybe he'll let us check the Register again. Hey - we really are making some progress, Cressida."

With renewed optimism they squeezed each other's hands, then stood up as they saw the bus approaching.

Although the experience at the Care Home had been positive, kindly and useful, they couldn't help their spirits rising as the bus turned in to the outskirts of Chilminster and they saw the cathedral tower emerging above the rooftops.

When they got there they decided to go straight in before lunch, hoping the verger might be around. He wasn't, but Tolly handed over the leaflet, pointing out the relevant passage, and said they would return later.

"He'll probably come back before Evensong, like he did yesterday," Tolly said as they walked over the Cathedral Green towards the bistro Cressida had mentioned.

At this point, she found that she was out of money. She had put her last coins into the donation tin at the museum. How embarrassing was that, especially as it was she who had recommended the place for lunch!

"Oh dear, Tolly, I've just realised that I might not be able to pay my way this afternoon, I'm afraid. I seem to have got through an awful lot of money, with all our to-ing and fro-ing; bus fares, coffees, snacks, lunches and donations etcetera. So sorry - I can pay you back …. ".

"Oh, don't worry about it, Cressida! You provided the sandwiches yesterday, anyway. And as I've said before, my father gives me a generous allowance, and I can easily pay for us both. In fact I should really have been subsidising you all week, in return for the generosity of your parents having me to stay."

"But it's not fair on you - anyway I don't believe it's right to assume the man ought always to pay."

Tolly stopped and put his hands on her shoulders, looking down at her quite seriously,

"Not another word, my darling. It's my pleasure and my privilege to pay for you. Don't even think of paying me back. You have no idea how much you've changed my life for the better; no amount of money can go anywhere near the joy of what falling in love with you has given to me."

Cressida hadn't expected this! She felt herself blushing bright red, put her hands to her cheeks and then suddenly buried her head against Tolly, overwhelmed by this declaration. His arms went around her and held her still, till she raised her head and looked at him with shining eyes,

"Thank you, thank you - that's the nicest thing anyone has ever said to me."

Gently he cupped her face in his hands and kissed each cheek, then took her hand and they proceeded to the bistro.

It was a joyful and delightful lunch. Tolly ordered a bottle of sparkling elderflower; pouring it out for them both, he raised his glass, as did Cressida. They toasted themselves, first together, and then each other.

"Just to say thanks, Cressida, for changing my life, and here's to us both!"

"And my thanks to you, dearest Tolly, for everything."

Cressida was reminded again of that drink in the Troycombe pub, weeks ago, when things were just beginning for them. Once again they were toasting one another, as they had done then.

"Isn't it extraordinary, Tolly," said Cressida, "that it often feels as if we've known each other for ever - but in fact it's only about three months! "

"I know - but somehow I feel we've subliminally always known each other, but we just didn't know we knew. Does that sound a bit mad? I mean, I would dream and daydream about a girl like you - a kind beautiful clever girl who would be my soulmate; fantasising about her - well, in a way, really about you. It kept me going during the bad times. And when I saw the real you at Louise's party I think I knew instantly that you were the one."

"Oh Tolly, I hate to think of you going through those bad times. But yes, I do sort of know what you mean. I also had secret romantic daydreams about finding a kindred spirit who would become my lover - but they were really just adolescent fantasies. Unlike you I hadn't been through bad times, so I was much more simple and naïve."

She paused, then continued thoughtfully, smiling at him,

"What has happened to me since being with you, Tolly, has been a sort of miracle. I feel as if I've opened up on every level, in my heart, in my head, through all my senses - it's a whole magical new world of feeling and understanding. And every day I think how lucky we are, and what an incredible gift to us both all this is. Because I think it's probable that a lot of people never experience this sort of specialness."

Tolly had been listening closely; he now stretched his hand across the table and clasped hers, saying,

"You put it so well. love. We must cherish this special gift, and ensure that even when we're physically apart we continue to nurture it."

At this point their food arrived, postponing any more such contemplations for the time being. The less romantic but equally necessary need for nourishment took over as they shared a *mezze* platter - olive bread, humus, Greek salad, tzatziki, halloumi and chicken skewers. After finishing it all, much fortified, they headed back to the cathedral.

They were in luck. As they'd hoped, the verger was back. He greeted them like old friends, remembering them from their previous visit, and how they had then stayed for Evensong. When Tolly showed him the leaflet from the Care Home Museum, he retracted his previous scepticism and agreed to take them once more into the Chapter House to look again at the historic Register.

This time there was no doubt. Again, the white gloved hands of the verger lifted the huge book from its oak box and laid it out on the table. Following Tolly's recollection of the relevant date in the Births section, he soon reached that smudged 1735 birth entry. This time it seemed to jump out at them. There was the baby, *E.... S....a*, born *to A...... a.d S....a Ma.lin....,* - now unmistakably recognisable as: *Emily Sophia*, born to *Anthony and Sophia Marlington*.

"You were right, sir, no doubt about it," the verger said, turning to Tolly. "Congratulations. We must correct the record by slipping in an insert. Obviously we can't alter the original, but when errors are discovered we insert a slip of paper with the correction on it."

Cressida now had an idea.

"Do you think," she began, " that it would be possible to commemorate Lady Marlington and that poor little baby in the cathedral here? We know little Emily died in infancy, and we've also seen the notice of Lady Marlington's death decades later, in a page from a newspaper of the time, the Wessex Courant. Lady Marlington outlived her husband - she died of typhus in 1765. There's a memorial to him here, but no mention of her."

Tolly, listening, was simultaneously amazed and thrilled by this suggestion. He looked over at Cressida with a smile of gratitude and turned to hear what the verger was saying.

"Out of my remit, miss, I'm afraid," the man said, "You would probably need to talk to the Dean and other members of the senior clergy. But given what you've discovered, it would certainly be worth a try."

When Tolly and Cressida left the cathedral, after once again thanking the verger for his patience and perseverance, they had a lot to think about.

"A brilliant idea of yours, Cressida! If we could do it, it would be righting a historic wrong, and making sure she and her child were remembered. It would be a legacy of acknowledgement, dignity and respect."

"Yes, I agree. But first, Tolly, we need to find out how to go about it. Of course it's outrageous that Sir Anthony should be interred here, with a distinctive commemoration plaque, while his wife and child, both innocent of any wrong-doing, have been - well - sort of cancelled out. But as we've seen, she was obviously a good, kind person despite all that had happened to her. Maybe Mum might be able to help again; as an archivist, though her work isn't directly related to the church, there are often overlaps when you're dealing with past times. And now I think about it, Dad might also have some ideas. He's a lawyer and occasionally gets roped in to legal ecclesiastical stuff. We'll ask them later."

"Anyway," she went on, "I don't know about you, Tolly, but now I'm ready for a break! Ice cream, the Minster Gardens, perhaps even a go on the swings in the playground there!"

"What useful parents you have! But yes, let's take some time out."

The Minster Gardens were still beautiful, although the multi-coloured floral glory of their previous visit in July was now more muted. Some of the trees were beginning to turn, and the roses were past their best - but the sun was shining and it felt delightful to be there. An Italian ice cream van, strategically stationed at the gates to the gardens, supplied them each with a large cornet. It felt to them both almost as if they were on holiday, as they ambled towards one of the benches and sat down to finish their ices.

"This is so nice," Tolly said, happily relaxing in the early autumn sunshine. Enjoying the last delectable traces of his ice cream, he stretched his legs out and put an arm round Cressida. But she had already finished hers, and soon stood up.

"Come on Tolly, Race you to the swings!" And she was off, running like a hare across the gardens, past the children's playpark, and towards the recreation ground beyond, where there were larger swings, a climbing frame, a rope grid, a zipline and a long twisting slide. She could hear Tolly's feet pounding behind her as she reached the swings, and just before he got to her she pulled herself onto one of them, launching herself into action and laughing.

Tolly, taken by surprise, nevertheless caught up quickly. While Cressida soared up and down, higher and higher on the swing, he headed for the rope climb. Fairly soon he was clawing his way up. aiming for the metal bars at the top where he would be able to swing himself over to the next frame.

They had the place more or less to themselves. Because Cressida was used to the simpler, more limited playground in Troycombe village - the setting for frequent visits with her little brothers - she was thrilled to experience this much larger and more challenging space. Flying up and down on the swing she got breathtaking glimpses of the cathedral and the hilly countryside around, before sinking down again.

Tolly, determinedly making his way swinging hand-to-hand along the parallel bars toward the final rope grid, was also relishing the experience. He'd had to get used to fairly extreme gymnastics and compulsory competitive outdoor races when at boarding school. While acknowledging that such activities had been good for his physical fitness, he'd never enjoyed them very much. But here, with Cressida, it was altogether different! It might be challenging, but it was fun!

He reached the bottom of the grid and dashed over to the zipline. Meanwhile Cressida had abandoned her swing and was heading for the long slide.

Later they noticed a sort of obstacle course of tyres placed at intervals, zig-zagging in and out of a small stream running along the edge of the area. Tolly and Cressida both tested it out. She was lighter and more agile, but he had the advantage of longer legs, so could sometimes step from tyre to tyre when two were close enough together.

With a lot of giggling, they invented several silly extra rules, including having to do one circuit with bare feet, another while singing a song, and a third which involved doing it with a folded handkerchief on the head.

"Ok, Cressida - now I'll challenge you! The first one to complete four clear runs is the winner."

The barefoot circuit was the simplest, achieved by both with ease and poise. "Easy-peasy!" said Tolly as he leapt off the last tyre.

The song followed. It was surprisingly difficult to sing and spring at the same time, as Cressida found, realising that she had to time her jumps with the stresses of the tune. 'The Grand Old Duke of York' proved a safe choice, much safer than Tolly's more ambitious pick of 'Sur le Pont d'Avignon'. The pulse of that song was much too fast, so he hurtled along chaotically and frantically, finishing with wild shouts and gasps as he tumbled off the final tyre and rolled onto the grass. The handkerchief on head also proved challenging - it was surprisingly difficult to keep one's head still while jumping. Here Cressida was at her least successful, as she had to do much more jumping, while Tolly was able to stride over several of the tyres.

In the end they declared a draw, and collapsed on the ground chuckling, as they went over the disasters and triumphs of one another's performances. "That was such fun!" said Tolly, "What a brilliant place!"

"Isn't it! I knew it was there but had never gone over to it before. But we should probably be heading home now, the twins'll be back from school and I promised Mum I'd be around to help with them after their tea."

"Well, anything I can do - story reading, football etcetera - I'm willing and available!" Tolly said cheerfully. He was now accustomed to the Curtis family routines and felt quite at home there. "And after the twins have gone to bed," he added, "we need not only to properly look through all the data your mum gave us, but also to ask her for some advice on the possible memorial for Lady Marlington."

They caught the next bus back and were soon absorbed into the mixture of bustle and domesticity which was all part of Curtis family life.

CHAPTER TWENTY-NINE

Winding Down

"Your father rang, Tolly," Helen said, as they arrived home. "He wants you to call him. Use the phone in the study if you like - it's more private and you'll be less likely to be interrupted by the twins. As soon as they realise you're home they'll be all over you!"

"Oh, thanks. But wouldn't it be better if I went out to the phone box - after all I don't see why my call should go onto your phone bill," Tolly replied, wondering what the call was about. He'd talked to Pa the previous evening when he and Cressida got back from Chilminster.

"Don't worry, dear. Given the hours Cressida spends on the phone one extra call won't make all that much difference!"

Cressida, looking slightly abashed, smiled wryly at Tolly and disappeared into the kitchen to put the kettle on. Tolly headed for the telephone.

"Hi Pa. Is everything OK?"

Tolly tried to sound off-beat and casual, but he couldn't ever entirely suppress a feeling of anxiety about Pa whenever he was away from home. There was also now a permanent small niggle of guilt lurking inside him, given that he himself was now so much happier and more optimistic, thanks to Cressida, but his father was still alone and often unhappy.

This time, however, there was no need for anxiety. Pa sounded upbeat and cheerful as he outlined the plan he had made to take Tolly to France for a few days to visit prehistoric sites in Brittany.

"Avebury and all around was so fascinating, and since then I've been reading about other such places. The French megaliths and passage graves in the Carnac area sound quite extraordinary. It's a pity we can't take Cressida with us too - but I thought of driving down to Troycombe on Friday, so we could maybe take her and her parents out to lunch. Then perhaps you and she might like to show me the castle and the area round about, where the dig took place. We would spend the afternoon there then drive down to the coast to get the night ferry to France. What do you think?"

"Oh Pa, how exciting! It sounds like a lovely plan. I'll just check with Cressida's mum. Could you ring me back - say in about twenty minutes?"

It was indeed a lovely plan, and Tolly was delighted that his father would now be able to meet Cressida's parents. He returned to her and her mother, both now in the kitchen preparing supper. The twins, who'd finished their tea before Cressida and Tolly got home, were upstairs in their bedroom playing with Lego. Amazingly, both boys were so absorbed in their game that they hadn't yet realised that Tolly and Cressida were back.

Tolly told Cressida and her mother about his father's proposal. He was fairly certain that Helen didn't work on Fridays, but wasn't so sure whether Graham would be able to get away. The twins would of course be at school, which would make a lunch date much more manageable.

"How very kind of your father," Helen said. "We'd love it, wouldn't we, Cressy? And with any luck Dad might be able to get the afternoon off, things sometimes wind down a bit at the office on Fridays."

"Yes! Brilliant!" Cressida agreed, trying not to show the spurt of envy which had shot up inside her, when she heard that while she was back at school Tolly and Bart would be exploring French prehistoric sites.

Tolly however now knew her far too well not to have sensed how she was feeling, so when they returned together to the study to await Bart's next call, he put an arm round her.

"I know what you're thinking, Cressida, and I do understand. It would be wonderful if you could have come with us - but we always knew that I'd have to leave on Friday, and that there's no way of dodging your return to school. On the plus side, I would've gone back to Salisbury on the morning train on Friday. This way we have longer together and Pa gets to meet your family. And we do still have the whole of tomorrow."

" I know, I know, Tolly. And of course I'm glad for you both - and also for the extra time this gives us. Just make sure you take lots of photos and tell me all about those amazing Breton menhirs and alignments - in fact, I've got some books about them upstairs which I'll lend you."

"That'll be great; thank you. And, Cressida, in the future, when we're both free, I promise that you and I will go together to see them. None of these places are going to go away - the time will come one day when we can both go to Greece, to Italy, to France - all over Europe in fact, and visit lots of ancient sites for as long as we want."

"We will, Tolly. Thanks. And sorry. I really do hope you both have a marvellous time."

At this point the phone rang again, so Cressida quickly went back to the kitchen, leaving Tolly to talk to his father about practicalities including bringing some clean clothes and finding Tolly's passport.

That evening, after the twins were in bed, Tolly having obligingly read them the usual quota of bedtime stories, he and Cressida sat in the sitting room and went through the papers Helen had photocopied for them earlier in the week.

"We're actually doing quite well," Cressida said, "Just a few loose ends to tie up, but we've got more or less enough data to start writing our reports for Penny. Tomorrow we'd better make more photocopies of all this stuff so when you go back to university you'll have your own copies. And of course we'll talk together regularly about what progress we're making, won't we?"

She was trying to be very businesslike and practical, but the thought of life without Tolly beside her was a bleak one. They had known for weeks that the day would come when they would have to part; now, suddenly, it was imminent.

Tolly tried to be equally pragmatic.

"Of course we will, " he agreed, then continued, "There are really only two aspects outstanding, as I see it; the possible memorial plaque for Lady Marlington, and the missing links in the history of the necklace. Perhaps tomorrow we should make those our main priorities."

"Yes, absolutely. We could ask Mum and Dad for a bit of advice on the memorial plaque - and also, I suggest that when we get to Chilminster again tomorrow we go back to the second-hand shop where I got the necklace. We need to find out if they have any information as to when. and from where, it ended up there. Actually, I thought it might be an idea to bring the blue skirt that the beads were tangled up in, it might just jog someone's memory."

"That's a really good idea. I've also been thinking that it might be worth our while contacting a member of the Dean and Chapter of the cathedral regarding the plaque, perhaps this evening. With any luck we might be able to arrange a meeting for tomorrow."

"Yes, we'll talk to Mum and Dad at supper, after all, they both have professional links which might help. Oh, Tolly, will we get it all sorted out in time, I wonder. And are we getting it right?"

"Oh Cressida, I hope we are - we're very nearly there." And suddenly, they were clasping one another's hands, clinging together and both very much aware of time running out.

Supper time yielded a bit more hope. Cressida's father, who confirmed that he could take time off to join them for lunch on Friday, was also able to help them with a connection to one of the cathedral clergy.

"Canon Wilcox is a good man," he said "I've been able to sort out a few legal problems for him in the past, and I'm sure he'll be interested in what you're proposing. I'll give him a call after supper and see if you can meet up with him sometime tomorrow."

Helen added that if they didn't get any more information from the second-hand shop about the necklace, it might be worth writing an article to send to the local paper, the Chilminster Gazette, about it. She suggested providing a description of the necklace, referring to the painting in the City Art Gallery, and asking if any readers had clues as to its whereabouts before it turned up in the charity shop.

This was a practical proposal, and Cressida thanked her mother for the idea. But the last thing she wanted was for information about the hallucinogen to become public knowledge, so she was secretly reluctant to follow through with this suggestion. She was also aware that, having gifted the necklace to the museum, it was now up to the management there rather than for her to make those sort of decisions.

"Good idea, thanks Mum. I'll ask Penny what she thinks," she responded, thinking that the museum itself might be preparing some sort of news feed about the necklace as a lead-up for the planned exhibition.

A good night's sleep worked its usual healing magic, meaning that both Tolly and Cressida arose the next morning feeling much more optimistic. Tolly, as he so often did, had awoken early and, hearing the twins chattering to one another, had dressed and visited them in their bedroom. They were thrilled, and were about to launch themselves loudly and delightedly onto him, but he put his finger to his lips and said in a secret, whispering sort of voice,

"Sh, Shhh, boys. I wondered if you'd like to come downstairs with me and help me make a surprise for your Mummy and Daddy and Cressida."

"Yes, yes, we will, we will," they whispered back, thrilled at the prospect. He helped them get dressed, then the three of them crept downstairs.

"Now, I thought I'd like to do something a bit special, to say thank you to everyone for having me to stay, so will you help me sweep the floor and lay the table for breakfast? Then we'll go into the garden and pick some flowers, to look pretty in the middle of the table."

The twins remembered the last time they'd got up very early, and how Tolly had found them in the castle. Mikey said,

"But this time we won't go off like we did before. We'll make a nice picture message to go on the table so if anyone comes down they'll know that we're in the garden."

"Good scheme," said Tolly, echoed by Jo-jo, who thought any phrase uttered by Tolly was rather cool.

The kitchen was soon looking much cleaner and neater, as the twins got busy as quietly as they could with brushes and dustpans, and Tolly laid the table for breakfast. The boys then created their colourful picture message, before all three of them going into the garden and picking the brightest flowers they could find, which they then placed in a large vase on the kitchen table.

"Great work, guys," said Tolly. "I've also got some special breakfast treats for everyone." He had bought croissants, brioches and pains-au- chocolat in Chilminster the previous day, and now laid them out temptingly on a large platter on the table.

At this point he heard someone coming downstairs.

"Shhh, boys, quick, let's hide in the pantry," he whispered. There wasn't enough room for him, but the twins disappeared inside, and Tolly stood quietly by the pantry door as he saw Graham, in his dressing gown, coming into the kitchen to make morning tea. He caught Graham's eye then tiptoed over.

"The twins' breakfast surprise," he mouthed, and crept back to the pantry. Graham, quickly getting the gist of it, said, sounding astonished,

"Goodness me! What's happened here? Have some elves got in and prepared our breakfast! Or maybe it's more likely to be clever little monkeys! Oh, here comes Cressida. Look darling - there's been magic happening here this morning!"

The little boys could contain themselves no longer. Shrieking with excitement they erupted out of the pantry.

"It was us!" "We did it, Tolly helped us make a surprise!" "Do you like it?" "There's special treats for breakfast!"

Cressida had just noticed Tolly lurking by the pantry, and realised immediately what had happened. She gave him one of her sweetest and most radiant smiles before hugging both twins. Helen was the last to come down, aware of the growing commotion which was now filling the kitchen.

"Mummy, Mummy , we did a breakfast surprise with Tolly. And we made you a picture."

They had drawn and coloured a garland of flowers around this message:

"Don't worry we are just in the garden".

It made Helen smile, as she remembered again that catastrophic early morning awakening only a few weeks ago.

"We didn't want you to think that we'd gone again," Mikey explained.

"Thank you, darlings - what an amazing surprise! Let's put these lovely looking delicacies in the oven to warm up and then we can all have a delicious breakfast together. What a wonderful way to start the morning!"

Later, Tolly and Cressida set off again for their last complete day together in Chilminster. They were still smiling about the success of the twins' breakfast party.

"!t was a brilliant idea, and so kind of you, Tolly. And actually they both did a really good job! What made you think of it?"

"Well, I thought I'd like to provide something a bit special for breakfast, just as a sort of 'thank-you' to your family, so yesterday I bought the French stuff from the continental boulangerie in town - the one next door to where we had lunch - before we went back to the cathedral. I think you'd gone to the loo just then, so I just nipped in to the shop before you got back. Then, when I woke up early this morning, as I started to get dressed I heard the twins prattling away, so I decided I'd get them to help me make the festive breakfast. I thought that taking them downstairs might ensure a bit more sleep for all of you! I'm so glad it worked!"

"It was lovely of you. Such a nice start to the day. And they were so proud of themselves, bless them. They went off to school feeling like heroes!"

CHAPTER THIRTY

Steps towards an Ending

The first visit of this final full day took place in the cathedral refectory. Canon Wilcox, after his conversation with Cressida's father the previous evening, had agreed to meet them there. The refectory was in the cathedral undercroft, which been turned into a pleasant café, with a flight of steps leading up outside into the cloisters and the grassy quadrangle beyond.

As Tolly and Cressida arrived a smallish, balding man in a cassock and clerical collar stood up and came towards them, smiling.

"Good morning. I'm Simeon Wilcox. And you, I presume, are Miss Curtis and Mr Henderson. Good to meet you."

They shook hands, begged him to call them Cressida and Tolly, and thanked him for agreeing to see them.

"I'll order coffee, then you can tell me how I can help you, Milk? Sugar? Biscuits? Or perhaps you'd like a slice of our cathedral ginger cake. Sally Merton here makes it and it is extremely good!"

Despite the lavish breakfast they'd had earlier, neither could resist such a tempting offer.

"Oh yes, that sounds lovely," said Cressida. "And thank you very much," added Tolly, ever polite.

It was indeed delicious, as was the coffee brought over with it by Sally Merton, the plump lady who presided over the canteen.

"Now, how can I help you?" asked Canon Wilcox

"You start, Tolly," Cressida said, knowing how important it was to Tolly to try and achieve a sort of posthumous justice for Lady Marlington.

Tolly, as succinctly as he could, gave an account of the sad story of her married life, beginning with the death of her baby daughter at just a few weeks old, her incarceration in the Chilminster Asylum at her husband's behest, and his subsequent rejection of her, never visiting, discarding her out of his life as if she had never lived.

"He paid for her, but that was all," said Tolly. "But he's buried here, in this cathedral, with an impressive memorial plaque, while she has been totally blanked out. She might have never been born, as far as he was concerned."

Cressida could hear from Tolly's voice that he was starting to become upset, so she took over, linking her hand into his as she did so.

"We're shocked that he effectively abandoned her, with no kindness, no contact, no care; when she became ill he basically dumped her. We've been doing quite a lot of research about attitudes to episodes of dementia and illness, and the treatment of the 'insane' in the past. It's a pretty depressing story.

"Yesterday we visited the Minster Care Home - which was once the Chilminster Asylum, where Lady Marlington spent the final thirty years of her life. And we got just a glimpse of what kind of a person she was, despite everything. Tolly, have you got your copy of that bit of paper we found on display in the museum there?"

Tolly, who had now regained control of his emotions, brought out his copy of the paper scrap they had found and read while they were at the Care Home Museum.

"It's just a few words," he said, "but it gives, I think, an idea of what a good woman she was despite the circumstances of her life.

It says "*Lady Sophia continues kindly and gentle with the most deranged souls and is able to calm...* and that's all there is." He handed it to the canon.

There was a short silence after this. Then Canon Wilcox spoke.

"Thank you, both of you, for your moving and eloquent account of this sad story. I completely understand why you feel so strongly about the plight of this poor woman, and the inexcusable cruelty and disregard with which she was treated by her husband."

He paused for a moment, then went on, "To me, it seems that there are some significant insights about her character and generosity of spirit, very clearly demonstrated in that small fragment of paper. I quote: *Lady Sophia* **continues** *kindly* etc - the implication being that she is always so, that it's part of her personality. Going on, we hear that she is gentle even with the most unbalanced inmates, and that she has the ability to soothe and calm. Rather a remarkable woman, I should say."

Cressida and Tolly exchanged glances.

"So what do you think can be done? Is there a chance of some sort of memorial for her," Tolly asked.

"There's a lot of protocol which has to be gone through; the first step being to put it before the Diocesan Advisory Committee. If they are agreed, then a formal application for a faculty has to be made. Usually recent cases have less chance of success than historic ones, so in this instance that wouldn't be a problem. I would certainly endorse putting this forward, and if you could provide a written account of everything you've just told me - with the compassion and fluency that you have demonstrated this morning - I'll discuss it with colleagues and recommend that it is submitted for consideration by the DAC."

They gasped. "Oh, wonderful!" "That's amazing, thank you so much!".

Canon Wilcox looked at them benignly.

"It's been a pleasure to meet you both; and well done, for your concern and perseverance in taking on a bygone injustice which could easily have disappeared without trace into the void of history. Here's my card, and would you each give me your contact details so I can keep you updated."

Once outside the cathedral again, Tolly and Cressida hugged one another ecstatically, dancing around as they did so in a sort of crazy hornpipe.

"Yey Cressida, we've done it!!! Wasn't he brilliant?"

"Fantastic, Tolly, and good for you for making it such a serious priority."

"You too, my love, for your encouragement and understanding."

Tolly knew that Cressida had been aware all the time of how his distress about Lady Marlington was somehow tied up with his mourning for his beloved mother. He was also acutely conscious of the fact that for centuries it had been acceptable for women to be domineered over, abused and ignored, by members of the male sex. As a man himself he felt deeply ashamed of the entrenched historic injustice which had effectively relegated half the human race to second-class status.

All the important women in his life - his mother, cousin Charlotte, Stella, Louise and now Cressida - he could only think of with gratitude and admiration. With regard to Cressida, as with most women, there was only one way in which he was more able than she - his greater physical strength. Cressida was as intelligent as him, as capable, as imaginative, as creative and as resourceful. In fact, Tolly reflected, with her natural empathy and kindness, her ability in solving problems, her practicality and quick-wittedness, she was almost certainly in many ways a more useful and impressive human being than he was.

While these thoughts jostled about in his head, he looked over at this beloved girl with thankfulness and gratitude. What alchemy, what providence, what magic had brought them together?

"OK, Tolly?"

Cressida was watching him a bit anxiously, as he stood deep in thought.

"Never better, darling, just thinking yet again how lucky I am to have you by my side."

"Ditto, ditto, my lovely Tolly! What shall we do now? It's a bit early for lunch, so I suppose we could go over to the second-hand shop. I brought the blue skirt in this shopping bag."

"Yes, let's do that."

It was over three months since Cressida had found the necklace, while rummaging through boxes of miscellaneous clothing in the charity shop in Chilminster High Street. Now she and Tolly headed away from the cathedral, down the cobbled passageway which led to the High Street and that charity shop. On their way they passed the museum.

"If we have time, on the way back p'raps we could call in to see if Penny's around," Cressida suggested. "I'm sure she'd like to hear about our meeting with nice Canon Wilcox."

"That's a really good idea," Tolly agreed, thinking that he'd also like Penny to know that his angry distress about Sir Anthony's treatment of his wife had led to what could turn out to be a just resolution. He still felt bad about having lost his temper, but now, between them he, Cressida and Canon Wilcox might have achieved some retrospective justice for a much wronged, and completely innocent woman.

To Cressida, the second-hand shop looked unchanged. There were still those racks of clothes hanging on coat hangers, the jumble of shoes and boots lined up on one side of the shop, and the wall of assorted books crammed into shelves on the opposite side. At the back, as before, there were a few large cardboard boxes full of miscellaneous stuff.

Cressida and Tolly went straight to the counter. The woman behind it, Cressida felt certain, was not the same person who had been there when she bought the skirt.

"Good morning," she began, pulling the skirt out of her bag, "You won't know me, but I bought this about three months ago, with one or two other things - a blouse and a brooch - to wear at a fancy-dress party."

"We don't take returns, as a rule, unless they have been laundered and are in good condition."

"No, I understand - that's fine - but I wondered if there was any way you could tell me who brought it in originally."

Cressida had planned her approach. Tolly, standing beside her, kept quiet.

"You see," she continued, "I discovered some jewellery knotted in with it, and I thought if possible I might be able to find out who the original owner was."

The woman now looked more closely at Cressida, saying,

"I don't remember you - one of my colleagues must have served you. You say you were going to a fancy-dress party? And you bought the skirt and one or two other bits - a blouse, was it?"

"Yes, that's right, and a brooch. But it's really this skirt that I'm concerned about. Do you keep any sort of record of the people who bring stuff in?"

"Well, yes, we do. If the clothing is new or nearly new, we make a note of the donor. That's in case it turns out to sell at quite a high price, in which case we offer a percentage back to the donor. On the whole, they don't want it, but a few do. Were you hoping to return this skirt?"

"No, but if you could put me in touch with the donor it would be great."

At this point Tolly joined in, deploying his natural charm and courtesy, and smiling sympathetically at the woman.

"It's really kind of you to listen to us, and I know you must get absolutely fed up with people making enquiries, but we would be most awfully grateful if you could just look to see if you have contact details for the person who brought in this skirt."

"Wait a bit, I'll check the book. You bought it three months ago, you say."

Cressida had been working out the exact date. Lou's birthday had been on the twentieth of June, which was a Tuesday - definitely a school day, so the party must have been the weekend before. Yes, it had been on the seventeenth, so it was on the previous Saturday, the tenth, just after she had finished her GCSE's, that she had bought the clothes. Tolly, looking in his diary, also had a note of the party date, and confirmed it as the seventeenth of June.

"I'm pretty sure it was on Saturday the tenth of June that I bought it," she said.

"Now I remember about that skirt," the woman said suddenly. "It looked both vintage and unworn, so we'd put it in one of the boxes at the back, we needed to agree an appropriate price for it and a percentage for the donor if necessary, before putting it on sale. We realised it was rather a classy garment, made of heavy silk, so as I say, we set it aside. It seems as if one of my colleagues didn't realise we hadn't yet priced it, so she would have estimated a price and sold it to you there and then."

At this point, some other customers claimed the woman's attention.

Tolly and Cressida waited, Tolly idly wishing that he could somehow get hold of the book to search. He knew this was unlikely to be permitted, but he secretly thought he just might be able to find what they needed more quickly than she.

However at last she was free to deal with them again, and fairly soon she did have an address and phone number for them - a local number. The owner was called Angela Penwood, she lived at 49 Westdown Lane, Chilminster. They each wrote down those details.

"Thank you, thanks so much," Tolly said, shaking the woman's hand.

"You've been wonderful - and really patient with us." Cressida added, and the pair of them left the shop, Cressida once again carefully folding up the blue skirt and putting it back in her bag.

"What next?" said Cressida. "The museum? Food?"

"Both, I think, in that order! In fact, we might be able to phone from the museum, once we've updated Penny. She'll be interested to hear about Canon Wilcox, and intrigued that we've got a possible lead on the provenance of the skirt."

Penny was delighted to hear about their meeting with Canon Wilcox, and its positive outcome. They also told her about their visit to the Care Home, the meeting with Professor Sheldon and the precious fragment about Lady Marlington which they had found in the little museum there.

"I think that was the clincher, really," Tolly said, "When we told the Canon what it said, he was really moved."

"Well done. I'm so glad your passion and determination led to such a positive outcome, you must feel much better about it all now, Tolly."

"I do, thanks. And we've also made a bit of progress today about the necklace, haven't we, Cressida?"

"Yes," Cressida agreed, continuing, "We went back to the charity shop where I bought the skirt - which originally had those beads tangled up around the waist and tied in by the ribbons at the end. We didn't say much about the beads, though, as of course they now belong to the museum. The lady in charge looked through the record of donors to the shop, and eventually managed to find contact details for the person who brought the skirt in. So this afternoon we'll give her a call."

"I'll be interested to hear what she has to say; I suppose it's too much to hope that you manage to trace it all the way back to the eighteenth century, but you never know! We do have a phone booth downstairs, so you could try from here if you like. And now I have a bit of rather extra- ordinary news for both of you. It's about the drug in the spacers."

"Oh gosh, Penny, have they identified it?" Both Cressida and Tolly were curious and excited.

"Not precisely, though the botanists have now discovered traces of a similar drug in another group of plants, so they're getting a little closer. But the interesting thing for you, Cressida, is that they have named this mysterious ancient and as yet unidentified plant after you: *Nepenthe Archaea Cressidae*! What d'you think of that!"

"Oh goodness me! Really! But why?" Cressida was taken aback, but also intrigued by this unexpected revelation.

Penny explained, "Well, every plant has to be classified, and in order to continue trying to trace this one, it needs to have a name, even though as yet the plant hasn't actually been located. As you effectively bought the necklace with the skirt, and thus became the owner of it, your name is the one they've given it. Quite a nice surprise, don't you think?"

Tolly was thrilled! "Yey Cressida!" he said, clapping her on the shoulder, "Fame at last!"

"Well, yes, it is sort of exciting and completely unexpected - but also a bit weird," Cressida said, "Until - and if ever - they find the plant, I can't see that it's going to make all that much difference to me!"

Penny had more to say, "Well, it will certainly need to be mentioned in our exhibition, so you may have to put up with a bit of questioning then, Cressida! Also, there's another, more serious thing to consider. I think we'll all have to allude to the hallucinatory qualities of the necklace when we prepare our documentation for the exhibition. That doesn't mean full details of the various effects it has had, but rather, an acknowledgement of the presence of the drug - that ancient psychedelic component - in the spacer beads."

Tolly nodded slowly, "I see, and yes, I agree. As historians we need to tell the truth. That doesn't mean giving full details of what it did it to you, Cressida, or to Penny, or indeed Lady Marlington but, as you say, an acknowledgement."

"Quite right, Tolly. And don't worry, Cressida, everything you have told me and Tolly about your own experiences, and also mine, remains confidential between the three of us."

"Yes, I agree too, to all that. And actually, I did mention to my mother months ago that it had made me feel strange when I tried it on in the shop. It'll be interesting to find out whether the previous owner had any similar experiences. So perhaps we'd better make that phone call now, don't you think, Tolly."

They did, but met with this recorded response:

"This is the answerphone of Ralph and Angela Penwood. I'm afraid we aren't available at the moment, but please leave a message, name and number and we'll get back to you as soon as we can."

They decided to leave a brief message, but would also try again later. Presumably the Penwoods were at work. So the pair thanked Penny yet again for her time and attention, and left the museum.

"Lunch time! Tolly said. "Don't know about you, Cressida my love, but despite that delicious breakfast and the cathedral ginger cake, I'm starving!"

"That's the problem with being so big and tall," Cressida said teasingly, "Now I am merely just a bit peckish! Anyway, why don't we go back to the cathedral refectory. I can have a salad and you can have something much more substantial."

They were both feeling upbeat and positive, despite the inexorable dwindling down of their time together. It had been a good day so far, with this morning's successful meeting, the possible link to finding out more about the necklace, and Penny's revelation about the plant name.

"Mum and Dad will be thrilled," Cressida said while they were eating. "In fact, telling them about it will give me a bit of a lead-in to explaining about the hallucinogen. I'll go as far as talking about the buzzing feeling I got from it, but no further. And the fact that I've now given it to the museum should reassure them that their daughter is not about to become a drug addict."

"Bravo, that's a great idea. Do you want me to stay with you when you tell them, or would it be better if I kept out of the way?"

"Oh no, Tolly, you're never in the way. Of course I want you to be there, this is our story, our search for the truth, our shared research project. And anyway it 'll be good to have your input as an independent witness."

"Ah, thank you. And certainly, regarding your parents, I'll support what you say and endorse everything you tell them."

"That's brilliant, Tolly, exactly what I'll need. Now for coffee and pudding – and whether you like it or not, this bit's on me! No, don't protest, I went and got some money out of the post office before we left this morning, and I'm solvent again."

"What can I say, other than thanks - that's very kind of you. Could I have a bit of ginger cake and a scoop of ice cream. And a black coffee?"

"Of course, Tolly, whatever you like." She stroked his hair as she went over to the canteen.

When they had both finished eating, and were drinking their coffee, Cressida said suddenly,

"We do spend a lot of time sitting opposite one another at tables, don't we? First it was the pub at Troycombe, then various cafés in Chilminster, the Greek place yesterday - and now here, today - the last time before we have to part. Oh my goodness, I'm really going to miss holding your hands and looking at your lovely kind face across the table."

He immediately stretched his hands to hers and once more they sat, face to face and hands linked together.

"Last time for the moment, but not for too long. There's still most of tomorrow to come. And I've worked out some future timings; in just over six weeks' time, with any luck we'll be together again for the two Shakespeare plays near Oxford. I know your mother has been in touch with Charlotte, Mum's cousin, about it, so that's something to look forward to. Then not long after that it'll be

Christmas, we'll definitely spend time together then - oh, my darling love, don't cry."

"I'm not, well not really - just thinking how much I'm going to miss you. But I'll get used to it, we'll write and phone of course. I know we'll manage - well, there's no alternative is there? We have to manage because now we can't really do without each other, can we?"

"No, my sweetheart, we can't do without each other."

Both were silent for a moment after this, then Cressida, becoming practical again, said,

"We mustn't waste time. As we can't ring the Penwoods till later, why don't we stay here for a bit and work on our submission for Canon Wilcox. Have you any blank sheets left of the photocopier paper in your backpack?"

For the next half hour they both scribbled away. At first they each made a list of the points to be included, then they worked together to create an effective and expressive account of what had happened to Lady Marlington. They concluded first by quoting verbatim the fragment about her they'd seen in the Care Home Museum, then finally added a brief but eloquent plea for justice and recognition.

"Is it too sentimental, do you think?" asked Cressida when they had finished.

"Well, it isn't really sentimental, because all we've done is to tell the truth. But it's a really sad story, isn't it? I think that the death of the poor little baby is probably the most emotive bit - truly tragic. That loss must have been devastating for her - and then to be packed off to the asylum without compassion or understanding; it doesn't bear thinking about. And it triggered off everything that happened afterwards. I can't help feeling that if the baby had been a boy, and had survived, things might have been very different."

Again Tolly was considering historic attitudes to women and girls.

"I suppose so," responded Cressida, "but even so it would still have seemed as if poor Lady Marlington was going mad, because as we now know, it was the necklace, not the baby's death, which caused her delusions. Sir Anthony would therefore still have had her committed to the Asylum and would most likely have hired a nurse to care for the baby, boy or girl, if it had lived. He was a nasty selfish misogynistic character and I'm actually glad he had no legitimate descendants to carry on the line."

"Hear, hear! Good for you - I absolutely agree! So let's go through it again and tweak any bits we aren't satisfied with. Why don't we read it aloud to one another and if something doesn't quite work, we can change it as we go along."

They worked on it until they were both satisfied with the content, and planned to type it out when they got back home.

"After that we'd better both sign it too ," said Cressida, "then I can send it to Canon Wilcox; I expect Dad's got his contact details. Well done us! Another box ticked! If we manage to have a useful conversation with Mr or Mrs Penwood this evening, we'll have got to the end of our list of chores. Though of course we might never be successful in tracing the necklace right back to its disappearance after Lady Marlington's death"

"But still, well done us! We make a pretty amazing team, Cressida, don't we? And now, why don't we go out into the cloister for a bit of fresh air. It looks beautiful out there."

"Let's do that. An oasis of calm and tranquillity - just what we need."

A gentle stroll, hand in hand, around the cloister, was peaceful and undemanding. They paused to look at some ancient gravestones, many of which lay on the grassy green rectangle of the cloister garth.

"For non-churchy people, we seem to be spending a lot of our time in and around this cathedral." Tolly observed.

"You're right - it's mainly because of the historical context, isn't it, but also the beauty, the ambience, and the feeling of calm and benevolence...."

"And the music," Tolly added, as a procession of choirboys and men emerged from the Song School into the other side of the cloister, and began to walk round towards the choir entrance behind the high altar.

"Practice for Evensong, I suppose," he said, "Shall we go in and listen?"

It would be a pleasant and gentle way to fill the time before making the call again to the Penwoods. So that was what they did, welcomed by the priest and their old friend the verger, who was delighted to see them and insisted on ushering them into a pew right up by the chancel, close to the choir and near the organ.

"I know you appreciate the music, sir," he said to Tolly, "Sitting here you can see the choir as well as hearing them, and also enjoy the organ playing."

Tolly and Cressida were touched. They both spoke at the same time.

"That's really kind, thank you very much! " "Yes, and also thanks so much for all your help the last few days."

Sitting contentedly together they listened to the majestic organ voluntary while reflecting on the success, so far, of the day.

CHAPTER THIRTY-ONE

A Bit of a Setback

The call to the Penwoods proved interesting but inconclusive. After getting back home, Cressida waited for some time in case they weren't yet back from work, then rang them, feeling slightly nervous.

"Hello. Angela Penwood here. Who's speaking, please?"

"Oh, hello. You don't know me but my name is Cressida Curtis; I left a brief message on your answering machine this afternoon. I'm ringing about a skirt you donated to the second-hand shop in Chilminster some months ago."

"Yes, what about it?"

This was difficult. Angela sounded neither very forthcoming or very interested. Cressida tried to be as friendly and polite as she could.

" Well, the thing is, I bought that skirt to wear to a party, and I found an old string of beads knotted up in the waist, so I wondered who the skirt had belonged to and whether you could tell me any more about it."

"Not really. I never wore it, it wasn't mine. It was with a lot of other old fashioned rubbish which came from my grandmother. When she died, we had to clear her house. There was loads of stuff - most of it junk - clothes, books, papers and so on. The clothes, those that were in reasonable nick, we took to the second-hand shop, most of the rest of the stuff we put into boxes and took to the town tip."

"Oh, thanks. Do you remember your grandmother wearing that skirt?"

"No, never. It actually wasn't hers either. In fact I think most of the stuff had come from *her* mother and grandmother or even further back, my Gran never threw anything away. I'm sorry but I really can't help you much more."

"I'm sorry too, to have bothered you, and thank you for your patience. Could I leave you my phone number in case you remember anything else?"

"I suppose so, but we probably won't; however, do give it to me if you like."

When she had done this, Cressida thanked Angela, replaced the phone, and turned to Tolly, shrugging her shoulders.

"Not much to go on there," she said, as she gave him the gist of the conversation. After her earlier confidence, she was now feeling rather cast down, but Tolly, assessing what she had told him, was much more hopeful.

"Look at it this way, Cressida - we now have a possible provenance for that blue skirt going back about five generations - all the way back to Angela Penwood's great, great grandmother. That's way back into the nineteenth century. It's also intriguing that Angela mentioned taking stuff to the tip. As they did that only a few months ago, some of it could still be there. It might be worth us going there first thing tomorrow morning, before my Pa gets here. What do you think?"

"Oh Tolly, thank goodness for your optimism! You're right, of course we should go. Gosh, we really are going right up to the wire with this one, aren't we? But I haven't a clue where the tip is, or how to get there. And now, I should be clearing up the twins' tea then helping with their bedtime, and our supper...."

What Tolly had no idea of, or indeed any knowledge about, was that the main reason for Cressida's oncoming feeling of weary depression was that her period was due. This was a dimension of her life that she had not yet felt able to share with him. Completely unaware of it, but as ever sensitive to her apparent anxiety, he continued,

"Don't worry, leave it all to me, I'll find out where it is and work out a way of getting there and back before Pa arrives here at midday tomorrow. You go and do your chores, I'll sort this one out."

"Thanks Tolly, and thanks too for being so positive. Good luck!" and Cressida departed to see to her early evening responsibilities.

Tolly meanwhile left the house again to make some enquiries locally as to the location of the tip, and whether it was on a bus route. He also planned to make a few calls from the village phone box. If they couldn't get there by bus, he decided, he would order a taxi. Cressida would probably be shocked at such extravagance, but time was of the essence, and he could afford it. Sometimes he felt slightly uneasy at the fact that, thanks to his generous father, his financial situation was so much more secure than hers.

When he returned Cressida had just gone upstairs to read to the twins and her parents were together in the kitchen preparing supper.

"Can I help?" he offered. Helen looked up at him with a smile.

"Yes, thank you, Tolly, would you mind laying the table in the dining room. After this morning's delightful breakfast extravaganza I'm sure you know where everything is kept."

"I think I probably do," he agreed, also smiling and remembering the twins' breakfast surprise.

"And after that," put in Graham, "get yourself and us a drink. Gin and tonic for me, a glass of white wine for Helen and whatever you like for yourself. I expect Cressy'll also have a glass of white, she should be down quite soon."

Tolly laid the table and mixed the drinks, taking them to the kitchen for Graham and Helen, but decided to wait for Cressida before he had one himself. Meanwhile he popped into the study, typed out the letter for Canon Wilcox and also found and addressed an envelope for it. When Cressida eventually did come down she looked anxious and tired.

"OK, love?" he asked, putting an arm round her and kissing her cheek.

"Just about. They took ages to settle down and are now demanding you, they want you to say goodnight and tuck them up. Sorry Tolly, I should think you must have had your fill of them by now."

"Not at all, I'll really miss them when I go. Well, I'll miss you all, but most especially you, of course. Back in a minute."

He dashed up the stairs two steps at a time to do as she requested. Firmly he tucked both boys in, ruffled their hair and said good night, turning the main light off and closing the door behind him before returning downstairs to the sitting room, where she was waiting for him.

"Now, my sweetheart, your dad has delegated me to get us a drink. What would you like?"

"Anything to perk me up a bit, Tolly, I must confess I'm now feeling really sad about you going tomorrow. I'm going to miss you so much."

"Oh darling, come here," - and she was in his arms, the tears that she had been keeping under control for the last couple of hours now spilling out as she sobbed her heart out against him. He held her close, stroked her hair and murmured words of love and comfort as she tried to pull herself together.

At last she looked up at him, smiling apologetically. "Sorry Tolly, didn't mean to fall apart. Let's have that drink."

Gently, he wiped her eyes then kissed her on each cheek. Next, he held her in his arms again for a moment, before relaxing them and looking down at her, clasping both her hands in his. Trying to explain her sudden emotional collapse, she said,

"It's been a long day; a good day, but a challenging one, what with Canon Wilcox and all the Lady Marlington stuff, the visit to the charity shop, then that rather unsatisfactory conversation with Angela Penwood. Even sitting in the cathedral today with you, listening to the music and the beautiful singing - and knowing that this time tomorrow you'll be gone - it just all seems to have caught up with me. Sorry for being such a wimp. And thank you for being so kind."

"My love, you are absolutely not a wimp. You're brave, brilliant and generous, full of ideas and solutions, you've been the mainstay of all our explorations and plans. What we both have to do now is to keep remembering that nothing, *nothing*, is going to come between us, whether we are together or apart. We have got trials ahead, but we must and will cope with them, and stay strong, and one day, one day, Cressida, we really will be properly together, I promise."

"Yes, Tolly, we will - and thanks again."

When Helen and Graham came into the room Tolly and Cressida were sitting together on the sofa, sipping their drinks and looking slightly self-conscious. Were there traces of tears on Cressida's cheeks? What had happened? Had they had a row or something?

Before any questions could be asked, Tolly put an arm round Cressida's shoulders and said,

"You'll never guess what we were told today when we popped into the museum to say hello to Penny. Your daughter is going to be famous - well, to botanists at least!"

"What on earth do you mean? What's all this about?" Baffled and curious, Graham and Helen looked at them from one to the other in complete bewilderment. They then both sat down to listen to what the pair had to say.

Cressida began, "Well, Mum, it all goes back to Lou's birthday party and that Ancient Faience necklace. You remember when I first got it, and I told you I'd had a weird fuzzy feeling when I put it on?"

"Yes, I do remember - although when we tried it round your neck again, nothing happened. But didn't we then discuss the faint possibility of there being something peculiar about it, which was one of the reasons why you took it to the museum?"

Tolly and Cressida, talking in turn, now described how Cressida, having again felt that strange sensation while she was at Louise's party, had returned to the museum again to find that Penny too had experienced the same odd effect.

"She'd restrung it for me, for the party, you see, then she'd tried it on herself," Cressida explained. "Actually I was really relieved when she told me it had happened to her too - it meant I wasn't going crazy!"

"Anyway, to cut a long story short," Tolly continued, "in the end Penny had it scientifically examined, and the verdict came back that there were traces of a powerful ancient psychedelic drug on the necklace."

Graham and Helen, listening, were both spellbound! Cressida then said that she had decided to make a gift of the necklace to the museum, where it could be displayed in a protective glass cabinet, to ensure no-one else suffered the odd effects both she and Penny had experienced. Next, Tolly explained that subsequently botanists had been searching worldwide to identify the plant which had secreted the hallucinogen.

"And this is where Cressida comes in again, because all plants have to be classified, whether extant or extinct, so they've named this as yet unidentified ancient plant after your daughter!"

"It's because I found, then bought the necklace, and as far as they were concerned, that made me its official owner," Cressida explained, "So they've decided it should be named after me. It's called '*Nepenthe Archaea Cressidae.*' It all seems a bit unreal really, as so far they haven't yet identified any living specimen of it. In fact it may well be - and probably is - extinct."

"But," put in Tolly, "they're still searching - so watch this space!! Isn't that all utterly extraordinary and unbelievable?"

"Absolutely astonishing!" said Helen, "But why on earth didn't you tell us any of this before?

Cressida knew this was coming, and she had her response planned.

"Well, at first I was in a sort of denial about how it made me feel, thinking that I must have had some sort of a panic attack, but as soon as Penny told me she'd felt it too, we realised that something had to be done. I didn't want to worry you, when we didn't really know for certain, but that was why I gave it to the museum rather than keeping it at home, because I realised it wasn't safe. And once the presence of the drug was confirmed, I was so glad that I had."

"And how did you come in to it all, Tolly?" was the next question, from Graham this time. Cressida looked over at him, knowing that they hadn't rehearsed a response to this. But Tolly, as ever, was clear and composed.

"I too was at Louise's party, and had been introduced to Cressida. We'd clicked immediately, found we had a lot of interests in common, and were getting on really well, talking happily together about all sorts of things, when suddenly she had what I also thought was a panic attack. It was in fact, that necklace, buzzing away again. But she was very scared, and I was shocked and worried about her - anyway that's really the start of how we got together. Later we began to meet up more regularly on the dig, and it was then that she told me in detail the whole saga of the necklace."

"Well, " said Helen, "It seems to me that you've both behaved extremely sensibly over the whole extraordinary experience. And tell me, is all this research you've both been so busy with in any way related to it?"

Tolly and Cressida, in fleeting eye contact, shared simultaneous relief that the story was told, with no recriminations or extra explanations requested. It was now easy for them, taking turns as usual, to explain how the effect of the necklace linked in to the tribulations of poor Lady Marlington and her subsequent sad fate.

"Goodness me, what a fascinating story," said Graham, standing up. "Thank you, both of you, for such an enlightening and intriguing account. But now do let's all go and have something to eat, or that casserole which has been simmering away in the oven all this time will be spoilt! Get a bottle of red from the cupboard, will you, Tolly. I think we need another drink after all those extraordinary revelations! And Cressy, I completely agree with Mum, I too feel that congratulations are in order to the pair of you for dealing with it all so intelligently, and for the conscientious and meticulous research you have undertaken to date."

Later that evening Tolly and Cressida slipped out for a walk together. She was quiet, calm but still subdued, particularly about their oncoming separation. He was feeling very protective about her, much moved by her distress earlier, and was determined to make the final part of their quest as stress-free as he could.

"Now, my love, this is what I've planned for tomorrow morning," he began. She looked at him anxiously, wondering how they could possibly fit in another search when his father was due at lunch time, they had still got paperwork to finish, and Tolly also needed to find time to sort out and pack all his stuff ready to go to France with his father later that day.

"I've booked a taxi to pick us up here early tomorrow morning and take us to the tip, where we can have a good look round - just hear me out, Cressida, and trust me.. " - for she was about to interrupt, alarmed at the extravagance of a taxi.

"I know you're probably shocked at my profligacy in arranging transport, but honestly, Cressida, I can afford it, and it's the easiest and most logical thing to do it this way. The Chilminster tip is right over the other side of town and nowhere near a bus stop. Our driver will take us there, then return to pick us up again soon after 11 o'clock, to bring us back here in good time before Pa arrives. Is that OK?"

"Yes of course, Tolly, and it's really generous of you to be prepared to spend your money in this way..."

"Not generous at all, Cressida - after all, what's money for? We haven't exactly been splashing the cash so far - on trips to the cinema or the theatre, buying luxury goods, eating in fancy restaurants - or buying top hats, fur coats and tiaras, staying in grand hotels, having posh massages, betting on the horses, visiting amusement arcades and casinos....... Oh, darling, it makes me happy to see you smiling again!"

That was because Cressida, listening to this catalogue of possible expenditures, couldn't help laughing; it was all so unlike anything either of them would consider doing!

"OK, Tolly, I agree with your plan, and thank you for sorting it all out. What time have you booked the taxi for?"

"It'll pick us up at 8.30 a.m. I've told your parents, and they agree that it's by far the most practical way to complete our mission. We might not find anything, but at least we'll have tried. And anyway we've made enormous progress in these last few days and will have plenty to write about when we prepare our papers for the exhibition."

Cressida gave a little skip and linked her arm in Tolly's, feeling much more cheerful.

"Thanks Tolly, as usual your kindness has made me feel lots better. And now I suppose we'd better go home and type out the submission for Canon Wilcox, so we can get it into the post as soon as possible."

"Done," said Tolly, explaining how he had slipped into the study and typed it out while waiting for her to come down after reading to the twins. He'd also addressed and stamped the envelope, and had brought it with him ready to post.

"Luckily I had a stamp in my wallet," he said. "I've signed it but haven't yet sealed it, as you need to sign it too. I've brought a pen."

"Oh goodness me, Tolly, you are a star! And to bring a pen too! I'll sign it now, then let's go down to the post-box and pop it in. And after that, before it gets too dark, why don't we walk up past the old windmill to where all the blackberry bushes are. I've got a plastic bag, so we can pick enough for everyone to have with breakfast tomorrow morning."

CHAPTER THIRTY-TWO

Visiting the Tip

Neither Cressida nor Tolly had ever before been to a municipal tip - or rather 'Household Recycling Centre' - which was its official name. It was an absolute hive of activity! They hadn't really known what to expect, but quickly realised what an orderly and well-run establishment it was. It was situated in a large yard with car parking spaces down one side, leaving plenty of room in the middle to unload.

The first thing they saw was a row of huge skips, each of which was labelled; there was one for electrical goods, one for furniture, one for kitchen appliances, one for clothing and so on. A constant flow of cars was arriving, the drivers dumping goods into the skips, then leaving. On the opposite side of the yard, beyond the car parking spaces, was a wall over a deep wide trench into which garden waste could be emptied.

Of most interest to Tolly and Cressida was the far end of the tip. Here, as well as containers full of discarded toys and other bits and pieces, there were large cardboard boxes of printed matter: books, paperwork, magazines and newspapers. It all looked rather daunting. Where on earth were they going to start?

In charge of this section was a young man in overalls who was constantly tidying up stuff as it arrived, swiftly consigning different objects to specific parts of the area. He looked over at the pair of them.

"Hi! Can I help? Are you looking for anything in particular?" he asked.

"Oh yes please," Cressida began, "What we're really interested in is notebooks and papers - not just newspapers but any sort of discarded print or paperwork."

"We're trying to find some lost stuff which we think arrived here about three months ago - it was brought by a couple who were having a clear-out of old bits and pieces which had been in their attic." Tolly explained.

Cressida had a sudden idea. "You might have heard them talking to one another," she said. "They were called Angela and Ralph. It was mainly old paperwork, we think, newspapers, notices - that sort of stuff."

The young man smiled, "Sorry, we get so many people coming in, can't really remember names. But do have a rootle through those big cardboard boxes under the tarpaulin over there. Quite a bit of that stuff's been here since before the summer so you might find what you're looking for."

Tolly and Cressida applied themselves forthwith to what seemed as if it could be a fruitless and thankless task. But they were young, they were keen, and they were together, so they thanked the young man, and began in an optimistic frame of mind.

"We've got about two hours," Tolly said, as he heaved a large dilapidated cardboard box towards him. "Between us we could get through quite a lot of this, I should think."

"And he did say there was still some stuff here from last spring. So - fingers crossed!" Cressida added. Her natural optimism was re-asserting itself as she and Tolly, of one mind as they had been throughout their quest, began their search.

For quite a long time they worked steadily and silently, meticulously making their way through piles of discarded bills, correspondence, invoices, children's scribbles and pictures, and old school exercise books. It was painstaking work. Sometimes it was hard not to get sidetracked, as one or other of them would come across an interesting document or get a glimpse into sad, intriguing or touching elements in people's lives - a school report, a funeral notice, a charity fund-raising initiative, a plea for donations for life-saving treatment, among others.

Then Cressida noticed something, having come to the end of one box and pulling over the next.

"Hey, Tolly, look at this!"

This box had obviously originally contained some sizeable bulky pieces of hardware, and had an address label on the outside: *Penwood, 49 Westdown Lane, Chilminster, Dorset* - the address of Angela and Ralph Penwood! There were a few shabby old fashioned children's books on the top, and below them it looked as if it was crammed full of paper; faded, yellowed paper; handwritten, ancient paper, piles of it.

"Oh my goodness, Cressida. This could be it!"

Kneeling down, they crouched over the box. It was obviously part of the stuff which had been stored in the Penwoods' attic. Before beginning to explore its contents, Tolly made a thorough inspection of all the other boxes in case there were any more with the Penwood address on them. He found one, a slightly smaller box, addressed to Angela Penwood this time.

The two of them stared at one another, excited, relieved and also rather nervous. Would these boxes yield anything of interest or would they just be full of slightly older versions of the sort of junk they had spent their time sorting through so far?

"We've still got about an hour before the taxi's due to come back to pick us up," Tolly said. "Not enough time to go through it all, but perhaps between us we can get some way through the bigger box."

"Oh Tolly - how exciting! It looks promising, doesn't it. Let's see how much we can do now, then maybe take the boxes away with us."

"Yes, we'll do that. But also, Cressida, I suppose there could be more - it's perfectly possible that the Penwoods filled other boxes which didn't have their address...."

" I know, I've been thinking just the same thing. But let's do what we can now, then take these two boxes home, so I can go on with them after you've gone. And if necessary I'll come back here over next weekend and check the other boxes. We can ask the man not to get rid of them till I've come back and been through them all."

"Are you sure, love? That's quite an undertaking on your own - oh if only we had a bit more time."

"My Dad might be able to take me; of course it won't be the same as you and me doing it together, but it'll be better than leaving it unfinished. And in a way, it'll be a help to me, to carry on when you aren't here anymore. I'll be continuing with our joint work, so it will seem a bit as if you're still with me." She looked up at him as she said this, smiling slightly, at which he smiled back and stroked her hair, then they carried on.

By the time the taxi returned they had made a basic search though the contents of the larger box. Much of it, while giving them fascinating glimpses into bygone times, was not relevant to their investigations.

There was, however, quite a bit of material which looked more promising, or at least worthy of further scrutiny, including a few papers actually dating from the late eighteenth century. They also came across some later documents referring to the time when the building was a workhouse.

"So much to find out about," said Cressida as they left the tip, carrying the two Penwood boxes over to the waiting taxi. "I'll send you details of everything I discover, Tolly, although you might have to wait for it till you get back from France."

"I'll try and phone you at least once each day we're over there, so you can update me. And I just might be able to snatch a visit to you after Pa and I are home again and before I go back to Durham. I do need to call in on the Jacobs's, so we could maybe fit in some time together. Or even just an evening, if it's a school day."

They couldn't hold hands or hug one another in the car, being so loaded with the two boxes, but they leaned close together, feeling one another's warmth, and Cressida laid her head on his shoulder.

"Making the most of you, dearest Tolly, while you're here. In a way, school next week will be helpful, choosing my A level subjects and starting in the Sixth Form. And it will be great to see Lou again. No substitute for you, but still lovely."

"Well done, love, for being so positive and pragmatic. I'll be really excited to hear what else you manage to glean from the stuff in those boxes! And of course I'll want to hear all about life in the Sixth Form, your choice of A levels, and what advice about the future might be suggested regarding university and so on. With those impressive GCSE results I should imagine Oxbridge might well be on the cards."

"Wouldn't that be great! One thing I'm determined to do if possible, is to see if there's any way I can do Latin."

"I hope you can, then I can send you some of Catullus's love poems to read! But seriously, Cressida, it's been quite a productive morning, and thanks so much as ever for everything."

"And thanks to you, Tolly, for organising it all and helping me out of my depression. I'll try to stay upbeat and cheerful this afternoon!"

Much later, Cressida lay in bed looking back on the events of the day. Everything had gone to plan after she and Tolly had got back home from the tip. Tolly disappeared upstairs to sort out his stuff and clear his room, ready for leaving with his father later.

Bart arrived soon after midday and was warmly welcomed by her parents. He was in a very cheerful mood, with kindly hugs for Cressida and Tolly, and firm handshakes for Graham and Helen, as well as laughingly expressing regret that he wouldn't have the pleasure of meeting the twins!

They then all headed off to the pub, where there was a dining area in a separate room behind the bar, offering a varied and appetising looking menu. Drinks were ordered, everyone sat down, and a lot of conversation ensued. There were tender memories associated with this pub for both Tolly and Cressida. As they exchanged glances, each knew that the other was remembering that momentous evening weeks ago, when the first green shoots of their love affair began to take root.

Cressida tried her very best to play her part in this atmosphere of friendly conviviality, but was finding it all quite a challenge. She really wasn't feeling at all well.

She and Tolly couldn't squeeze each another's hands as they would have liked to, being at different ends of the table, but as usual they gleaned some of the gist of one another's thoughts through eye contact. Tolly realised that Cressida was finding it all a bit overwhelming; however he also felt protective and supportive of his kind father, who had planned this event. He exerted his natural charm and social skills as best as he could, describing some of the more lighthearted aspects of the past weeks.

It had been, Helen and Graham later agreed, a very pleasant occasion. Bart was good company; easy-going and friendly. Tolly had felt slightly embarrassed but also flattered by Cressida's parents' fulsome praise of him as a house guest as well as his heroic rescue of the twins. This incident was news to his father, who beamed at Tolly with benevolent pride when he heard about it.

Poor Cressida, however, had been all the time secretly coping with strong menstrual cramps. She ate very little, and while both her mother and Tolly knew something wasn't right, they each thought that the separation to come was the cause of it. Perhaps, Tolly hoped, the planned walk up the hill to visit the castle would cheer her up.

Out in the fresh air, Cressida did feel slightly better. She wished she could tell Tolly what was wrong, but her parents and Bart were all around. She also felt a natural timidity about divulging something so intimate and private. Tolly, she knew, would be kind, but he came from a masculine world, and a wholly male household. It was possible, she thought, that he knew nothing about this aspect of a woman's life. So she did her best to be cheerful, linked arms with Tolly, chatted to the adults about the dig, and pointed out the ghostly remains of the trenches, all now grass-covered again and growing back to normality.

Bart was fascinated by it all, and particularly intrigued when they reached the castle. Cressida and Tolly took him round the outside to look through the windows into that large chamber where the twins had trapped themselves. He was also interested in the little kitchen garden, identifying both wild and non-native plants, some of which were still just managing to survive despite decades of neglect.

Cressida and Tolly did manage to drift away from the others for a short time on their own.

"Tell me, Cressida, please - what's the matter?" Tolly asked, stroking her windswept hair away from her face and putting his hands on her shoulders.

"Just sad, Tolly, and not feeling a hundred percent. Sorry - but anyway it's been lovely seeing your father again, and so kind of him to have taken us all out - oh look - they're waving at us - we'd better get back. Oh, dearest Tolly, I do love you so much…"

"As I do you, my sweetheart, as I do you," he responded, kissing her forehead. "Yes. we'd better get back. But look after yourself, darling, and remember, whether absent or present, you have my heart."

"And you have mine, Tolly. Please keep in touch, as much as you can, and - could I just kiss you one more time?".

After that, the remainder of the afternoon suddenly accelerated. Graham departed to collect the twins from school. Tolly loaded his stuff into his father's car. Cressida brought down a couple of her books about the French megaliths and alignments to lend them, then she and her mother stood waving, as the car and its passengers disappeared down the road and out of sight.

"Are you OK, Cressy," Helen said, looking slightly anxiously at her daughter as they turned to go back into the house.

"As OK as I can be," Cressida replied, "But, oh Mummy, I've had the most awful period pains all day. I think I'm just going to lie down upstairs for a bit."

It was such a relief to tell her mother - and with relief came tears.

"You poor darling, how horrid for you - today of all days. Come on, lovey, let's get you more comfortable."

Her mother knew exactly what Cressida needed. She came upstairs with Cressida, ran her a bath, re-made her bed, plumped up the pillows and lit a couple of scented candles.

"Now, you go and have a nice warm bath, sweetheart, then get into bed. I'll bring you up a hot water bottle and a hot drink, and some paracetamol to dull the pain. Do you want to listen to some music?"

Tolly rang the next morning in a state of some anxiety. He'd been worrying about Cressida all night. He and his father had arrived in France after the overnight crossing from Poole to Cherbourg, and as soon as he could he telephoned the Curtis family's number. Helen, touched by his obvious concern, reassured him and explained the situation. Cressida was fine, still asleep but all was well, she said.

As a doctor's son, Tolly did know about the workings of the female body, but it was still a shock to him to realise what was happening to Cressida. He now understood why she had been more tearful and anxious than usual over the last couple of days, and wished that she'd felt she could have told him what was going on.

But this was private feminine business, and as such she must have been too shy to share it with him. Fair enough, he thought, but nonetheless he urgently requested Helen to give Cressida his love and sympathy, and could Helen also let her know that he understood completely why she had kept it to herself. But, he added, as far as he was concerned, Cressida need never feel embarrassed about such things again.

Cressida awoke later that morning just as her mother arrived with a mug of tea for her. She was feeling much more normal, the pain had subsided and she had slept well.

"Oh, thanks Mummy, I feel miles better!"

"I'm so glad, lovey. All the same I suggest you stay put for a bit and I'll bring you some breakfast. The twins are rampaging around downstairs but Dad'll be taking them swimming quite soon so you might as well make the most of a bit of peace and quiet!"

"Oh, that would be really nice. And thanks again Mum, for being so kind, looking after me yesterday. But - did Tolly ring?"

"Yes, about an hour ago. I explained everything and he sends you lots of love. Of course, he'd had no idea what was wrong but he knew something was. And he specifically asked me to tell you that there's no need ever again for you to be embarrassed about it - nice, understanding guy that he is! He's going to ring again later on today. Now, what would you like for breakfast?"

By mid-morning Cressida had got dressed and come downstairs. She'd decided to make a start on properly scrutinising the contents of the boxes she and Tolly had brought home from the tip. It would be wonderful, she thought, if, by the time he rang, she had discovered something significant.

Her father was still out with the twins, so all was quiet and orderly. After a cup of coffee with her mother, Cressida heaved the boxes up to her bedroom one by one, and set to work. She started on the larger box, the one they had briefly looked through at the tip. Meticulously she removed the contents, page by page, and started to pile them in separate heaps, according to context, antiquity (if apparent), and subject matter.

It was laborious but fascinating work. Cressida found herself drawn into long gone legal disputes, criminal trials and feats of bravery and sportsmanship. One of the most antiquated papers was an advertisement for a newly opened fencing academy in the 1760's! Round about that time both Sir Anthony and Lady Marlington had died; somehow it brought the world of the late eighteenth century strangely close. Cressida wished that Tolly could have been with her when she came upon it; she knew he would have been as awestruck as she was.

She then found a tattered, yellowed copy of the Wessex Courant newspaper. It was dated May 1765, a month later than the one they'd seen in the Care Home Museum. It was a four-sided production, on one large folded sheet of paper, with the final back page mainly devoted to advertisements, Cressida felt a rush of anticipation as she scanned the closely written print.

'If only, oh if only Tolly was here too and we could look at it together,' she thought again. But she knew that he would want her to carry on without him, so she went downstairs to the study to see if she could find a magnifying glass to read the columns of printing. And while she was there, the phone rang, She knew, by some sort of instinctive intuition, that it was Tolly calling.

"Hello. Is that you, Tolly?"

"Darling, darling - how wonderful to hear you! How are you feeling? Are you any better? And how did you know it was me?"

His beloved voice, deep and clear, came down the line to her.

"I just knew! And I'm fine, Tolly - much better. And don't worry, it isn't always that bad - it was just unfortunate that it was a particularly painful one on such a special day. It's sweet of you to be so concerned, but all is well now - and after all, it's not an illness! It's just one of the features of being a woman! Anyway, my Mum was wonderful - she looked after me and was really kind - and she also told me she'd spoken to you and explained things. But thanks again, Tolly, for being so sympathetic. Oh, goodness, it's so nice to be talking to you! How are the megaliths?"

"Pretty amazing. I'm taking plenty of photos so you'll be able to see how extraordinary they all are. Very different from Avebury, but just as strange and otherworldly. And your books are proving really useful and informative. But Cressida, I'm afraid I can't talk for much longer, I'm in a phone box and haven't many francs left, and also I need to go and find my Pa. But I'll ring again as soon as I can."

"Of course, Tolly, and please give him my love, and apologise to him from me for not being at my best yesterday. But quickly, before you go, I've started properly going through the big box and have found some intriguing and interesting stuff - including another slightly later Wessex Courant, from the end of May 1765 - which I'm going to try and read - in fact I was just about to look for a magnifying glass when you rang."

"Oh wonderful, that sounds promising! It's so reassuring to know that you're carrying on with it, and you will make sure you keep me up to date with everything you find, won't you? I'll ring again later - probably early evening - and I'll make sure I have plenty of francs this time so we can talk for longer. Meanwhile, so much love to you. I'm thinking of you all the time and sending you lots of kisses - goodbye, my love."

"Bye, dearest Tolly, goodbye." And that was that.

CHAPTER THIRTY-THREE

More Findings

Tolly and his father were staying in a small hotel in Carnac, at the very heart of the '*Région des Mégalithes*' not far from the Quiberon peninsula in southern Brittany. It was a fascinating area, with the famous stone alignments - long lines of menhirs (standing stones) - marching in parallel formation across the landscape. Altogether there were eleven rows of these gigantic granite megaliths, probably contemporary with the Avebury stones, and just as mysterious.

Local tradition said that they had once been a massive army of Roman legionaries, who'd been turned to stone by the wizard Merlin. There was also a Christian take on this story, stating that the menhirs were originally pagan soldiers marching to war against the Pope, and it was he who turned them all to stone.

Tolly and Bart wandered through the Menec alignments - the nearest of three groups of those strange stone avenues. The rows stretched away towards what might have been a stone circle at the end. It was all so enigmatic, so baffling, thought Tolly, wishing that Cressida was by his side to appreciate them with him! He had been reading the books she'd lent him; just leafing through them seemed to bring her a bit closer to him as he turned pages that she had also turned.

Despite Tolly's lovesick yearnings, he was finding this second foray into prehistory fascinating, and he and his father were getting on very well. Bart, a generous and kindly companion, was sympathetic to his son's state of mind. He encouraged Tolly to talk to him about Cressida, as well as the research they had been working on, and was understanding when Tolly told him about her recent sufferings.

"Poor girl. Do give her my love when you call her, won't you?" he said, as the pair of them sat together looking out to sea, and enjoying an al fresco lunch of local seafood together.

"Of course, Pa, and thanks for not minding me talking about her! It does help, you know, to be able to tell you things. One thing I've learnt from Cressida is to be much more open about emotions and feelings - she does seem to have an innate ability to empathise - she's certainly done a lot for me."

"Yes, I can understand that," his father responded, remembering the conversation he and Cressida had been having on the last afternoon of her visit to Salisbury. After a brief pause, he continued,

"I know I failed you after your mother died, Tolly. I realise now that I was on the verge of a breakdown during the aftermath of her death - not really in my right mind at all. I should have reached out to you, but I was so demented with grief and anger that I couldn't. I also know that I shouldn't have sent you away to boarding school - and, as I said to your wise and kindly Cressida, I can't forgive myself for that."

Tolly was moved by this confession. "Oh Pa," he said, putting an arm over his father's shoulders, "It's OK, I'm OK - and I think Mum would be very glad to see you and me spending time together now so companionably. As Cressida would say, we can't change the past, but we can make the best of the present and the future. And I love yours and my relationship now, so please, don't worry about it any more."

"Funnily enough, she did say something very much like that to me," said Bart. "Thank you, Tolly - you're a wonderful son and I can see much of the kindness and gentleness of your mother in you. If you can forgive me I can try to forgive myself."

"Of course I can, Pa. And, although boarding school wasn't a bed of roses, it wasn't all bad, and it did give me an excellent education which has stood me in good stead so far. Please don't be too hard on yourself! "

"Thanks again for all that, Tolly - as I say, you're a good, kind, thoughtful son. And now, what about a coffee and some pudding? Crêpes, gateaux, meringues, sorbets - what d'you fancy? And perhaps a small glass of cognac each - as we won't need to use the car this afternoon."

" Great! That'd be lovely, Pa. Do you want me to get them - oh, here's the garçon........ "Excusez moi.."

In reasonable French Tolly ordered a slice of Breton gateau, with ice cream, for his father, and crêpes with honey and lemon sauce, also with ice cream, for himself. After they'd finished eating, they sat together chatting, sipping their cognac and enjoying the mild September sun.

Meanwhile, across the channel Cressida had returned to her bedroom with the magnifying glass. She laid the ancient, fragile broadsheet carefully on the floor, title side up, and smoothed it out as gently as she could. The front of it, the right hand side of the paper as it lay, looked very similar to the Wessex Courant edition they'd seen at the Care Home Museum, with a large heading followed by three closely packed small print columns. Only the date and the heading were different.

"LAUNCH OF THE NEW FIRST-RATE WARSHIP HMS VICTORY" was the arresting title-page heading. Cressida, using the magnifying glass, couldn't resist reading on, even though it had nothing to with her current research. The account of the launch from Chatham dockyard in May 1765 of this historic ship, which Cressida herself had visited on a school trip to Portsmouth a couple of years ago, was absolutely fascinating.

Reading it, Cressida felt that she really was back in the eighteenth century, almost as if she had been an onlooker on that historic day in May more than two hundred years ago. What an extraordinary twist in her explorations into the past this was! If only Tolly had been with her, so they could marvel together at what felt like a momentous revelation.

She was desperate to share it with someone, and was about to rush downstairs and show the paper to her mother, but she remembered that her father would soon be back home with the twins after swimming. They would all be hungry; and it wouldn't be a good idea to introduce a fragile old newspaper into the mêlée of food and chatter which would shortly ensue. Better to carry on for the time being, she decided.

So she took a quick look at the opposite face of the same side of the sheet, which would have been the back page of the newspaper. It was full of advertisements; examples included corduroy clothing, hats, gloves and hair powder, worsted stockings, tobacco and wigs among the offerings for sale. There were also promotions for patent medicines, all promising miraculous cures for a variety of ailments and 'disorders'.

Cressida then turned the whole broadsheet over and tried to apply herself to the news articles on what would have been the two inside pages. The first half was fairly mundane, focusing on local events. One section had lists of recent births, marriages and deaths, followed by obituaries for some of the notable local individuals recently deceased. There were also reports of events such as cricket matches, cockfighting, theatrical performances and dances. Lower down the page were a few announcements placed by employers requiring employees, plus other notices posted by people in search of employment.

Then, down at the foot of this page, Cressida found an intriguing notice.

"Laundry and kitchen workers are now urgently required for the Chilminster Lunatic Asylum," it read. There was no further information but below was an address for the asylum. It was, of course, the same place that she and Tolly had visited just a few days ago.

Cressida sat back on her feet. She was cramped and stiff from having knelt on the floor for so long searching through the news-sheet. But her thoughts were racing as she pondered this notice. What was the work turnover at these institutions? What sort of people would have applied for these posts? And why were workers urgently needed?

Noise from below indicated the return of her father and the twins. She looked at her watch. To her surprise it was past one o'clock, and she realised that she was very hungry. Perhaps it was time to shelve her research and go and join the rest of her family for lunch. With any luck, she thought, she could grab a sandwich and carry on her explorations as soon as she'd eaten. Reluctantly she carefully laid the paper on her bed and went downstairs.

In the end it wasn't until late afternoon that Cressida was able again to apply herself to her research. After lunch she'd agreed to take the twins to the playground, while her parents worked together in the garden. It wasn't really what she wanted to be doing, but once she was out in the fresh air she found that it was just what she needed.

Running around and kicking a football, pushing the boys on the swings, helping them climb onto the sturdy horizontal branch of one of the trees, which then became an imaginary horse as they both sat astride it, while she jiggled it up and down - all this turned out to be invigorating and fun!

By the time the three of them set off to walk back home, the twins were ready for a bit of television before tea, and Cressida planned to spend the remains of the afternoon once again studying the ancient Wessex Courant newspaper.

Soon she was again completely immersed in antiquated reports about life and times in May 1765. She now focused on the second side of the internal sheet, the third of the four pages of the broadsheet. It too had a local focus to its articles, but the pieces were fewer, longer and more detailed. There was a lengthy report about the effect a period of very unseasonably cold weather had been having on farming, with grim descriptions of frosted crops and dead lambs.

All this was fascinating but challenging work. The tiny newsprint was making her eyes ache despite the help of the magnifying glass. She closed them for a moment, hoping that such intensive scrutiny wasn't damaging them.

Then suddenly, came the bombshell! The final article on the page, several lines long, was headed: "*Continued theft of valuables from Chilminster Lunatic Asylum.*" Her heart started to beat faster - was this the breakthrough? With slightly shaking hands she scanned the brief article though the magnifying glass.

It read thus: "*Valuable jewellery and other items, belonging to a recently deceased noble lady inmate of the Asylum, disappeared some time after her death several weeks ago. Larceny has become all too frequent in recent years, and over time has led to the dismissal of several domestic servants judged to be guilty of theft. A laundry worker and a scullery maid were eventually identified, tried and convicted. They were both summarily dismissed, then committed to the punishment of having their hands burnt with a red-hot iron and branded with a T for thievery."*

At that moment the phone rang. She knew it would be Tolly - he'd said he would ring again in the early evening. She sprang up and dashed downstairs and into the study, grabbed the phone and said breathlessly,

" Hello - is that you, Tolly, is it you?"

" Yes - it's me. You sound agitated. Are you alright?"

" Tolly, Tolly - you won't believe it - I think I've found it!"

" Oh Cressida - tell me, tell me - what have you discovered? I've got plenty of francs this time so you can tell me everything."

Tolly was absolutely fascinated as she filled him in with everything she'd been reading - beginning with the launch of HMS Victory and proceeding all the way through to that final article on the second-last page, which she read out loud to him. He was simultaneously thrilled and shocked.

"Oh my goodness, Cressida, how utterly amazing and exciting. Such a fantastic discovery! You clever, wonderful girl - what tremendous work! Wow! Who would have thought that at last we may be on the verge of solving the mystery of those beads?"

He paused, then continued, more soberly,

"But, you know, I can't help feeling terribly sorry for those two poor souls who were branded. What a brutal punishment - it would probably mean they could never work again. What would have happened to them after that? Maybe we can find out. But anyway, of course it's all wonderful news for us! I want to hug you and hug you and hug you and dance and dance for joy!"

"Me too! I had to keep thinking of you to spur me on, but it's been so interesting, Tolly - I feel almost as if I've been an invisible eavesdropper and witness to the events of 1765. And of course, like you, I'm absolutely horrified by that vicious punishment. But it might actually help us find out who they were - we may be able to trace them through some sort of historic record of criminality and sentencing."

"Yes indeed, good idea. And when I'm back, I can get involved with more reading and researching too. I need to visit the Jacobs's anyway before I go back to Durham, so I could collect the data from you then - I know you'll be back at school but we might be able to snatch a bit of time together. Oh, goodness me, my brilliant, marvellous Cressida! I'm utterly overwhelmed with what you've achieved, we truly are very nearly there!"

"Yes, I think we are, I really do think we are. And d'you know, Tolly, I've been wondering - those papers Penny wants us to write - well, there's so much to say - it could be enough for a book, a book to be written jointly by us both. What do you think?"

"Wow, Cressida, what a great idea! You and me collaborating on a book together; I can't think of anything more appropriate - or more exciting! And it'll be a wonderful way for us to keep in regular, creative and meaningful contact with one another even when we're far apart."

" I know - I'm excited just thinking about it! But now, before we stop talking, I want to hear about how your trip is going. Have you enough francs to tell me what you've been doing, and what you've seen? And is your dad OK? Is he enjoying it all too?"

CHAPTER THIRTY-FOUR

Moving On

"Well done, Cressida. These are extremely impressive results!"

It was the first day of the autumn term, and Miss Marshall, Cressida's headmistress, was conducting brief one-to-one interviews with aspiring A level candidates.

She went on, "With those very high grades for English, History and French I suggest that you continue with them for your A levels. I also think that you should consider working towards applying for both Oxford and Cambridge entrance."

This was really exciting! It was also gratifying to receive such praise from Miss Marshall, who had always seemed rather distant and formidable. However, Cressida had a request.

"Is there any way that I could study Latin? I've been doing a lot of reading over the summer about the ancient world, as well as Homer and Virgil in translation, and I would really love to be able to read some of them in the original."

Miss Marshall was surprised and quite impressed. Even in the days when it was still on the curriculum, she couldn't remember when she had last heard anyone asking to do Latin. However, bearing in mind Cressida's long record of diligence and achievement, she had a possible solution.

"As you know, we no longer teach Latin here. However, I understand that there is still a member of staff at the Boys' School who is a Classics scholar. He mainly teaches Ancient History now, but I believe from time to time he is able to run a Sixth Form Latin class. It would be quite challenging, as you'd have to start from scratch, not having studied it at GCSE. But as the Sixth Forms of our school and the Boys' School do often merge for certain subjects, it may be possible. I'll make some enquiries."

"Oh, thank you so much. I wouldn't mind the hard work. I suppose my French might help quite a bit, mightn't it?"

"Indeed it might. Am I therefore to assume that if possible you'd prefer to take Latin than French?"

"Yes, I can keep up with my French through reading and French films and going to France - and also I could continue going to the French Conversation Circle with Mme Cléret after school on Tuesdays."

"That's true - of course you could. Very well, Cressida. I'll see what can be arranged. Now off you go and send in the next person, please."

"Thank you, Miss Marshall," and Cressida left the office, feeling excited and optimistic about her chances.

At break she and Louise rushed to their usual place to catch up with one another. Lou's family had only returned from London the previous day so they hadn't had a chance to chat until now.

"I did try ringing you yesterday evening - but it was engaged for ages," said Louise. Cressida felt slightly abashed.

"It was Tolly - he's still in France till Wednesday but he tends to ring me in the early evening - sorry Lou, he and I always seem to have so much to talk about."

"I thought that was probably it - goodness me, he must be getting through his cash, ringing from France! So it's still true love, Cressy?"

Cressida nodded, "More than ever, Lou. I'll tell you all soon, but first I want to know about you. How was London, did you have fun? And how is Duncan getting on? And, what did the Marshmallow have to say when she saw you? She was actually pretty human with me, and promised to find out how I can do Latin."

"Yes, she was really nice. But Cressy, I don't think we'll be able to be in the same class any more, because I've decided to concentrate on sciences. In fact, what I want to do in the end is to study medicine.

"I talked to my parents a lot about it while we were away, and actually visited a couple of hospitals which were running open days for aspiring students. It was really fascinating! I've been vaguely thinking about it for ages, but going to those open days really crystalised it. I'm now certain that it's the right career choice for me."

"Oh, goodness, Lou, I never realised any of this. I suppose I've been too wrapped up in my own concerns; I'm so sorry. And I'll also really miss you in class. Actually I'm now feeling a bit ashamed of myself, obsessing about Latin, yearning for Tolly, dreaming about our researches and our future together - while you've been planning to enter a career which will truly benefit humanity and make people's lives better. You are caring and kind and clever - I think you'll make a brilliant doctor."

"Thanks Cressy - and don't beat yourself up - I only started considering it seriously quite recently. But the more I thought about it, the more sure I became that this was what I wanted. After all, it does sort of run in the family, doesn't it? But I don't want to follow directly in my Dad's footsteps - my intention is to be a hospital doctor."

Louise's father was a GP, and her mother a child-psychologist. Both were capable, thoughtful and kind. Cressida remembered

Tolly's account of the whole family's sensitivity and support for him after his mother's death, and recognised too, that Lou had found her true vocation. She was filled with renewed admiration and respect for this much-loved, generous, clever and practical good friend.

They went on talking about friends and family: Duncan's first concert, Charlie's current girlfriend, Cressida's twin brothers' oncoming eighth birthday in November, and Tolly's twentieth only a few weeks away. Cressida didn't say much about the research she and Tolly were working on but she did tell Louise about the proposed exhibition at the museum to showcase the necklace and its extraordinary history.

She was also able at last to fill Louise in about the mysterious hallucinogen which had had such a profound effect on the events of the last few months. This was a complete revelation to Lou, but also a relief. Now she appreciated why Cressy had felt the need to be so secretive.

The pair of them then arranged to go together to the museum's oncoming exhibition about the finds from the Troycombe Castle dig, when it opened. Time flew as they carried on talking. In the end Louise looked at her watch and jumped up.

"Nearly the end of break." she said. "But why don't you come over to ours sometime for a sleepover. We've only just scratched the surface – there's so much more to talk about! And we're also expecting a visit from Tolly soon, before he heads off back up north. Oh, there we go, that's the bell."

They both dashed back inside for the rest of the school day. But there was still plenty that they needed to chat about, so instead of getting the bus after school, they ambled together through town towards Lou's home, so as to have a bit more time catching up with one another.

Somehow, talking to her closest friend, sharing news about their summer experiences, as well as knowing that Tolly was also almost a surrogate member of Lou's family, was a very comforting thought for Cressida. His departure for Durham in a few weeks' time, while inevitable, somehow now didn't seem quite as devastating as it had done previously.

Discussing their future plans made both girls realise what an enriching and maturing experience the summer had been for them both. Now, as they entered the Sixth Form, it felt as if they really were on the brink of the crucial next stage of their lives.

They hugged one another before Louise headed for home and Cressida walked to the nearest bus stop.

" 'Bye Cressy, see you tomorrow."

" 'Bye Lou, give my love to your family."

A couple of days later Tolly was home again. He and his father had taken the Wednesday morning sailing from Cherbourg to Poole and driven straight back to Salisbury. Early the following evening, after Cressida got home from school, he rang.

"Hello my darling - here I am back in the UK."

"Oh Tolly, it's always so good to hear your lovely voice! Tell me everything you've been doing, I've been imagining the two of you scrambling around the dolmens and exploring the alignments .... I hope the books I lent you were helpful?"

"They really were, thanks, Cressida. You and I will definitely have to go there together one day. And I'm sending you some photographs so you can actually visualise the things we saw. So - where do I start......?"

For the next half hour Cressida listened, fascinated, as Tolly described his and his father's experiences, the tombs - dolmens - that they had visited, the lines of alignments and the spectacular broken menhir - *'Le Grand Menhir Brisé'* - it was called, and was thought to have been the largest megalith in the world. He also regaled her with descriptions of delicious meals and long companionable conversations with his father.

"Honestly, Cressida, he really does seem to have turned a corner. He was on great form and we got on so well. The whole trip was a real success."

"I'm so glad, Tolly - with any luck it'll mean you won't need to worry quite so much about him when you go back to Durham. Anyway, compared to all that, I've been having a pretty uneventful time - but there's one thing that I'm really thrilled about. My headmistress was very complimentary about my results, and she's arranged for me to learn Latin! I'll have to go over to the Boys' School for it, three times a week, but that's fine as it's in the town centre, not far from the cathedral. Apart from that I haven't had much time to carry on going through the boxes since term started - maybe next weekend..."

"That's brilliant news about Latin!" said Tolly; "You wanted it so much, didn't you? And regarding those boxes - well, you've already done so much - now somehow I must devise a way to come over so we can work on them together. I'm definitely going to spend a few days with the Jacobs's soon - is there any possibility that you could get over there sometime? Oh, Cressida - I'm just longing to see you again!"

"Me too, Tolly, me too. Actually Lou has suggested I go over there soon for a sleepover - perhaps we can work things out so we coincide there. Or I suppose if we can't meet up I could parcel up some of the stuff and send it to you in Salisbury."

"Oh, no, I wouldn't expect you to do that! How about, Cressida, if I came to you over the weekend - say on Saturday - the day after tomorrow. As I said, I'm planning to spend a bit of time with the

Jacobs's next week, so if they were to agree to me going there earlier, I could come over to you on Saturday from their house, and if necessary also on Sunday. I would then be back with them properly for a few days after that. Then I'd go home for a week with my Pa - from about the twenty-first till the twenty-eighth, before heading off to Durham a day later."

"It sounds possible, Tolly, but an awful lot of to-ing and fro-ing for you. Having said that, of course it would be heavenly if you came over at the weekend, and we just might be able to complete our work! If necessary, we'd also have time for another visit to the tip on the Sunday. Or, here's a better idea - how about if I ask Mum and Dad if you can stay with *us*, for tomorrow night and Saturday night, then you could go on to the Jacobs's on Sunday evening. The twins would be around of course, but they go swimming on Saturday mornings, and I think they're going to a friend's birthday party that afternoon. I can also probably keep them out of your way the next day if need be! Needless to say, they'd be absolutely thrilled to have you back!"

"Yes, oh yes, Cressida - that might work, and of course it would be amazing to be staying at yours again for the final stretch of our research together. Might you be able to ask your parents this evening, and let me know? Then if I can't stay, I'll ask Stella if I can go to them at the weekend and come over to you each day - so we might still be able to finish our investigations."

Later, having helped both with the twins' bed time and preparing the evening meal, Cressida broached the idea of another visit from Tolly, from Friday evening till Sunday evening. It would be their final time together before he went back to Durham, she said, and they still had a bit more research to complete. She clasped her hands together imploringly.

"Please, Mummy, please! We'll behave ourselves, I promise, but we're so very nearly finished with our research, and although I did a lot on my own last weekend it's much, much better if we work together. And after that we won't be seeing each other for weeks and weeks."

"What about homework?" Helen asked, "Now you're in the Sixth Form there's bound to be quite a lot more of that."

"Yes, I know - and I'll fit it in, I promise, Mummy. Actually, he can probably give me a hand with some of it. Oh please..."

Helen had no reason really to object to this request; after all, Tolly had proved himself to be a helpful and charming guest on his previous visit. She also remembered that the upstairs attic bedroom had been empty since Tolly was last there, so really all that needed to be done was to tidy up the bed and check the towels and toiletries.

"OK, Cressy, he can come, as long as you promise to get your homework done. I do understand, lovey, that you both want to fit in as much time together as you can before he goes back to college, and luckily we all like him very much, so give him a call and tell him he'll be welcome. And you'd better go up to the attic and straighten things up there."

Cressida, overjoyed, gave her mother a hug.

"Thanks, Mummy, thanks so much - you really are the best mother in the world! I'll go up there now and sort it all out. And then I'll ring Tolly with the good news."

Tolly had left the attic very neat and tidy so there wasn't all that much to be done. Cressida put a clean towel and a new cake of soap in the little bathroom, and couldn't resist lying for a few moments on the bed, breathing in what she felt to be the spirit of Tolly and visualising him back there, before remaking the bed. She then rushed to the phone.

"It's fine, Tolly. Mum says you can come and stay again! Isn't that fantastic? So if you get here tomorrow evening we'll have the whole of Saturday and nearly all of Sunday."

"Wonderful, Cressida, perfect! What a kind mother you have! Can't wait to see you again!"

Conversation then became less practical and more romantic as they shared tender thoughts and loving reflections with one another before duty called for them both. Cressida addressed herself to her homework, then brought the boxes down from her bedroom and put them in the study, where her parents had agreed she and Tolly could work together. At his home Tolly set about unpacking and re-packing, sorting out his clothes and loading the washing machine with his and his father's laundry.

After school the next day there was an early and totally unexpected surprise for Cressida. Louise had arranged to meet up with her mother for some shopping together, so Cressida set off alone to get her bus.

She'd come out of the school gates and was walking down into town, towards the High Street in the direction of the bus stop. Then suddenly, to her amazement and joy, Tolly emerged from just around a corner. She wasn't expecting him till that evening, so was simultaneously thrilled and overwhelmed.

"Tolly, Tolly - what are you doing here so early .. how lovely - oh Tolly!" she stammered as they fell into each other's arms. To be together again, to feel the closeness of his firm body and see his much loved face again in the flesh, was the most unexpected delight!

"Oh Cressida – oh, I've missed you so much!" he responded, equally fervently, bending to kiss her.

Then, as they both began to surface from this sudden ardent encounter, Cressida realised that it wasn't the best place to be exchanging hugs and kisses. Other people, including some girls from school, would probably be around. Luckily, now that she was in the Sixth Form she no longer had to wear school uniform, but it was still possible she might be recognised. Had any members of staff also been nearby, and seen them?

"We'd better get further down towards the town centre before I get into trouble for inappropriate behaviour," she said. "But dearest Tolly, what a brilliant and heavenly surprise! How come you're here so early?"

"Well, as soon as I woke up this morning I just knew I needed to see you as soon as I could! I'd been terribly worried about you when you were feeling so awful last Friday, and though of course now I know you're fine, and we've talked, and it's nothing to worry about, I still really wanted to see you in the flesh. So I thought I'd get here early and catch you after school. I was hoping maybe we could have a bit of time on our own together, here in Chilminster before going on to your home."

What Tolly didn't divulge was the fearful and intense panic he had felt that day when Cressida was unwell. Not far below the surface of the renewed optimism and happiness of his life now, there was still a lurking innate anxiety. He had seen his mother declining and dying. He remembered her in the last weeks of her life, her thick dark curls, so like his, all gone, her body emaciated, and her face gaunt and pale. He remembered too how he'd been almost afraid to hug her, she had become so frail and weak.

The terrifying thought that Cressida too might be terminally ill was one which he'd tried to rationalise and dismiss, but it wasn't really until he had spoken to her mother on the phone and heard the reason for her temporary malaise, that he could entirely shed his fears.

He decided not to mention any of this, as the pair of them rejoiced together in their happy reunion. One day, Tolly thought, he would be able fully to share with Cressida the anguish he had suffered during that terrible time when his mother was dying. For now, he was back, joyfully reunited with this most beloved girl.

Cressida went on, "I can't believe it - how amazing and romantic that was, thank you, dearest Tolly - how lucky am I! But I promised Mum that I'd do my homework before you came - could you bear it if we went to a café somewhere, so I can look over what I need to do. Actually, it's not much - I can do my English reading on the bus, but I've also got a bit of Latin - I've had my first Latin classes this week. Pretty simple stuff, mainly a few first declension verbs."

"Yes of course. I'll tell you what - why don't we go and have a cup of tea somewhere and I can help you with that? After all, now we both know about 'Amo, Amare, Amavi, Amatum', don't we? Then, if you like, I'll see you onto the bus, and get a later one myself, so you can do your English before I arrive."

"What a good idea! I'd really enjoy doing some Latin with you! I must say, when the lessons started with words meaning love, I was thrilled - it seemed like a good omen! And much as it would be nice for us to travel back home together, it *is* a better idea for you to wait for a bit, so I can do my chores and the rest of my homework. Mum won't worry if I'm slightly late getting home, she knows Lou and I often dawdle our way through town."

All of that worked well, so by the time Tolly arrived at the Curtis's home Cressida had finished her homework, read to the twins and was laying the table for supper. She'd told her mother about Tolly's unexpected early arrival, how he'd met her from school, how they'd looked at her Latin together, and how he'd agreed to come to Troycombe on a later bus so she could complete the rest of her homework beforehand. Helen couldn't help but be impressed by her daughter's diligence and Tolly's patience. For obvious reasons Cressida had not included an account of their passionate embraces and loving kisses.

CHAPTER THIRTY-FIVE

Searching for Final Evidence

After supper they retired to the study to search for what they hoped might be the final pieces in the jigsaw of their investigations. First, Cressida showed Tolly the Wessex Courant broadsheet which had yielded such interesting information last weekend. As she had expected, he was awed by the account of the launch of HMS Victory.

"I completely understand just how you must have felt," he said, turning to her after reading the account of that pivotal event.

"Goodness me, Cressida, when one thinks of the part that the Victory was to play a few decades later - the Battle of the Nile, the Napoleonic Wars, the death of Nelson... and here we are, as it were, sort of experiencing its very beginnings!"

Cressida nodded, "Yes, I know! And I knew you'd get it - it's pretty mind-blowing isn't it? And of course, it was history in the making; unknown as yet to them, but a crucial part of our country's past to us. Anyway, now have a look at the inside of the paper - if we turn it over, you 'll see at the foot of the first half there's a piece about needing more workers at the Asylum, then on the next half there's that crucial article about thefts."

Tolly was very soon up to date with her findings, then they carried on searching painstakingly through the remaining material in the box. Thanks to Cressida's careful sorting out and detailed examination of the content in that first box, there was only about a quarter left to explore.

It was hard, however, not to be continually sidetracked by many of the articles they came across. It wasn't all as ancient as the Wessex Courant, but to these two young historians, the glimpses they were getting into past lives and long gone events were proving irresistible. They kept stopping to read bits and pieces aloud to one another - both of them continually enthralled and fascinated, as they shared these strange fragmented forays into the past.

"It's possible that we may not need to go back to the tip, since there seems to be so much info in the stuff we've already got," Tolly observed.

He paused, pushing his fingers through his hair as he considered the next steps. They had now reached the end of the first box.

"Still at it, you two? It's nearly eleven o'clock, you know. Don't you think it might be time to call it a day?"

In the doorway stood Graham, Cressida's father.

"Is it really, Dad? We must've completely lost track of the time. It's all so fascinating..."

"Sorry - we've been centuries away," added Tolly, standing up and stretching.

"You'll have plenty of time tomorrow - come on, time to shut up shop for tonight," Graham said.

"Yes, OK Dad, of course we will. Tolly, I'll just come up with you to your bedroom to make sure you've got everything you need."

"Not too long, Cressida, and be as quiet as you can. We don't want the twins waking up."

It had been a good start, they both agreed. After a last hug and kiss they separated, each secretly wishing that they could spend the night together, but at the same time knowing that this wouldn't be possible for a long time.

Tolly was awoken the next morning by the sound of eager feet on the landing below his attic. 'The twins', he thought with a slight smile, and got out of bed quickly to get to the bathroom in case they were planning to pay him a visit. They were! Excited footsteps bounded up the stairs, and just as he regained his bed and pulled the duvet back over himself, the door flew open and in they rushed.

"Tolly, Tolly, you've come back! Hello Tolly, hello!" They launched themselves onto his bed, landing on his legs and stomach.

"Hey, hey chaps - careful - don't squash me," he pleaded, trying to shift himself into a more comfortable position. At nearly eight years old they were no lightweights. A good thing he'd gone to the loo when he did, Tolly thought, as Mikey settled himself down right over his bladder. To his relief they then did move themselves, one to either side of him. It was quite a narrow bed so a bit of a squeeze, but better than having them actually sitting on top of him. Next they submitted him to a barrage of questions - how long was he staying, would he take them to the park to play football, could he come swimming with them this morning, was he coming to their eighth birthday party in November...?

Tolly tried to answer everything as clearly and honestly as he could, explaining that he and Cressida had important research to do over the weekend. However he promised that they'd take the boys to the park one afternoon, once they had finished their work. Tolly also found himself half-agreeing to come to their birthday party, circumstances permitting, thinking to himself that it was several weeks away, so no need for much planning at the moment.

The little boys chatted away happily, thrilled to be with him, and telling him about everything they'd been doing in and out of school over the last few days. Cressida, waking up to hear those two shrill voices and the occasional deep toned interjection from Tolly, swiftly got out of bed, pulled on her dressing gown and headed up the attic stairs herself.

"What on earth are you two doing up here? Poor Tolly - he looks completely squashed between the pair of you. Anyway, it's time you got dressed and cleaned your teeth - you'll see Tolly later, Go on - off you go." As they scampered away she turned to him,

"I'm so sorry - did they wake you up? Are you OK, Tolly?"

"Yes, fine, if just a bit crushed! I'm always rather flattered by their devotion! They've asked me to their birthday party in November, and they want us to take them to the park sometime this weekend! I said we would, if we get through our work in time! Anyway, love, how are you? Do I get a morning kiss?"

"Of course, darling Tolly, of course!"

After that she disappeared, to get dressed herself and to help with preparing breakfast, very much aware that her parents wouldn't approve of her spending too much time upstairs with Tolly while he was still in bed and she was in her nightwear.

By 9.30 they were back at work. When they'd finished the first box, Tolly suggested they list the contents before starting on the second one. To create a logical archive, he said, they should try as far as possible to classify the findings alphabetically with regard to date and context.

"So if we have to go back and check anything we have it easily to hand."

Cressida was impressed. She'd been punctilious and thorough when working alone but hadn't thought of creating an index.

A couple of hours later, Helen appeared, offering coffee. Nothing could have been more welcome! It was immersive, fascinating work, but, with the study being quite a small room, they were both stiff and cramped, and had also become rather ink-stained by much of the antique printed material they'd been handling. They followed her to the kitchen.

Helen, as an archivist, was genuinely interested in their research, and had some useful suggestions. She advised them to photocopy the more fragile documents and suggested that the May 1765 Wessex Courant newspaper should be given to the museum. It was, she said, a valuable, and possibly unique example of historical journalism, particularly due to that eye-witness cover-story about the launch of the HMS Victory. There was also a lot of other content which was of notable local interest.

"I think the various articles about people's lives and recreations, the world of work, from farming to manufacture to commerce, as well as all those glimpses into everyday life, are of huge significance. I could see them being used in schools, for instance - so much more evocative than the stuff you get in a lot of school history books."

"Really, Mum? That's amazing."

Cressida was intrigued. It was good to know that the work they were doing could have a useful function beyond their own research.

"So, although we haven't yet found the crucial link we're looking for, all this won't have been in vain. That's very encouraging," added Tolly, "Thanks, Helen - it's reassuring that you think what we're doing is worthwhile."

"Very much so, Tolly. And now I have a suggestion for you both. Take a break for a few hours. Go for a good walk, get some fresh air, re-charge your batteries! Dad and the twins will be back from swimming quite soon and wanting lunch, so all will be noise and confusion here! I've made you a picnic so you can both have a bit of freedom and privacy, rather than being taken over by those two little boys. And by the time you get back they'll be at their friend's party, so you'll be able to get on with your work in peace."

Cressida was touched. "Oh, Mum," she said, "That's so lovely and thoughtful of you, what a great idea! And I'm sure it's just what we need, a bit of a break!"

"Just what we need, as Cressida says; thanks so much. And the sun is shining - come on, let's make the most of it!"

Within a few minutes the two of them had left the house, with the picnic and a rug in Tolly's rucksack on his back.

"How very kind of your mother," Tolly said. "And she's right. I always feel that it's impossible to come back from a walk and not feel better than one did when setting out! So where are we going, Cressida ?"

" I think we'll climb the hill past the old windmill and reach the downland higher up. From there we can actually get onto part of the Wessex Ridgeway, and there are amazing views in all directions. Oh, Tolly, how lovely it is to be with you, just us two, out in the countryside.... " She felt for his hand and held it briefly against her cheek. He then closed it over hers as they made for the hills, both feeling a bit like children who had been let out of school early.

It was a stiffish climb, taking them nearly three-quarters of an hour. But they were both young and fit, and Cressida knew all the paths through the fields and the way to the track which zig-zagged up the hill to join up with part of the ancient Wessex Ridgeway at the top.

When they arrived there, invigorated and energised, they stopped to look at the spectacular panorama spread out on both sides. Cressida pointed out Troycombe village far down in the valley below, surrounded by a patchwork of fields and farms, woodlands, streams and water meadows. There wasn't a breath of wind or a hint of mist in the clear air.

"And look, Tolly, there, can you see - there's our castle." Tolly stood behind her, his hands on her shoulders, as the two of them gazed down at the crenellated dark mass on its hill - reminding them both of so many memories forged during that enchanted summer.

"We can't see the sea, but it's to the left, due south, miles further down below all this farmland and woodland." Cressida indicated the direction.

They then turned to face the other side: "Towards your Wiltshire countryside, Tolly," said Cressida.

"Oh, look - it's fascinating, Cressida - you can see far beyond the hilly landscape to where it begins to flatten out at the start of Salisbury Plain. It's just a misty purplish-green line in the far distance, d'you see?"

They found a little dell by an outcrop of trees just below the crest of the ridge on the Wiltshire side, which was where they spread out the rug. They were both now ready for lunch. Unpacking the picnic that Helen had provided, they found a substantial meal: a variety of sandwiches, crisps, a bag of salad, some fruit and a few little cakes - and as well as a bottle of water she had included a half-bottle of rosé wine. There were also paper picnic plates and even a couple of plastic wine goblets.

"Goodness me," said Tolly "What a banquet! I think we need to open that wine and toast your mother! It's like being on holiday!"

"Good old Mum, she's really done us proud. Do we need a corkscrew?"

"No, it's a screw-top. Here we go," Tolly opened the wine and poured it into the two goblets while Cressida opened the bag of crisps and emptied it onto one of the plates.

"To Mum," "To Helen." "And now," said Tolly, "to us and to the future."

It was a truly carefree interlude. They sat together, eating and drinking while reminiscing about the past few months. When they'd finished lunch they lay down on the rug facing one another, relaxed and contented, and carried on chatting. Cressida confessed to Tolly how when she'd gone up to his bedroom to freshen it up again ready for him, she had lain down for a few moments on the bed, to re-envisage him.

"Oh, that's amazing, Cressida," Tolly exclaimed, enchanted by this revelation, "I did just the same - after you'd been staying with us in Salisbury. When I came back from taking you to the station I went upstairs, to tidy things up and strip the bed... but first I lay down where you had been and tried to conjure up the essence of you!"

"We really are a pair of hopeless cases, aren't we, Tolly? Before I met you I often used to think about boyfriends, and whether I would ever have one - and I wondered how many there might be before I had a proper long-term relationship. Now here I am, with you, the first boy I've ever been with, the one I love with all my heart, the only one I ever want to be with. But what about you, Tolly? Surely there must have been other girls you fancied before you met me?"

"You'd think so, wouldn't you, considering I'm nearly twenty. But no, there's never been anyone. I suppose it's mainly because of my state of mind as Mum was declining, then afterwards trying to cope after she'd gone. I couldn't look outwards at all, but just had to concentrate on keeping my head above water. Also, as I told you before, I kept myself going by secretly fantasising about the girl of my dreams - who turned out to be you! So I'm as inexperienced as you are. I've never even kissed another girl - apart from friendly kisses to the likes of Lou and her mum. When I kissed you on your birthday, it was the first time I'd given a proper, long, deep kiss. I'd wanted to kiss you like that for some time, but I was quite nervous about it - it felt wonderful to have got it right!"

Cressida moved closer to him, cheek to cheek, and reached for his hand.

"It was a beautiful, magical kiss, Tolly, and my first one too. But I do feel so sorry when I think of what you went through, and it makes me both overwhelmed and humble to know how our falling in love with one another is helping to heal some of that grief. And for a pair of innocents we aren't doing too badly, are we? We now have plenty of wonderful kisses and cuddles! And I know we'll have to wait for quite a time till we can entirely fulfil our relationship but I think we'll probably do fine when that time comes. We're learning together about the art of love."

"We are, sweetheart. Of course, I'm longing to make love with you. but the sensible side of me says that we must wait. What we both have together now is much too precious to jeopardise by doing it too soon, while you're still at school and living with your family. They've all been so good to me, and I have far too much respect for your parents to take advantage of their trust. So we have to be content for the moment with our wonderful kisses and cuddles."

"Dearest Tolly, I understand, and of course you're right - what we've got now is so very special, we have to hang on to that and not let our desires get the better of us. I long for it too, but I agree with your principles over this - I can wait! Maybe when I'm eighteen .. oh my God, what's that!"

A large dog had bounded up to them and was sniffing around the bag containing the remains of their picnic. They both leapt up, Tolly grabbing the picnic bag and cramming it into his rucksack and Cressida picking up the rug they had been lying on.

The dog was friendly and harmless. It stood wagging its tail and looking at them with dark beseeching eyes.

"He's rather a lovely dog," Cressida said, patting him.

"Hello old chap - what's happened your owner, I wonder," Tolly added, trying to get a look at the dog's collar to see if he had an identification disc. All of a sudden they heard shouting.

"Morris! Morris! Come back, you bad dog, come here!"

Down below, on the north face of the ridge, they could see a man and woman struggling up the slope. Tolly grasped Morris's collar and they waited, Tolly still hanging on to the dog, till the couple reached them.

"Oh, thanks so much! You bad boy, Morris, running away like that!" said the woman, while the man fastened Morris's lead, saying, "He's a bit of a devil for dashing off - he's young and we haven't had him long. Our old dog died recently, so we're all still getting to know each other."

"That's OK, he's a nice friendly fellow isn't he?" said Tolly with a smile.

"Yes, he's got a lovely nature - but he's a bit too keen on making a bid for freedom! Lucky that you were here - he could have gone charging all the way down the other side and we might have lost him. Thanks again," the man responded.

The three of them - man, woman and dog - then left to continue walking along the ridge. Soon afterwards Tolly and Cressida decided that they too should be on the move. It was time they headed back home to finish their work, so they packed up again and set off down the slope. The descent was much faster than the upward climb had been; each gripped the other's hand as they ran downhill, and twenty minutes later they were back again on the undulating downland. As they ran, both remembered that first exhilarating run they'd done together down the Castle Hill, and how their relationship had begun to develop.

As they got their breath back Cressida smiled and looked at Tolly, saying,

"I was so thrilled then, when you grabbed my hand as we ran down to the village, and then you kept on holding it after we got to the end....." "... and I said I was so glad I'd found you again and was absolutely elated when you agreed," Tolly added.

"Even though it's only been a few months, already we have lots of really special memories," Cressida said as they continued towards the village.

The final field, part of the farmland behind the village, was now full of sheep. They heard a chorus of gentle bleating as they approached.

"I think we'd better walk round the edge so as not to upset them," Cressida advised.

They were just about to climb the stile into the field when suddenly, at breakneck speed, Morris the dog reappeared hurtling down the slope, and leapt right over the hedge into the field of sheep. The peaceful bleating turned into a cacophony of alarm as he rushed though the flock, scattering them far and wide.

"Oh no!" exclaimed Tolly, "Here, take the bag, Cressida," He vaulted over the stile and sprinted into the field to try and grab the dog.

Cressida climbed over the stile herself, put the rucksack down, and, also moving quickly, prepared to get hold of Morris if he came anywhere near. It was a tense few minutes. The sheep were becoming increasingly panic-stricken, but it was all over fairly quickly when Tolly, who'd noticed that the lead was trailing behind the dog, managed to jump onto it and stop him in his tracks. Quickly, Tolly then seized the lead and halted the chase, bringing Morris back over to Cressida, who'd returned to the stile to pick up the rucksack.

"I think we ought to wait here for a few moments, till the sheep have calmed down," he said, panting slightly as he sat on the step of the stile.

" Phew, that could have been catastrophic! Thank goodness you stopped him before he got hold of any of them," Cressida said, "Luckily I think it's the wrong time of year for them to be in lamb, lucky too that the farmer doesn't seem to be around. We need to get this naughty chap back to his owners as soon as possible; I wonder who and where they are."

Earlier, Tolly had been looking for Morris's identity disc after that first sudden arrival when they were on the top of the ridge, but the dog's owners had reached them before he found it. Now once again he bent down to feel around Morris's collar. The dog, seeming somehow to know that he had transgressed, sat passively with his tongue hanging out, humbly watching them with his limpid brown eyes.

Cressida couldn't help stroking him. "Ah, he's a very sweet dog. I don't think he actually wanted to harm them, it was just the thrill of the chase, wasn't it, Morris? "

"Oh my goodness, Cressida," Tolly said suddenly, "This is the name and address of his owners: Penwood, 49 Westdown Lane, Chilminster. It looks as if there's also the remains of a phone number as well, but it's almost completely rubbed off."

CHAPTER THIRTY-SIX

A Conclusion

They stood staring at one another. The Penwoods - the couple they had telephoned about that blue skirt from the charity shop, and whose boxes of long forgotten and discarded stuff they had since been examining. What a strange coincidence!

"Well, at least we know how to get in touch with them," said Tolly. "Not just with this address - but we both took their phone number, didn't we? Maybe we should go down to the village phone box and call them."

"But they're probably still out on the hills, frantically looking for Morris. Shouldn't we hang around for a bit in case they come down?"

"I suppose so, but it's rather a nuisance, isn't it. We need to get back soonish or your mum will wonder where we are - it's nearly two hours since we left. Oh Morris, what a muddle you've landed us in!" Tolly patted the dog, and smiled wryly at Cressida. It really was something of a dilemma.

Cressida was weighing up options.

"Obviously we must contact the owners, but we're going to have to hang onto him till we get through to them - and that could be hours. There's no point in us going back up to the top, we've got no idea where they'll be. So what I think we should do, is take him back home with us, and keep on trying to get hold of them on the phone. I did write the number down but it's not in my pocket, have you got it?

I think I was wearing a skirt when we went to the charity shop; maybe it's at home in there."

Tolly felt around in both his side and back pockets. He also often slipped bits and pieces into his wallet or his diary for safekeeping, but equally it could be in the back pocket of the jeans he'd been wearing the day they'd been to the charity shop. They were also the jeans he'd later taken to France and which he'd put in the washing machine at home in Salisbury, before coming back to Chilminster and Troycombe.

"Oh dear, Cressida - no sign of it I'm afraid. It's not in my wallet either, and I have an awful feeling that it may have gone into the wash with my other jeans after Pa and I got back from France. I'm so sorry."

"No matter really, Tolly, I'll be able to find it at home. And in any case, we have their name and address so we'll definitely get hold of them somehow - we probably just need to look in the phone book. But, Tolly, I've been thinking, all this could actually be beneficial for our research. By rescuing their dog and then saving the sheep from a possible dog attack, we've gained a bit of an advantage....."

"You mean they might be more willing to talk to us about any possible historic links to the Chilminster Asylum, in gratitude to us for finding the dog? Yes, I was just thinking along those lines too, but wondered if it was a bit unscrupulous."

"I know. Anyway, at the moment we've got no real alternative other than taking him home with us, then keeping on trying to contact them. I wonder what Mum'll say when we arrive; luckily he's a very nice natured dog! The twins would be really excited - but it's probably just as well that they are out for the afternoon, at Sammy's birthday party."

Morris, bored by this interlude of inactivity, was lying down taking a nap. He sprang up joyfully as they got going again, and soon the three of them were heading back into Troycombe and the Curtis family home. They'd agreed that Cressida would go on ahead to warn her mother about the unexpected canine visitor, and that Tolly would follow, taking Morris around the back of the house and into the garden.

Helen was now on her own at home, as Graham, after bringing the twins home from swimming for a quick lunch, had then dropped them at their friend's party before heading off for a planned meeting with a client. She was somewhat taken aback when Cressida explained the situation, but agreed that really they'd had no alternative. When Tolly and Morris arrived in the garden she stroked the dog's silky head.

"I must admit, he is rather a charming dog, " she said, smiling.

Tolly was apologetic, "Really sorry about this, Helen," he said, "but I think we'll have to bring him inside, he's made two bids for freedom so far - the first when Cressida and I had just finished our lovely picnic. The dog suddenly arrived out of nowhere - luckily his owners appeared soon afterwards. But the next time, well, we were on our way home, right at the foot of the hill - when suddenly he careered past us at a rate of knots and leapt into a field full of sheep....."

Cressida then took over.

"Tolly was amazing, he dashed into the field and got him pretty quickly, then we waited a bit till the sheep calmed down again. We wondered what to do next, and in the end we thought the best thing was bring him home and try to contact his owners. Hopefully he won't be here for too long - with any luck he'll have gone before the twins get back."

"They're being brought home after the party at about five, by another friend's mother," Helen said. "Meanwhile he can come into the kitchen. I'll put down an old blanket for him, and get him a bowl of water. Perhaps he'll take a bit of a rest after all that activity."

Morris had a long drink, then settled down peacefully on the blanket. Tolly and Cressida decided to wait a little longer before trying to ring the Penwoods, judging that they might still be out and about, searching for Morris. So Helen made a pot of tea, then they all sat round the kitchen table and discussed what to do. Cressida explained the coincidence regarding the Penwoods. It went back to June, she said, when she'd bought the skirt to wear at Louise's birthday party.

"My blue silk skirt was part of a pile of old stuff the Penwoods found when clearing up after her grandmother's death, Angela Penwood told me when I rang recently - I'd been given their phone number by the shop. She didn't mention the necklace - I don't think she even knew it existed. Anyway she confirmed that they'd taken the clothes to the charity shop and the rest of the stuff to the tip, which of course was where we found the boxes that we've been investigating.

"Well, getting back to today, obviously we didn't exchange names with those two strangers who had lost their dog, we just handed him over and they went on their way. We had no idea that they were the Penwoods, till their dog escaped for the second time. After getting him away from the sheep Tolly looked at the ID disc and found their name and address. Anyway then of course we realised who they were. It was a complete surprise, but we couldn't help thinking that it could be a real stroke of luck for us!"

Tolly continued, "Yes, because Angela had said before, when we'd phoned to ask her about the skirt, that some of that stuff went back several generations, to her great, great grandmother and beyond

- back in fact, as we've worked out, to sometime possibly before the start of the nineteenth century. Also, as we've since discovered, there was lots of other ancient stuff in the boxes too - the Wessex Courant paper for example. But Angela hadn't been interested in any of it, so they'd just taken all the paperwork to the tip, which was where we found the boxes. We don't know how many there were, but we identified the two we've got because they happened to have Penwood address labels on them, probably they originally contained goods sent by post or delivery van."

Cressida went on, "So now we're wondering whether we might take the chance to ask them for a bit more information about Angela's ancestors - hoping that they'll be so relieved to have their dog back safe and sound that they might be prepared to help us. We've found that a lot of thefts happened in the asylum during the eighteenth century, some of the poor people working there would steal the possessions of recently deceased inmates.

"We'd also discovered that the skirt and the bead necklace disappeared some weeks after Lady Marlington died. The two female thieves, who were probably destitute themselves, were eventually found out, dismissed, convicted and tried, then appallingly and brutally punished by being branded on their hands. Our hunch is that one or other of those thieves might have been an ancestor of Angela Penwood. What do you think we should do, Mum?"

Helen was again both surprised and impressed by the painstaking research that the two of them were doing, and how much they had already achieved. She was also concerned about the problem of the dog, and how to return him to his owners as soon as possible.

"Well, you need to get Morris back home pretty quickly. Maybe try and ring them now, obviously if there's no answer you'll have to leave a message. Regarding the information you want, perhaps it might be worth taking him back to them at home rather than hanging on here waiting. It could then give you a chance to mention that previous phone call and explain a bit of what you're working on."

Tolly and Cressida exchanged glances. This could well be the best course of action; to take the dog back into Chilminster by bus.

The next thing was to find the Penwoods' phone number. It wasn't in the telephone book; it seemed they were ex-directory. In the end Cressida located her copy after a slightly harassed search. It turned up at the bottom of the bag in which she'd been carrying the blue skirt, when they revisited the charity shop over a week ago. As soon she'd found it she remembered dropping it back in there after her unsatisfactory phone conversation with Angela later the same day.

"What an idiot I am," she said, "Sorry, of course that's where it was."

"No more of an idiot than me," Tolly cut in, remembering Cressida's bout of depression that day. "I'm pretty sure my copy of it went through the washing machine when I got back from France."

"Anyway, we need to make the phone call. We'd better be quick though, the next Chilminster bus goes in about ten minutes," said Cressida.

"I've got a better idea," interjected Helen, " Both of you leave now with Morris, give me the phone number and I'll call them. I'll tell them you're bringing him back, or if they're still out, I'll leave an answerphone message for them saying their dog is safe, and on the way home. That means we get him away from here before the twins arrive.

"Also, Dad will be returning through Chilminster later, so he may be able to pick you up there. I imagine it'll take you the best part of an hour before you find the Penwoods - Westdown Lane is a bit of a trek from the bus terminus in town. They should have got home by then."

"Fantastic - we'll do that!" said Cressida, "Thanks Mum - OK, Tolly?"

"Fine. Come on, Morris, let's get you back where you belong!"

"Make sure you ring me once you've returned him. I'll have spoken to Dad by then and agreed a pick-up place; the bus station would probably be best. 'Bye Morris, nice to have met you!" She patted the dog as Tolly fastened his lead again.

Leaving the phone number with Helen, they left hastily to catch the next bus, Tolly again keeping a firm hold of Morris's lead as they ran to the bus stop.

"Gosh, I hope they're home when we get there. What are we going to do if not? We can't possibly bring him back with us again," Cressida said anxiously, as they boarded the bus.

"If they aren't back we'll wait for a bit, then leave a note for them, and take the dog to the Police Station. We'll give them the Penwood's address and phone number. That's all we can do really. Goodness me, Cressida, we didn't anticipate this, did we? Thank heavens we've still got most of tomorrow to carry on our research."

"Poor old Morris," Cressida said, stroking the dog, who was sitting passively between them as the bus rumbled on towards town. "What a lot of bother you've caused. Let's hope your owners are home by now!"

It was after four o'clock by the time Tolly and Cressida arrived at 49, Westdown Lane in Chilminster. There was a light on in the house, maybe a hopeful sign, Cressida thought. Morris clearly recognised his surroundings, he waved his feathery tail and made few excited whiney sounds as she rang the doorbell.

The door was flung open and an anxious looking man appeared. They recognised him immediately.

"Hello Mr Penwood!" Tolly said with a smile, "Here is Morris!"

"It's a relief to see you're back!" Cressida added. "We thought you might still be scouring the downs for him. Did you get my Mum's message?"

"Yes, yes we did - thank you all so much. But where did you find him? We spent ages calling and calling; he'd jerked his lead out of my hand and immediately dashed off. In the end we just couldn't cope any longer, so we decided we'd come home and put some 'Lost Dog' notices up."

Angela Penwood now arrived behind her husband.

"Come in, do come in, thank goodness you found him. Let's get him inside so he doesn't escape again. Oh Morris, Morris - what have you been up to?"

Tolly and Cressida exchanged covert glances as they followed the pair in. Cressida showed Tolly her crossed fingers, he responded with a slight nod and a faint smile.

Once inside, they were ushered into the sitting room at the back of the house. Then, as usual taking it in turns, they told the full story of Morris's escapade, from his leap into the field full of sheep and Tolly's capture of him, all the way to the decision to deliver him back home, leaving Cressida's mother to contact them on the phone.

"We brought him on the bus," Tolly said. "It was the fastest way to get him here, as Cressida's father's at work, and her mother's at home waiting for Cressida's brothers to come back from a birthday party."

"Yes, it seemed the best thing to do, we just hoped you'd have got back home by now. And he might be a bit of a naughty boy, and a brilliant escapologist, but what a lovely dog he is!" Cressida added.

"So it's been not one, but two rescues of our dog that we owe to you both. I don't know how we can possibly thank you enough," said Angela. "it could have been absolutely catastrophic if he'd harmed any sheep....

" ... and if the farmer had been around and had seen it happening he would have been well within his rights to shoot him," added Ralph Penwood, continuing, "Honestly, if there is any way in which we can recompense you for doing all this....."

Tolly's mentions of Cressida's name had awakened a memory. Angela realised that this was the same girl who'd telephoned her recently.

"Oh my goodness, now I remember you - didn't you phone me the other day? You were asking about some old clothes and other stuff I took to the charity shop several months ago, weren't you?"

Unexpectedly Cressida felt herself blushing. Was this an entirely ethical thing that she and Tolly were embarking on? Angela would be totally within her rights to deny them any further information. She glanced quickly at Tolly, who immediately took over.

"That's right!", he said, with a smile, "And what an extraordinary coincidence! Yes, it was Cressida who called you that day. We're working together on a research project, you see, and are particularly interested in some things that happened over two hundred years ago in the old asylum - which is now the Minster Care Home on the outskirts of town. It seems that the blue skirt, with a necklace which was tangled into its waist, disappeared a few weeks after the death of one of the female inmates. There was typhus fever around at the time, and the lady we're researching was among those inmates who caught it and died of it.

"The people who worked there - laundresses, kitchen staff, washer women and so on - were very badly paid. After the typhus outbreak most of them fled, some taking with them pieces of clothing and other items, including jewellery, which had belonged to some of the deceased inmates. One can't blame them really - it must have been a miserable life working there. But the awful thing is, that the two who were eventually found out were punished by being branded with hot irons. We're trying to trace the stories of those poor women." He paused, looking over at Cressida, who continued:

"Yes, that was why I phoned you that day. The woman in the charity shop had given me your contact details, and we've been trying to fill in the gaps. Because the blue skirt was in your grandmother's stuff, though probably dating from much earlier, we wondered there were any clues handed down in family reminiscences or memoirs about that time.

"We were so shocked to find out about the dismal lives those poverty-stricken workers led, and were of course horrified by the fact that at least two of them were branded. That would have meant that, with such damaged hands, they might never have been able to work again, making them even more destitute. We want to tell their story too. History's full of the tales of the rich and famous, but underpinning all that are the forgotten lives of lots of ordinary people. Tolly and I wondered if you would be able to give us any insights from your family history which might shed a bit of light on all this."

Both Angela and her husband were temporarily silenced by this account. Then she spoke, sounding apologetic,

"I'm really sorry I was so dismissive of you when you made that call. I suppose I didn't want to be bothered raking up all that stuff from the past again. But yes, I do have some evidence which might be of use to you. You see, my mother's great, great grandmother, who was born in 1845, made a sort of scrapbook - just a collection really, of things she had heard from her own grandmother and other family members. There are little drawings, bits of poetry, pressed flowers, and other reminiscences.

"She'd moved up in the world. Her family was very poor - in the scrapbook there's a sketch she later did of herself as a child - barefoot, ragged and unkempt looking, poor little thing. She worked as a carder in a wool mill from the age of nine or ten, but over time she was promoted to weaving; then when machinery took over the more routine work, she was promoted again. But her big break came not through work, but when she attracted the eye of the new supervisor; he wooed and wed her and that was the end of her life of poverty! She learnt to read and write and became a respected member of her local community.

"She never forgot her origins, though. In the scrapbook there's a cutting from a newspaper dating from about a hundred years earlier, which mentions thefts from the Chilminster Asylum. No names are given, but under the report she's written the names of the two thieves and some details of what happened to them. They were branded with red-hot irons and had the letter 'T' for thief burnt onto their palms. Both of them were very young - still in their teens. One of those women, Martha Corston, was her mother's great, great aunt."

Tolly and Cressida had listened spellbound to Angela's narrative. For a few moments they were both so overwhelmed by everything they'd heard that it was hard to say anything. They looked at one another, both temporarily stunned. Then Cressida spoke, sounding quite emotional:

"Oh Angela, thank you so much for telling us all that! What a moving, and at times, truly heartrending story. And what a heroine your great, great, great grandmother was, to find her way out of poverty, as much through her own hard work and ability as by marrying the boss! Good for her! Oh dear, though, it's horrifying to imagine the fate of those poor girls - I wonder what happened to them after such a brutal punishment. They must have been in agony."

After a short pause Tolly added, "And also how amazing it was of your wonderful great, great, great grandma to create that record. Have you still got it?"

Ralph went over to a built-in bookcase at one side of the room and pulled out a leather folder which he handed to Tolly.

"This is it," he said. "Obviously we had no intention of getting rid of it with all the other stuff, it's far too fascinating and informative. We understand that poor Martha Corston didn't live long after the branding, maybe she also got typhus - or perhaps the wound got infected. Anyway as she had no husband or children - she was only about fifteen - all her possessions went to her sister - Ange's six or seven times great grandmother – sorry, I'm afraid I find all those 'greats' a bit confusing!"

"Yes," Angela confirmed, "So that must be how the skirt, along with other bits and pieces, eventually ended up here. Before hearing about it from you I'd had no idea how old it was, so I just bundled it up with the other bits and pieces of clothing and took it to the charity shop. But of course, as Ralph says, we've kept the scrapbook - it's very much a family treasure. I'd be OK about lending it to you for a week or so, maybe to photocopy the bits of info you need. Consider it Morris's thank you for rescuing him and bringing him home!"

Tolly was quite overcome. Neither he nor Cressida had expected this!

"Really? Are you sure? That's incredibly generous of you. And it's marvellous news for us, because it's given us the final missing piece of the jigsaw in our research. Of course we'll take great care of it, and will return it to you as soon as we can - certainly within a few days. And also, once the exhibition about all this happens at the museum, we'll make sure you get invitations to the private view. Thank you again, thank you both very, very much! Honestly, we're not only incredibly grateful, but also quite overwhelmed - we never imagined such an outcome! And all due to Morris!"

"Well," said Angela, "after all that, would you like a cup of tea?"

"It's very kind of you," Cressida replied regretfully, "We'd have loved it, but we'll have to go as we're being picked up by my father in town, he'll be on his way home. Perhaps another time - it would be lovely to keep in touch. But anyway, thank you both again so much - quite apart from everything else it's been really nice to meet you both. Good old Morris! He's not only enabled us to finish our research but he's also made us two new friends!"

CHAPTER THIRTY-SEVEN

Farewell

Cressida and Tolly left the Penwoods' house with that precious folder, carefully wrapped, in Tolly's rucksack. He had earlier emptied out the picnic stuff back at Cressida's home, and, practical as ever, had reloaded it with writing pads and pens, to be available if necessary for possible note-taking.

They both kept a grip on themselves until they'd turned the corner out of Westdown Lane, but then gave way to mutual expressions of triumph and excitement, embracing one another and joyfully dancing around as they had done after their meeting with Canon Wilcox!

Calming down a bit, Cressida then said,

"I'd better ring Mum; she'll probably have had a phone chat with Dad by now, about picking us up."

They located the nearest telephone box and she got through to Helen, who confirmed that Graham would pick them up at the bus terminus at around 6 o'clock. It was quite a long walk back there, but in contrast to their earlier anxious journey taking Morris home to the Penwoods, they were both now full of elation and excitement. Hand in hand, they bounded blithely along the street back towards the bus station.

When they were nearly there Tolly noticed an Off-License. He stopped suddenly and grinned at Cressida.

"I'm just going in to buy a bottle of champagne," he said, "I need to get something for your parents, and we two have also definitely got something to celebrate, don't you think?"

"How lovely, Tolly, and how generous of you!"

There was more for Tolly and Cressida to celebrate when they got home. On the drive back they'd given Graham a brief account of the day's events - the picnic, the runaway dog, the field of sheep, eventually getting Morris back to his owners, and finishing with a succinct and tantalising mention of the amazing revelation which had completed their research. They were both feeling euphoric and excited, and were looking forward to sharing their news in full.

"We'll tell you all about it in detail later," Cressida promised.

At home Helen and the twins were waiting for them. The twins shrieked with delight and immediately leapt onto Tolly, urging him to come and play with them.

"Wait a minute, boys," their mother said, "I've got what's possibly some more good news for you, Tolly. Stella Jacobs rang to ask if you'd mind coming to them a day later - on Monday rather than tomorrow. An old university friend from America has been in touch with them to ask if he and his wife can pay a flying visit tomorrow - they are briefly in the UK. I said that was fine - that you could stay an extra night here and get the bus into Chilminster with Cressida on Monday morning, when she's off to school. I'm sure it will be no hardship for the two of you to have a bit more time together!"

Tolly and Cressida exchanged delighted glances.

"Oh, wonderful! And much, much nicer to leave here the next morning rather than getting a taxi tomorrow evening!" Tolly said, smiling as he looked over at Cressida, and rejoicing that they would now have another precious evening together.

Good naturedly, he then agreed to play a bit of Lego with the twins before their bed time.

"Not long, boys - you can have twenty minutes at the most," Helen called, adding to Tolly that it had been a very full day for the twins, who had only got back from the party about an hour ago. "They're still pumped full of adrenalin I'm afraid, they need to calm down. Actually they're absolutely exhausted but of course they won't admit it. I'll come and sweep them off to bed before long. Thanks, Tolly."

Later, when the twins were in bed, and the shepherd's pie - prepared earlier that afternoon by Helen - was baking in the oven, Graham brought glasses, olives and nibbles into the sitting room and Tolly followed with the champagne in a bucket of ice. They made a contented and relaxed foursome. Graham described his frustrating meeting with a verbose, tetchy and repetitive client. Helen relayed her initial surprise and momentary alarm when the dog arrived in her kitchen, and described her phone conversation with a very agitated Ralph Penwood. Lastly Tolly and Cressida, taking in turns as was their custom, gave a full and enthusiastic account of the afternoon's extraordinary revelations.

Now that they had another whole full day ahead of them, they decided to allow themselves the rest of the day off. Tomorrow they'd finish going through the contents of the second box, as well as investigating that potentially intriguing scrap book. But this evening was theirs to enjoy together. They had an early supper and headed out, leaving Cressida's parents to enjoy a more leisurely and relaxing evening meal.

Without having discussed it, they both instinctively knew exactly where they were going. When they got to the footpath leading up to the castle they turned to one another and exchanged grins.

"A bit of telepathy!" Tolly said, putting an arm round Cressida and kissing her cheek. She nodded, smiling, and slipped her hand into his as they began to climb the Castle Hill.

The whole site was empty when they reached the top; all the weekend visitors had gone. It was sunset. Deep pink trailing clouds streaked across the sky, with the shadowy waning moon faintly visible in the east. Jagged black against the roseate sky stood the castle, stark and still. Reddish gold light from the setting sun shed a magical glow all around, illuminating their faces and burnishing Cressida's dark auburn hair.

"My darling beautiful Cressida - you look like an enchanting spirit from the Islands of the Hesperides," Tolly said, stroking her hair.

She looked up at him, "And you look like a Greek hero, with your dark curly hair and classical features - your straight nose and beautiful brown eyes.. ... ah, Tolly, my dear love... let's go and sit down for a bit...we need to make the most of these last hours together."

They found a bench and sat there for a long, affectionate interlude, with hugs, kisses and caresses, as they softly shared tender words of love with one another. Although they'd spent a lot of time together in the last twenty-four hours, it had all been busy and action-packed. They were also both acutely aware that intense and lengthy embraces were not acceptable when Cressida's family was around, or when they were out and about in a public or crowded place. It was wonderful now to have this romantic, peaceful, private time.

it was also a time for exchanging confidences. Cressida had heard from her mother how very distraught and agitated Tolly was when he'd first phoned from France, and his relieved reaction once he heard the reason for her feeling unwell. She remembered his anxiety about her when they were all on the Castle Hill, before he and his father left for their French trip, and how she had felt too embarrassed to tell him what was wrong.

"Tolly, I've been wondering why you were so distressed when you talked to Mum from France, the time when I'd had such bad period pains. Tolly, we don't need to keep things secret from each other - and I'm really sorry, I should have told you what was happening. Maybe you could also explain a bit more about what made you so upset and worried. I have an inkling that it might have been something to do with your mother."

"Oh Cressida - yes, I didn't want to load you with my private emotional troubles - but you're right, it was about Mum. My fears about you feeling ill brought back all the awful memories of when she was dying, when I visited her in the Hospice for the last time, she was so tired, so weak.......

Anyway, during that night when Pa and I went over to France, all those demons came back to scare me. Even though I knew I was over-reacting, I couldn't get to sleep, and couldn't stop myself from thinking over and over again about how devastating it would be if I lost you too ... I'm sorry, !'m sorry ..."

Tolly, now in tears, leaned forward and hid his face in his hands.

Cressida, deeply moved by his confession, put an arm round him and kissed the top of his head. She remembered how he had always been ready with comfort and support whenever she needed it; it was now her turn to comfort and support him.

"Tolly, darling Tolly – there's nothing to be sorry about, it was all my fault for not telling you. And there's no way that you're going to lose me. I love you with all my heart, Tolly! I'll always be by your side, no matter whether we are together or apart. I'll support you, cherish you, share everything with you, work and play with you, laugh and cry with you, for as long as we are both on this earth. I also feel, in some weird inexplicable way, that I owe it to the spirit of your dear mother to ensure that her beloved son stays happy and is loved. We're together for good, Tolly. Your troubles are my troubles. Your joy is my joy.

"And as for my health - well, I'm a pretty hardy creature, so I don't think you need have any worries in that direction. I'm mortified that my embarrassment - over a perfectly normal aspect of being female - meant I didn't tell you why I was feeling so rotten, which led to you going through all those hours of stress and anxiety. So I think that from now on, what we must make sure we do is to *always* tell one another about our worries, doubts, regrets, uncertainties - even disagreements if we ever have any.... "

Tolly had lifted his head while she was speaking, so she wiped his tears away with her hands, looking compassionately at him and smiling gently as he responded in a slightly shaky voice,

"Yes, yes, we always will. Thank you, thank you my darling, my love - oh, thank you so much."

Eventually they were ready to come back down to earth again, and to walk on round to the castle, arm in arm, heading first for the walled kitchen garden - overgrown and secretive. Inevitably they began to reminisce about the events of the summer, and once again re-living the fairy-tale early blossoming of their love affair.

Tolly, his equilibrium restored, mused on their shared researches.

"We're also a creative partnership now, Cressida. We've been working so happily and harmoniously together - and between us we've already achieved a huge amount. And that's something we'll be able to continue even when we're far apart - we'll pool ideas, send each other stuff we've written, and regularly talk on the phone. We can each be one another's proof readers and copy editors."

As the sun receded, disappearing behind the woods on the other side of the hill, they watched the silvery gibbous moon rising in the eastern sky.

"It'll always be a place of enchantment for us, here," said Cressida. "I remember the night of my birthday party, walking alone in the dark, looking up at the moon, then seeing you coming back towards me, and feeling so peaceful and so uplifted....."

"We will treasure all these memories, and keep adding to them as time goes on. Although hundreds of miles will soon separate us, our souls will stay close to one another," was Tolly's gentle reply.

"Yes I know - and we do sometimes seem to experience a sort of spiritual communication which transcends normality, don't we? Hopefully it'll still work for us when we're a long way apart. And somehow I don't feel quite so sad about it all as I did, because I know that every passing day brings the time closer when we'll be able to be properly together."

"My dearest love, we will, we really will."

Darkness had fallen before they got home. It had been an intense and challenging interlude, but it left each of them emotionally fortified and enriched, contemplating their commitment to one another as well as their readiness together to tackle any more trials yet to come.

The next morning, having promised the twins that they would take them out that afternoon, Cressida and Tolly returned to the study to complete their investigations. They now began to tackle the smaller box, listing its contents, and classifying and indexing them as they had done with the other one.

It took rather longer than it should have done, because they were waylaid into spending quite a lot of time reading a tattered newspaper article about changes to the asylum system in the nineteenth century. It was rather a depressing story. An Act of Parliament in 1808 had established publicly funded asylums for 'pauper lunatics' across the nation, and over time there was a huge increase in such establishments. The aim was to have one in every county. However, institutionalisation didn't seem to have led generally to more humane treatment, although the ideas of social reformers like Harriet Martineau and Samuel Tuke did achieve some improvements. More time had to pass before changes in attitude to mental disorders led to real reform.

"Oh dear, Tolly, here we are again dipping in to more accounts of human misery," Cressida said despairingly. "Much as we need to know about such things, we can't do anything about it...."

"Of course we can't, darling, we must stick to what we *are* trying to do something about. Let's move on from this - finish the box and look through the scrapbook to decide what bits we need to photocopy."

This made sense. They were eager and curious to explore that handmade album created over a hundred and thirty years ago. So as soon as they'd completed the second box Cressida unzipped the leather folder, lifted the book out and laid it on the desk.

It turned out to be a surprisingly engaging and quite moving experience, looking through the reminiscences of Angela's ancestress, Sarah Daisy Collins, she was called. Her name, surrounded by a hand-painted wreath of daisies, decorated the front cover, and a miscellany of contents including keepsakes, sketches, newspaper cuttings and bits of fabric were carefully pinned, glued and sometimes sewn into the inside pages.

"*I am Sarah Daisy Collins eighteen years old, born Sarah Daisy Morley 3rd April 1845 and this is my book of memories,*" was inscribed in largeish, slightly uneven but perfectly legible script on the inside front cover. Underneath, below that introduction, she had listed the names and birth dates of her six brothers and sisters, and the names of her parents. Three of her siblings had died in childhood.

"So she was married by the time she was eighteen," Cressida observed. "I wonder what happened to the rest of that large poor family."

They soon found out. After her marriage Sarah had been able to support her parents financially with monthly sums of money, and to ensure that her remaining siblings were lifted out of the extreme poverty of their earlier years.

"She seems to have been a pretty impressive person," Tolly said, leafing through the book and finding drawings of those younger brothers and sisters, as well as the sketch of herself as a little girl that Angela had mentioned when talking about Sarah's life.

He went on, "All that stuff about her family - and the small mementoes she's also included about the ones who didn't survive - it's really heartwarming, isn't it? This, for instance."

He indicated a little patch of woollen fabric, which was labelled "*From little Lennie's baby blanket,*" and sewed onto the page. Underneath Sarah had added, "*Little Lennie died of a quinsy 1852 aged two.*"

"Oh, Tolly, heartwarming but heartbreaking too. Quinsy - I think it's a complication of tonsillitis. When the twins were small they both caught tonsillitis badly, and the doctor was worried it might turn into a quinsy, but thanks to penicillin, they got better pretty quickly. Poor little Lennie. And what a kind and loving sister she must have been!"

"We're so lucky today, aren't we? Antibiotics such as penicillin must've saved millions upon millions of lives - those killer diseases of the past, many of which now are now reduced to treatable minor infections. When I was younger I wondered if penicillin would work for Mum..... but of course her cancer couldn't be cured that way."

Cressida, now even more sensitive to Tolly's emotions when he talked about his mother, immediately moved closer and stroked his arm.

"Thanks, sweetheart, - and hopefully soon there might be a cure for cancer," he said, "Of course I still think of Mum every day but the sadness is mostly getting easier to manage, apart from the odd setback, which we've talked about. I know she'd rejoice to see me so happy now."

Cressida squeezed his hand, then continued scrolling through the album which lay open before them.

"Let's try and find out what we can about Sarah's wider family," she said, "Her ancestors - grandparents, great aunts and uncles etcetera - and also we need to locate the newspaper cutting about Martha Corston."

They soon found it, glued onto a page about halfway through the scrapbook, headed 'In the Olden Days'.

Sarah had listed some of the names of previous generations of her family that she knew of. It was quite a short list - other than her parents and one grandmother (the grandfather had died young) there was a great aunt and a few female cousins, and, decades further back, Martha Corston and her sister Rosie. It was possible, Tolly and Cressida thought, that some of these relationships had been transitory ones; brief affairs which left the girl pregnant while the man moved on.

The article from the Wessex Courant about thefts from the asylum was stuck in below the list of relations. It was identical to the account Cressida had found in her explorations while Tolly was in

France, obviously from another copy of the same newspaper. But, as Angela had told them, at the foot of the cutting Sarah had added a handwritten insert with the names of the two thieves: Hatty Singer and Martha Corston, and this explanation:

Martha Corston was my mother's great, great aunt. Her family was destitute, the father had gone, and her mother and the three younger children ended up in the parish workhouse where they all died of cholera. Of the two older girls Martha, the eldest child, aged fifteen, worked as a scullery maid at the Chilminster Insane Asylum until she was dismissed for thievery. She was branded on her palms and died soon afterwards. Her sister Rosie, a year her junior, inherited Martha's few possessions. Rosie worked as a milkmaid, until she became with child by the farmer. He married her.

"Oh dear, more sadness," said Cressida, "I wonder if it was typhus, or as a result of the branding, that poor Martha died - maybe the wound became infected. Or perhaps she was affected by the hallucinogen in the necklace she had stolen, and thought she had gone mad. But at least Rosie survived, and thank goodness the farmer who'd made her pregnant then married her. I wonder if there were any more babies. Rosie and her farmer husband were obviously the couple who Angela is descended from, generations and generations ago."

"Yes, and that means we've done it, Cressida, we've done it!! We've established the timeline as clearly as we can, starting with Sir Anthony's return from Greece with all those treasures, including the necklace; then his banishment of his wife to the Chilminster Asylum together with the necklace, the skirt, and that single portrait among her possessions. Then, after the death of Lady Marlington, Martha's theft of the skirt with the necklace now knotted into its waist, her sister's inheritance of her stuff after her death, all the way down though her sister's family and descendants, to Angela's grandmother, ending up by being taken by Angela to the charity shop where you bought it. How about that!"

"Amazing!" Cressida said, "Wow, just amazing! Aren't we clever!! But I think I need to have a good look at that skirt again, to see exactly how those beads were fixed into the waist. I think that after Martha took them, she must have sewed them into the top of the skirt to hide them. By the time I found it, the beads were still there but I don't remember any trace of stitches."

"Why don't we go and look now," Tolly replied, "I remember thinking how marvellous and stylish you looked in it and how elegantly late Victorian you seemed. Little did we know that the skirt was more than hundred years older than that."

They went upstairs to Cressida's bedroom where she took the skirt out of her wardrobe and spread it out on her bed. It really was rather spectacular, with its elegant ruched hemline, and its heavy ultramarine silk fabric gleaming in the light from the window. She remembered how smart and sophisticated it had made her feel, but also the terrifying effect of the beads which had shattered her tranquillity that memorable afternoon.

Now, she bent over and examined the waist fastening. Obviously there were no such things as zips or even buttons to fasten the skirt, just a pair of ribbons, one on either side of the gap. She then turned the flaps over and looked all the way round the inside of the waist.

"Yes, look, Tolly - there are traces of stitches here and there, all the way along. Most of them are broken, but this must surely have been how poor Martha concealed the necklace. She would also then have secured it by knotting it with those ribbons at the side."

"Lucky that the ribbons didn't deteriorate like the stitching," Tolly observed, "especially as you'd been dancing in it, then when you dashed off ....."

"We had realised how fragile the ribbons were, Mum and I. This is why it didn't suddenly come undone or break." Cressida pointed out that on either side of the waist opening her mother had attached three small Velcro stickers - one trio on the outside, the other on the inside, so as to close the gap securely.

"Probably an act of cultural vandalism," Tolly laughed, "but given all you went through that day thank goodness the skirt didn't lose its moorings, as it were!"

"Thank goodness!" Cressida echoed him, also laughing, "That would have been the ultimate humiliation! But you know, Tolly, despite that skirt and those beads giving me such a terrifying experience, they also brought you and me together. So really I feel incredibly grateful that it happened as it did. It's unimaginable now to think of my life without you." She paused, smiling at him, then continued,

"But what I'm thinking now, is that I probably ought to give the skirt to the Museum to go with the necklace. It is, after all, an antique, and should be cared for and preserved properly rather than hanging here in my wardrobe. It's a bit of a responsibility - just think how awful it would be if something happened to it - if it got damaged in any way."

"Yes, you're probably right. Maybe see what Penny thinks - it would undoubtedly be much safer at the museum. But first, don't you think we ought to mention it to Angela as she's been a co-owner of it, as it were."

"That's a good idea. I'll have a chat with her about it when I take the folder back to them - probably next weekend after I've photocopied the bits we need. I'm also thinking that we need to update Penny on everything, now that we've completed our research. As you're going to be in Chilminster for a few days with the Jacobs's maybe you might be able to do that," Cressida suggested.

"Why don't we ring Penny this afternoon, and suggest both coming in on Tuesday, we could mention the skirt then. I could meet you after school - and that would really round off our time together," Tolly said.

"Yes, oh yes, that would work. But we'll have to be very sober and decorous if you meet me straight out of school! No more romantic ambushes like on Friday, wonderful and magical though that was! And of course, after that, we'll be apart again."

Cressida tried to sound pragmatic and sensible, but Tolly could hear the sadness in her voice. He responded gently, putting his arms around her.

"Apart in body, but not in mind, my darling. We've known this was ahead of us, and we'll keep in touch as much as we can. As we agreed, we need to - we know that we can't really do without each other, don't we. What sort of a state would I have continued to be in yesterday, without you to reassure me and care for me? Anyway, we've got the rest of today ahead of us, and we'll make the most of that, starting with taking the twins out this afternoon."

Two days later, after their visit to the museum, Tolly and Cressida said their final farewells. At first they tried to remain self-controlled, waiting together quietly at the bus stop. Then, suddenly turning face to face, they clasped each other's hands and pledged their love for one another. With a final embrace, as the bus approached to take Cressida home, they were each close to tears. Clinging to one another for a few more precious seconds, they kissed, then parted.

THE END

© Eliza Merry 2025

www.ingramcontent.com/pod-product-compliance
Lightning Source LLC
Chambersburg PA
CBHW020927260626
47169CB00006B/1610